Praise for Marian Keyes:

'The fabulous Marian returns with her unique brand of hilarious,
heartbreaking fiction' *Cosmopolitan*

'Keyes writes brilliantly, as always, about love, grief, jealousy
and friendship' *Daily Mail*

'Marian Keyes at her emotionally savvy best' *In Style*

'She is a talented comic writer . . . laden with plot, twists, jokey
asides and nicely turned bits of zeitgeisty observational humour . . .
energetic, well-constructed prose delivers life and people in
satisfyingly various shades of grey' *Guardian*

'Keyes [is] a virtuoso who can deftly mix dark and light, tragic and
comic in a way that only a handful of writers can' *Irish Times*

'High-quality entertainment' *Marie Claire*

'A rare blend of genres, a richly enjoyable satire and an inspirational
take of one woman's triumph over despair' *Daily Telegraph*

'Another beautifully written triumph' *Heat*

'Emotional and entertaining' *Closer*

'[A] hilarious, touching novel' *Sun*

'Keyes can blend heavy and light together in a style that's smart, sassy and thoroughly absorbing' *Irish Independent*

'Marian Keyes is the queen of feel-good fiction. Her hip, heart-warming comedies have made her the hottest young female writer in Britain and the voice of a generation' *Daily Mirror*

'A romantic comedy with dark twists' *Bella*

'A wonderful, subtle, hilarious and highly sophisticated novel' *Evening Standard*

'This is scalpel-sharp comic writing – laden with juicy plot twists, sparking dialogue and hilarious helping of zeitgeisty observational humour' *Ireland on Sunday*

'Wildly funny, romantic and nearly impossible to put down. Elbow your way to the front of the queue to get a copy' *Daily Mail*

ABOUT THE AUTHOR

Marian Keyes is the international bestselling author of *Watermelon*, *Lucy Sullivan is Getting Married*, *Rachel's Holiday*, *Last Chance Saloon*, *Sushi for Beginners*, *Angels*, *The Other Side of the Story*, *Anybody Out There?*, *This Charming Man*, *The Brightest Star in the Sky*, *The Mystery of Mercy Close* and *The Woman Who Stole My Life*. Her two collections of journalism, *Under the Duvet* and *Further Under the Duvet*, are also available from Penguin. Marian lives in Dublin with her husband.

Find out more about Marian and keep up to date with what she's doing:

Follow her on Twitter @MarianKeyes
Sign up for her newsletter
www.mariankeyes.com
Like her Facebook page
Facebook.com/MarianKeyes

Rachel's Holiday

MARIAN KEYES

PENGUIN BOOKS

PENGUIN BOOKS

UK | USA | Canada | Ireland | Australia
India | New Zealand | South Africa

Penguin Books is part of the Penguin Random House group of companies
whose addresses can be found at global.penguinrandomhouse.com.

Penguin
Random House
UK

First published in Penguin Books 1997
Reissued in 2015

001

Copyright © Marian Keyes, 1997

Printed in Great Britain by Clays Ltd, St Ives plc

A CIP catalogue record for this book is available from the British Library

ISBN: 978–1–405–92477–1

www.greenpenguin.co.uk

MIX
Paper from
responsible sources
FSC® C018179

Penguin Random House is committed to a
sustainable future for our business, our readers
and our planet. This book is made from Forest
Stewardship Council® certified paper.

ACKNOWLEDGEMENTS

Several people deserve a damn good thanking.

Thanks to my editors Kate Cruise O'Brien and Louise Moore for their enthusiasm, support, vision, patience, friendship and belief in me while I wrote this book. Thanks to the staff at Poolbeg, Michael Joseph and Penguin for all their hard work and huge amounts of enthusiasm.

Thanks to Jenny Boland, Rita-Anne Keyes and Louise Voss, who read the book as I wrote it and supplied advice and – much more importantly – praise. It was often painful to write, and whenever I indulged in self-pity and despair (about 87 per cent of the time) their support was a lifeline.

Thanks to Belinda Flaherty, who for the third year running was persuaded to act as a guinea pig and read the finished product. Thanks for the comments and the enthusiasm.

Thanks to all those brave men and women who volunteered to ingest cocaine for research purposes and reported back to me of their experiences. Their sacrifices will not go unremembered.

Thanks to Mags Ledwith for letting me use her 'Dance of the Stolen Car'.

Thanks to Siobhán Crummey for letting me use her 'Singing in the Decorated Kitchen' story.

Thanks to Jonathan Lloyd and Eileen Prendergast for all the hard work done sorting out my contracts, etc. Much appreciated because I'm not exactly a legal eagle. More like a legal sparrow, in fact.

Thanks to all the other 'Rachels' who have shared their story with me.

Thanks to Dr Geoff Hinchley for the medical advice.

Finally, thanks to Tony – my husband, best friend, sounding-board, pyschiatrist, lexicon and punch-bag. God love him – is there anything more awful than being the spouse of a neurotic writer? I couldn't have written this book without him. He has praised, consoled, advised, cajoled – he's especially good at cajoling – fed, watered, chocolated and ice-creamed me though the whole experience. On bad days he almost had to wash and dress me.

This book is for him.

Of course he may not *want* it after all he had to go through, but he's getting it anyway.

For Tony

I

They said I was a drug addict. I found that hard to come to terms with – I was a middle-class, convent-educated girl whose drug use was strictly recreational. And surely drug addicts were thinner? It was true that I *took* drugs, but what no one seemed to understand was that my drug use wasn't any different from their having a drink or two on a Friday night after work. They might have a few vodkas and tonic and let off a bit of steam. I had a couple of lines of cocaine and did likewise. As I said to my father and my sister and my sister's husband and eventually the therapists of the Cloisters, 'If cocaine was sold in liquid form, in a bottle, would you complain about me taking it? Well, would you? No, I bet you wouldn't!'

I was offended by the drug-addict allegation, because I was nothing like one. Apart from the track marks on their arms, they had dirty hair, constantly seemed cold, did a lot of shoulder-hunching, wore plastic trainers, hung around blocks of flats and were, as I've already mentioned, *thin*.

I wasn't thin.

Although it wasn't for the want of trying. I spent plenty of time on the stairmaster at the gym. But no matter how much I stairmastered, genetics had the final say. If my father had married a dainty little woman, I might have had a very different life. Very different thighs, certainly.

Instead, I was doomed for people always to describe

me by saying, 'She's a big girl.' Then they always added really quickly 'Now, I'm not saying she's *fat*.'

The implication being that if I was fat, I could at least do something about it.

'No,' they would continue, 'she's a fine, big, tall girl. You know, *strong*.'

I was often described as strong.

It really pissed me off.

My boyfriend, Luke, sometimes described me as magnificent. (When the light was behind me and he'd had several pints.) At least that was what he said to *me*. Then he probably went back to his friends and said, 'Now, I'm not saying she's *fat* . . .'

The whole drug-addict allegation came about one February morning when I was living in New York.

It wasn't the first time I felt as if I was on *Cosmic Candid Camera*. My life was prone to veering out of control and I had long stopped believing that the God who had been assigned to me was a benign old lad with long hair and a beard. He was more like a celestial Jeremy Beadle, and my life was the showcase he used to amuse the other Gods.

'Wa-atch,' he laughingly invites, 'as Rachel thinks she's got a new job and that it's safe to hand in her notice on the old. Little does she know that her new firm is just about to go bankrupt!'

Roars of laughter from all the other gods.

'Now, wa-atch,' he chuckles. 'As Rachel hurries to meet her new boyfriend. See how she catches the heel of her shoe in a grating? See how it comes clean off? Little did Rachel know that we had tampered with it. See how she limps the rest of the way?' More sniggers from the assembled gods.

'But the best bit of all,' laughs Jeremy, 'is that the man she was meeting never turns up! He only asked her out for a bet. Watch as Rachel squirms with embarrassment in the stylish bar. See the looks of pity the other women give her? See how the waiter gives her the extortionate bill for a glass of wine, and best of all, see how Rachel discovers she's *left her purse at home*?'

Uncontrollable guffaws.

The events that led to me being called a drug addict had the same element of celestial farce that the rest of my life had. What happened was, one night I'd sort of overdone it on the enlivening drugs and I couldn't get to sleep. (I hadn't meant to overdo it, I had simply underestimated the quality of the cocaine that I had taken.) I knew I had to get up for work the following morning, so I took a couple of sleeping tablets. After about ten minutes, they hadn't worked, so I took a couple more. And still my head was buzzing, so in desperation, thinking of how badly I needed my sleep, thinking of how alert I had to be at work, I took a few more.

I eventually got to sleep. A lovely deep sleep. So lovely and deep that when the morning came, and my alarm clock went off, I neglected to wake up.

Brigit, my flatmate, knocked on my door, then came into my room and shouted at me, then shook me, then, at her wit's end, slapped me. (I didn't really buy the wit's end bit. She must have known that slapping wouldn't wake me, but no one is in good form on a Monday morning.)

But then Brigit stumbled across a piece of paper that I'd been attempting to write on just before I fell asleep. It was just the usual maudlin, mawkish, self-indulgent poetry-type rubbish I often wrote when I was under the influence. Stuff that seemed really profound at the time, where I thought I'd discovered the secret of the universe, but that caused me to blush with shame when I read it in the cold light of day, the bits that I *could* read, that is.

The poem went something like 'Mumble, mumble, life . . .' something indecipherable, 'bowl of cherries, mumble, all I get is the pits . . .' Then – and I vaguely remembered writing this bit – I thought of a really good title for a poem about a shoplifter who had suddenly discovered her conscience. It was called *I can't take any-more*.

But Brigit, who'd recently gone all weird and uptight, didn't treat it as the load of cringe-making rubbish it so clearly was. Instead, when she saw the empty jar of sleeping tablets rolling around on my pillow, she decided it was a suicide note. And before I knew it, and it really *was* before I knew it because I was still asleep – well, asleep or unconscious, depending on whose version of the story you believe – she had rung for an ambulance and I was in Mount Solomon having my stomach pumped. That was unpleasant enough, but there was worse to come. Brigit had obviously turned into one of those New York abstention fascists, the kind who if you wash your hair with Linco beer shampoo more than twice a week, say that you're an alcoholic and that you should be on a twelve-step programme. So she rang my parents in Dublin and told them that I had a serious drug problem and that I'd just tried to kill myself. And before I could intervene and explain that it had all been an embarrassing misunder-standing, my parents had rung my painfully well-behaved older sister, Margaret. Who arrived on the first available flight from Chicago with her equally painful husband, Paul.

Margaret was only a year older than me but it felt more like forty. She was intent on ferrying me to Ireland to the bosom of my family. Where I would stay briefly before being admitted to some Betty Ford type place to sort me out 'For good and for all', as my father said when he rang me.

Of course I had no intention of going anywhere but by then I was really frightened. And not just by the talk of going home to Ireland and into a clinic, but because my father had *rung* me. *He* had rung *me*. That had never happened in the whole of my twenty-seven years. It was hard enough to get him to say hello whenever I rang home and it was one of the rare occasions when he answered the phone. The most he ever managed was 'Which one of you is that? Oh Rachel? Hold on till I get your mother.' Then there was nothing except banging and bashing as he dropped the phone and ran to get Mum.

And if Mum wasn't there he was terrified. 'Your mother's not here,' he always said, his voice high with alarm. The subtext being, 'Please, *please* don't let me have to talk to you.'

Not because he didn't like me or was a cold unapproachable father or anything like that.

He was a lovely man.

That I could grudgingly admit by the time I was twenty-seven and had lived away from home for eight years. That he wasn't the Great Withholder of Money For New Jeans that my sisters and I loved to hate during our teenage years. But despite Dad's lovely manness he wasn't big on conversation. Not unless I wanted to talk about golf. So the fact that he had rung me must have meant that I'd really messed up this time.

Fearfully, I tried to set things right.

'There's nothing wrong with me,' I told Dad. 'It's all been a mistake and I'm fine.'

But he was having none of it. 'You're to come home,' he ordered.

I was having none of it either. 'Dad, behave yourself. Be ... be ... *realistic* here, I can't just walk out on my life.'

'What can't you walk out on?' he asked.

'My job, for example,' I said. 'I can't just abandon my job.'

'I've already spoken to them at your work and they agree with me that you should come home,' he said.

Suddenly, I found myself staring into the abyss.

'You did WHAT?' I could hardly speak I was so afraid. What had they told Dad about me?

'I spoke to them at your work,' repeated Dad in the same level tone of voice.

'You big stupid eejit.' I swallowed. 'To who?'

'A chap called Eric,' said Dad. 'He said he was your boss.'

'Oh God,' I said.

OK, so I was a 27-year-old woman and it shouldn't matter if my father knew I was sometimes late for work. But it *did* matter. I felt the way I had twenty years earlier when he and Mum were called up to the school to account for my on-going dearth of completed homework.

'This is awful,' I said to Dad. 'What did you have to go ringing work for? I'm so embarrassed! What'll they think? They'll sack me for this, you know.'

'Rachel, from what I can gather I think they were just about to anyway,' said Dad's voice from across the Atlantic.

Oh no, the game was up. Dad knew! Eric must have really gone to town on my shortcomings.

'I don't believe you,' I protested. 'You're only saying that to make me come home.'

'I'm not,' said Dad. 'Let me tell you what this Eric said . . .'

No chance! I could hardly bear to think about what Eric said, never mind *hear* it.

'Everything was fine at work until you rang them,' I lied frantically. 'You've caused nothing but trouble. I'm going to ring Eric and tell him that you're a lunatic, that you escaped from a bin and not to believe a word you said.'

'Rachel.' Dad sighed heavily. 'I barely said a thing to this Eric chap, he did all the talking and he seemed delighted to let you go.'

'Let me go?' I said faintly. 'As in, fire me? You mean I've got no job?'

'That's right.' Dad sounded very matter-of-fact.

'Well, great,' I said tearfully. 'Thanks for ruining my life.'

There was silence while I tried to absorb the fact that I was once more without a job. Was God Beadle rerunning old tapes up there?

'OK, what about my flat?' I challenged. 'Seeing as you're so good at messing things up for me?'

'Margaret will sort that out with Brigit,' said Dad.

'Sort out?' I had expected the question of my flat would totally stump Dad. I was shocked that he'd already addressed the matter. They were acting as if something really *was* wrong with me.

'She'll pay a couple of months' rent to Brigit so that Brigit has breathing space to find someone new.'

'Someone new?' I shrieked. 'But this is my home.'

'From what I gather yourself and Brigit haven't been getting on too well.' Dad sounded awkward.

He was right. And we'd been getting along a whole lot worse since she'd made that phone call and brought the interference of my family tumbling down on top of me. I was furious with her and for some reason she seemed to be furious with me too. But Brigit was my best friend and we'd always shared a flat. It was out of the question for someone else to move in with her.

'You've gathered a lot,' I said drily.

He said nothing.

'An awful bloody lot,' I said, much more wetly.

I wasn't defending myself as well as I normally would have. But, to tell the truth, my trip to the hospital had taken more out of me than just the contents of my stomach. I felt shaky and not inclined to fight with Dad, which wasn't like me at all. Disagreeing with my father was something I did as instinctively as refusing to sleep with moustachioed men.

'So there's nothing to stop you coming home and getting sorted out,' said Dad.

'But I have a cat,' I lied.

'You can get another one,' he said.

'But I have a boyfriend,' I protested.

'You can get another one of those too,' said Dad.

Easy for him to say.

'Put me back onto Margaret and I'll see you tomorrow,' said Dad.

'You will in your arse,' I muttered.

And that seemed to be that. Luckily I had taken a couple of Valium. Otherwise I might have been very upset *indeed*.

Margaret was sitting beside me. In fact, she seemed to be constantly by my side, once I thought about it.

After she finished talking to Dad, I decided to put a stop to all the nonsense. It was time for me to grab back control of the reins of my life. Because this wasn't funny, it wasn't entertaining, it wasn't diverting. It was unpleasant, and above all it was unnecessary.

'Margaret,' I said briskly, 'there's nothing wrong with me. I'm sorry you've had a wasted journey, but please go away and take your husband with you. This is all a big, huge, terrible mistake.'

'I don't think it is,' she said. 'Brigit says . . .'

'Never mind what Brigit says,' I interrupted. 'I'm actually worried about Brigit because she's gone so weird. She used to be fun once.'

Margaret looked doubtful, then she said, 'But you do seem to take an awful lot of drugs.'

'It might seem an awful lot to you,' I explained gently. 'But you're a lickarse, so any amount would seem like lots.'

It was true that Margaret was a lickarse. I had four sisters, two older and two younger and Margaret was the only well-behaved one of the lot. My mother used to run her eye along us all and sadly say, 'Well, one out of five ain't bad.'

'I'm not a lickarse,' she complained. 'I'm just ordinary.'

'Yes, Rachel.' Paul had stepped forward to defend Margaret. 'She's not a lickarse. Just because she's not a, a . . . junkie who can't get a job and whose husband leaves her . . . Unlike some,' he finished darkly.

I spotted the flaw in his argument.

'My husband hasn't left me,' I protested in my defence.

'That's because you haven't got one,' said Paul.

9

Paul was obviously referring to my eldest sister, Claire, who managed to get ditched by her husband on the same day that she gave birth to their first child.

'And I have a job,' I reminded him.

'Not any more, you don't.' He smirked.

I hated him.

And he hated me. I didn't take it personally. He hated my entire family. He had a hard job deciding which one of Margaret's sisters he hated the most. And well he might, there was stiff competition among us for the position of black sheep. There was Claire, thirty-one, the deserted wife. Me, twenty-seven, allegedly a junkie. Anna, twenty-four, who'd never had a proper job, and who sometimes sold hash to make ends meet. And there was Helen, twenty, and frankly, I wouldn't know where to begin.

We all hated Paul as much as he hated us.

Even Mum, although she wouldn't admit to it. She liked to pretend that she liked everyone, in the hope that it might help her jump the queue into Heaven.

Paul was such a pompous know-all. He wore the same kind of jumpers as Dad did and bought his first house when he was thirteen or some such ridiculous age by saving up his First Communion money.

'You'd better get back on the phone to Dad,' I told Margaret. 'Because I'm going nowhere.'

'How right you are,' agreed Paul nastily.

2

The air hostess tried to squeeze past Paul and me. 'Can you sit down, please? You're blocking the aisle.'

Still Paul and I lingered awkwardly. Margaret, good girl that she was, had already taken her allocated seat by the window.

'What's the problem?' The air hostess looked at our boarding cards, then she looked at the seat numbers.

'But these are the right seats,' she said.

That was the problem. The boarding-card numbers had me sitting beside Paul and the thought of being next to him for the entire flight to Dublin revolted me. I wouldn't be able to let my right thigh relax for a whole seven hours.

'Sorry,' I said. 'But I'm not sitting beside him.'

I indicated Paul.

'And I'm not sitting beside her,' he said.

'Well, how about you?' the air hostess asked Margaret. 'Have you any objections to who you sit beside?'

'No.'

'Fine,' she said patiently. 'Why don't you go on the inside.'

She said this to Paul.

'Come out, you,' she said to Margaret. 'Then you go in the middle.'

'And then you,' she said to me.

'OK,' we all said meekly.

A man in the seat in front of us twisted his neck for a good look at the three of us.

He stared at us for a while with a puzzled look on his face. Then he spoke.

'Do you mind me asking,' he said. 'But what age are you?'

Yes, I had agreed to go home to Ireland.

Even though I had had absolutely no intention of doing so, a couple of things changed my mind. First, tall, dark and sexy Luke arrived at the apartment. I was delighted to see him.

'Shouldn't you be at work?' I asked, then proudly introduced him to Margaret and Paul.

Luke shook hands politely, but his expression was tight and tense. To put the smile back on his face, I launched into the story of my escapade in Mount Solomon. But he didn't seem to find it funny. Instead he gripped my arm hard and muttered, 'I'd like a word with you in private.'

Puzzled, I left Margaret and Paul sitting in the front room and took Luke into my bedroom. From his grim air I didn't think he was going to clamber all over me and say 'Quickly, let's get you out of these wet clothes,' and expertly remove my garments, like he usually did.

Nevertheless I still wasn't prepared for what *did* happen. He indicated that he wasn't at all amused by my hospital visit. In fact, he sounded disgusted.

'When did you lose your sense of humour?' I asked bewildered. 'You're as bad as Brigit.'

'I'm not even going to answer that,' he hissed.

Then, to my utter horror, he proceeded to tell me our relationship was over. I went cold with shock. *He'd* ended it with *me*?

'But why?' I asked, as every cell in my body screamed '*NO!*' 'Have you met someone else?'

'Don't be so stupid,' he spat.

'Why then?' I asked.

'Because you're not the person I thought you were,' he said.

Well, that told me precisely nothing.

He went on to viciously insult me, trying to make out it was *my* fault. That he had no choice but to end it with me.

'Oh no.' I wasn't going to be manipulated. 'Break it off with me if you're determined to, but don't try and blame me.'

'God,' he said angrily, 'there's just no getting through to you.'

He stood up and moved towards the door.

Don't go.

Pausing only to throw a few more nasty comments my way, he slammed out of the apartment. I was devastated. It wasn't the first time a man had ditched me for no obvious reason, but I hadn't expected it from Luke Costello. We'd had a relationship for over six months. I had even begun to think it was a good one.

I struggled to deflect waves of shock and grief and pretend to Margaret and Paul that everything was fine. Then in the midst of my stunned, stomach-churning misery, Margaret said 'Rachel, you've *got* to come home. Dad's already paid the deposit for you at the Cloisters.' And I felt like I'd been thown a life-line.

The Cloisters! The Cloisters was famous.

Hundreds of rock stars had been admitted to the converted monastery in Wicklow (no doubt tying in some handy tax exiling while they were at it) and stayed the requisite couple of months. Then, before you could say

'Make mine a fizzy water', they'd stopped wrecking hotel rooms and driving cars into swimming pools, had a new album out, were on every talk show going, speaking gently and being serene, with their hair cut and neatly combed, while reviewers spoke about a new quality and an extra dimension to their work.

I wouldn't mind going to the Cloisters. There was no shame attached to that. On the contrary. And you never knew who you might meet.

Being blown out by Luke caused me to rethink my entire life.

Maybe it would be O K to leave New York for a while, I thought carefully. Especially as there seemed to be a move towards a ban on enjoying yourself there. I didn't have to go for ever, just for a couple of months until I felt better.

What harm could it do now that I had no job and no boyfriend to hold me? It was one thing to lose my job, because I'd always get another one. But to lose a boyfriend . . . well . . .

'What do you think, Rachel?' Margaret asked anxiously. 'How about it?'

Naturally, I had to put up a bit of a protest. I couldn't admit that my life was so worthless that I could walk away from it without a backward glance. I made a show of resisting, but it was mere bravado, empty posturing.

'How would you like it,' I demanded of Margaret, 'if I marched into your life and said "Come on now, Mags, say goodbye to Paul, your friends, your flat, your job and your life. You're going three thousand miles away to a madhouse, even though there's nothing wrong with you"? Well, how would you like that?'

Margaret was nearly in tears. 'Oh, Rachel, I'm sorry. But it's not a madhouse and . . .'

I couldn't keep it up for long because I hated upsetting Margaret. Even though she was weird and saved money and hadn't had sex until she got married, I was still very fond of her. So by the time I got round to saying 'Margaret, how can your conscience let you do this to me? How can you sleep at night?' my capitulation was complete.

When I said 'OK, I'll go,' relieved looks shot between Brigit, Margaret and Paul, which annoyed me because they were acting as if I was some kind of incapacitated half-wit.

Once I had a good think about it, a rehabilitation place seemed like a good idea. A great idea.

I hadn't had a holiday in ages. I could do with a rest, some peace and serenity. Somewhere to hide and lick my Luke-shaped wounds.

The words of Patrick Kavanagh's *Advent* floated around in my head, *We have tested and tasted too much, lover, through a chink too wide, there comes in no wonder.*

I'd read loads about the Cloisters and it sounded wonderful. I had visions of spending a lot of time sitting around wrapped in a big towel. Of steam rooms, saunas, massage, seaweed treatment, algae, that kind of thing. I'd eat lots of fruit, I vowed, nothing but fruit and vegetables. And I'd drink gallons of water, at least eight glasses of water a day. To flush me out, to cleanse me.

It would be good to go for a month or so without a drink and without doing drugs.

A whole month, I thought, clenched by sudden fear. Then the calming effect of the Valium soothed me. Anyway, they probably had wine with the meals in the evenings. Or maybe people like me, the ones that didn't have serious problems, would be allowed out to walk down to the local pub.

I would stay in a simple converted monk's cell. Slate floors, whitewashed walls, a narrow wooden bed, the faraway sound of Gregorian chant floating on the evening air. And, of course, they'd have a gym. Everyone knows that exercise is the best cure for alcoholics and the like. I'd have a stomach like a plank when I came out. Two hundred sit-ups a day. It would be great to have time to spend on myself. So when I returned to New York, I'd look fabulous and Luke would be on his knees begging me to take him back.

There was bound to be some kind of therapy, as well. *Therapy* therapy, I mean, not just cellulite therapy. The lie-down-on-the-couch-and-tell-me-about-your-father kind. Which I'd be quite happy to go along with. Not to actually *do*, of course. But it would be very interesting to see the real drug addicts, the thin ones with the anoraks and the lank hair, nurturing themselves as five-year-olds. I would emerge cleansed, whole, renewed, reborn. Everyone who was currently pissed-off with me wouldn't be pissed-off anymore. The old me would have gone, the new me ready to start all over again.

'Will she, er, be going, you know, cold turkey?' Margaret tentatively asked Brigit, as we prepared for the snow-lined drive to JFK.

'Don't be so ridiculous.' I laughed. 'You're all over-reacting wildly. Cold turkey, my foot. You only get that with heroin.'

'And you're not on heroin, then?' asked Margaret.

I rolled my eyes at her in exasperation.

'Well, how am I supposed to know?' she shouted.

'I've got to go to the loo first,' I said.

'I'll come with you,' offered Margaret.

'No, you won't.' I broke into a run.

I reached it just before she did and slammed the door in her face.

'Get lost,' I shouted from behind the locked bathroom door. 'Or I'll start shooting up just to annoy you.'

As the plane took off from JFK, I settled back in my seat and I was surprised to find that I felt intense relief. I had the strange feeling that I was being airlifted to safety. I was suddenly very glad to be leaving New York. Life hadn't been easy lately. So little room to manoeuvre.

I was skint, I owed money to nearly everyone. I laughed to myself because for a minute there I really did sound like a drug addict. I didn't owe *that* kind of money, but I was up to the limit of both my credit cards and I'd had to borrow from every single one of my friends.

Work in the hotel where I was an assistant manager had become harder and harder to do. There were times when I walked through the revolving doors to start my shift and found myself wanting to scream. Eric, my boss, had been very bad tempered and difficult. I had been sick a lot and late a lot. Which made Eric more unpleasant. Which, naturally, made me take more time off sick. Until my life had shrivelled down to two emotions. Despair when I was at work, guilt when I wasn't.

As the plane cut through the clouds over Long Island, I thought fiercely 'I could be at work now. I'm not and I'm glad.'

I closed my eyes and unwelcome thoughts of Luke came barging in. The initial pain of rejection had shifted slightly to make room for the pain of missing him. He and I had practically been living together and I felt his absence like an ache. I shouldn't have started thinking about him and what he had said because it made me feel a bit hysterical. I became seized by an almost uncontrollable compulsion to find him *that very minute*, tell him how wrong he was and beg him to take me back. To get such an uncontrollable compulsion on an airborne plane at the start of a seven-hour flight was a foolish thing to do. So I fought back the urge to pull the communication cord. Luckily the air hostess was on her way round with the drinks and I accepted a vodka and orange with the same gratitude that a drowning girl might accept a rope.

'Stop it,' I muttered as Margaret and Paul stared at me with white, anxious faces. 'I'm upset. Anyway, since when wasn't I allowed to have a drink?'

'Just don't overdo it,' said Margaret. 'Promise me?'

Mum took the news that I was a drug addict very badly. My youngest sister, Helen, had been watching daytime television with her when Dad broke the news. Apparently after he had got off the phone from Brigit, he ran into the sitting-room and, all of a dither, blurted out 'That daughter of yours is a drug addict.'

All Mum said was 'Hmmm?' and continued watching Ricki Lake and the big-haired trailer-park trash.

'But I know that,' she added. 'What are you getting your knickers in a knot about?'

'No,' said Dad, annoyed. 'This isn't a joke. I'm not talking about Anna. It's Rachel!'

And apparently a funny expression appeared on Mum's face and she kind of lurched to her feet. Then, with Dad and Helen watching her – Dad nervously, Helen gleefully – she felt her way blindly into the kitchen and put her head on the kitchen table and started to cry.

'A drug addict,' she sobbed. 'I can't bear it.'

Dad put a comforting hand on her shoulder.

'Anna maybe,' she wailed. 'Anna *certainly*. But not Rachel. It's bad enough having one, Jack, but two of them. I don't know what they do with the bloody tinfoil. I really don't! Anna goes through it like wildfire and when I ask her what she does with it, you can't get a straight answer out of the child.'

'She uses it to wrap the hash into little parcels when she's selling it,' supplied Helen helpfully.

'Mary, shut up about the tinfoil a minute,' said Dad, as he tried to formulate a plan for my rehabilitation.

Then his head snapped back to Helen. 'She does *what*?' he said, aghast.

Meanwhile, Mum was furious.

'Oh "shut up about it" is it?' she demanded of Dad. 'It's all very well for you to say shut up about the tinfoil. You're not the one who has to roast a turkey and goes to the press to get a sheet of tinfoil to cover the fecker with and finds there's nothing there only a roll of cardboard. It's not your turkey that ends up as dry as the Sahara.'

'Mary, please, for the love of God . . .'

'If she only told me she'd used it, it wouldn't be so bad. If she left the cardboard roll out I might remember to get more the next time I went to Quinnsworth . . .'

'Try and remember the name of the place that that fellow went in to,' he said.

'What fellow?'

'You know, the alcoholic, the one who embezzled all that money, he was married to that sister of the one you go on the retreats with, you *know* him.'

'Patsy Madden, is that who you're talking about?' asked Mum.

'That's the lad!' Dad was delighted. 'Well, find out where he went to, to get help for the jar.'

'But Rachel doesn't have a problem with drink,' protested Mum.

'No,' said Dad. 'But they do a whole load of stuff in whatever the name of the place is. Drink, drugs, gambling, food. Sure you can get addicted to nearly anything these days.'

Dad bought a couple of the glossy women's magazines every month. Ostensibly for Helen and Anna, but really for himself. So he knew about all sorts of things that fathers really shouldn't: self-mutilation, free radicals, AHAs, Jean-Paul Gaultier and the best fake tans.

So Mum got on the phone and made discreet enquiries. When pressed she said that a distant cousin of Dad's was showing a bit too much fondness for alcohol, thanked the woman for her concern and quickly got off the phone.

'The Cloisters,' she said.

'The Cloisters!' Dad exclaimed in relief. 'It was driving me mad not being able to remember. I wouldn't have got a wink of sleep, I would have just lain there all night racking my brain . . .'

'Ring them,' Mum interrupted tearfully.

3

The Cloisters cost a fortune. That's why so many pop stars went there. Some people's health insurance covered the costs but, as I'd lived away from Ireland for about eight years, I didn't have any. I didn't have any in New York either, come to think of it. I'd always intended to get round to it, some day, when I was mature and responsible and grown-up.

Because I had neither health insurance nor a penny to my name, Dad had said that he'd foot the bill, that it was worth it to sort me out.

But that meant that as soon as I arrived home and staggered in through the front door, jetlagged and depressed with a Valium and vodka hangover, Helen greeted me by yelling from the top of the stairs, 'You stupid cow, that's my inheritance money you're using to dry out with, you know.'

'Hello, Helen,' I said wearily.

Then she said in a surprised voice, 'God, you've got thin. Emancipated looking, you skinny bitch!'

I nearly said 'thanks' but remembered in time. The usual scenario was that I would say 'Really? Have I?' And she'd say 'No! Nah haaah! You fall for it every time, don't you? You big thick.'

'Where's Pollyanna?' asked Helen.

'Out at the gate, talking to Mrs Hennessy,' I said.

Margaret was the only one of us who spoke to our

neighbours, happy to discuss hip replacements, grand-children's First Communions, the unusually wet weather and the availability of Tayto in Chicago.

Then Paul pushed into the hall, loaded down with bags.

'Oh Christ, no,' said Helen, still at the top of the stairs. 'No one said *you* were coming. How long are you staying for?'

'Not long.'

'Better not be. Or else I'll have to go out and get a job.'

Despite sleeping with all her professors (or so she said), Helen had failed her first-year exams in university. She'd repeated the year but, when she failed the exams again, she gave the whole thing up as a bad job.

That had been the previous summer, and she hadn't managed to get a job in the meantime. Instead she spent the time hanging round the house, annoying Mum, badgering her to play cards.

'Helen! Leave your brother-in-law alone,' came my mother's voice. And then she appeared at the top of the stairs beside Helen.

I'd been dreading meeting my mother. I had the sensation that there was a lift in my chest that had plummeted out of control to the pit of my stomach.

Faintly I could hear Helen complaining 'But I hate him. And you're always telling me that honesty is the best policy . . .'

Mum hadn't come to the airport with Dad. It was the first time since I had left home that she hadn't come to the airport to meet me. So I figured she was dangerously cross.

'Hi, Mum,' I managed. I couldn't quite look at her directly.

She gave me a sad, little, martyrish smile and I felt a

violent pang of guilt that nearly sent me groping for my Valium bottle there and then.

'How was your journey?' she asked.

I couldn't bear the pretend politeness, the skirting round the really big issue.

'Mum,' I blurted, 'I'm sorry you got a fright, but there's nothing wrong with me. I don't have a problem with drugs and I didn't try to kill myself.'

'Rachel, WILL YOU STOP LYING!'

The lift inside me was going haywire by then. I was getting the plummeting sensation so often that I felt sick. Guilt and shame mingled with anger and resentment.

'I'm not lying,' I protested.

'Rachel,' she said with an edge of hysteria to her voice, 'you were rushed to hospital in an ambulance and had your stomach pumped.'

'But there was no need for it,' I explained. 'It was a mistake.'

'It was not!' she exclaimed. 'They checked your vital signs in the hospital, it *needed* to be done.'

Really, I thought in surprise. Was that true? Before I could ask she was off again.

'And you have a drug problem,' she said. 'Brigit said you take loads and so did Margaret and Paul.'

'Yes, but . . .' I tried to explain. While simultaneously feeling a burst of explosive rage at Brigit, which I had to file away for a later date. I couldn't bear it when my mother was upset with me. I was used to my father shouting at me and it didn't affect me in the slightest. Except maybe to make me laugh. But Mum giving me all this 'I'm disappointed in you' stuff was very unpleasant.

'OK, I take drugs now and then,' I admitted.

'What kind?' she asked.

'Oh, you know,' I said.

'I don't.'

'Er, well, maybe a line or two of cocaine . . .'

'Cocaine!' she gasped. She looked stricken and I felt like slapping her. She didn't understand. She was from a generation that went into spasms of horror at the mere mention of the word 'drugs'.

'Is it nice?' asked Helen, but I ignored her.

'It's not as bad as it sounds,' I pleaded.

'It doesn't sound bad at all.' I wished Helen would go away.

'It's harmless and non-addictive and everyone takes it,' I beseeched Mum.

'I don't,' complained Helen. 'Chance would be a fine thing.'

'I don't know anyone who does,' said Mum. 'Not one of my friends' daughters has done anything like this.'

I fought back the rage that filled me. From the way she was going on, you'd swear that I was the only person in the whole world, ever, who had been out of line or made a mistake.

Well, you're my mother, I thought belligerently. You made me the way I am.

But mercifully – Jeremy must have been having a rest – I somehow managed not to say it.

I stayed at home for two days before I went to the Cloisters.

It was not pleasant.

I was not popular.

Except for Margaret, who hadn't got past the qualifying rounds, the position of Least Favourite Daughter passed from one of us to the next on a rotating basis, like the

24

presidency of the EU. My brush with death ensured that I had toppled Claire from her position and I now wore the crown.

Almost the moment I was off the plane Dad told me that they'd do a blood test at the Cloisters before I was admitted. 'So,' he said nervously, 'now, I'm not saying you will, mind, but if you were thinking of taking anything, and I'm sure you're not, it'll show up in the test and you won't be allowed in.'

'Dad,' I said, 'I keep telling you, I'm not a drug addict and there's nothing to worry about.'

I nearly added that I was still waiting for the condom full of cocaine to clear my digestive tract but, as he wasn't showing much of a sense of humour, I thought better of it.

Dad's fears were unfounded because I had no intention of taking any drugs.

That's because I didn't have any to take. Well, no illegal ones anyway. I had my economy-size, family-pack of Valium but that didn't count because I got it on prescription (even if I had to buy the prescriptions from a dodgy doctor in the East Village who had an expensive ex-wife and an even more expensive smack habit). I certainly hadn't been fool enough to risk smuggling cocaine and its illicit ilk into the country. Which was very adult and sensible of me.

And not actually the great sacrifice that I'm making it sound. I knew that I'd never go short of a narcotic while Anna was around.

The only thing was, Anna *wasn't* around. From Mum's terse little sentences, I gathered that Anna was as good as living with her boyfriend, Shane. Now, there was a boy who knew how to enjoy himself! Shane, as they say, 'lived life to the full'. To overflowing. To bursting point.

Oddly enough, it wasn't cocaine I missed. It was Valium. Not that that was surprising, I was shaken by the recent and rapid changes my life had undergone and the tension between me and Mum wasn't pleasant. I would have appreciated something to take the edge off it all. But I managed not to take any of my little magic white pills because I was really looking forward to going to the Cloisters. If I'd had more time (and any money) I would even have bought new clothes in honour of it.

Such willpower! And they were calling me a drug addict? I ask you.

I slept an awful lot in the two days. It was the best thing to do because I was jetlagged and disoriented and everyone hated me.

I tried to ring Luke a couple of times. I knew I shouldn't. He was so angry with me the best thing to do was give him time to calm down, but I couldn't help myself. As it happened, I just got his answering machine and I had enough of a grip of myself not to leave a message.

I would have tried ringing him a lot more. I had compulsions to do so for most of my waking hours. But Dad had recently got a very large phone bill (something to do with Helen) and had mounted a twenty-four-hour guard round the phone. So any time I dialled a number, Dad tensed no matter where he was, even if he was four miles away playing golf, and cocked his ear intently. If I dialled more than seven digits, I would barely be started on the eighth when he would come barrelling into the hall to shout 'Get off the fecking phone!' Which ruined my chances of talking to Luke but was worth its weight in gold in the nostalgia stakes. My teenage years came rushing back to me. All I needed was for him to say 'Not a minute past eleven, Rachel. Now, I mean it this time. If you keep me waiting in that car like the last time you're never going out again' for me to be fourteen all over again. Although why would I want to be that? You try being fourteen and five foot seven, with size eight feet.

Relations were even more strained with my mother. My first day at home, as I undressed for a post-flight snooze, I caught her staring at me as if I'd just grown another head.

'Lord preserve us.' Her voice was shaking. 'Where did you get all those terrible bruises?'

I looked down and thought I was seeing someone else's body. My stomach and arms and ribs were a mess of dark purple blotches.

'Oh,' I said in a little voice. 'I suppose that must have been from having my stomach pumped.'

'God above.' She tried to take me in her arms. 'No one said . . . I just thought they . . . I didn't realize it was so *violent.*'

I pushed her away. 'Well, now you do.'

'I feel sick,' she said.

She wasn't the only one.

When I got dressed or undressed after that I avoided looking in the mirror. Luckily it was February and it was freezing, so, even in bed, I could wear long-sleeved, high-necked things.

During those two days, I had one horrible dream after another.

I had my old favourite, the There's-someone-scary-in-my-room-and-I-can't-wake-up dream. Where I dreamt – surprise, surprise – that there was someone in my room, someone menacing, who meant to harm me. And when I tried to wake up to protect myself, I found I couldn't.

27

The force got closer and closer until they were leaning over me and, even though I felt panicky terror, I still couldn't wake up. I was paralysed. I tried and tried to break through to the surface, but I suffocated under the blanket of sleep.

I also had the I'm-dying dream. That one was horrible because I could actually feel my life force spiral out of me, like a tornado in reverse, and I couldn't do anything to stop it. I knew I'd be saved if I woke up, but I couldn't.

I dreamt that I fell off cliffs, that I was in a car crash, that a tree fell on top of me. I felt the impact every single time and jerked awake sweating and shaking, never knowing where I was or whether it was day or night.

Helen left me alone until the second night I was back. I was in bed, afraid to get up, and she arrived into the room, eating a Cornetto. She had an air of loose-endness about her that spelt trouble.

'Hello,' she said.

'I thought you were going for a drink with Margaret and Paul,' I said warily.

'I was. I'm not now.'

'Why not?'

'Because stingy bastard Paul says he's not buying me any more drinks,' she said viciously. 'And where am I going to get money for drinks? I'm unemployed, you know.

'That Paul wouldn't give you the steam off his piss,' she said, as she sat down on my bed.

'But didn't they take you last night and get you totally locked?' I asked in surprise. 'Margaret said you were drinking double Southern Comforts all night and you didn't buy a single drink.'

'I'm unem*ploy*ed!' she roared. 'I'm poor! What do you expect me to do?'

'OK, OK,' I said mildly. I wasn't up to a row. Anyway, I agreed with her. Paul was as tight as a nun's gee. Even Mum once said that Paul would eat his dinner in a drawer and peel an orange in his pocket. And that he wouldn't piss on the road in case the little birds warmed their feet. Even though she was drunk when she said it – she'd had a quarter pint of Harp and lime – she meant it.

'God, imagine!' Helen smiled at me, as she settled herself on the bed and looked as if she'd be there for some time. 'My own sister, a mentaller, in a loony bin.'

'It's not a loony bin,' I protested weakly. 'It's a treatment centre.'

'A treatment centre!' She scoffed. 'That's nothing but a loony bin by another name. You're fooling no one.'

'You've got it all wrong,' I tried.

'People will cross the road when they see you coming,' she said gleefully. 'They'll say "That's the Walsh girl, the one that went mad and had to be locked up," so they will.'

'Shut up.'

'And the people will be confused because of Anna and they'll say " *Which* Walsh girl? I believe there's a couple of them that are gone in the head and . . ."'

'Pop stars go there,' I interrupted, playing my trump card.

That stopped her in her tracks.

'Who?' she demanded.

I named a couple of names and she was visibly impressed.

'Really?'

'Yes.'

'How do you know?'

'I read about them in the papers.'

'How come I never heard about it?'

'Helen, you don't read the papers.'

'Don't I? No, I suppose I don't, what would I want to read them for?'

'To find out about pop stars going to the Cloisters?' I said archly. I was rewarded with a sour look from Helen.

'Shut up, you smart arse,' she said. 'You won't think you're so great when you're bouncing around in your padded cell wearing one of those lovely jackets with the long sleeves.'

'I won't be in a padded cell,' I said smugly. 'And I *will* be hobnobbing with celebrities.'

'Do pop stars really go there?' Her excitement was starting to show, no matter how hard she tried to hide it.

'Yes,' I promised her.

'Really?' she asked again.

'Really.'

'Really, really?'

'Really, really.'

There was a little pause.

'Janey.' She sounded impressed.

'Here, finish this.' She thrust the remains of the Cornetto at me.

'No thanks,' I said. The thought of food made me feel sick.

'I'm not asking you to take it,' said Helen. 'I'm telling you. I'm sick of Cornettos and no matter how many times I tell Dad to get Magnums at the freezer centre, he always comes back with bloody Cornettos. Except for the one time and what does he bring back? Mint Magnums. I ask you, *mint . . .*'

'I don't want it.' I pushed the offending Cornetto away.

'Well, on your head be it.' Helen shrugged and put it on my bedside table where it proceeded to melt all over the place. I tore my thoughts back to happier things.

'So, Helen, when I'm best friends with the likes of Madonna,' I said airily, 'you'll be . . .'

'Be realistic, Rachel,' she interrupted. 'Although I suppose that's one of the reasons you're going to the bin in the first place, because you can't be realistic . . .'

'What are you talking about?' It was my turn to interrupt.

'Well,' she said, with a pitying smile, 'they're hardly going to put the famous people in with rest of you, are they? They have to protect their privacy. Otherwise the likes of you would go to the papers as soon as you're out and sell their story. *Sex in my cocaine hell* and all that.'

She was right. I was disappointed, but not too disappointed. After all I'd probably see them at mealtimes and on social occasions. Maybe they had dances.

'And of course they're bound to have much nicer bedrooms and nicer food,' said Helen, making me feel worse. 'Which you won't be getting because Dad's much too stingy. You'll be in the economy rooms while the celebrities will be living it up in the deluxe wing.'

I felt a burst of rage at my tightfisted father. How dare he not pay the extra for me to be in with the celebrities!

'And there's no point asking him to cough up.' Helen read my thoughts. 'He says we're poor now, because of you, and we can't get real crisps anymore, just yellow-pack ones.'

I felt very depressed. I lay in silence. So, highly unusually, did Helen.

'All the same,' she finally said, 'you're bound to bump

into them at some stage. You know, in the corridors and in the grounds and such places. You might even get to be friends with some of them.'

Suddenly I felt joyous and hopeful. If Helen was convinced, then it had to be true.

4

I'd been on nodding terms with Luke Costello long before the night I ended up in bed with him. He was Irish and I was Irish and, although I didn't know it at the time, we lived about four blocks away from each other.

I used to see him around because we went to the same bars. Irish bars, but not the type of Irish ghetto bar where you sing 'A Nation Once Again' and 'Spancil Hill' and cry and collect money for The Cause. These bars were different. They were actually *fashionable*, in the same way that brasseries were a few years back. They were called tongue-in-cheek, Irishy things like Tadgh's Boghole and Slawn Che. Apparently an Irish pop star owned one of them, although I'm not sure which bar it was. Or which pop star, either, for that matter.

Being Irish in New York has a perennial cachet, but while I lived there it was actually groovy.

Anyway, Brigit and I used to 'hang out' (we emulated the vernacular, but always with a snigger) in these places and see Luke and his friends and have a good laugh at them.

Not because Brigit and I were unkind, but really, you'd want to have seen them. None of them would have looked out of place in any of the rock bands that were fashionable in the early seventies. The type that played huge stadiums and drove Ferraris into swimming pools and were photographed with a string of interchangeable skinny blonde girls.

Luke and the boys were all about the same height, around six foot, and had regulation-issue longish, curlyish hair. At the time long hair on a man was only OK if it was all the same length, middle-parted and lank. *Nul points* for layered, curly and shiny.

In the time we knew them, not once did any of them appear with this month's cut. Whether it was short, brushed forward and bleached white. Or the crewcut to end all crewcuts. Or a shaved head with sideburns almost joined under the chin. Or whatever.

And their clothes were as old-fashioned as their hair. Denim, denim and more denim, and an occasional splash of leather. With the emphasis on *tight*, if you follow me. On a good day, you could tell which of them had been circumcised.

They were completely immune to the fashion of the outside world. Tommy Hilfiger suits, Stussy hats, Phat-pharm jackets, Diesel satchels, Adidas skateboard shoes or Timberlands – I don't think these boys even knew such things *existed*. Anyone worth their sartorial salt would. The only thing I can say in their defence is that none of them had a suede fringey jacket. At least I never *saw* any of them wearing one.

Luke and his pals were too anachronistic-looking for our taste. We called them 'Real Men', but with heavy irony.

And as for the aforementioned occasional splash of leather, well . . . thereby hangs a tale. What happened was that after we had observed and laughed at the lads for many months, Brigit and I slowly became aware of something strange. Whenever they were out en masse only *one* of them was wearing his leather trousers. How do they organize that, we wondered? Do you think they ring each other up before they go out? And ask each other what they're wearing, the way girls do?

Over the months we tried to see if there was a pattern to it. Did they have a rota system going, we puzzled? With Joey being allowed to wear his pair every Wednesday, Gaz every Thursday, something like that? And what would happen if two of them turned up *both* wearing theirs?

But one night we noticed something even stranger than their foolproof rota. The back pocket on Gaz's pair was ripped. Nothing remarkable there. Except that when we had seen Shake the previous weekend, *his* pair had had a rip in exactly the same place. Interesting, we mused, *very interesting.*

Two days later when we saw them at the Lively Bullock, Joey's pair had an identical rip.

Open-mouthed from the wonder of it all, we resolved to withhold judgement until it had happened to a fourth one. (Oh ye, of little faith . . .) And sure enough, not long after that we saw Johnno in the Cute Hoor. Except he was sitting down for hours and we thought he would never stand up and show us his bum. How we eked out that one beer between the two of us! We didn't have a bean, but we would have gone demented stuck in the apartment all evening. Eventually, several hours later, when our beer had nearly *evaporated,* Johnno of the camel-like bladder finally got up. As Brigit and I clutched each other and held our breath, he slowly turned around and there it was! The rip! The identical rip on the identical pocket!

We both let out a shriek of laughter and triumph. So it was true!

Through my convulsions I vaguely heard someone

complain in an Irish accent, 'Christ ALMIGHTY! Is there a banshee on the premises?'

As we rolled around the place, tears pouring down our cheeks, we were watched by the rest of the pub which had fallen completely silent.

'Oh God,' gasped Brigit. 'And we thought they all had a . . . a . . . a . . .' She couldn't really speak she was laughing so much.

'Pair!' she finally snorted at last.

'We thought . . . we thought . . .' I heaved with shaking shoulders. 'That only one of them was allowed to wear their pair at . . . at . . .' I had to put my head down on the table and pound with my fist for a while, 'at any one time.'

'No wonder only one ever turned up wearing his pair . . .' I croaked.

'Because,' convulsed Brigit, her face bright red. 'Because . . . because . . . *there was only one pair to* WEAR!!!'

'Stop,' I begged. 'I'm going to puke.'

'Come on, girls,' a man's voice exhorted. 'Share the joke.'

We were suddenly very popular. There were thousands of men in the bar who were over from Mayo for a conference on beef. They had thought mistakenly that, because the bar was called the Cute Hoor, they'd have a night of singing 'Four Green Fields' and holding forth on Irish politics ahead of them. They hadn't enjoyed being sniggered at and snubbed by New York's finest and trendiest. They hadn't liked it at *all*. After all, they were very important men in Ballina or Westport or wherever it was they hailed from.

So when Brigit and I had our convulsions they thought it was a breath of fresh air. Every single one of them wanted to buy us a drink and find out what was so funny.

But, while we accepted the jars, after all a free drink is a free drink, we couldn't possibly tell them what we were laughing at.

We managed to calm down slightly. Except now and again, Brigit would grab my arm and almost unable to speak, would manage 'Imagine owning a ... a ... a timeshare in a pair of trousers!' And we'd be gone for the next ten minutes, twitching and convulsing, tears pouring down our red, shiny faces. While the circle of Mayo men watched us in bemusement.

Or I'd say 'You can only be in their gang if you have the right waist and leg measurements!' And we'd be off again.

Actually, it was a great night. All the trendy people upped sticks en masse as a protest against the hick Mayo men. So Brigit and I were able to let our hair down and enjoy ourselves without the fear of being thought uncool.

We were there until at least three and, God, we were *pissed*. So pissed that we even joined in with the mandatory, misty-eyed singsong. Isn't it funny the way Irish people, whenever they go away from home, even if it's only a daytrip to Holyhead for the duty-free, end up singing sorrowful, poignant songs about the leaving of the Emerald Isle and how they wished they were back there?

Even though the Mayo men were only in New York for four days, we had 'From Clare to Here', 'The Mountains of Mourne', 'The Hills of Donegal', Ireland's Eurovision entry and – unusual choice this – Oasis's 'Wonderwall'. *And* we had an ill-advised and very, very drunken attempt at dancing the Walls of Limerick. Which the proprietor put a stop to. ('Come on lads, settle down, let ye, or ye can all feck off back to Westport for yeerselves.') After two of the men nearly came to blows over the number of times you meet and go back before you cross over. Apparently one of them was confusing the Walls of Limerick with the Siege of Ennis, the way you do . . .

5

All in all, the idea of sleeping with Luke or any of his pals was laughable. Unimaginable, really. Little did I know . . .

The night in question was about a month after the Great Mirth with the Mayo men in the Cute Hoor. Brigit and I were going to – well crashing, if I'm honest – a party at the Rickshaw Rooms. We had tried very hard to look sexy because we hoped, as we did wherever we went, that there might be some attractive and, more importantly, *available* lads there.

New York was a poor hunting ground for boyfriends. You couldn't get one for love nor money. (Naturally, I was prepared to offer both.) Reports from a friend in Australia and a friend in Dublin indicated that pickings were slim everywhere, but New York just took the biscuit. Not only were there a billion women to every straight man, but every one of the billion women was heart-stoppingly beautiful. I'm talking *exquisite*. And the explanation of such incredible beauty usually went something like 'Oh, her mother's half Swedish, half Australian Aboriginal and her father is half Burmese, quarter Eskimo and quarter Italian.'

As Brigit and I were both a hundred per cent Irish, how could we possibly compete? On a regular basis we despaired of our looks. Especially because we were both tall and big-boned. All we really had going for us was our hair; mine was long and dark and hers was long and blonde. Some of hers was even natural.

What we did have in our favour, however, was that most of the New York girls were completely neurotic. We weren't.

We were only *mildly* neurotic. (Pathological fear of goats and an obsession with potatoes cooked in any way wasn't as bad as begging to be beaten about the face and neck with a broken bottle during sexual intercourse.)

Anyway, despite our lack of ethnic diversity, on the night in question we thought we looked pretty hot. As I remember, Brigit's exact words when we surveyed each other before the off were 'Not bad for a pair of heifers.' I agreed, and all without any self-esteem-enhancing snow in our systems! Of course, we would have loved some but it was two days from Brigit's payday and we barely had enough money to feed ourselves.

I had a pair of beautiful new shoes on their maiden voyage. With my size feet, it was impossible to get nice shoes to fit me. Even in New York where they're used to dealing with freaks. But I was befriended by the season. It was summer and the shoes were mules. Lime-green, not-too-high mules. So it didn't matter that they were two sizes too small for me, because my toes could stick out the front and my heels out the back. Excruciating to walk in, of course, but who cared. Beauty is pain.

So along to the Rickshaw Rooms for ourselves! Where they were holding a launch party for a new television series. Brigit had heard about it through her job and apparently it would have a couple of famous, good-looking men, enough free drink to sink a battleship and, hopefully, countless people with a cocaine habit who might be willing to share their stash.

We didn't have an invitation but we got in because Brigit offered to not have sex with the bouncer.

That's what she actually said. 'My friend and I don't have invitations but, if you let us in, you needn't sleep with either of us.'

And, as Brigit had promised me, we certainly had his attention after that.

'You see,' Brigit explained to his bemused face, 'in your line of work, you must have hundreds of gorgeous women saying "If you let *me* in, I'll let you in," if you follow me?' She gave him a leery wink that involved every muscle in her body, just in case he didn't.

'You must be sick of it,' she told him firmly.

The bouncer, a young, not-unattractive Italian man, nodded, as if in a daze.

'My friend and I here,' Brigit went on, 'our unique selling point is that we're *not* gorgeous, so we thought we'd make the most of it. Can we come in?'

'Of course,' he mumbled. He looked puzzled and confused.

'But wait,' he called after us. 'You'll need these.' And he pressed two invitations upon us, just as we were about to break into a run for the lift.

When we got upstairs we had to run the gauntlet of a second set of bouncers but by then we had invitations.

And in we swept. We tried not to look too overwhelmed. The beautiful art deco room! The fabulous view! The vast quantities of strong drink!

Seconds after we arrived, laughing and buoyed up by our success, Brigit froze and grabbed me.

'Look,' she hissed, 'it's the Time Warp Boys.'

I looked and sure enough, there, in a proliferation of hair and red Levi's tabs, were Gaz, Joey, Johnno, Shake

41

and Luke. As usual, they were accessorized by a couple of blonde girls with legs so skinny they looked as if they had rickets.

'What are the Real Men doing here?' I demanded. Suddenly our victory over the bouncer became meaningless, all the good went out of it. They were obviously letting any old eejit in.

Luke was earnestly distributing their drinks. 'Joey, man, JD straight up, there you go.'

'Thanks, Luke, man.'

'Johnno, man, JD on the rocks, that's yours.'

'Good one, Luke, man.'

'Gaz, where are you, man? Oh right, here's your tequila, salt and lemon.'

'Nice one, Luke, man.'

'Melinda, babe, no pink champagne, but they had some ordinary stuff and they put some Ribena in it, nice guy that barman.'

'Thanks, Luke.'

'Tamara, babe, JD straight up, sorry, babe, no umbrellas.'

'Thanks, Luke.'

Am I painting a clear enough picture here? Yes, that's right, they *did* call each other 'man', they *did* call women 'babe', they *did* drink Jack Daniels almost incessantly, and naturally, of course, they abbreviated 'Jack Daniels' to 'JD'. I won't malign the boys by saying that whenever they met, they highfived each other, but at times, I'd say it was touch and go.

'Who's wearing the timeshare trousers tonight?' asked Brigit. Which put paid to the next five minutes as we held each other and laughed.

Finally, I managed to look at them.

'It's Luke,' I said. I must have said it louder than I had intended because Luke looked up. He stared at us both, and then, while we watched in disbelief, he winked at us. Brigit and I looked blankly at each other for a moment, before *exploding* again. 'The *state* of him,' I whimpered, through tears of mirth.

'Who does he think he is?' Brigit guffawed.

Then, to my horror, I saw Luke detach himself from the others and, with the same loose-limbed insouciance with which he usually perambulated himself, made his way in our direction.

'Oh God,' I snorted, 'he's coming over.'

Before Brigit could answer Luke was standing in front of us. He was all smiles and eager, puppy-like friendliness.

'It's Rachel, right?'

I nodded because if I opened my mouth I would have laughed all over him. Vaguely I registered that I had to tilt my head back to see him. Something tickled inside me.

'And Brigit?'

Brigit nodded mutely.

'I'm Luke,' he said and stuck out his hand. Dumbly, Brigit and I shook it.

'I've seen the pair of you around a lot,' he said. 'You're always laughing, it's great!'

I searched his face for a trace of irony, but there didn't seem to be any. Then again, I hadn't taken any of them to be Einstein.

'Come on over and meet the rest of the lads,' he invited.

And although we didn't want to, because we were wasting valuable time when we could have been trying to get off with some of the lovely men there, we traipsed over behind him.

Where we had to do the Irish person meets other Irish person abroad thing. Which involved first of all pretending that we hadn't realized the other was Irish. Then we had to discover that we had been brought up two minutes' walk from each other, or that we'd gone to the same school, or that we'd met on our summer holidays in Tramore when we were eleven, or that our mothers were each other's bridesmaids, or that his older brother had gone out with my older sister, or that when our dog got lost his family found it and brought it back, or that my father once drove into the back of his father's car and they had a row on the Stillorgan dual carriageway and they were both due up in court for causing a public affray, or whatever. But our paths would have already crossed in some way, of this there would be no doubt.

Sure enough, within seconds, we found out that Joey and Brigit had met at Butlin's nineteen years before, when they had come first and second respectively in the fancy-dress competition. Apparently the nine-year-old Joey had gone as Johnny Rotten and was so good that even Brigit agreed he had deserved first prize. (Brigit had wanted to go as Princess Leia, but she didn't have a gold bikini or long hair. But in keeping with the *Star Wars* theme her mother made her go as Luke Skywalker instead. She wore one of her father's white shirts and the bottom of her pyjamas and held a long white stick and when the judges came round she had to mumble 'Can you feel the force.' And they didn't hear her the first time so she had to say it again. And one of the judges said, 'The what, lovie? The fort?' To this day, she says she hasn't recovered from it. But at least she wasn't as bad as Oisin, her older brother, who had to wear a black bucket on his head and breathe heavily and go as Darth Vader.)

A few seconds later, Gaz and I established a link. He said 'You look familiar,' and then proceeded to interrogate me. 'What's your second name? Walsh? Where do you live? Have you an older sister? Did she ever go to Wesley? Long hair? Huge pair of ... er ... eyes? Very friendly girl? What's her name? Roisin? Imelda, something like that? Claire! That's right! Yeah, I rode her one night at a party in Rathfarnham about ten years ago.'

A chorus of outrage erupted.

'You can't say that!' we all exclaimed. 'The cheek of him.'

We turned to each other with disgusted expressions. 'The *cheek* of him,' we nodded vigorously. 'The cheek of him.'

I looked at Shake and he looked at me and we both said, 'The cheek of him!'

Brigit turned to Joey and Joey turned to Brigit and they both exclaimed 'The cheek of him!'

Luke and Johnno looked aghast and said in unison 'The cheek of him!'

Melinda looked at Tamara and Tamara raised her eyebrows at Melinda and Melinda said 'We must remember to buy some milk on the way home.'

'Gaz, man,' said Luke, when the hue and cry had died down slightly. 'I keep telling you, man, you can't go round saying things like that about the ladies, it's not what a gentleman does.'

Gaz was puzzled and annoyed. 'What have I done?' he demanded.

'You're insulting her by talking that way about her,' explained Luke gently.

'I'm not insulting her,' said Gaz hotly. 'She was a *great* ride.'

45

'Are you anything like your big sister?' he asked, moving perceptibly closer to me.

6

I enjoyed talking to the Real Men. In New York I found it so hard to get men to show any interest in me that it was balm to the ego to be the centre of some male attention. Even if you wouldn't touch said males with a ten-foot pole. In fact, Brigit and I were so popular that Melinda marched off in a huff, wriggling her six-year-old-child's bum. *The lucky bitch!* Then Tamara flounced off a second later, looking as though her legs might break.

'The blonde leading the blonde,' I remarked. Which had everyone in stitches. Like I said, I hadn't thought any of them were Einstein.

'Poor Tamara,' I continued. 'She must have a terrible sex life.'

They all demanded 'Why?' Fair enough, as at least three of the lads present were responsible for Tamara's horizontal fun.

'Because,' I explained, 'Tamara never comes.'

Luke, Shake, Joey and Johnno nearly had to be hospitalized. Gaz looked bewildered and bleated plaintively 'What does she mean?' until Luke, doubled over with laughter, took him aside and explained it to him.

Eventually, the time came to say goodbye to the boys. It had been a pleasant interlude, but Brigit and I were on a mission. There were too many chiselled hunks in that room for us to be wasting time talking to this crowd of hairy eejits, nice and all as they were.

But just as I was about to slip my moorings, Luke remarked to me, 'When I was nine, I wouldn't have dared dress up as Johnny Rotten. I was more likely to have gone as Mother Teresa.'

'Why's that?' I asked politely

'I was an altar-boy then and I wanted to be a priest.'

With his words, a youthful memory ignited in my head.

'That's funny, when I was nine I wanted to be a nun,' I burst out, before I could stop myself.

Straightaway, I was sorry I'd said anything. After all, this wasn't something I was proud of. On the contrary, it was something I had kept well hidden and that I wished had never happened.

'Is that right?' Luke gave a big, amused smile. 'Isn't that a blast, altogether? I thought I was the only one.'

His relaxed attitude, as if it wasn't something to be ashamed of, mollified me.

'So did I,' I admitted.

He smiled again, drawing me into an intimate little circle of identification. I felt a flower of interest begin to unfurl within me, and I decided not to leave just yet.

'How bad did it get for you?' he urged. 'Because I don't think you could have got any worse than me. Would you believe I was actually sorry that Catholicism wasn't still banned because I would have loved to have been martyred? I used to fantasize about being boiled in oil.'

'I used to draw pictures of myself covered in arrows,' I admitted, on the one hand amazed at how bizarre my behaviour had been and on the other remembering how real and important it had seemed at the time.

'Not only that,' Luke said, his eyes twinkling at the

memory, 'but I was into mortification of the flesh, tying stuff too tightly on me, and all that. Sort of like, Junior S and M, you know?' He cocked a questioning eyebrow at me, and I smiled encouragingly.

'Only I couldn't find any ropes in the garage, so I had to steal the cord of my mother's dressing-gown and knot it round my waist. I had a couple of days of good, purifying agony until my brother found out and accused me of being a transvestite.'

I found myself drawing nearer to Luke, as I wondered how other people dealt with scornful older siblings.

'Did he really?' I asked, intrigued. 'And then what happened?'

'I suppose I should have done the decent thing,' he said thoughtfully.

'What?' I asked. 'Pray for him?'

'*No!* Head-butt the fucker.'

I burst out laughing in surprise.

'But instead I made a great show of turning the other cheek, then I said I'd do a novena with his name on it. The joys of a Catholic childhood.'

I laughed and laughed.

'I was an awful eejit, wasn't I, Rachel?' He invited me, with a charming, disarming smile.

I liked the way he said my name. And I decided to wait a while longer before cruising the room. I discreetly shifted so that I was in a corner, with Luke facing me. That way, no one who mattered could see me.

'Why do you think?' I asked awkwardly. 'Why did we want something so peculiar? Could it have been incipient puberty? Hormones gone haywire?'

'Could have been,' he agreed, as I searched his face for answers. 'Although maybe we were a bit young. I think

49

with me it had something to do with having just moved house and having no friends.'

'Me too.'

'You'd just moved house?'

'No.'

We looked at each other for a few bemused seconds. He didn't know whether to feel sorry for me, or to laugh or to offer advice. Then, luckily, we both laughed, holding each other's eyes, united by the laughter, encircled by it.

And for the next couple of hours Luke had me in hysterics. He told me about an Indian restaurant on Canal Street where he said he had a curry so hot he swore he went blind in one eye for three days. Talk of food led to the revelation that, like me, Luke was a vegetarian. That opened up an entire new pasture of shared experience, and we talked at length about how vegetarians were discriminated against and not taken seriously. And we enthusiastically told great stories of Times I Was Nearly Forced To Eat Meat.

Luke took the biscuit with a tale of a guest-house in County Kerry where he asked for a vegetarian breakfast and the plate arrived with the best part of a cooked pig draped seductively across it, almost grinning up at him.

'So what happened?' I asked gleefully.

'I said to Mrs O'Loughlin "Woman of the house, didn't I say I'm a vegetarian?"'

'And what did she say?' I asked, thoroughly enjoying myself.

'She said "You did, alanna, you did. And what's up?"'

'So what did you say?' I joyously fed Luke his lines.

'I said "Rashers, missus, is what's up."'

'And what did she say?'

'She nearly burst into tears and said, "But it's not right,

and you a growing lad, to be only ating a few oul'
musharoons and four or five oul' eggs. What harm can a
rasher or two do?"'

We energetically threw our eyes heavenward and tisked
and pshawed and felt great.

We complained for a bit about how people overcon-
sumed protein anyway, and how alfalfa sprouts were a
much-maligned foodstuff and were actually a wonderful
source of everything.

'What more do we need?' I demanded rhetorically.
'Only alfalfa sprouts?'

'Exactly,' Luke agreed. 'An adult male can survive on a
handful of alfalfa sprouts every couple of months.'

'Cars can run on them,' I pointed out.

'Not only that,' I went a step further. 'But alfalfa
sprouts give you X-ray vision, superhuman strength and
. . . and . . . let's see . . .'

'A glossy coat and tail,' Luke offered.

'That's right.'

'And the secret of the universe.'

'Exactly,' I smiled. I thought he was great, I was great,
alfalfa sprouts were great.

'It's a shame they taste so horrible,' I added.

'Isn't it?' he nodded.

I tripped over myself to match Luke hilarious anecdote
for hilarious anecdote. He had a marvellous turn of phrase
and did a great line in accents so that one minute he was
a Mexican bandit, the next a Russian president, the next
an overweight Kerry policeman making an arrest.

He seemed to exist in vivid colour in a world of black
and white.

And I, too, was at my entertaining best because I was
totally relaxed. Not just because massive amounts of

alcohol had been ingested, but because I didn't fancy Luke.

In the same way that I never felt nervous with a gay man, no matter how extravagantly good-looking he was, I just couldn't take Luke or his pals seriously as potential boyfriend material. Try as I might, I simply could *not* make myself blush or become a brain-dead mute or pull my wallet out of my bag only to find it was a folded sanitary towel or run my fingers through my hair leaving a false nail trapped in it or try to pay for a round of drinks with a phonecard or any of the other things I did as a matter of course when I fancied a fella.

It's tremendously *liberating* when you don't fancy someone because you don't have to try and make them fancy you.

With Luke, I was able to be myself.

Whatever that was.

Not that he was *bad*-looking. He had nice dark hair, well, it would have been nice if he'd had it cut properly. And he had twinkly eyes and a very animated, mobile face.

I told him all about my family because, for some reason, people found that amusing. I told him about my poor father, the only man among six women. How he'd wanted to move to a hotel when my mother's menopause arrived on the same day as Claire's puberty.

How he'd bought a cat to try and even the sexes up, only to discover that the cat wasn't a male. And how he'd sat at the bottom of the stairs and wept 'Even the shagging cat is a girl.'

Luke laughed so much I thought he deserved to be told about the school trip to Paris I'd gone on when I was fifteen. How the tour bus got caught in a traffic jam in the Pigalle and the nuns who were guarding us nearly had apoplexy at their proximity to neon signs advertising totally nude bars.

'You know the sort of thing,' I told Luke. '"Girls, girls, girls, in their pelt!"'

'I've heard such things exist, all right,' he said, his eyes wide with contrived innocence. 'Although of course, I've never actually seen them.'

'Of course.'

'So what did the good sisters do?'

'First they went round and closed the curtains on the bus.'

'You're joking!' Luke looked stunned.

'And then . . .' I said slowly, 'You're not going to believe what happened next.'

'What happened next?'

'Sister Canice stood in the aisle and, all business, announced "Right girls, the Sorrowful Mysteries; first, The Agony in The Garden. Our father who art in heav – Rachel Walsh, come away from that window! – who art in heaven . . ."'

Luke choked, in hysterics. 'They made you say the rosary!'

'You can see it, can't you,' I said, making him laugh even more. 'Forty fifteen-year-old girls and five nuns, on a bus in a traffic jam in the red-light district of Paris, with the curtains closed, intoning the fifteen decades of the rosary.

'That,' I said solemnly to his red, shiny-with-laughter face, 'is a true story.'

Like a magnet, Luke drew lots of me to the surface, so that I told him things I'd never tell a man that I fancied.

Somehow, I even let slip that I kept *The Collected Works*

of Patrick Kavanagh by my bed. As soon as I'd said it, I wished I hadn't. I knew what was cool to read and what wasn't.

'Not because I'm a clever clogs,' I hastened to tell him. 'But I like to read *something* and my attention span is only long enough to concentrate on something short like a poem.'

'I know what you mean,' he said, giving me a wary look. 'There's no problem trying to remember plot developments or different characters with a poem.'

'I think you're humouring me.' I smiled.

'There's nothing wrong with reading poetry,' he insisted.

'You wouldn't say that if you had my sisters,' I said ruefully, then I made a scrunched-up face so that he'd laugh.

Now and then, the others interrupted and tried to join in with funny stories of their own, but it was no contest, really. No one was as funny as Luke or I. At least that was what Luke and I thought and we gave each other knowing looks as Gaz laboured to tell us about the time his brother nearly choked on a Rice Krispie. Or was it a Frostie? No wait, it might have been a Weetabix. Not a whole Weetabix, couldn't have been a *whole* Weetabix, although maybe again it was . . .

All the others, including Brigit, did at least one trip to the bar to get drinks for everyone, but Luke and I didn't. We ignored Gaz as he called, time after time, 'Your shout, you stingy bollix.' (Eventually Joey managed to make him understand that the drinks were free and he shut up.)

Meanwhile, Luke and I were so busy out-hilariousing each other that, when our drinks were pressed into our gesticulating hands, we barely noticed. We hardly even heard the several mutters of 'You could at least have said thanks.'

I just kept thinking to myself, *he's so nice. He's so funny.*

He launched into another story 'So, Rachel, there I was, wearing one of my mother's flowery skirts . . .' (He had broken his leg.) 'And who do I meet, only my ex-girlfriend . . .'

'Not the one who caught you and Shake tying each other up?' I exclaimed. (They had been practising knots, not indulging in bondage.)

'The very same,' said Luke. 'And she looked at me and shook her head and said "Now it's women's clothes. You're one sick bastard, Luke Costello."'

'And what did you say?' I gasped.

'I decided to go for broke, so I said to her "I suppose a ride is out of the question?"'

'Any luck?'

'She threatened to break my other leg.'

That had me in hysterics. All in all, I was delighted with my new friend.

Of course, I realized, I'd have to do something about the way he looked. What would people think of me if I was seen with the likes of him? I wondered. Wasn't it a pity? Because if he didn't dress like such a fool he could nearly be attractive.

I found myself discreetly checking out his body, flicking my eyes away from his face and back again, really fast, so that he wouldn't notice what I was doing. And I had to say that, while leather trousers are rather unsubtle, there was no denying that he had tall, strong legs and . . . I waited for him to turn slightly to accept another drink from Joey, so that I could get a good look . . . a very cute bum. I found myself thinking that if, just say, I was a

RockChick and if, let's pretend, I was looking for a mate, then he'd be a good one to pick.

After ages of non-stop mirth, there was a small let-up in the talk. The hum of the outside world broke through the magic circle that Luke and I had drawn round ourselves.

Out of the corner of my ear I heard Johnno calling to Brigit, 'Hey, The Brigit of Madison County, get cigarettes as well.'

'Isn't it funny,' Luke remarked, 'how this is the first time we've ever spoken to each other?'

'I suppose.' I smiled.

'Because I've been watching you for a long time, you know,' he said, holding my eyes for far longer than was necessary.

'Have you?' I simpered, as my brain screamed, *He fancies me, one of the Real Men fancies me, what a blast!* I wondered how soon I could tell Brigit so that we could laugh our heads off about it.

'So tell me,' he said confidentially, 'what it is you and Brigit find so funny about me and my friends?'

I could have died. That lovely, warm feeling ebbed away at high speed. He didn't fancy me at all, how could I have thought he did? Even though my emotions were well upholstered by the twenty Seabreezes I'd had, I stammered and blushed.

'Because I've seen you, you know,' he said. He didn't sound half as friendly, all of a sudden. He didn't look it either.

He was like a different person, grim and annoyed. One worthy of respect.

I dropped my eyes and found that I was looking at his midriff. His white T-shirt had worked its way free of his waistband and I could see his flat, tanned stomach and the line of black hair that led down to his . . .

Quickly, my heart beating fast, I looked up again and met his eyes. He glanced down, at where I'd just been looking, then held my gaze again. We stared at each other in silence. I couldn't think of a thing to say. Then suddenly lust just *exploded* within me.

In an instant, Luke ceased to be a figure of fun. I didn't give a damn about his unfashionable haircut or his stupid clothes. Everything about him, including his tight trousers and, more importantly, their contents, had become inexplicably and unbearably sexy. I wanted him to kiss me. I wanted to drag him away from the Rickshaw Rooms. I wanted him to throw me in a taxi and tear my clothes off. I wanted him to fling me on a bed and fuck me.

He must have felt the same because, although I don't know who made the first move, one moment we were staring angrily at each other and the next his mouth was on mine. For a second cool and gentle, then hot and sweet and hard.

My head swam with shock and pleasure. Christ, was I glad I had come tonight! His arms were around me and underneath the hair at the back of my neck, his fingers on the sensitive skin sent desire racing through me. I slid my arms around his waist and pulled his body close to me. With a shock I realized that the hard thing against my stomach was his erection. I soared as I realized that I wasn't imagining this. He fancied me as much as I fancied him. This was real.

He pulled my hair and tilted my head back. It hurt and I loved it. He scraped his stubble along my face and bit the side of my mouth. I nearly fainted.

'You sexy bitch,' he murmured into my ear, and I nearly

fainted again. I *felt* like a sexy bitch. Powerful and desirable.

'Come on,' he said. 'Get your bag, we're leaving.'

We didn't say goodbye to anyone. I was vaguely aware of the rest of the Real Men and Brigit staring in astonishment at us, but I didn't give a damn.

This kind of thing didn't happen to me, I thought in confusion, this kind of uncontrollable lust. Or at least it wasn't usually reciprocated.

We got a taxi immediately and as soon as we were in, he pushed me flat on my back onto the seat and slid his hands up under my top. I wasn't wearing a bra and when he put his hands on them, my nipples were already rock hard. He pinched them between his thumb and finger and two shocks of pleasure zipped through me.

'Jesus,' I croaked.

'Rachel, you're beautiful,' he whispered.

Frantically I pulled my skirt up and forced his groin down on top of mine. Through my knickers I could feel his erection. I put my hands on his bum and pressed him down into me, so hard it hurt. Delicious pain.

'I have to have him in me,' I thought.

Feverishly I put my hands under his T-shirt to touch his skin, then I put my hands back on his bum because I couldn't bear to not feel it.

In a daze I realized the taxi had stopped and I thought the driver was telling us to get out because of our terrible antics. But we had actually arrived at Luke's apartment. I should have known better. A New York taxi driver doesn't care what you do, so long as he gets paid and tipped. You can murder someone in the back of the cab for all he cares, just so long as you don't get blood on the seats.

I can hardly remember getting into his apartment. All I know is that, holding hands, we ran up the four flights of stairs because we couldn't bear to wait for the lift. We went straight to his bedroom and he kicked the door shut behind him, a gesture that I found unbearably sexy. Although I was so filled with desire for him by then that he could have done anything, he could have thrown up, and I would have found it sexy.

Then he shoved me onto the bed and in seconds all his clothes were off. They were nearly off anyway. His big, sexy man's buckle on his leather belt was already open and so were the top two buttons of his leather trousers. I supposed I must have done this in the taxi, although I barely remembered doing so.

Without his clothes he was beautiful.

I went to take off my clothes but he stopped me. First he pulled up my top so that my breasts rolled free, but he didn't take it off. Grinning, he knelt on my arms so that I couldn't move. He played with my nipples, running the slick tip of his erection over them, the slightest touch sending me twitching with desire.

'Now,' I said.

'Now what?' he asked innocently.

'Now can we do it?'

'Do what?'

'You know,' I begged, as I arched against him.

'Say, please.' He smiled evilly.

'Please, you bastard!'

So he tore off my clothes. As soon as he entered me, I started to come. And come and come. It went on for ever, I'd never known anything like it. I held onto his shoulders, paralysed, as my body contracted with waves of pleasure. And then his breathing became hoarser and more ragged and he groaned and started to come. 'Oh Rachel,' he panted, his fingers tangled in my hair. 'Oh Rachel!'

Then all was silence. He lay on top of me, goosepimples prickling his skin, his head in the curve of my neck.

Finally he sat up on his elbows and stared into my face for a very long time. Then he smiled, a wide, beautiful, almost beatific smile. 'Rachel, babe,' he said, 'I think I love you.'

7

'That's it, that's the Cloisters.' Dad slowed down the car (which was rather hard as he had driven the entire way from Dublin at about twenty miles an hour, much to Helen's disgust) and pointed into a valley. Helen and I clambered for a look. As we gazed silently across bleak winter countryside at the big, grey, Gothic house below, I noticed that I had a knot in my stomach.

'Janey, it looks just like a laughing house.' Helen sounded impressed.

Frankly, I was slightly alarmed. Did it really need to look so much like an asylum? The house looked scary enough but, to make matters worse, it was totally surrounded by a high stone wall and dense, dark evergreens. I wouldn't have been surprised to see bats circling its turrets against a backdrop of a full moon, even though it was eleven o'clock on a Friday morning and it hadn't any turrets.

'The Cloisters,' I murmured, trying to hide my anxiety with a flip remark, 'where I finally meet my Nemesis.'

'Nemesis?' asked Helen, in excitement. 'What do they sing?'

Although, I thought, trying hard to tune her out, it had a certain kind of austere charm. It couldn't go round just looking like a luxury hotel, even if that was exactly what it was. No one would take it seriously.

'Are any of them good-looking?' clamoured Helen.

It was great to be out in the countryside, I told myself, determinedly refusing to hear Helen. Just think! Clean air, simple living and the chance to get away from the hustle and bustle of the city.

'Are they all here?' whinged Helen. 'Or only som . . .?'

My anxiety overflowed. 'Shut up!' I shouted. I wished Helen hadn't come, but she had been insistent ever since she had heard about the pop stars.

Helen looked thunderous and Dad intervened quickly. 'Go easy on her, Helen.'

She glared, then wavered. 'OK,' she said, in a burst of rare altruism. 'I suppose it's not every day she's committed.'

When we got out of the car, Helen and I did a quick scan of the grounds, looking for stray celebrities, but nothing doing. Dad, of course, had no interest. He had once shaken Jack Charlton by the hand and nothing could top that. He trudged ahead of us up the grey stone steps to the heavy wooden door. He and I weren't speaking much, but at least he had come with me. Not only had Mum refused, but she hadn't let Anna come either. I think she was afraid they'd keep Anna in too. Especially after Helen swore blind she'd read that the Cloisters was doing a special 'Two for the price of One' offer for the month of February.

The front door was good and heavy and wooden and swung open with solemn weight. Just as it should. But then I was surprised to find that we were suddenly in a modern office reception area. Photocopiers, phones, fax machines, computers, thin cardboard walls, a sign on the wall that said 'You don't have to be a drug addict to work here, but it helps.' Although maybe I imagined that bit.

'Good morning,' sang a bright young woman. The type

of young woman who answered ads looking for someone 'Bubbly'. Blonde curly hair, bright smile, although not too bright as to seem insensitive. After all, this was not a happy occasion.

'I'm Jack Walsh,' said Dad. 'And this is my daughter, Rachel. We're expected. And that's Helen, but don't mind her.'

The bubbly one flicked a nervous glance at Helen. She probably didn't often find herself in a room with a girl who was better looking than herself. Then she gathered herself enough to smile a professionally sympathetic smile at Dad and me.

'She's, ah, had a bit of trouble with, you know, drugs . . .' said Dad.

'Mmmm, yes.' She nodded. 'Dr Billings is expecting you. I'll just let him know you're here.'

She buzzed Dr Billings, smiled brightly at Dad, smiled sadly at me, scowled balefully at Helen, and said. 'He'll be with you in a moment.'

'It's not too late, is it?' asked Dad. 'For Rachel. She can be helped, can't she?'

Bubbly looked alarmed. 'It's not for me to say,' she said quickly. 'Dr Billing will do the assessment and only he would be qualified to . . .'

Mortified, I elbowed Dad. What was he doing asking this child if I could be saved?

My father always behaved as if he knew everything. What had I done to reduce him to this?

While we waited for Dr Billings I picked up a glossy leaflet on her desk. 'The Cloisters. Deep in the ancient Wicklow hills . . .' For a minute I thought I was reading the back of a mineral-water bottle.

Dr Billings looked uncannily like John Cleese. He was

about eight foot tall and nearly bald. His legs ended somewhere up around his ears, his bum was up around the back of his neck and his trousers only came to mid-calf where they flapped around showing a good six inches of white socks. He looked like a lunatic. I found out later that he was a psychiatrist, which made perfect sense.

To a backdrop of Helen's sniggers, he ferried me off to be 'assessed'. Which consisted of convincing both of us that I was bad enough to be admitted. He did a lot of staring thoughtfully, saying 'Hmmm' and writing down nearly everything I said.

I was discomfited to find that he didn't smoke a pipe.

He asked me about the drugs I took and I tried to be truthful. Well, truthful*ish*. Strangely, the amount and variety of drugs I took sounded far worse when described out of context, so I toned it down a lot. I mean, *I* knew my drug-taking was perfectly under control, but he mightn't understand. He wrote stuff on a card and said things like 'Yes, yes, I can see that you have a problem.'

Which I didn't like to hear. Especially considering I'd lied. Until I remembered that me being a drug addict was worth several thousand pounds to him.

Then he did something that I'd been tensed for him to do since I went into his office. He rested his arms on the desk and made a steeple of his fingers. Then he leaned forward and said 'Yes, Rachel, it's obvious that you have a chronic drug-abuse problem, etc, etc . . .'

Basically, I was in.

Then he gave me a lecture about the place.

'No one is forcing you to come here, Rachel. You're not being sectioned. Perhaps you have experience of other institutions?'

I shook my head. The cheek of the man!

'Well,' he continued. 'Many of our clients do. But once you have agreed to come here, there are certain conditions that we expect you to adhere to.'

Oh yes? Conditions? What kind of conditions?

'The usual length of time people stay here is two months,' he said. 'Occasionally, they may want to leave before the two months have elapsed, but once they've signed in they're committed to staying three weeks. After which they're free to go, unless we think it would be against their best interests.'

That started an icy little trickle of something akin to apprehension. It wasn't that I minded staying three weeks. In fact, I planned to stay the full two months. It was just that I didn't like his tone of voice. Why did he take it all so seriously? And why would people want to leave before their two months were up?

'Do you understand this, Rachel?' he asked.

'Yes, Dr Cleese,' I mumbled.

'Billings,' he frowned, and dived for my card and wrote something. 'My name is Dr Billings.'

'Yes, Billings,' I blurted. 'Of course, Billings.'

'We don't take anyone against their will,' he went on. 'Neither do we take anyone who doesn't want to be helped. We expect your cooperation.'

I didn't like the sound of that either. I just wanted a nice, hassle-free rest. I wouldn't cause any trouble. But I didn't want any demands made on me either. I'd been through a lot and I was here to regain my strength.

Then Dr Billings went extra-weird on me.

'Rachel.' He stared deep into my eyes. 'Do you admit that you have a problem? Do you want to be helped to recover from your addictions?'

I figured it was OK to lie. Just not as OK as I had expected.

To hell with it, I thought uncomfortably. Think of the magazine reading, the jacuzzis, the exercise, the sunbeds. Think flat stomachs, lean thighs, clear glowing skin. Think of rubbing shoulders with celebrities. Think of how Luke will miss me, and how he'll suffer when he sees me on my triumphant return to New York.

Dr Billings continued outlining the conditions of my stay.

'Visitors on a Sunday afternoon, but not for your first weekend. You will be allowed to either make or receive two phone calls a week.'

'But that's barbaric,' I said. '*Two* phone calls. A *week*?'

I usually made two phone calls an hour. I had to speak to Luke and I might have to make lots of calls. Did it count as a phone call if I got his answering machine? Surely it couldn't because I wouldn't have actually spoken to him? And what if he hung up on me? That wouldn't count either, would it . . .?

Dr Billings wrote something on my card and said, looking at me carefully, 'That's an interesting choice of word, Rachel. Barbaric? Why do you say barbaric?'

Oh ho, I thought, as realization dawned and I prepared to nimbly sidestep his trap of a question. I'm wise to your psychoanalytical tricks. I'm not your usual poor eejit. I've lived in New York, you know, second only to San Francisco, for shrink-speak. *I* could probably psychoanalyse *you*.

I fought back the urge to stare steadily at Dr Billings and say 'Do I threaten you?'

'Nothing.' I smiled sweetly. 'I meant nothing by it. Two phone calls a week? That's fine.' He was annoyed, but what could he do?

'You will refrain entirely from mood-altering chemicals during your stay here,' he went on.

'Does that mean that I won't get wine with my dinner?' I thought I'd better bite the bullet.

'Why?' he pounced. 'Do you like wine? Drink a lot of it?'

'No, indeed,' I said, although I never usually said things like 'No, indeed.'

'Just asking,' I added.

Dammit, I thought in disappointment. Thank God I'd brought my Valium with me.

'We'll have to search your suitcase,' he said. 'I hope you don't mind?'

'Not at all,' I smiled graciously. Good job I'd stashed the Valium in my handbag.

'And your handbag, of course,' he added.

Oh no!

'Er, yes, of course,' I tried to sound calm. 'But first, can I use the ladies?'

There was a smug, knowing look about him I didn't like. But all he said was 'Down the corridor on your left.'

My heart pounded as I rushed to the ladies and banged the door behind me. I wheeled around the little room in panic, looking for somewhere to get rid of my precious little bottle or – far preferably – somewhere to hide it so I could retrieve it at a later date. But there was nowhere. No bin or sanitary-towel disposal thing, no handy little nooks and crannies. The walls were smooth and even, the floor empty and exposed. It occurred to me that perhaps this dearth of hiding places was deliberate. (I found out later that it was.)

How paranoid were they here? I thought in a burst of

impotent anger. Fucking paranoid, fucking lanky, fucking mad, fucking fucking fuckers!

I stood with the bottle in my hand and felt lightheaded as anger swam into fear and back again. I had to get rid of it somewhere. It was very important that I wasn't caught with drugs, however mild and harmless, on me.

My handbag! I thought joyfully. I could put it in my handbag! No, wait a minute, that was why I was standing here, sweating, in this small toilet, because I *couldn't* put it in my handbag.

I looked around again, hoping that I might have missed something on the last twirl. I hadn't. Regretfully I realized that I'd better at least get rid of the tablets. And quickly. Dr Billings was probably wondering what I was doing and I didn't want him to think badly of me. At least not yet. I mean, he was bound to eventually, everyone in authority always did, but it was too soon, even for me . . .

A voice in my head interrupted, urging me to get moving and remove any identifying details. I don't believe this is happening to me, I thought, as, with sweaty hands, I tore the label off the bottle. I felt like a criminal.

I threw the label into the toilet and then, with a brief, though fierce, spasm of loss poured a small torrent of little white pills in after it.

I had to turn my head away as I flushed.

As soon as they were gone I felt naked and exposed, but I couldn't dwell on it. I had bigger worries. What was I supposed to do with the empty brown glass bottle? I couldn't leave it there, someone was bound to find it and they'd probably be able to trace it to me. There was no window that I could open and throw it out of. I'd better bring it with me, I thought, and hope that I got a chance to get rid of it later. My handba . . .! Oh no, I kept forgetting. Better carry it on my person and hope – little laugh – that they didn't do a body search.

My blood ran cold. They *might* do a body search. Look at how thorough they were being with my suitcase and handbag.

Well, I'd refuse to let them do a body search, I thought. How dare they!

In the meantime, where on my body would I carry it? I'd left my coat in reception and I had no other pockets. Hardly believing what I was doing, I lifted up my jumper and stuck it under my bra, between my breasts. But that was agony because my chest was so badly bruised, so I took it back out. I tried it in one of the cups of my bra, then the other, but you could see the outline clearly through my clingy angora jumper ('my' being a figure of speech, of course. The jumper was actually Anna's), no matter which cup I chose, so out it came again.

There was nothing else for it, there was nowhere else it could go. I put it in my knickers. The glass was cold against my skin and I felt foolish in the extreme, but I took a couple of steps and it stayed secure. Success!

I felt quite good until I caught a quick mental image of myself and something seemed wrong.

How did I end up like this? Surely I was living in New York, young, independent, glamorous, successful? And not twenty-seven, unemployed, mistaken for a drug addict, in a treatment centre in the back arse of nowhere with an empty Valium bottle in my knickers?

8

'Poor bastards,' I thought in sympathy, as I looked at the long wooden table where the alcoholics and addicts sat eating their lunch. 'Poor, poor bastards.'

I was now an official inmate.

I had had my blood test and passed with flying colours, my knickers hadn't been searched, my bags *had*, but nothing untoward had been found, and Dad and Helen had left with the minimum of affection and tears ('Behave yourself for Christ's sake. I'll be up on Sunday week,' said Dad. 'Bye bye, you mentaller, weave me something nice,' said Helen.)

As I saw Dad's car pull, very slowly, out of the grounds, I congratulated myself on how calm I was and how the thought of a drug hadn't even crossed my mind. Drug addict, indeed!

Dr Billings interrupted my staring out the window and told me that the other clients, as he called them, were having their lunch. He just missed Helen making grotesque faces at him out the back window as the car disappeared.

'Come and have lunch,' he invited. 'And I'll show you to your room afterwards.'

A thrill of excitement ran through me at the thought of seeing some pop stars. Despite Helen convincing me that the famous rich people would be segregated from the ornery folk, hope jumped in my stomach like a frog.

And, of course, the mad addicts and alcoholics and compulsive overeaters and gamblers who made up the rest of the clientele would be worth a look at also. It was with a light step that I followed Dr Billings up the stairs and into the dining-room, where he introduced me by saying 'Ladies and gentlemen, meet Rachel, who'll be joining us today.'

A sea of faces looked up at me and said 'Hello'. I did a quick sweep of them and, at first glance, there was no one that was obviously a pop star. Pity.

Neither did anyone seem very *One Flew Over the Cuckoo's Nest*. Even more of a pity.

In fact the alcos seemed very friendly. They made a great show of making space for me at the table.

Once I got a proper look at the room, I found it was surprisingly unglamorous. Though it was always possible that the interior designer had meant the yellow, shiny, institutional walls in an ironic, postmodern way. And, of course, lino was very fashionable again. Even if the buckled brown tiles on the floor looked as if they'd been there from first time round.

I had a quick look round the table and there seemed to be about twenty 'clients'. Only about five were women.

The fat old man on my right was shovelling food into his mouth. A compulsive overeater? The fat young one on my left introduced himself as Davy.

'Hello, Davy.' I smiled with dignity. There was no need to be completely standoffish. I would keep a strict distance, but I would always be pleasant and polite, I thought. After all, I was sure that their lives were miserable enough. There was no need for me to add to it.

'What are you in for?' he asked.

'Drugs,' I replied, with a 'Would-you-believe-it?' little laugh.

'Anything else?' asked Davy hopefully.

'No,' I said, puzzled. He looked disappointed and stared down at his plate of food. Mountains of turnip and spuds and chops.

'What are you in for?' I asked. I felt it was only polite.

'Gambling,' he said gloomily.

'Alcohol,' said the man beside him, although I hadn't asked.

'Alcohol,' said the man beside him.

I had started something. Once you asked someone what they were in for, it had a domino effect and the whole place felt obliged to tell you the nature of their addiction.

'Alcohol,' said the next man, although I couldn't see him.

'Alcohol,' came another voice, further away.

'Alcohol,' said another voice, even further.

'Alcohol,' came a faint voice at the end of the table.

'Alcohol,' came another voice, this time slightly nearer. They'd started working up the other side of the table.

'Alcohol,' a tiny bit louder.

'Alcohol.' All the time the voices were getting nearer.

'Alcohol,' said the man sitting opposite me.

'And drugs,' interrupted a voice from further back. 'Don't forget, Vincent, you found out in group that you've a problem with drugs too.'

'Fuck off, you child-molester,' said the man opposite me angrily. 'You're a fine one to talk, Frederick, you shirt-lifter.'

No one batted an eyelid at the fight. It was just like dinner in our house.

Was Frederick really a child-molester and shirt-lifter? But I was not to find out. At least, not yet.

'Alcohol,' continued the next man.

'Alcohol.'

'Alcohol.'

'Drugs,' came a woman's voice.

Drugs! I craned my neck to get a good look at her. She was about fifty. Probably a housewife addicted to tranquillizers. Pity that, for a second I thought I might have someone to play with.

'Drugs,' said a man's voice.

I got a look at him and my blood quickened perceptibly. He was young, the only person I'd seen so far who was about my age. And he was really good-looking. Well, maybe he wasn't, but he seemed good-looking in comparison to the gang of bald, fat, undeniably unattractive – although I'm not for one moment saying that they weren't nice people – men that the table was packed with.

'Drugs,' came another man's voice. But he looked like a bit of an acid casualty. The bulgy, staring eyes and backcombed hair gave it away.

'Alcohol.'

'Food.'

'Food.'

And eventually everyone had introduced themselves to me. Or at least they'd let me know what they were in for. The alcoholics outnumbered the drug addicts by about four to one and there were a couple of overeaters. But there was only one gambler, Davy. No wonder he was disappointed.

A fat woman in an orange overall banged a plate of chops and turnip down in front of me.

'Thank you.' I smiled graciously. 'But I'm actually a vegetarian.'

'And?' She curled her lip at me in an Elvisesque manner.

'I don't eat meat,' I explained, unsettled by her aggression.

'That's tough,' she said. 'You'd better start.'

'P . . . pardon?' I asked nervously.

'You'll eat what's put in front of you,' she threatened. 'I've no time for any of that nonsense, not eating or eating too much or eating it and then making yourself sick. I never heard the like! And if I catch you in my kitchen trying to find where I hide the jelly, you're straight out.'

'Sadie, leave her alone,' said a man diagonally across from me. I immediately warmed to him, even though he looked like a prizefighter, and, even worse, had tight curly hair in the style favoured by Roman Emperors. 'She's here for drugs, not food. So knock it off.'

'Oh, I beg your pardon, miss.' Sadie was effusive in her apologies. 'But you're very thin and I just assumed that you were one of the not-eating brigade and they give me the pip, so they do. If they knew about real hunger they'd quickly put a stop to their carry-on.'

The warm glow of being mistaken for an anorexic momentarily overrode my anxiety.

'Sadie wishes she was a therapist, don't you, Sadie?' joked the man. 'But you're too thick, aren't you, Sadie?'

'Shut up with yourself, Mike.' Sadie sounded in remarkably high spirits for a woman who'd just been insulted by (if I'd remembered correctly) an alcoholic.

'But you can't even read and write, can you, Sadie?' said the man – Mike?

'I can so.' She smiled. (Smiled! I would have belted him.)

'The only thing she can do is cook and she can't even do that,' said Mike, gesturing to the table at large and receiving enthusiastic agreement.

'You're crap, Sadie!' someone shouted from the end of the room.

'Yeah, bleedin' useless,' called a young boy who didn't look a day over fourteen. How could he be an alcoholic?

After she had assured us that 'None of yiz will be getting any tea this evening,' Sadie moved off and I was surprised to find that I felt like crying. The good-natured insults, even though, for once, they hadn't been directed at me, nearly reduced me to tears.

'Talk to Billings after lunch,' advised the Mike man, who must have seen my wobbly lip. 'In the meantime why don't you eat the spuds and the turnip and leave the chops.'

'Can I have them?' A moonfaced man stuck his head around the fat old man on my right.

'You can have the lot,' I said. I didn't want turnip and potatoes. I wouldn't eat that kind of thing at home, never mind in a luxury place like this. While I knew that the fashionable restaurants had re-embraced sausages and mash, onion gravy, steamed puddings and similar, I still couldn't bring myself to like it. Even though it might no longer be fashionable, I had been looking forward to fruit. Where was the help-yourself salad buffet? Where were the delicious calorie-counted meals? Where was the freshly squeezed fruit juice?

I shoved my plate towards the fat man and it caused uproar.

'Rachel, don't give it to him.'

'Someone stop her.'

'Eamonn isn't allowed.'

'He's a compulsive overeater.'

'Please do not feed the elephant.'

'It's not our policy to do special food for anyone,' Dr Billings said.

'Isn't it?' I was astonished.

'No.'

'But,' I protested, 'it's not special food, I'm a vegetarian.'

'Most people who come here have eating disorders and it's very important for them to learn to eat what's put in front of them,' he said.

'I quite understand,' I said nicely. 'You're worried about the anorexics or bulimics or overeaters or whatever. They might get upset when they see my special dinner.'

'No, Rachel,' he said firmly. 'I'm actually worried about you.'

Me? Worried about me? What on earth for?

'Why?' I struggled to sound polite.

'Because although your primary addiction is to drugs, you may well have unhealthy relationships with other substances, food and alcohol for example. And you run the risk of cross-addiction.'

But I wasn't addicted to drugs. Although I couldn't say that because he'd tell me to leave. And what was cross-addiction?

'Cross-addiction can occur when you try to tackle your primary addiction. You may get the primary addiction under control but become addicted to another substance. Or you may simply add the second addiction to your first one and remain addicted to both.'

'I see,' I said. 'I come here to get treated for drugs and,

76

by the time I leave, I'm an alcoholic and a bulimic. Sort of like going into prison for not paying a fine and coming out knowing how to rob a bank and make a bomb.'

'Not quite,' he said with a cryptic little smile.

'So what am I supposed to eat?'

'Whatever you're given.'

'You sound like my mother.'

'Do I?' He smiled neutrally.

'And I never ate what she gave me either.'

That was because my mother was the worst cook in the known universe. All that talk of tinfoil and turkeys when she first found out about my so-called suicide was just wishful thinking on her part. No matter how much tinfoil she had her turkeys always ended up shrivelled and dehydrated.

Dr Billings just shrugged.

'So how am I supposed to manage for protein?' I was surprised that he didn't seem worried.

'There's eggs, milk, cheese. Do you eat fish?'

'No,' I said. Although I did.

I was shocked that he didn't seem to care. Dr Billings ignored my obvious confusion.

'You'll be fine.' He smiled. 'Come and meet Jackie.'

Who was Jackie?

'The woman you'll be sharing your room with,' he added.

Sharing with? I thought, shock being heaped upon shock. Surely at the prices they were charging I'd get a private room? But before I could question him further, he had opened the office door and led me towards a blonde, glamorous woman who was half-heartedly rubbing the reception area with a hoover. So I stuck a 'I'm nice, you'll like me' smile on my face. I'd just have to wait until she was gone before I complained. Nicely, of course.

She extended a smooth, tanned hand. 'Pleased to meet you, I'm Jackie,' she smiled.

She was about forty-five but from a couple of feet away she could have passed for at least ten years younger.

'And that's spelt C-H-A-Q-U-I-E,' she added. 'Jackie's so common when it's spelt J-A-C-K-I-E, don't you think?'

I didn't know *what* to say to that, so I smiled again.

'I'm Rachel,' I said politely.

'Hello Rachel,' she said. 'And is that Rachel with a Y and two Ls?'

I was sharing a room with this lunatic?

And why was she hoovering? Wasn't she an inmate? I was certain that I'd seen her at the lunch table. My heart sank. Surely they hadn't taken that Betty Ford stuff to heart?

'You missed the bit by the door, Chaquie,' Dr Billings called and made for the stairs.

The look that Chaquie gave his disappearing back could, as they say, haunt a house.

'Don't forget your bag, Rachel,' reminded Dr Billings.

And off he went, up the stairs to the bedrooms, leaving me to carry my bag. And it weighed a ton. In case there were lots of famous people at the Cloisters, I'd taken the precaution of bringing all my own clothes, plus any of Helen's that fitted me. I would have borrowed everything Helen possessed but she was dainty and tiny and petite and I was five nine, so there was no point in taking anything other than her 'One Size Fits None' garments. Apart from the fact that it would be a right laugh when she opened her wardrobe and found every stitch she owned gone, of course.

As I bumped and banged my way up the lino-covered stairs and past walls with peeling paint, I cursed my bad luck that my stay coincided with the Cloisters being redecorated.

'When will the decorating be finished?' I shouted up to Billings, hoping that he would say 'Soon.'

He just laughed and didn't answer me. He really was a mad bastard, I thought in a sudden burst of rage.

With every breathless, puffing step I took, my heart sank further. I was sure that, when the walls were repainted and the new carpet laid, the place would look just like the luxury hotel I'd been expecting. But in the meantime I was uncomfortably aware that it was more like a Dickensian orphanage.

When I saw my bedroom I was even more disappointed. Downright puzzled, in fact. Surely it didn't need to be so small? It barely held the two tiny single beds that had been shoehorned into it. Apart from the size, or lack thereof, the similarity to a monk's cell ended there. Unless, of course, monks had pink nylon fitted bedspreads, the type that I remembered from my childhood in the seventies. Not exactly the crisp, white, Irish linen counterpane that I'd been expecting.

As I walked past the bed, I heard a faint crackle of static and the hairs on my legs stood up.

A white rickety chest of drawers was loaded down with bottles of Clinique and Clarins and Lancôme and Estée Lauder skin-care stuff. They must have been Chaquie's. There was no room for my pitiful couple of jars of Ponds.

'I'll leave you to it,' said Dr Billings. 'Group starts at two and you're in Josephine's. Don't be late.'

Group? In Josephine's? What would happen if I was late? Which bed was mine? Where would I get hangers?

'But what . . .?'

'Ask any of the others,' he said. 'They'll be happy to help.'

And he was gone!

The cheeky bastard, I thought in fury. Lazy, unhelpful layabout. Wouldn't get me vegetarian food. Wouldn't carry my bag. Didn't stay to help me settle in. I might have been very upset, you know. He wasn't to know that I wasn't really an addict. Ask any of the others, indeed. I'd write a letter to the papers when I got out and I'd name him by name. Lazy bastard. And he was probably being paid a fortune, out of *my* money.

I looked around the little room. What a dump. In misery, I flung myself on the bed and the forgotten Valium bottle nearly disembowelled me. When the agony abated I fished it out and decided to hide it in my bedside locker. But when I tried to get up, the pink nylon bedspread came with me. Every time I tore some off it swam back to me and reattached itself.

I was frustrated and disappointed and pissed-off.

9

Come now, come, I cajoled myself. Let's look on the bright side. Think of the jacuzzi, the massage, the seaweed treatment, the mud wraps, the funny stuff they do with the algae.

OK, I said grumpily, reluctant to let go of my self-pity.

I half-heartedly unpacked a couple of things until I found that the tiny wardrobe was already packed to bursting with Chaquie's clothes. So I redid my make-up, in the hope that I might find some celebrities in Josephine's group, and forced myself to go back downstairs.

It had been quite a battle to leave the bedroom. I felt shy and self-conscious and suspected that all the others were talking about me. When I got to the dining-room (hugging the wall and sucking a finger in a childish and unattractive gesture. A woman of my height just doesn't cut the mustard in the 'cute' stakes) I could barely see into the room for the cigarette smoke. But, from what I could hear, everyone seemed to be sitting around drinking tea and laughing and chatting and very obviously *not* talking about me.

I sidled in. It was just like going to a party and knowing nobody. A party where there was nothing to drink.

With relief I saw Mike and, even though I'd be afraid to give him the time of day in the outside world in case somebody thought I hung around with him, for the moment I was too scared to care. I was quite happy to overlook the fact that his trousers were Farrah slacks and that he looked like a bull wearing a curly wig, because he had protected me from Sadie of the orange pinafore.

'Where do I go for Josephine's group?' I asked.

'Come here and I'll show you how it all works.' He took me over to a notice board on the wall and pointed out a timetable.

I did a quick scan of it and it seemed to be very full. Group therapy both morning and afternoon, lectures, talks, films, A A meetings, N A meetings, G A meetings . . .

'Is that A A, as in Alcoholics Anonymous?' I asked Mike in disbelief.

'That's right.'

'And N A?'

'Narcotics Anonymous?'

'What the hell's *that*?' I asked.

'Like A A, but for drugs,' he explained.

'Get lost,' I said, greatly amused. 'Are you serious?'

'Yes.' He looked at me oddly. Try as I might, I couldn't decipher the look.

'And G A?'

'Gambling Anonymous.'

'And O A?' I could hardly keep from laughing. 'No, let me guess – Olivetti Anonymous – for people who can't stop using typewriters!'

'It's Overeaters Anonymous,' he said, looking far from amused. His ugly face was like a slab of granite.

'I see.' I tried to stop my snorting, embarrassed at having made fun of the A A and N A and G A and all the rest. It might have been funny to me, but it was probably a matter of life and death to these poor bastards.

'And this is where each activity is held.' He pointed out

another column. I forced myself to look interested. 'See, today, Friday, two o'clock, Josephine's group is in the Abbot's Quarter . . .' Everything was held in places with beautiful names like the Conservatory, the Quiet Room and the Reflections Pond.

'So this is our new lady,' interrupted a man's voice.

I turned round. I needn't have bothered. It was one of the short, tubby, middle-aged men that the place was awash with. Just how many brown acrylic jumpers could one building hold?

'How are you getting on?' he asked.

'Fine,' I said politely.

'My first day was awful too,' he said kindly. 'It gets better.'

'Does it?' I asked pitifully. His unexpected kindness made me feel like bursting into tears.

'Yes,' he said. 'Then it gets worse again.' He said it as though it was the punchline to a joke and threw back his head and laughed uproariously. After a while he calmed down a bit and reached out his hand and shook mine. 'Peter's the name.'

'Rachel.' I managed to smile back at him. Although I would have preferred to punch him.

'Don't mind me,' he said with a twinkle in his eye. 'Sure, I'm stone-mad.'

I soon discovered that Peter had a great sense of humour and laughed at everything, even the terrible things. Especially the terrible things.

I would quickly grow to hate him.

'Come and have a cup of tea before we start group,' he invited.

Self-consciously, I poured myself a cup of tea, the first

of several thousand (even though I hated tea) and sat at the table. I was instantly surrounded by men, unfortunately none of them either young or good-looking, who wanted to know all about me.

'You've lovely long hair,' said a man wearing a – no, it couldn't be! A pyjama top, yes, it *was* a pyjama top. And a mustard cardigan. His own hair was almost non-existent, but despite that he had some strands swept over his bald pate from the base of one ear right over to the other. It looked as if it had been superglued to his scalp. He gave me a sickly smile and moved slightly closer.

'Is it naturally that black?'

'Er, yes,' I said, trying to hide my alarm, as he began to stroke it.

'Hahaha,' went Peter the comedian from further along the table. 'I'd say that wasn't the colour you were born with, all the same. WHA-hahaha!'

I was too busy sitting rigid, waiting for the hairstroker to move away, to be badly offended by Peter. I pressed myself as far back into my chair as I could go but, when he didn't stop fawning and touching, pressed back even harder. Then Mike, who had been smoking a cigarette and staring moodily into the middle distance, seemed to come to, and shouted 'Down Clarence, down! Leave the girl alone.'

Clarence reluctantly unhanded me.

'He means no harm,' explained Mike as, for about the fifteenth time that day, I fought back the tears. 'Just tell him to piss off.'

'Of course I don't mean any harm,' exclaimed Clarence, looking hurt and surprised. 'She has beautiful hair. What's wrong with that?'

84

'What's wrong with that?' he asked again, thrusting his face into mine.

'No . . . nothing,' I managed, horrified.

'Whose group are you in?' A man with the reddest face I had ever seen skill-lessly changed the subject.

'What's this group thing?' I asked, breathing freely as Clarence pulled back from me.

'You might have gathered that we do a lot of group therapy,' explained Mike. They all laughed at that. I didn't know why, but I smiled anyway so they wouldn't think I was a stuck-up cow. 'And we're divided into groups of about six or seven. There's three groups, Josephine's, The Sour Kraut's and Barry Grant's.'

'The Sour Kraut?' I asked, bewildered.

'Her real name is Heidi,' said Puce Features.

'Helga,' interrupted Peter.

'Helga, Heidi, whatever,' said Redface. 'Anyway, we hate her. And she's German.'

'Why do you hate her?' That prompted an outburst of laughter.

'Because she's our counsellor,' someone explained. 'Don't worry, you'll hate your one too.'

Actually, I won't, I felt like saying, but didn't.

'And Barry Grant?' I enquired.

'She's from Liverpool.'

'I see. Well, I'm in Josephine's group.' I was disappointed that I hadn't got one of the ones with the funny names.

There was an immediate chorus of 'Not Sister Josephine!' and 'Oh Jaysus' and 'She's as tough as nails that one' and 'She'd make a grown man cry' and 'She *did* made a grown man cry.'

That last remark started a row between – if I had their

names right, and I mightn't have had, because most of the men seemed to blend into one – Vincent and Clarence, the hairstroker.

'I wasn't crying,' protested Clarence. 'I had a cold.'

'You were crying,' insisted Vincent, who seemed to be very argumentative.

You wouldn't catch me having a row with anyone, I thought. I'd just do my time and leave. In and out. Befriend no one. (Unless they were rich and famous, of course.) Offend no one.

The argument was interrupted by someone saying 'Here's Misty.'

All the men shifted uncomfortably. Misty, I presumed, was the beautiful girl, who had strolled languidly across the room, her head held high. Even though she was just wearing jeans and a green jumper, she was stunning. I immediately felt overdressed. She had long red hair, so long that she could sit on it. If she was so inclined, of course. And she was skinny and delicate and appeared to have aloofness down to a fine art.

She sat at the furthest end of the table, as far away as she could get from the rest of us, and ignored everyone. I gazed at her until I was so engulfed by envy that I thought I might puke. I would have loved to be good at being aloof, but I always ruined it. (Asking, 'How am I doing? Am I being aloof enough?' is undeniably counterproductive.)

It seemed as if the collection of men around me held their breath. They gazed raptly at Misty, as she took out a newspaper and started to do the crossword.

'She thinks she's great,' scoffed Mike. 'Just because she wrote a book when she was only seventeen.'

'Did she?' I was passionately intrigued, but tried hard

not to show it. It really wasn't *cool* to be interested and impressed.

'Surely you've heard of Misty?' asked Mike, with what sounded like irony, but I couldn't be sure.

'She used to be a right jarhead?' he enquired of me.

I shook my head.

'Then last year she stopped and wrote the book?'

Again I shook my head.

'And was only seventeen when she did it?' This was definitely said with irony.

'No? Well, she did. Then, the next thing you know, she's there every time you turn on the telly, telling how she knocked the drink on the head and became a writer and was only seventeen.'

Misty's story was starting to ring bells for me.

'And before you know it, she's back on the sauce, and ends up in here to be "recovered" all over again.' Mike's sarcasm was, by now, out in the open. 'By this time, of course, she's not seventeen anymore.'

Yes, in fact, I *had* heard of her. Of course I had. The newspaper that I had read out of hysterical boredom on the flight from New York was full of the story of her fall from grace. The implication being that it was nothing but a publicity stunt. Surely it was no coincidence, it suggested, that Misty's new book and photographs of Misty were plastered all over every shop?

'Why she expected to get so many claps on the back for just giving up the drink is beyond me,' continued Mike. 'It's a bit like Yasser Marrowfat winning the Nobel prize for Peace. You know, behave like a right bollix, then stop, then expect everyone to tell you you're great . . .'

Misty must have known she was being talked about because she suddenly looked up from her newspaper, and

87

stared in disgust, before raising two fingers at us. I was torn between excessive admiration and great jealousy.

'She does *The Irish Times* crossword every day,' whispered Clarence. 'The cryptic one.'

'And she never eats a thing,' said Eamonn of the moon face, and matching arse.

'Is her name Misty O'Malley?' I asked in an undertone.

'Have you heard of her?' Mike asked. He sounded almost afraid.

I nodded.

Mike looked as if he might cry. But he cheered himself up by saying, 'I believe no one could make head nor tale of that book she wrote.'

'It won an award, didn't it?' I asked.

'My point exactly,' said Mike.

'Givvus a clue, Misty,' shouted Clarence.

'Fuck off, Clarence, you fat old culchie,' she said malevolently, without looking up.

Clarence sighed, a look of naked, hungry, devotion on his face.

'I would have thought a writer would have been able to come up with a better insult than "Fat old culchie",' Mike called scornfully.

She looked up and smiled sweetly. 'Oh Mike,' she breathed and shook her head. Her red hair caught the light and became spun gold. She looked beautiful, vulnerable and appealing. I'd misjudged her. Mike obviously thought so too. He was so still that I was afraid to move while a long taut look stretched between the two of them.

But wait! She was going to speak again! 'When are you going to ask them to put bromide in your tea, Mike? You just can't leave me alone, can you?' She gave a savage little smile and Mike went grey. Smirking, she picked up her newspaper and slowly wiggled out of the room. All eyes were on her as she jutted one skinny little hip, then the other. None of the men spoke until she had disappeared. Then, looking slightly dazed, they reluctantly turned their attention back to me.

'She has our hearts scalded,' said Clarence, in what sounded annoyingly like admiration. 'Thank God you're here now. We can fancy you and you won't be mean to us, will you?'

Bigheaded, unpleasant, little bitch, I thought. You wouldn't catch me behaving like her, not in a million years. I'd be *so* nice, everyone would love me. Even though, of course, I had no intention of getting involved with any of the people here. Despite myself, I was uncomfortably aware that I felt very much in awe of her . . .

Then someone exclaimed 'It's five to two.' And they all said 'Jesus!' and, as they stubbed out their cigarettes and slugged back their tea, jumped to their feet. Good-naturedly they said things like 'Off to be humbled' and 'My turn to be hauled over red-hot coals this afternoon' and 'I'd rather be taken out into the yard and flayed alive with a cat o'nine tails.'

'Come on,' said Mike to me.

10

Mike grabbed me by the wrist and rushed me down a corridor and into a room.

'This is the Abbot's Quarter?' I asked doubtfully, looking round the draughty room that had nothing in it but a circle of threadbare chairs.

'Yes.' Mike sounded in a panic. 'You sit there. Quick, Rachel, quick!'

I sat down and so did Mike.

'Listen to me,' he said in an urgent tone. 'I'm going to give you some advice. The most important thing you'll probably learn in your whole time here.'

I drew nearer, nervous and excited.

'Never!' he declared, then took a deep breath. 'Never!'

Another deep breath. I drew even nearer to him.

'Never,' he pointed, 'sit in *that* chair, *that* chair, *that* chair or *that* chair. Group lasts for at least two hours at a time and your arse will be in rag order if you have the misfortune to be sitting on any of them. Now look and I'll point them out to you again . . .'

As he was doing so, the door burst open and a handful of the other inmates ran in and loudly set up a clamour of complaint that all the good seats were gone. I instantly felt guilty because they all had terrible things wrong with them and should at least have been afforded comfortable seats while they were being fixed.

There were six inmates, most of whom I recognized

from the dining-room. Unfortunately the young good-looking man who was in for drugs wasn't among their number. There was Mike, Misty the writer, Clarence, Chaquie, my room-mate, and Vincent, Mr Angry. My stomach went into a little knot when I saw Vincent because he positively bristled with aggression. I was afraid he might pick on me, not realizing I wasn't one of them. The sixth person was an old man whom I didn't remember seeing in the dining-room, but, at the same time, I was certain he wasn't from the pop-star wing. Either the pop stars had their own group, which seemed most likely, or they were in with Barry Grant or the Sour Kraut.

'It's nice to have another woman,' Chaquie said. 'It evens things up.'

I realized she was talking about me. Yes, it did even things up, *in theory* but, as I wouldn't be participating, it didn't really even things up at all.

Josephine arrived. I checked her out with great interest. But I couldn't see what they were so scared of, she was *harmless*. She was a nun, but a modern hip one, or so she liked to think. I see nothing hip whatsoever in wearing a grey flannel skirt which ends below the knees and having short, unstyled, grey hair with a brown clip stuck in the side. But she looked nice; sweet, actually. With her round, bright blue eyes she was just like Mickey Rooney.

As soon as she sat down, everyone stared at their feet in silence. All traces of the laughter and the conversation of lunch had disappeared. The silence stretched on and on and on. I looked from one face to another in amusement. Why so anxious, everyone?

Eventually she said 'Gosh, you're all very uncomfortable with silence. OK, John Joe, maybe you'd like to read your life story.' There was a collective sigh of relief.

John Joe was the old man. In fact, he was *ancient*, with huge eyebrows and a black suit that was shiny with age. I later discovered that this was the suit he wore on special occasions. Weddings, funerals, unusually profitable bullock sales or being incarcerated by his niece in rehabilitation centres.

'Er, right, I will,' said John Joe.

When would the shouting and recriminations start? I wondered. I had thought that group therapy would be a lot more dynamic and *nasty* than this.

John Joe's life story lasted about five seconds. He was brought up on a farm, had never married and now lived on the same farm with his brother. He had it written on what seemed to be a torn page of a child's copy book. He read slowly and quietly. It wasn't very interesting.

Then he said 'That's it,' gave a shy smile and went back to looking at his big black boots.

Another silence followed.

Eventually Mike said 'Er, you didn't go into much detail.'

John Joe peeped out from under his eyebrows, kind of shrugged and gave a gentle smile.

'Yes,' said Chaquie. 'You didn't even mention your drinking.'

John Joe shrugged and smiled again. More peeping. He was the kind of man who might hide in a bush when a car passed him on the road. A mountainy man. A man of the land. A bog maggot.

'Er, maybe you'd like to elaborate a bit,' Clarence nervously suggested.

Eventually, Josephine spoke. She sounded a lot more scary than her harmless exterior would lead you to expect.

'So that's your life story, is it, John Joe?'

A little nod from Himself.

'And no mention of the two bottles of brandy that you've drunk every day for the past ten years? No mention of the cattle you sold without telling your brother? No mention of the second mortgage you took out on the land?'

Did he really? I wondered in excitement. Who would have thought it? A harmless old lad like him?

John Joe didn't react. He sat as still as a statue, so I gathered it must be true. Surely, if it wasn't, he'd have been on his feet, passionately defending himself?

'And what about the lot of you?' She swept her glance around the room. 'Didn't any of you have anything to say except' – at this juncture she affected a singsongy, childish voice – '"It's a bit short, John Joe"?'

Everyone cringed under her glare. Even me for a moment.

'Right, John Joe, we'll try again. Tell the group about your drinking. We'll start with why you *wanted* to drink.'

John Joe was unfazed. I would have been raging. In fact I *was* raging. After all, the poor man had done his best. I considered telling Josephine to lay off him, but I thought I'd better wait until I'd been there a couple of days before showing them how things should be done.

'Well,' John Joe shrugged. 'You know how it is.'

'Actually, no, John Joe, I don't,' said Josephine, coolly. 'I'm not the one in a treatment centre for chronic alcoholism, don't forget.'

God, she was vicious!

'Er, well, you know,' attempted John Joe gamely. 'Of an evening, you'd be lonesome and you'd have a drink . . .'

'Who?' snapped Josephine.

John Joe just smiled that benign smile again.

'*Who* would have a drink?' Josephine pushed.

'I would,' said John Joe. He seemed to find it hard to talk. By the look of things there hadn't been much call for it in his life until now.

'I can't hear you, John Joe,' said Josephine. 'Louder. Tell me who had a drink.'

'I had.'

'Louder.'

'I had.'

'Louder.'

'*I HAD.*'

John Joe was distressed and was shaking at the exertion of having used his vocal chords so much.

'Own your actions, John Joe,' barked Josephine. 'You did them, so *say* you did them.'

Watch how she tries to break them down, I thought with interest. How cruel. I had to admit that I'd underestimated Josephine. She was not so much Micky Rooney as Dennis Hopper.

Although you wouldn't catch her getting the better of me. I wouldn't react to whatever she said to me, I'd just stay calm. Anyway she had nothing on me. I didn't drink two bottles of brandy a day and I never sold cattle without telling my brother.

Josephine pressed John Joe hard, firing questions at him about his childhood, about his relationship with his mother, all the usual stuff, I would imagine. But trying to get information out of him was like trying to get blood out of a turnip. He was all shrugs and 'Yerra's and not too many hard facts.

'Why didn't you ever get married, John Joe?' she demanded.

More shrugs, more gentle smiles.

'I s'pose I just never got round to it,' he said.

'Did you ever have a girlfriend, John Joe?'

'Yerra, I might have had one or two,' he admitted.

'Was it ever serious?'

'Sure, it was and it wasn't.' John Joe shrugged. (Again!)

He was starting to irritate me now. Couldn't he just tell Josephine why he hadn't got married. There was bound to be a good Irish economic explanation. Perhaps the farm wouldn't have been viable if it was divided between him and his brother, or he had to wait until his mother died before he could marry his sweetheart because he couldn't have two red-headed women under the one (thatched) roof. (This one seemed to be a common problem in rural Ireland, cropping up again and again in agrarian folklore. I had spent a summer in Galway once, I knew about these things.)

On and on whittled Josephine, asking questions that were ever more brazen. 'Were you ever in love?'

And finally she asked 'Did you ever lose your virginity?'

There was a collective intake of breath. How could she ask such a thing?

And was there really a chance that he hadn't?

A man of his age?

But John Joe wasn't telling. He gazed steadfastly at his boots.

'Let me put it another way,' Josephine pressed on. 'Did you ever lose your virginity to a woman?'

What was she implying? That John Joe had lost his virginity to a sheep?

John Joe sat as if made of stone.

The rest of us were much the same. I held my breath.

The voyeuristic thrill was nearly cancelled out by the feeling that I was trespassing. The silence stretched on for ever. Until eventually Josephine said 'Right, time's up.'

The disappointment was huge. How awful to be kept hanging on a thread. It was like a soap opera only worse, because it was real.

As we all filed out my head was racing. I caught up with Mike.

'What was that all about?'

'God knows.'

'When will we find out?'

'We've got group again on Monday.'

'Oh no! I can't wait.'

'Look.' He sounded annoyed. 'It mightn't mean anything. It's just a ploy. Josephine asks all kinds of questions in the hope that one of them touches a nerve. She casts her nets widely.'

But I wasn't buying it. I was used to the dénouement of soap operas.

'Oh *come* on . . .' I said scornfully, but I was talking to the air. I was annoyed to find that Mike had gone over to John Joe who looked shocked and shaken.

Now what happens? I wondered eagerly. *Now* do we go for the massages? I watched the others intently, anticipation zinging my nerve endings, to see where they were going. Down the corridor, round the corner and . . . oh no! . . . back to the dining-room. Everyone from Josephine's group and the other groups poured in and commenced to drink tea, talk loudly and smoke cigarettes with gusto. Maybe they were just having a quick cup before rushing to their session in the sauna? Maybe.

I sat down, perched on the edge of my chair, and refused a cup of tea. I didn't want to be dying to go to the loo during my aromatherapy session. My eyes darted anxiously from one cup of tea to another. Come *on*, I urged silently, drink them quickly! Otherwise, it'll be dinner time and we won't have long enough for a massage worth talking about. But the tea was consumed with excruciating slowness. I felt like frantically grabbing the cups and drinking it for them.

Then, as they drained the dregs in unbearably relaxed fashion, I was aghast to see them languidly pick up a teapot and pour a second cup which they sipped with lazy enjoyment.

OK, I reasoned nervously, maybe after the second cup?

But as the minutes ticked by and the second cups were sipped and cigarettes were lit and then, the dreaded third cups were poured, I reluctantly admitted that they all looked as if they'd settled in for a long stay. Maybe after tea was when it all happened?

Of course, I could just ask someone and find out for sure. But somehow I wasn't able to.

Perhaps I was afraid that the ordinary clients like Mike and John Joe would think I was shallow if I seemed too concerned with the luxury treatments or where the celebrities were housed? In fact, I realized, they were probably *expecting* me to ask about them. They were probably *sick* of people arriving and saying dismissively 'Get out of my way, I'm off to sit in the seaweed bath with the likes of Hurricane Higgins.'

Well, I'd pretend that I was perfectly happy to sit and drink tea with them for all eternity. That way they were bound to like me. I'd be here for two months, I calmed myself, *plenty* of time.

I looked around the table. They were still at it, heaping spoonfuls of sugar into cups and knocking back tea and remarking on how nice it was. How sad for them.

'Don't you smoke?' asked a man's voice. I was alarmed to discover that it belonged to Vincent, Mr Angry.

'No,' I said nervously. At least, not cigarettes.

'Given up, have you?' He moved closer to me.

'Never started.' I shrank back. Oh, how I wished he would go away! I didn't want to be friends with him. He scared me, with his black beard and his big teeth. *Lupine*, that was the word to describe him, if lupine meant wolf-like.

'You'll be on sixty a day by the time you leave here,' he promised me with a nasty grin and a whiff of BO. ('Oh Vincent, what a big smell you've got.')

I looked around for Mike to protect me but there was no sign of him.

I turned my back on Vincent as much as I could without seeming rude and found myself face to face with strange Clarence. Out of the frying pan into the fire. Although I was afraid there would be a repeat of the hair-stroking incident, I reluctantly spoke to him.

I suddenly realized that I'd been there a whole afternoon and the thought of a drug hadn't even crossed my mind. Hadn't even occurred to me! Which gave me a warm, self-satisfied glow which lasted while I had a succession of identical conversations with nearly every man in the place. They all wanted to corner me and find out everything about me. All except the good-looking one I'd seen at the lunch table. Because I would have actually *liked* to talk to him, he totally ignored me.

Well, to be fair, he wasn't even in the room.

I related my background countless times in the space of a couple of hours. I said over and over again, 'My name is Rachel. I'm twenty-seven. I'm not an anorexic, but thank you for asking, naturally I'm flattered. No, I haven't always been this tall, I was slightly shorter the day I was born. I've lived in New York for the past two and a half years. I was in Prague before that . . .'

'Where's Prague?' John Joe asked. 'Is it in Tipperary?'

'Jeee-zus.' Clarence sucked his teeth and shook his head in disgust. 'Did you hear him? "Is it in Tipperary?" You big thick.

'Doesn't everyone know,' he added, 'that it's in Sligo.'

I was sorry I'd let slip that I'd once lived in Prague because at the mention of it everyone always became excited and it was no different in the Cloisters. Say to anyone, anywhere, 'I've lived in Prague,' and brace yourself to be asked questions. Three questions. The. Same. Three. Questions. *Always.* It was unbearable. Whenever I came home from Prague on my holidays, I was a woman on the edge, tensed against hearing The Three Questions one more time. In the end what I wanted to do was, anytime Prague was mentioned, to circulate a photocopied sheet of paper, that said 'One: yes, you're right, Prague is beautiful. Two: no, actually, the shops are much better now, you can get most things that you can get over here. Although not Kerrygold, of course, ha ha ha.' (The Kerrygold question was the one that really, *really* annoyed me. And if it wasn't Kerrygold it was Barrys tea.) 'Three: yes, you really should get there before the Yanks have the place taken over.'

Talking about Prague always reminded me of what a philistine I was. I was ashamed that, even though Prague was beautiful and atmospheric, I hadn't been comfortable there. Too wholesome, outdoorsy and undebauched for me. If there had been slightly less of the weekend skiing and hill walking and a bit more of the staying out till dawn in a succession of clubs, I might have liked it more.

As I was being quizzed by Eddie, the man with the bright red face, about the price of everything in Prague, the good-looking man came into the dining-room.

'Here's Christy,' shouted a man with a luxuriant head of black hair and a huge Stalin moustache that strangely enough was grey. He pronounced it 'Chreeeeeeeesty' thus letting me know that he was a salt-of-the-earth, dyed-in-the-wool, born-and-bread-and-butthered (as he would have said) Dublin man. Christy sat down a couple of places away from me. This threw me into such excited confusion that I lost my conversational thread and told Eddie that beer was much dearer in Prague than in Ireland. Which, of course, it wasn't. He looked very surprised, and stepped up his interrogation.

'Vodka?' he demanded.

'What about it?'

'Dearer or cheaper?'

'Cheaper.'

'Whiskey?'

'Dearer.'

'Bacardi?'

'Ah . . . cheaper, I think.'

'But why would Bacardi be cheaper and whiskey be dearer?' he demanded.

I just ummed and ahhed vaguely. I was too busy giving Christy a thorough, if sidelong examination. I had been right. He *was* good-looking. Even outside the Cloisters he would be. He had blue eyes that burned with brightness and pale colour, as if he'd been swimming in over-chlorinated water.

A little voice protested that it still preferred Luke, but I immediately silenced it. I intended to fancy this Christy whether I liked it or not. I was desperate to wipe out the hurt that Luke had caused and what better way than to become fixated on someone else? It was just random good fortune that Christy was so attractive I couldn't take my eye off him. (I could only spare one because Eddie was such a demanding conversationalist.)

I stared sidelong at Christy as he talked energetically to the Stalin-moustache man. Christy had my favourite type of mouth, a Dave Allen one.

(Dave Allen was a dissipated raconteur whom I used to watch in the late seventies. My father regularly entertains people, i.e. bores them comatose, by telling them about how I used to scream my head off to be allowed to stay up to watch Dave Allen on telly.)

(I was twenty-five.)

(I was only joking about that last bit.)

Anyway, a Dave Allen mouth is a great thing on a man. It's an unusual mouth, because it looks as if it's slightly too big for the face that it belongs to. But in a highly appealing way. A quirky mouth, whose corners turn up or down as if they have a life of their own. People blessed with Dave Allen mouths always look slightly wry.

I continued giving Chris the discreet once over. Even his hair was nice. Wheat-coloured, and cut well.

Despite his mobile, quirky mouth, he looked like a *man*, one you could depend on. *Not* one that you could depend on to not ring you, the other kind of dependable, the 'I'll get you out of a burning building' kind.

I thought he was gorgeous, except, of course, for his height. When he stood up to reach the teapot from further along the table, I saw that he wasn't much taller than me. Which was a disappointment, but one I was familiar with.

But despite that, there was some very pleasing body action going on. He was thin. Not in a pale, concave, weedy, toast-rack-for-ribs, baguettes-for-thighs kind of way. Lean would be a better word to describe him. His sleeves were shoved up and he had strong-looking forearms that I wanted to touch. And he had great legs. They were a tiny bit shorter than would be considered ideal. Which was fine by me. If I thought a man was good-looking, the addition of shortish legs pushed him into the realm of very sexy. I wasn't sure why. It might have had something to do with an indication of sturdiness.

Or the suggestion of a thick willy. Even though I knew I was supposed to love them, I wasn't wild about men with very long legs. They were the caviar of the leg world. In other words, I couldn't see what all the fuss was about.

Men with lanky legs often put me in mind of giraffes and ballerinas and general effeminatry.

Christy was in no way effeminate.

I suddenly understood why they'd always made such a song and dance about Corpus Christy at Mass. Now that I'd experienced it first-hand, I certainly wouldn't ever again have any objections getting on my knees for it . . . but that was enough of that kind of talk. With a pang of loneliness, I realized that I missed Brigit, I missed Luke, I missed having someone to talk dirty with.

I wrenched my mind away from Luke and back to Christy and his body.

Wouldn't it be great, I thought, my mind wandering, if something happened with me and Christy. If we *fell in love*. And if he came back to New York with me and we met Luke. And if Luke was gutted, and found out that he really loved me and begged me to leave Christy. And I'd get to say something horrible to Luke like 'I'm sorry, Luke, but I've found out how shallow you are. What Christy and I have is *real* . . .'

I'd just got to the bit where Luke tried to hit Christy and Christy caught Luke's arm and said with great pity 'Come on, man, she doesn't want you, right?' when suddenly a couple of people threw handfuls of knives and forks onto the table with a great clatter. Christy was one of them, which surprised me because in my head he was still humiliating Luke.

'Teatime,' fatso Eamonn shouted joyfully.

What the . . .? What on earth . . .? What the *hell* were they doing? To my amazement, the inmates were setting the table! I had thought they were rattling the cutlery to let the kitchen staff know they were ready for their tea. But, no. The rattling had merely been a prelude to the table being set. They ferried jugs of milk, sliced bread and distributed dishes of butter and jars of jam the length of the table. ('Here, pass that down to the end and don't let Eamonn eat it.')

'Why are you setting the table?' I asked Mike nervously. Because they needn't think I'd help. I wouldn't set a table ordinarily and I certainly wouldn't do it while I was on holiday.

'Because we're nice people,' he smiled. 'We want to save the Cloisters money because we don't pay them much.'

Fair enough, I thought, so long as they don't *have* to do it. Although, for some reason, I wasn't convinced. It might have had something to do with the burst of raucous laughter that followed what Mike had said.

12

The dinner was lovely in a totally disgusting way. We got chips, fishfingers, onion rings, beans and peas. Unlimited quantities, according to Clarence.

'You can have as much as you want,' he advised, in a conspiratorial whisper. 'Just go down to the kitchen and ask Sadie the sadist. Now that she knows you're an addict you can have as much as you like to eat.'

I winced at the 'you're an addict' bit, but then my great love for chips took over and I started to devour them.

'I've put on a stone since I came here,' he added.

I felt a cold hand clutch my heart and my loaded fork came screeching to a halt just before I stuffed it into my mouth. I didn't want to put on a stone. I didn't want to put on any weight, I was bad enough as it was.

While I tried to convince myself that one fat-laden meal wouldn't do any real harm and that I'd start eating properly tomorrow, I became aware of an unpleasant noise to my left. It was the sound of John Joe eating!

It was really loud. In fact, it was becoming louder. How come no one else seemed to notice? I tried not to hear him but I couldn't help it. My ears had suddenly become like those powerful microphones used on the television programmes to hear ants breathing.

I concentrated on eating my chips but all I could hear was John Joe slurping and chomping and puffing like a rhino. My shoulders got tenser and tenser until they were nearly up around my ears. The smacking and chewing became louder and louder until it was all I could hear. It was revolting. I felt acute rage, boiling, killing anger.

'Say it to him,' I urged myself. 'Just ask him to keep the racket down a bit.' But I couldn't. Instead I fantasized about turning to him and belting him really hard, swinging my arm across his chest and thumping the chomping noises out of him.

No wonder no one would marry him, I thought, in a fury. Serves him right for never losing his virginity. It couldn't happen to a nicer guy. Who'd sleep with a man who made that kind of lip-smacking, disgusting racket three times a day?

The noise of a particularly enthusiastic mouthful reached me. This was unbearable! I threw my knife and fork down on my plate with a loud clatter. I would not eat another mouthful under these conditions.

To compound my annoyance, no one noticed that I had stopped eating. I had expected concern, 'Rachel, why aren't you eating?' But no one said anything. Least of all that stupid old slurpy bastard John Joe.

I couldn't understand *why* I was so angry. I'd been feeling red-hot rage on and off all day. As well as wanting to burst into tears. Neither of which were like me. I was a happy-go-lucky person most of the time. I should have been happy because I'd wanted to come to the Cloisters. And I *was* glad I was there. But maybe I'd be more glad when I'd clapped eyes on a couple of celebrities and perhaps had a little chat with them.

After the chips etc, there was cake. John Joe enjoyed it. They probably heard him in Peru.

But then, while I sat hunched into a ball of tense anger, imagining John Joe being tortured, the brown jumper who had been sitting on my other side got up and Christy appeared in his place. While I went all of a dither he called to Brown Jumper, 'Brown Jumper' (or whatever his name was) 'are you finished? Is it OK if I sit here for a while? I haven't had a chance to speak to Rachel yet.' And he sat down as if it was the most natural thing in the world. I immediately wiped John Joe and his chomping from my mind and forced myself to smile brightly.

'Hello, I'm Chris,' he said.

His chlorine-bright eyes were so blue they looked as if the light must hurt them.

'I thought your name was Christy.' I smiled, in what I hoped was a cheeky, intimate way at him. (*Like me, like me!*)

'No, that's Oliver's fault.' (Stalin, I presumed.) 'He can't call anyone a name without putting an "ey" on the end.'

Mesmerized, I watched his quirky, beautiful mouth as he asked all the usual questions. Where was I from, what age was I, etc., etc. But I answered with a great deal more enthusiasm than I had in any of the identical conversations I'd had earlier. ('Yes, haha, it's a beautiful city. No, you can get most things that you can get here. Except for *Kerrygold*, hahaha.')

He smiled at me at lot. It was gorgeous, wryness going on right, left and centre. He's so cool, I thought in admiration, much cooler than Luke. Luke just *thought* he was cool and dangerous and living on the edge. But he had nothing on Chris. I mean, Chris was a *drug addict*. Beat that, Luke Costello!

And while I was all for men being cool, and being drug addicts if needs be, I was middle-class enough to be relieved that Chris was well-spoken and articulate. It turned out he lived about ten minutes from where I'd been brought up.

'I believe New York is a great place,' he said. 'So much to do. Great theatre, great fringe productions.'

I couldn't have agreed less, but I was happy to overlook it to make him like me.

'Great!' I said with pretend enthusiasm. I was in luck because, a couple of months before, I'd gone with Luke and Brigit to this awful 'interactive installation'. A kind of a play thing that was on in a disused garage in TriBeCa. It had bodypainting and nipple piercing actually live on stage. Although when I say stage, I really mean the piece of greasy floor that the audience weren't allowed to stand on.

The only reason we'd gone was because Brigit was having dealings with a boy called José. (Pronounced Hose-ay, except Luke and I called him Josie to annoy Brigit.) Josie's sister was in the play thing so Brigit wanted to curry favour with him by going to see it. She begged Luke and me to come and provide immoral support, she even offered to *pay* for us. But the thing was so awful we left after half an hour, even Brigit. And went to the nearest bar, got jarred and made up pretend reviews. ('A pile o'shite,' 'Loan the usherette your clothes.')

I closed my mind to the feelings of loss as I remembered that evening. Instead I dredged up a flattering description of the play for Chris and threw in words like 'ground-breaking' and 'astonishing' (it was that, all right).

While I was still expounding he stood up and said, 'I suppose I'd better get on with the tidying. I can't let the lads down.'

Slightly dazed, I looked around. The inmates were scraping plates and loading them onto a trolley. One of them was tickling the lino with a sweeping brush. Why are *they* doing it? I wondered in confusion. How come the Cloisters haven't got a team of lackeys to clean up? And set up, for that matter? Are the inmates really doing it just because they're nice people?

Well, why not? I demanded of myself. People can be nice, you know. And I shook my head at my lack of faith in human nature. I must have lived in New York too long.

'Can I do anything to help?' I asked politely. Although I didn't mean a word of it. If they had said yes, I would have been highly annoyed, but I knew they wouldn't. And they didn't. There was a chorus of 'no's and 'not at all's. And I was pleased because they obviously sensed that I wasn't really one of them.

But then, as I ran up to my room to quickly re-do my make-up in honour of whatever happened after tea, I passed the kitchen. Where to my great surprise Misty O'Malley was washing a huge pot. She had to stand on a chair to do it. Although I was sure that she didn't *really* have to stand on a chair, she only did it to look cute and dainty.

I was instantly sorry that I hadn't insisted on helping with the tidying. I never felt that anything I did was right. If I had helped and Misty O'Malley hadn't, I would have felt like a right sucker. But the other way round, with Misty helping and me skiving, I felt lazy and worthless.

So when I got back I tried wandering aimlessly around with a butter dish until one of the jumpers stopped me.

'There's no need for you to do that.' He gently removed the dish from my happy-to-yield hand.

I was delighted. Beat that, Misty O'Malley!

'We've put you on Don's team,' he continued.

I wondered what that meant. Don's team? I supposed it must be something like Josephine's group.

'You're on breakfasts tomorrow, so I hope you're good at getting up, it's a seven o'clock start.'

He was obviously having me on.

'Ha ha.' I winked at him gamely. 'Nice one.'

13

I loitered in the dining-room as the remains of the tea disappeared. Whenever I wasn't actively involved in doing something, thoughts of Luke overwhelmed me. The pain of his rejection increased from a background hum to acute misery. I needed a distraction and fast. It *must* be time for the massage and the gym and all that, it really must. I could no longer sit quietly, drinking tea, tormented by the realization that Luke had ditched me, I just couldn't!

Hysteria rose from the pit of my stomach to contract my throat. Sweat prickled my scalp and I was suddenly propelled into positive action. I found myself on my feet, looking for Mike. Forgetting my earlier reluctance to seem too pally with him, I marched up to him and demanded, in a belligerent fashion, 'NOW WHAT?'

I managed to stop myself from grabbing the front of his jumper and, in an wild-eyed, out-of-control screech, adding 'And just in case you were thinking of suggesting it, I'm not drinking any more fucking tea!'

He looked taken aback at my aggressive stance, but just for a moment. Then he smiled easily and said 'Whatever we want. On Friday nights we've no lectures or meetings, so we can do whatever we want.'

'Like what?' I asked. Strangely, I found that the great rage had left me breathless.

'Come on and I'll take you on a little tour,' he offered.

I was torn between curiosity and reluctance to spend

time with him. But he was already racing out of the room, so, still gasping for breath, I followed him.

First stop was the sitting-room. Like the rest of the place, it was in the middle of being redecorated. But they'd really ripped this room asunder. All the furniture had been moved out except for a couple of threadbare couches and there were lumps of plaster on the carpet which must have fallen down from the ceiling. The windows were being replaced, but in the meantime a bitter wind rattled through the room. There was only one person there. I was surprised there was anyone at all, considering the Siberian temperatures. When we got closer I saw that it was Davy, the lone gambler. I hadn't recognized him because he was wearing his coat and a hat with earflaps. He was on the edge of the couch intently watching *You Bet Your Life*. 'All of it,' he muttered at the screen, 'go on, chance the lot.'

'What's on, Davy?' asked Mike, in an odd singsongy voice.

Davy jumped, he literally *jumped*, and hurriedly hopped up and turned off the television.

'Don't tell anyone, will you?' he beseeched.

'I won't this time,' said Mike. 'But for Christ's sake, be careful, you big eejit.'

I had not the slightest idea what either of them were talking about.

Next stop the Reading Room.

It too was being decorated. Despite that, there was a good number of the inmates there. Even though it was called the Reading Room, they were all writing. What were they writing? I wondered. Letters? But why would writing a letter make them slap the table with despair and shout 'I can't do this'? Because that was what they were all doing. I was only there for about three seconds and in that time at least five of them slapped the table. A few more crumpled pieces of paper into balls and flung them at the wall. The air was heavy with cigarette smoke and desperation. I was relieved to leave.

'And now,' said Mike, 'for the best bit.'

My heart leapt, chasing away the last few wisps of anger. What was he about to show me? The gym? The celebrity wing? The swimming pool?

His bedroom actually.

He dragged me up the stairs and threw open a door and said 'The piece de resistance.' He didn't even attempt a French accent. He just wasn't that kind of man.

Now that my anger had receded I was left with feelings of shame and a desire to be very nice. That was the usual sequence of events. So, while I might have drawn the line at giving him a blow job if that was why he'd taken me up there – I didn't feel *that* guilty – I was more than prepared to stick my head round the door and compliment his room to the hilt.

And I could hardly believe what I saw! It looked as if there had been a competition to see how many single beds you could fit into one room. It was crammed with beds. *Packed*. Each bed was in contact with at least one other.

'Nice and intimate, isn't it?' Mike asked drily.

I laughed. I thought he was funny. Although I would still have laughed even if I *didn't* think he was.

'Come on, let's go back downstairs,' said Mike after I had used every compliment I knew to describe his room.

'No, show me the rest of the place,' I protested.

'Ah no,' he said, 'it's dark and cold outside now. I'll show you tomorrow.'

The gym and pool and sauna must be in a separate building, I realized. So back down we traipsed. Back to the dining-room, where about ten of them were still sitting. *Still* drinking tea, *still* heaping spoonfuls of sugar into their mugs, *still* lighting cigarette after cigarette.

They loved the dining-room, it seemed to be some sort of spiritual home. With a sinking heart, I finally admitted to myself that these men probably never went to the gym. They probably never even left the dining-room. I wouldn't have been surprised to find that they slept there. None of them gave a damn about their bodies or the way they looked, that was glaringly obvious.

Except for Chris. He had disappeared, and I was willing to bet I knew where he was.

While I sat there I began to feel – there was no getting away from it – depressed. The yellow walls were getting to me, the tea-drinking was wearing me down, even though it wasn't me that was doing it. And thoughts of Luke were back in my head. The glamour that I was depending on to take my mind off him remained tantalizingly out of sight.

I tried to cheer myself up by asking Oliver, the man with the Stalin moustache, where he was from. Only because I wanted him to say that he was a 'Born and bread and butthered Dublin man'. And, when he replied 'Dublin, I'm a Dublin man. Born and bread and but-thered', it lifted my spirits, but only for a moment.

This wasn't the way I'd expected it to be, I thought with acute sadness.

Just as it occurred to me, accompanied by a violent lurch of my stomach, that there might be *two* Cloisters, and that I was in the wrong one, Clarence came in. His face was bright red, his sparse hair was wet and he was grinning fit to burst.

'Where were you?' Peter asked, with a forced bark of laughter that made me itch to pour a cup of boiling tea all over him.

'Beyond in the sauna,' said Clarence.

With those words my heart leapt with joy. And, I had to admit, relief. Now that I had proof, my fears seemed silly. Laughable even.

'How did you get on?' Mike asked.

'Great!' said Clarence. 'Just great.'

'Wasn't it your first time?' someone asked.

'Yes,' he said. 'And it went grand, so it did. I feel really good after it.'

'And well you might,' said someone else. 'Fair play to you.'

'It feels lovely to get rid of those impurities, doesn't it?' I asked, eager to be a part of this.

'Don't talk to me about impurities,' laughed Clarence. 'Sure, I hadn't a clean pair of jocks to my name.'

Ah, Jesus! I recoiled in disgust. Ugh! I was *revolted*. What did he have to mention his jocks for. I'd gone right off him. Which was a pity, seeing as I had just started to like him.

Clarence sat down and the conversation returned to whatever it had been before he arrived. I suddenly felt very, very sleepy and unable to concentrate on what the men were saying. All I could hear was the murmur of their voices, rising and falling, as conversation waxed and waned. It reminded me of when I was a little girl and used to stay in Granny Walsh's cottage in Clare. In the stillness of the evenings there were constant visitors, who quietly came and went, sat around the turf fire, drank tea and chatted into the small hours. Our bedroom was just off the main room and my sisters and I would fall asleep to the murmuring voices of the local men who came to visit Granny. (No, she wasn't a prostitute.)

Now, as the waves of mostly rural, mostly men's voices washed over me, I began to feel drowsy in the same way as I did back then.

I wanted to go to bed but I was paralysed by the fear that I would draw attention to myself if I stood up and said goodnight. I had made a big mistake by ever sitting down.

I'd always hated being tall. So much so that when I was twelve, and my sister Claire told me in tones of delighted horror, 'Mum's going to talk to you about The Curse,' I thought she meant that Mum wanted to talk to me about my height.

Although strangely enough, only about two months after she gave me my 'Introduction to Periods' talk (which included the sub-speech 'Tampons are the work of Satan'), Mum took me aside for another mother-daughter chat. This time it really *was* about my height and the fact that I hunched over so badly I was almost folded in two.

'Stand up, come on now, don't be like a tree over a blessed well,' she said briskly. 'Shoulders back, head up. God made you tall, there's nothing to be ashamed of.'

Of course she didn't believe a word of it. Even though she herself was tall, she thought that being twelve years old and five foot seven was freakish enough to deserve my own page in *The Guinness Book of Records*. But I mumbled 'OK' and promised that I'd try.

'No walking along inspecting the footpath,' she warned. 'Walk tall!' That sent her into a bout of what sounded like hysterical giggles. 'Sure, what other way *could* you walk?' she snorted and bolted from the room while I stared after her in bewilderment. She couldn't have been laughing at me, could she? I mean, my own mother . . .?

As soon as she had gone, Claire burst into the room and grabbed me. 'Come here,' she said urgently. 'Don't listen to a word she says.'

I hero-worshipped Claire who, at sixteen, seemed outrageously glamorous. Naturally, I believed everything she told me.

'*Don't* walk tall,' she urged, '*don't* hold your head up.'

'Not,' she added ominously, 'if you ever want a boyfriend.'

Well, *of course* I wanted a boyfriend, I wanted that more than anything in the whole world, even more than a rara skirt or a pair of tukka boots, so I listened to what she had to tell me.

'They won't go near you if you're taller than them,' she advised. I nodded solemnly. She was so wise! 'In fact, unless you're a lot shorter than them, they don't like it. It makes them feel threatened,' she finished darkly.

'Short and stupid,' she summed-up. 'They like that. That's their favourite.'

So I had taken Claire's advice to heart. And I found it to be true. In fact Claire would have been well-advised to heed her own words. I was convinced that Claire's marriage had broken up simply because when she wore high heels, she was the same height as James. His ego just wasn't able for it.

14

And so to bed. Cue: yawns, outstretched arms, rubbing of knuckles into eyes, smacking lips and muttering 'Myum, myum, myum', putting on a fleece-lined, *Care Bears* night-shirt and snuggling under the weight of a protective duvet to gratefully receive twelve hours of restoring, healing, happy sleep.

Fat chance!

Or if you prefer, Me arse!

There was a shock in store for me when I slumped into my room, all set to fling myself on the bed and not take off my make-up. (A special treat, the not-taking-off-my-make-up one, reserved for evenings of particular exhaustion. Or inebriation, of course.) To my dismay, I found Chaquie already in the bedroom. Dammit, I'd forgotten about her.

She was sitting on her bed, elegant ankles crossed, as she gave herself what appeared to my untutored eye to be a manicure. I had never needed a manicure to tidy up my nails. My life-long habit of biting them to the quick did just as well.

'Oh, hello,' I said nervously. Would I have to talk to her . . .?

'Hel*lo*, Rachel.'

Apparently I would.

'Come in and sit down.' She patted her bed invitingly. 'My heart went out to you at dinner, sitting next to that disgusting animal, John Joe. The noises that come out of that man. He must eat with the pigs at home.'

The relief! It was as though someone had just unlaced the tight, tight knot of tension in my chest.

'Yes,' I breathed, *delighted* to be with someone who felt the same way as I did. 'I couldn't believe it. I've never heard anyt . . .'

With pursed lips she nodded along with me for a moment or two as she did things with an ice-pop stick to her nails. Then, out of the blue, she demanded 'Are you married, Rachel?'

'No,' I said. I'd managed to stop thinking about Luke for two seconds, but her question had pitched me right back into it. My brain tightened because for a second I simply *could not believe* it was over with him.

'Are you married?' I managed to ask.

'Oh Lord, yes!' she tinkled. She rolled her eyes at me, to indicate long-sufferingness.

I realized that she wasn't interested in me at all. She had simply opened the conversation to bring it round to her.

'For my sins!' She gave me a dazzling smile. 'My husband's name is Dermot.' She pronounced it 'Durm't' to let me know she was posh.

I smiled weakly.

'Twenty-five happy years,' she said.

'I was married straight out of school,' she added hastily. 'A schoolgirl bride.'

I forced another smile.

Suddenly she flung down her ice-pop stick with force.

'I can't believe Durm't put me in here!' she exclaimed. She moved closer and to my alarm she had tears in her eyes. 'I just can't believe it. I've been a devoted wife all these years and this is how he repays me!'

'You're in for, er, alcoholism?' I asked discreetly. I didn't want to sound as if I was *accusing* her of anything.

'Oh please,' she said, with a dismissive wave of her hand. 'Me? An alcoholic?'

She opened her well-made-up eyes wide in disbelief.

'A few Bacardis and coke with the girls once in a while,' she went on. 'To let my hair down. God knows I deserve it, considering that I work my fingers to the bone for that man.'

'But why did Durm't put you in here?' I asked in alarm. A few Bacardis and coke didn't sound serious.

And I wished I hadn't called him 'Durm't'. It was an awful habit of mine. Talking in the same accent as the person I was with.

'Don't ask me, Rachel,' said Chaquie. 'Do I look like an alcoholic to you?'

'God, no.' I laughed with the warmth of understanding. 'Do I look like a drug addict to you?'

'I wouldn't know, Rachel.' She couldn't keep the disgust from her voice. 'I don't move in those sort of circles.'

'Well, I'm not.'

Stupid cow, I thought. I was hurt. Especially when I'd been so nice about her not being an alcoholic.

'Where are your family from?' she asked, with another abrupt change of subject.

'Blackrock,' I mumbled sulkily.

'What road?'

I told her. She obviously approved. 'Oh I know it. A friend of mine used to live there but they sold it and bought a lovely one in Killiney with a view over the bay and five bathrooms. She got a famous architect over from London to do it for her.'

'Is that right?' I asked snidely. 'Who is he? I know a bit about architecture, myself.' I didn't know the first thing, of course, but she had annoyed me.

'Oh, what's that his name is?' she said vaguely. 'Geoff something or other.'

'Never heard of him.'

She didn't turn a hair. 'You can't know that much about architecture, then,' she said airily.

Which served me right for being bitchy. I had learnt my lesson.

Oh yes, I thought bitterly, I had learnt my lesson, all right. Next time I'd be far nastier to her.

Then she started to talk about *her* house. She had an unnatural interest in en-suite bathrooms.

'Our house is perfect, an absolute showhouse!' she declared. 'Although *we* had no architect over from London to do it.' More humorous rolling of the eyes, inviting me to smile with her.

I did. I was anxious to please, even if I hated the recipient of my pleasing. My pleasee.

'It's in Monkstown,' she said with pride. 'You've been away for a good while, so you mightn't know, but Monkstown is very up and coming. Oh, pop stars galore. Chris de Burgh is only down the road.'

I shuddered.

'The singing eyebrow? Well, there goes the neighbourhood.' I mean, she couldn't *really* be glad, could she?

'I hope you don't hear him practising,' I went on. 'That would be just the pits alt . . .'

I trailed to a halt when I saw the expression on her face.

Oh dear. Oh, oh dear. We had not got off to a good start. I hoped to God she was getting out soon.

'Er, how long have you been here, Chaquie?'

'Seven days.'

Shite!

Then, to my great alarm, she started to talk. *Really* talk. I had thought my comment on Chris de Burgh had put an end to dialogue, which suited me more than I could say. But suddenly, before my weary eyes, she mutated into the Duracell bunny of trivial chat. The stuff about bathrooms and husbands had been mere messing around as she waited for the runway to clear. And now in response to some signal that only she could hear, she had gone into overdrive. Full throttle, firing on all cylinders, foot pressed firmly to the conversational floor.

The gist of her bitter monologue was that you couldn't trust anyone. From gynaecologists to milkmen to husbands.

Especially husbands.

Her words swam giddily at me.

'. . . I told him that there couldn't be two pints of milk for Tuesday because Durm't and I were away that day . . .' (Her milkman was under suspicion.)

'. . . And how am I supposed to trust him the next time he puts his hand up my skirt . . .?' (Her gynaecologist was having an affair with one of her friends.)

'. . . I still can't believe he put me in here! How could he!? . . .' (Durm't had upset her.)

'. . . I shudder when I think of all those times I took my clothes off in front of him . . .' (I think that was the roving gynaecologist. Although I later found out stuff about Chaquie which meant it could just as easily have been the milkman.)

I felt faint and queasy and kept losing the thread of what she was saying. I hoped I would pass out or have a fit or something but every so often I would come to, only to find she was still at it.

'. . . And they were full-fat pints anyway, and Durm't and I only have skimmed milk, well you've got to take care of yourself haven't you . . .' (The milkman again.)

'. . . Any time I'm with him now, I feel that he's looking *lustfully* at me . . .' (Either the gynaecologist or Durm't. Although on second thoughts maybe not Durm't.)

'. . . What did I do to deserve being shoved in here? How could he? . . .' (Definitely Durm't.)

'. . . And he said there was nothing he could do, that the bills were generated by a computer. And I said "Don't talk to me like that, young man" . . .' (Possibly the milkman.)

'. . . And they were six inches too short for the bay window. So I refused to pay . . .' (No idea, sorry.)

On and on she went, while I lay against the headboard as though flattened by centrifugal force. I wondered if I looked as desperate as I felt.

I nodded mutely, unable to speak. Just as well, because she didn't stop to draw breath.

Maybe it was just because I'd had a long, strange day, but I really felt that I hated her. I didn't blame Durm't for putting her into the Cloisters. If I was married to Chaquie, I'd be happy to incarcerate her in an institution. In fact, I'd want her dead. And I wouldn't pay a hired killer to do it, either. Why deny *myself* the pleasure?

Battling against the hail of her words, I dragged myself off the bed and decided to try to get some sleep. But I didn't want to get undressed in front of her. I mean, I didn't know the woman from Adam. Although, as Adam was the name of my sister Claire's live-in-lover, perhaps that was the wrong analogy. Because I *did* know Chaquie from Adam. And I would have been *delighted* to share a room with Adam. He was about eight foot ten, knicker-meltingly gorgeous and Claire had promised me that when she died I could have him.

As I wriggled like a contortionist into Mum's nightdress, trying not to let an atom of my shameful flesh show, Chaquie scolded, in a school teachery voice, 'You'd want to watch that cellulite, Rachel. At your age you can't afford to ignore it.'

As my face burned with shame, I climbed into the narrow bed.

'Have a word with Durm't,' she said. 'He'll sort you out.'

'PARDON?' I was shocked! What kind of woman was this who offered her husband to sort out the cellulite of a stranger?

'Durm't runs a beauty salon,' she explained.

That explained a lot. It certainly explained how she managed to look so glamorous.

'Well, I say he runs it,' she tinkled, 'I should really say he owns it. *We* own it. As Durm't always says "There's great money in cellulite."'

Then her face darkened. 'The louser,' she hissed.

Chaquie had no shame about getting undressed. She positively flaunted herself in front of me. I tried not to look, but it was unavoidable because she stayed in her knickers and bra for far longer than was necessary. And although it galled me to admit it, she was in pretty good shape. A bit saggy, but only a tiny bit. She was just *showing off*, I thought with gritted teeth, as I wished death and destruction to rain down on top of her and her lean, tanned thighs.

She spent several hours taking off her make-up, a lot of dabbing with fingertips and patting and stroking and gentle massage. On the rare occasions when I removed my slap *at all*, I just threw a lump of cold cream at my face, like a potter throwing wet clay onto a wheel, and swirled it round with the palm of my hand as if I was cleaning a window. Then gave it the briefest wipe with a tissue.

I desperately wanted to get to sleep. I've had enough of today, I thought, I really, poxing-well have. I'd like a bit of oblivion, please, any time you like. But Chaquie wouldn't let me. She kept talking, even when I tried to hide behind my Raymond Carver book. Which I'd only brought because Luke had given it to me, but all the same. I *might* have wanted to read it.

And even when I put the (scratchy, odd-smelling) blankets over my head and pretended I was asleep she *still* didn't stop. I tried ignoring her and faking deep, regular breathing, but she said 'Rachel, Rachel, are you asleep?' Then when I didn't answer she shook my shoulder and said sharply 'Rachel! Are you ASLEEP?'

It was awful, I was nearly in tears with exhaustion and frustration. I felt as if I was a thin sheet of glass about to shatter under unbearable pressure. If only she would SHUT UP! I thought, as molten rage surged through my veins.

I was so angry that I would have glowed in the dark. At least I would have if she ever put the fucking light out!

Then I wanted a drug. Or twenty. I would have given anything for a couple of handfuls of Valium. Or sleeping tablets. Or heroin. Or anything really. All contributions gratefully received.

I craved chemicals. I didn't think that wanting drugs

under such unbearable conditions made me a drug addict. Because I also craved a sawn-off shotgun. And that didn't make me a murderer. Not under normal circumstances, anyway.

To drown her out and the awfulness of it all, I tried to think of something nice. But the only thoughts that came to me were ones of Luke.

15

The first morning I found myself in bed with Luke I could have died.

It took me a moment or two, after I woke up, to realize that I wasn't in my own bed. 'Mmmm,' I thought contentedly, my eyes still closed, 'I wonder who's bed I *am* in? I hope it's somebody nice.' Then, with the shocking impact of a bucket of ice-cold water, it all rushed back to me. The Rickshaw Rooms, the Real Men, the carry-on in the taxi, the sex with Luke, and worst of all, the fact that I was currently located in his bed.

In my head, I sat bolt unright, tore at my hair and screamed, *How could I?* In reality though, I lay quiet and still, very keen not to wake Luke. Very keen indeed.

My senses had returned with the daylight and I was in the horrors. Not just that I'd slept with one of the Real Men, but that I hadn't had the wit to wake up in the middle of the night, dress in the dark and tiptoe from the room, leaving the man, my earrings and something embarrassing like my cold sore ointment behind me, never to be again retrieved. Not that I'd have cared, I'd have happily left a tube of piles ointment on his pillow as a farewell note, if I could only have been spirited out of there.

Trying not to move, I carefully opened my eyes. I was facing a wall. From the heat and the sound of someone else's breathing, I gathered there was another person in the bed.

Someone between me and escape.

Like a caged rat, my brain lurched hither and thither, wondering where my clothes were. Oh, how I bitterly rued that I hadn't woken at three in the morning!

No, I had to be honest and admit that the problem had started a bit earlier than that. How I passionately regretted the moment I let Luke Costello kiss me. In fact, I decided the rot had set in the moment I put foot inside the Rickshaw Rooms. Why couldn't the bouncer have just told us to fuck off like they did usually? The more I thought of it, it became clear that the day I'd first heard of New York was the start of all the trouble. If only I'd liked Prague none of this would have happened. If only they'd had a couple more night clubs there.

I lay rigid, my head racing back through my life. If only I'd got that place on the hotel-management course in Dublin, if only I'd never met Brigit, she was a bad influence, that girl, if only I'd been born a boy . . .

Just as I had traced the origin of my problem back to the great disaster of my mother giving birth to me, I heard a voice. 'Morning sweetheart,' someone – Luke, I could only hope, unless the boys shared more than their leather trousers – said. So he was awake. That scuppered the last of my remaining hope that I could slink out without disturbing him. If I hadn't been pretending to be a mute quadraplegic I would have put my face in my hands and wept.

To my alarm, I felt an arm snake around my naked body and pull me across the bed. Very macho behaviour, as I was no featherweight.

I slithered smoothly over the sheets until I came into

contact with another body. A man's one. I bristled at the nerve of him. I had no intention in joining Mr Hairy Real Man Luke in an early morning romp. He had got lucky, very, *very* lucky with me the previous evening. For a moment I wondered if I would get away with saying he took advantage of me, maybe even accuse him of a bit of date rape, and reluctantly decided against it. But it had been a terrible mistake on my part and it would never happen again.

'Hello,' he murmured to the side of my head. I didn't answer. I had my back to him and I would not, *could* not look at him.

Instead I squeezed my eyes shut and prayed for him to go away or die or something.

I had arrived at his side in exactly the same position as I had been in at the far side of the bed. While I lay as stiff and unyielding as a corpse he began to slowly stroke my hair away from the tender skin of my neck. Appalled at his cheek, I barely allowed myself to breathe. How dare he, I thought in anger. Well, he needn't think I'll be soft and pliant and malleable and eager. I'll keep perfectly still so that he'll lose interest in me and I'll be able to escape.

Then I felt a strange sensation on my thigh, so gentle and faint that at first I thought that maybe I was imagining it. But I wasn't. Luke was lightly running his other hand along the side of my thigh, raising all the downy little hairs. Tingly and shivery. Up to my hipbone, down to my knee, back up to my hipbone . . .

I swallowed.

I was almost hysterical to get out of there. But I didn't want to make any grand gesture like flinging back the sheet (and maybe allowing myself the luxury of elbowing

Luke in the kidneys) until I knew where I could locate at least some of my clothes.

Why couldn't we have drawn the curtains the previous evening? There was no hiding any of my nakedness in the harsh morning light.

Luke's hand strayed along my thigh and his other hand tickled and tingled at the nape of my neck. Then a very pleasant sensation around my neck sent electric sparks through my body. What was going on? Further investigation showed that Luke had started to gently bite me.

It had gone too far!

I *had* to leave. But how?

I could brazen it out, I thought desperately. I could just hop out of bed and act as if I wasn't mortified about groping round on the floor looking for my clothes. If I could only find my knickers and at least get my arse under wraps, I wouldn't be so worried about the rest of me . . .

Or I might try and be funny about it, and pull the sheet around myself like a toga and . . . just a minute, what was he doing?

I swallowed with difficulty. The bastard had somehow managed to get his hand under the rigor mortis barrier of my arm and was stroking my nipples with the lightest, feathery strokes, so they were standing out like football studs.

But still I remained like an inanimate lump. He moved closer to me, lying the front of his body along the back of mine. All the better for me to feel the stirrings of his early-morning erection.

I love semi-tumescent penises, I thought dreamily. Obviously they're not as much use as fully tumescent ones, but they feel so fat and swollen and *alive*, you never know what they're going to do next, well you do, of course, but all the same . . .

To my surprise my groin seemed to be awake.

Not just awake but demanding its breakfast.

I couldn't see Luke but I could *smell* him. Cigarettes and toothpaste and something else, something musky and sexy, a male smell. Essence of man.

And I felt the stirrings of my own arousal. He *did* feel good – big and solid, smooth and tender.

But he could fuck off with himself, I decided firmly. Last night had been a mistake.

He moved his legs so that his thighs were lying close against mine. I was acutely aware of the size and hardness of them. I was so sensitive to every touch from him it was as if I'd had a layer of skin removed. Nothing like a bit of desire to make me feel as if I'd spent the past hour exfoliating like mad.

To my surprise I didn't feel fat and hideous, the way I often did in bed with a man. I held the balance of power because I knew Luke was dying for me.

I could feel his erection behind me, not quite touching my bum.

He nipped my neck again and moved his hand lower, down over the curve of my stomach (a quick suck in!), then lower still. I found myself catching my breath again, for quite different reasons.

He moved his hand over my stomach, barely touching me, circling to my hip bone, to my thigh, a quick brush over my pubic hair (I bit back a gasp and it escaped sounding like the high-pitched noise a dog makes when it gets its tail caught in a door), back to my stomach, over to my hipbone, on the inside of my hipbone, sliding down, moving in ever-decreasing circles.

But not ever-decreasing enough for my liking.

My head was telling me to slap his hand away and tell him to piss off but my groin was whimpering like a small child.

Oh keep going, I thought frantically, as he moved his fingers lower. *Oh no!* He'd returned to my stomach again. Then my thigh, this time slightly higher than where he'd been the last time, but not yet high enough.

I could feel the place between my legs fizz and melt, it was almost radioactive down there.

And still I lay unmoving.

The blood had left my head and moved en masse, like migrating refugees to my pelvic region, pouring in and filling and swelling. My head was dizzy and light, my crotch swollen and supersensitive.

While I lay, crouched on my side, wondering what to do, everything suddenly changed! Without any warning Luke put his arms under me and flipped me over. One minute I was in a rigor mortis foetal curl, the next I was flat on my back, Luke crouched above me.

'What are you doing?' I croaked. I was annoyed. Disturbed. I had to admit he was looking pretty good, the early morning stubble suited him and his eyes were dark and blue in the daylight.

I looked down and caught a glimpse of his erect member. Quickly, I looked away, appalled and excited.

'I want someone to play with,' he said simply. He smiled, had ever a smile been so melting? And I felt the last small remnants of my resolve totter and keel over. 'I'm going to play with you.'

From the moment I'd woken up I'd kept my legs firmly clamped. But now he placed both his hands between my thighs and gently pushed them apart. And desire rippled through me. *Ripped* through me.

A sound escaped from my throat before I'd known I was going to make it.

'Unless you don't *want* to play?' he said innocently. He bent down and bit one of my nipples, gentle but sharp, and again I whimpered with want.

I felt swollen and raw with desire for him. I could feel my clitoris throbbing, burning, as if it was both melting and on fire. *Now I know what it's like to have an erection*, I thought dazedly.

He looked at me, and said 'Well?' Then he bit my other nipple.

If I'd tried to stand up and walk I knew I wouldn't be able to. Everything about me felt heavier than usual. I was dreamy, dopey, *drunk* with desire.

'Well?' he said again. 'Do you want to play?'

And I looked at him – blue eyes, white teeth, sexy thighs, big purple knob.

'Yes,' I admitted weakly. 'I want to play.'

16

After it was over I stumbled out into the hall in search of the bathroom. I was badly disoriented when the first person I came face to face with was Brigit.

'But . . .' I mumbled. 'But we're not at home, are we?'

'No,' she said briskly. 'We're in the Real Men's apartment.'

'But what are *you* doi . . .' Suddenly I understood.

'Which one?' I asked gleefully.

'Joey.' She was tightlipped and grim.

'What happened?' I demanded. I could have danced with joy. I wasn't the only one.

'Plenty,' she muttered.

'Did you shag him or just get off with him?'

'I shagged him.

'Twice,' she added.

She looked wretched. 'I shouldn't have. I could kill myself. How could I? After the way he beat me.'

'He *beat* you?' I couldn't believe my ears.

'In *Butlin's*, you thick, not last night.'

As I was leaving, Luke asked for my phone number. In silence I tore a page from my diary, neatly wrote my phone number on it, then, as he watched in astonishment, crumpled it up into a ball and threw it into the bin. 'There,' I said, with a dazzling smile, 'that's saved you the trouble.'

He was in bed, sitting with his back against the wall. Nice chest, I thought vaguely. For a fucking eejit.

He looked shocked.

'Bye now,' I said, with another blinding smile and swivelled on the backs of my mules. Agony cut into my heels and calves.

'Wait,' he called.

What now? I wondered. I supposed he wanted a farewell kiss. He could want all he liked, it wouldn't do him any good.

'What?' I asked, barely able to keep the impatience out of my voice.

'You forgot your earrings.'

Brigit and I hobbled home, scuzzy and slit-eyed, still in our party dresses. Although it was only eight in the morning, it was already hazy and hot. We stopped at Benny, the Early Morning Jew's stand, where we always got our coffee and bagels on the way to work and underwent intensive interrogation regarding our dishevelled states.

'Well, lookee here, lookee here, whadda you two goils bin doin'? Huh? Huh?' he demanded. He came out from behind the stand to inspect us. Half the street was looking and traffic was almost at a standstill as Benny gesticulated at the passers-by.

'I yask myself,' he thumped himself in the chest, 'what's goin' on heah.' General flailing of his arms to indicate Brigit and me, our uncombed hair and make-up that had run amok.

'And what do I see?' Gestures at his eyes.

'I see a mess, dats whad I see.' More flailing of the arms.

'I taut youse two was nice goils,' he complained.

'Get a grip on your head, Benny,' I said. 'You did not.'

Great sex or no great sex, I had no intention of seeing Luke again. I could never live it down. I had a post-mortem with Brigit. Not one of the nice ones where we shivered with delicious recall as we discussed a sexual encounter in minute detail and sometimes used the aid of diagrams to describe the man's penis.

It was more of a damage-limitation type of chat.

'Do you think anyone saw him kissing me?' I asked Brigit.

'Plenty of people saw you,' she said in astonishment. 'Me, for one.'

'No,' I said. 'Anyone who might, you know . . . *matter*.'

Luke rang me. Of course he did. The ones I wanted to ring me never did. He must have fished the crumpled piece of paper out of the bin after I left.

Brigit answered the phone.

'Who's speaking please?' She asked it in such a strange voice that I looked up. She was waving frantically at me.

'It's for you,' she said in a strangled voice.

She put her hand over the mouthpiece, made an agon-ized face, bent at the groin and turned her knees inwards the way men do when they get a cricket ball in the goolies.

'Who is it?' I asked. But I already knew.

'Luke,' she mouthed.

My head swivelled round the room, looking for an escape.

'Say I'm not here,' I begged in a whisper. 'Say I've moved back to Dublin.'

'I *can't*,' she whispered back. 'I'd laugh. I'm sorry.'

'You whore,' I hissed, as I took the phone from her. 'I'll remember this.'

'Hello,' I said.

'Rachel, babe,' he said. Funnily enough his voice was

136

nicer than I'd remembered. Deep and with the suggestion of a laugh in it. 'It's Luke. Remember me?'

I was pierced by the 'Remember me?' How many times had I said that to men I knew weren't interested in me, but that I'd persisted in ringing anyway?

'I remember you, Luke,' I said.

Which was more than some of the men had said to me.

'So how've you been?' he asked. 'Was work OK for you on Wednesday? I was in rag order all day myself.'

I laughed politely, and toyed with the idea of hanging up and pretending that the phone had suddenly broken.

He told me about his week and I was sure he could sense my wild impatience barely concealed under my forced courtesy. I responded in the same wary, over-polite way that men who weren't interested in me had done. A lot of 'Is that right?'s and 'Really?'s. It was fascinating to see it from the other side.

Eventually he got to the point. He'd like to see me again. Take me out for dinner, if I liked.

For the entire phone call, Brigit stood a few feet from me and energetically played an air guitar. She stood with her legs apart and wildly shook her hair up and down.

As I clumsily, awkwardly, declined Luke's invitation, she thrust her groin at me repeatedly and waggled her tongue. I turned my back but she followed me.

'Er, no, I don't think so,' I mumbled to Luke. 'You see, I, ah, don't want a boyfriend.' A large lie. It was just him I didn't want as a boyfriend.

Brigit was on her knees, playing frantically and facing the ceiling with an expression of 'I'm having an orgasm' that those guitarists are always going around with.

Luckily Luke didn't try to persuade me that we could meet as friends. Boys that were Mistakes often tried that.

They pretended they didn't mind that I'd told them to stick it and insisted they'd be happy just to be friends. I usually felt guilty enough to meet them. And the next thing I knew, I was slaughtered drunk and in bed with them.

'I'm sorry,' I said. I felt ashamed, emotionally itchy, because he *was* very nice.

'Not at all,' he said easily. 'Sure, I'll see you round anyway. We'll have a chat.'

'OK,' I said. 'Bye,' and slammed down the phone.

'You bitch!' I shouted at Brigit, who by then was trying to slide along the kitchen tiles on her knees. 'You wait until Joey rings you.'

'Joey won't ring,' she said smugly. 'He didn't ask for my number.'

I sat down and rooted through my bag, looking for my Valium. I tipped three into my hand, then thought better of it and added another two. What an ordeal! I hated him for having rung, for putting me through that. Why was my life such a series of unpleasant events? Was there some sort of curse on me?

17

In the middle of a lovely dream, I was woken by a strange woman sticking a flashlight into my face.

'Rachel,' she said, 'it's time to get up.'

It was pitch-dark and freezing and I had no idea who she was. I decided I must be hallucinating, so I turned my back and closed my eyes again.

'Come on, Rachel,' she whispered loudly. 'Don't wake Chaquie.'

The mention of Chaquie brought reality crashing in on me. I wasn't in bed in New York. I was in the Cloisters where a roving madwoman was trying to rouse me in the middle of the night. She must have been one of the more deranged inmates, who'd escaped from her locked room in the attic.

'Hello,' I said to her. 'Go back to your own bed.' Friendly but firm. Now, hopefully, I could resume my sleep.

'I'm the night nurse,' she said.

'And I'm Coco the Clown,' I said. I could out-derange her any day she liked.

'Come on, you're on breakfasts.'

'Why isn't Chaquie on breakfasts?' I had heard some-where that it was best to reason with lunatics.

'Because she's not on Don's team.'

Suddenly the words 'Don's team' rang a strange and unfriendly bell.

'Am I . . . am I . . . on Don's team?' I asked haltingly. It had dawned horribly that perhaps I was. Didn't I agree to something yesterday evening . . .?

'Yes.'

A sensation of great loss descended upon me. I might have to get up after all.

'Well, I've just resigned,' I offered, hopefully.

She laughed in what might in other circumstances be described as a kindly way. 'You can't just resign,' she cajoled. 'Who's going to do the breakfast if you don't? You can't let everyone down.'

I was too tired to argue. In fact, I was too tired to understand what was going on and get annoyed about it. I grasped one point and one point only. If I didn't get up, people might not like me. But I was going to find this Don, whoever he was, and tender my resignation forthwith.

I was so tired and cold that I thought I might die of shock if I had a shower. And I was afraid to turn on the light and wake Chaquie in case she started talking at me again. So, in the darkness, I put on the same clothes that I had thrown on the floor the night before.

I wearily went to the bathroom to clean my teeth but there was already someone in it. While I shivered on the landing, waiting for the bathroom to be empty, the flash-light lunatic reappeared.

'You're up, good girl,' she said, when she saw me. 'Sorry I had to introduce myself like that. I'm Monica, one of the night nurses.'

I moved my toothbrush to my other hand so that I could shake hands with her. She seemed nice and kind. Motherly. Although not like my mother.

The bathdoor finally opened and, in a cloud of Blue Stratos, Oliver the Stalin lookalike waltzed out. He was just wearing his trousers and a facecloth slung jauntily over his plump shoulder. He looked nine months pregnant. His huge, bare, grey-haired stomach seemed to have a life of its own. He winked at me and said 'Clean and Polish, wha'? It's all yours.'

After I had half-heartedly thrown some water at myself, I dragged myself down the stairs. I was all set to find this Don and explain firmly to him that it was my sad duty to have to tender my resignation . . .

The moment I got into the perishingly cold kitchen, a plump, middle-aged, little man rushed up to me. He was wearing a tank-top and again I had that feeling that I had taken some hallucinogens a short time before.

He panted, out of breath, and said 'Good girl yourself, I've got the black and white puddings on, will you do the sausages . . .?'

'Are you Don?' I asked in surprise.

'Who else would I be?' He sounded annoyed.

I was confused. Don was an inmate, I had seen him several times the previous day, in the thick of the brown jumpers. How come he was one of the team leaders? Haltingly, I said as much.

And he explained what I had already suspected. In the tradition of the Betty Ford Clinic, the inmates of the Cloisters did the majority of the housework themselves.

'It's to teach us responsibility and teamwork,' he said, hopping from foot to foot. 'And I'm *this* team leader because I've been here nearly six weeks.'

'How many teams are there?' I asked.

'Four,' said Don. 'Breakfasts, that's us, Lunches, Dinners and Hoovering.'

I started to explain that I couldn't be on this team. Or on any team for that matter. I was allergic to housework, and, anyway, there wasn't anything wrong with me, I knew all there was to know about responsibility and teamwork. But Don interrupted.

'We'd better get cracking,' he said. 'They'll be down any minute, bellyaching and demanding to be fed. I'll just go and get the eggs.'

'But . . .'

'And keep an eye on Eamonn, would you?' He said anxiously. 'He'd eat the raw rashers if he could get his hands on them.' With that he rushed away.

'It's not fair on the team leaders putting an O E on the breakfasts . . .' he called back over his shoulder.

'What's an O E ?' I shouted after him.

'Overeater,' said a muffled voice. I turned and found Eamonn was also in the kitchen. I didn't know why I hadn't noticed him until then. Christ knows, he occupied about half of it.

The reason his voice was muffled was because he had the best part of a loaf of bread in his mouth.

'I suppose you'll report me for this?' he said, with a hangdog expression, as he stuffed slice after slice into his mouth.

'*Report* you?' I exclaimed. 'Why would I report you?'

'Why not?' He looked and sounded hurt. 'You're supposed to care about me, you're supposed to help me overcome my addictions, like I'm supposed to help you.'

'But you're a grown man,' I said in confusion. 'If you want to eat a family-sized sliced-pan . . .' I paused and touched it. '. . . a *frozen*, family-sized sliced-pan in under a minute, that's up to you.'

'Right then,' he said belligerently. 'I will.'

I had said the wrong thing. And I was only trying to be nice.

'Wum!' He glared at me as he crammed his mouth full with more slices of bread, 'Um eat unuther wum now!' Muffled but adamant, he started on a second loaf. At least it was only the second that I was aware of. God alone knew how many he'd eaten before I arrived.

There was the sound of footsteps coming down the corridor and Don arrived back. He had Stalin in tow and both of them had their arms full of cartons of eggs.

'Ah lads, lads.' Don didn't look too happy, as he took in the breadless scene.

He turned to me with an outraged expression. 'What's going on here? Ah now, lookit, Rachel, he's after eating nearly all the bread, there won't be any left for the TOAST!' His voice had risen in pitch throughout the sentence, with the grand finale 'TOAST' uttered in a soprano that could have shattered glass.

I felt sick. I felt miserable. I was jetlagged, for God's sake! And this was supposed to be a bloody holiday. I hadn't had to get up this early when I was going to work! And I was sorry about Eamonn eating all the bread, I hadn't realized that that was all there was, I might have tried to stop him otherwise. Everyone would hate me . . .

'I'm sorry,' I said, close to tears.

'Ah never mind,' said Don, with awkward kindness. 'Sure the divil himself couldn't stop him.'

'Sorry,' I whispered again. I looked down at Don with tear-filled eyes, batted my eyelashes just once and thus closed the deal.

'Don't worry at all,' he reassured me. 'He's done it every morning this week already. Sure, they're used to not having any toast.'

Then he started to break eggs into a bowl. It was too early to look at thirty-six raw eggs. My stomach heaved.

'Are you all right?' Stalin asked anxiously.

'She's not well!' Don declared, all of a dither. 'You big eejit. The girl's not well. For God's sake, let the child sit down!'

Fussing, and sending us on a detour as he skidded on a piece of rasher rind, Don led me to a chair.

'Will I get the nurse for you? Get the nurse!' He ordered Stalin and Eamonn. 'Put your head between your ears! . . . I mean your knees.'

'No,' I said weakly. 'I'm all right, it was only the eggs and I didn't get enough sleep . . .'

'You're not up the pole, are you?' asked Stalin.

'What a question!' Don was shocked. 'Of course the child isn't up the pole . . .'

He thrust his plump worried face into mine. 'You're not, are you?'

I shook my head.

'You see,' he declared triumphantly to Stalin.

I later learnt that Don was forty-seven and lived with his mother and was a 'confirmed bachelor'. Somehow it came as no surprise.

'Are you sure you're not on the bubble?' Stalin asked again. 'My Rita couldn't look at an egg when she was expecting the first four.'

'I'm not.'

'How do you know?'

'I just do.'

He could get lost for himself if he thought I was going to discuss my menstrual cycle.

So, Don, Eamonn, Stalin and a young boy called Barry that I remembered seeing all those years ago – yesterday – prepared the breakfast. I sat on a chair, sipping water, took deep breaths and tried not to puke. Barry was the one who looked about fourteen and had shouted 'Yeah, bleedin' useless,' at Sadie yesterday.

Just before breakfast I realized that I would shortly see Chris and I wasn't wearing a scrap of make-up. Through my exhaustion, nausea and misery, there broke through a faint glimmer of self-preservation. But when I tried to crawl back upstairs to throw on some blusher and mascara, my way was blocked by motherly Monica, the nurse. Breakfast was about to start and I was going nowhere until it was over.

'But . . .' I said weakly.

'Tell me what you want from your room and I'll get it,' she offered with a warm, but very, very firm, smile.

But of course I couldn't tell her. She'd think I was vain. So I had to slink back into the dining-room with my head lowered in case Chris saw me full-on without my make-up and realized what a dog I was. I managed the entire breakfast without making eye-contact with one other person.

They were all so jovial. Even about the lack of toast.

'What, no toast? AGAIN!' Peter laughed. But of course he would have laughed even if he heard that his house had been burnt to the ground and all his family were wiped out in a massacre.

'No toast, again,' said someone else.

'No toast, again.'

'No toast, again.' The message passed down the table.

'That fat fucker, Eamonn,' mumbled someone bitterly. I was surprised to find it was Chaquie.

Between the stomach-turning eggs and the non-vegetarian sausages and rashers, I ate almost nothing. Which couldn't be bad, I decided.

But I was so tired and weirded-out by it all that it wasn't

until late that evening that I realized that there hadn't been one piece of fruit for breakfast. Not even a bruised apple or a black banana, let alone the mile-long buffet of fresh tropical fruits that I'd expected.

18

The day never really got on track for me. I was dizzy and queasy, and I didn't ever manage to wake up properly.

Thoughts of Luke were with me all the time. I was too tired to have the loss centred clearly in my mind, but the pain constantly buzzed away just under the surface.

Everything was weird and peculiar, as though I'd landed on another planet.

When the revolting breakfast finished, I had to scrub several large, greasy frying-pans. Then I bolted to the room and spent twenty minutes larding on make-up. I had a difficult job on my hands.

Whenever I didn't get enough sleep I got patches of red, flaky skin on my face. They were hard to cover because, even if I put tons of foundation on them, the flaky bits just flaked off, taking the foundation with them and leaving the red blotches centre stage again. I tried my best but even with make-up on I looked like a corpse.

I crawled back downstairs, forced a smile and bumped into Misty O'Malley. She was slouching around wearing a sour look and no make-up. With my brown sticky grinning face I instantly felt like a toffee apple and a gobshite.

Don scuttled over and grabbed me by the sleeve.

'Have you your hands washed?' he anxiously demanded.

'Why?'

'Because it's the cookery CLASS,' he shrieked, his eyes apop at my stupidity. 'It's Saturday morning, hobbies' TIME!'

A mirage of me having my pressure points gently massaged wavered and evaporated. I wasn't at all happy. A cookery class was only one step up from basket-weaving.

'It's great fun,' someone said, eyes ashine, as we were swept along to the kitchen and handed an apron.

'You'll love Betty,' someone else promised me.

Betty was the teacher. She was blonde and fragrant and popular.

Stalin grabbed her and waltzed her around the room. 'Ah, me darlin' girl,' he said.

Clarence elbowed me. 'Isn't she lovely?' he whispered, like the halfwit he was. 'Hasn't she lovely hair?'

'Work stations, everyone.' Betty clapped her hands.

As we were about to start, Dr Billings came and crooked a finger at Eamonn, who stood gleaming acquisitively at a bag of raisins, and took him away.

'Where's he going?' I asked Mike.

'Oh, he's not allowed to bake,' said Mike, 'because he went berserk last week and ate a whole bowl of pastry.

'Before it was cooked,' he added.

He looked pained at the memory. 'It would turn your stomach to see it,' he said, 'so it would. And he had the tightest hoult a that bowl . . .'

'Jayzus, it was desperate,' said Stalin, with a shudder. 'Like feeding time at the azoo. It took the night's sleep offa me.'

'So where is he now?' I asked. I didn't like the peremptory manner in which Eamonn had been led away.

'Don't know,' shrugged Mike. 'Doing some other hobby.'

'Maybe he's learning to make homebrew,' suggested Barry the child.

That caused uproarious laughter. They slapped their thighs and snorted 'Making homebrew, that's a good one.'

'Or doing . . . or doing . . .' Clarence was laughing so hard he could barely speak. '. . . or doing some wine appreciation,' he finally managed. The brown jumpers exploded into convulsions. They wheezed with mirth, laughing so hard they had to hold on to each other.

'I'll eat a bowl of raw pastry if they'll let me do wine appreciation,' Mike guffawed.

More hysterics.

I didn't laugh. I wanted to lie down and sleep for a very, very long time. The last thing I wanted to do was bake something.

The rest of them bantered happily with each other while I prayed to die. I could hear what they were saying, but their voices sounded a long way off.

'I'm making this great kind of . . . like . . . bread stuff that I had in Islamabad,' mumbled Fergus the acid casualty.

'Have you any wacky baccy to put into it?' Vincent enquired.

'No,' Fergus admitted.

'Then it's *not* like the bread you had in Timbuctoo, is it?'

Fergus turned away, his dead wasteland eyes emptied further.

'If me wife could see me now, wha'? Harharhar!' said Stalin, as he weighed out some caster sugar. 'She's never even seen me boil a kettle.'

'No wonder she's got a barring order out against you,' said Misty O'Malley.

And everyone tutted and said 'Oh, *Misty*,' but in a good-natured way.

But then aggressive Vincent said 'It's not because he can't cook, it's because he keeps breaking her ribs.'

There was a roaring in my ears and I thought I was going to faint.

That couldn't be true, could it? I thought in horror. Stalin was a nice, friendly man, he wouldn't do that, Vincent must be joking. But nobody laughed. Nobody said anything at all.

A long time passed before people began to speak and joke again. And Stalin didn't utter another word.

I continued to feel mighty pukey. If I hadn't known better I'd have sworn I'd been out on the rip the night before.

Luckily Betty was nice. She asked me if there was anything in particular I'd like to make. I mumbled 'Something easy.'

And she said, 'What about coconut buns? You could make them in your sleep.' Feeling like that was exactly what I was doing, I did.

'I've been planning this all week,' Mike announced with glee, as he pointed at a picture in a book. 'It's a tart tatin.'

'What's that?' demanded Peter.

'Some class of a French upsidedown apple tart.'

'And what's wrong with having it the right way up?' Peter wanted to know. ' 'Twas far from French upside-down yokes you were reared. AHAHAHAHAHAH AHAAAAAARGH!'

Betty moved around the room, helping here, making suggestions there. ('That's enough butter, Mike, you don't want to give yourself a heart attack.' 'No, Fergus, I'm sorry. You'll have to use a normal oven, fire regulations don't cover us for two bricks on a hillside. I'm sorry if it won't be authentic.' 'No, Fergus, I *am* sorry.' 'No, Fergus, I'm *not* patronizing you.' 'No, Fergus, I have nothing against drugs.' 'I'll have you know, Fergus, that I smoked pot once.' 'Do you mind? I *did* inhale.') Awful as I felt, there was something comforting about measuring and sieving the flour and sugar and desecrated coconut (as Mum called it), breaking in the eggs (pausing momentarily for a brief gag), stirring it all around in a bowl and putting the sticky mixture into little paper cases that had sprigs of holly on them. It make me think of when I was a little girl and I used to help my mother, in the days before she gave up baking for ever.

I stayed away from Chris because I knew he'd go right off me if he got too close a look at my cadaver's face and red blotches. But it was hard because the attention he'd paid to me the evening before had made me feel infinitesimally better about Luke. If another man wanted to talk to me, surely I wasn't as worthless as Luke made out I was? Surreptitiously, I watched Chris as he kneaded brown bread. I sighed, wishing it was my nipples he had on the floured board.

At one stage I saw him talking to Misty O'Malley and she must have said something funny, because he laughed. The sound of his laughter and the flash of blue of his eyes cut me to the quick. *I* wanted to be the one to make him laugh.

As soon as I felt jealous and excluded by Chris, it was only a moment before I remembered how excluded I felt by *Luke*. Then depression dragged me down.

After the cookery class, there was lunch, a film about

drunk people, followed by more tea-drinking. I moved through it all as though in a bad dream.

What am I doing here? flashed through my brain regularly. And then I'd take my brain aside and give it a good talking to, reminding it about pop stars and detoxifying and the general wonderfulness of the Cloisters. Deeply relieved, it would all come back to me and I'd realize how lucky I was. But a short time later I'd find myself staring in astonishment at the middle-aged men, the yellow walls, the thick fog of cigarette smoke, the terrible *dinginess* of it all, and again I'd wonder *What am I doing here?*

It was like wearing shoes with slippery soles. I kept thinking that as soon as I finished whatever I was doing, I'd get a grip on the day and do something nice. But I didn't. The minute one thing ended, the next thing started. And I hadn't the energy to fight it, it was easier to just follow the herd.

Something was worrying me. There was a thought in my head that I couldn't quite get a hold on, it kept slithering away.

19

In the afternoon a nice man I hadn't seen before came and spoke to me.

'Howya,' he said. 'Neil's the name and I'm in Josephine's group too. I didn't meet you yesterday because I was at the dentist.'

Normally I wouldn't give the time of day to anyone who introduced themselves by saying 'Neil's the name,' but there was something about him I liked.

He was twinkly, smiley and quite young. I found myself sitting up straight and making a bit of an effort for him. Although, even before I saw the wedding ring on his finger, I knew he was married. It was something to do with the smoothness of his jumper and the uncreasedness of his trousers. I had a strange pang of disappointment.

'How are you getting on with this crowd of headcases?' He jerked his head round the room at the brown jumpers.

A warmth filled me. A normal person!

'They're OK,' I giggled. 'For a crowd of headcases.'

'And what did you make of Josephine?'

'She's a bit scary,' I admitted.

'Ah, she's another headcase,' he said. 'She puts thoughts in people's minds, makes them admit to things that aren't true.'

'Really?' I said. 'You know, I *thought* she was a bit odd.'

'Yeah, you'll see for yourself,' he said intriguingly. 'Anyway, what are you in for?'

'Drugs.' I made a rueful face to let him know that there wasn't *really* anything wrong with me.

He laughed understandingly. 'I know what you mean, I'm in for alcohol myself. My poor deluded wife doesn't drink and she thinks that because I have four pints on a Saturday night it makes me an alcoholic. I came in here to get her off my back. At least now it'll prove to her there's nothing wrong with me.'

And we laughed together conspiratorially at other people's foolishness.

A couple of times during the day, I noticed the Sour Kraut and Celine the day nurse talking about me. At tea-time, just before the chips-fest, Celine appeared and said 'Can I have a word, Rachel?'

Impending doom descended. While the inmates shouted 'Oooh, Rachel, you've done it now' and 'Can I have your chips?' Celine took me, head lowered, to the nurses' room.

It was like being taken to the Principal's office at school. But, to my surprise, Celine didn't seem to be annoyed with me.

'You don't look well,' she said. 'You haven't looked well all day.'

'I didn't get much sleep last night,' I exhaled, euphoric with relief. 'And I think I might still be jet-lagged.'

'Why didn't you say anything?'

'I don't know,' I grinned. 'I'm used to feeling terrible, I suppose. Most days in work I feel like hell on wheels . . .' I stopped abruptly when I saw the expression on her face. This was *not* the right woman to discuss wild nights out on the town with.

'Why do you feel bad in work?' she asked, and for a

moment her easy-going voice nearly had me fooled. But not quite.

'I'm not a morning person,' I said briefly.

She smiled. She passed judgement on me with that one look. My euphoria dissipated. She knows, I thought uncomfortably. She knows everything about me.

'I think you should go to bed after tea,' she said. 'The counsellor on duty and I have discussed it and we think it's OK if you miss the games this evening.'

'What games?'

'Every Saturday night there are games. Musical Chairs, Twister, Red Rover, that kind of thing.'

She can't be serious, I thought. It was the most squirmy thing I'd ever heard.

'It's marvellous fun.' She smiled.

You poor, sad woman, I thought, if that's your idea of fun.

'Everyone lets off a bit of steam,' she went on. 'And it's the one time in the week when there are no nurses or counsellors present, so you can do impersonations of us . . .'

When she said that, I realized one of the things that had niggled me all day. The inmates were rarely alone. Even at mealtimes, one of the staff sat quietly in their midst.

'So after tea, go straight to bed,' she ordered.

Maybe I could have a sunbed or a massage first, I thought hopefully.

'First, could I . . .?' I asked.

'Bed,' she interrupted firmly. 'Tea, then bed. You're tired and we don't want you getting sick.'

It felt all wrong to find myself in bed on a Saturday night at seven o'clock. You'd usually only find me in the scratcher at that hour when I still hadn't got up from the night before. (Not that rare an event, actually. Especially if it had been a late one and strong cocaine had been taken.)

The sensations of isolation and alienation that I'd had all day intensified as I sat in bed, listlessly leafing through Chaquie's magazines, the rain cracking against the rattly, draughty window. I was lonely and afraid. *And* a failure. It was Saturday night and I should've been dressing up and going out and enjoying myself. Instead I was in bed.

My big worry was Luke. I had never felt so powerless in my life. I knew he'd be going out tonight and having a good time without me. He might even – my insides shrank with fear – he might even meet another girl. And take her back to his apartment. And shag her . . .

At this thought, an almost uncontrollable urge seized me, to jump out of bed, pull on some clothes and *somehow* get to New York to stop him. Frantically I grabbed a handful of Pringles and stuffed them into my mouth and the panic abated slightly. The Pringles were a great comfort. Neil had donated them when he heard I was being sent to bed early. I had only meant to eat a couple but I ended up ploughing my way through the lot. I can't sleep easy if there's an open container of savoury snacks in the house.

I would have loved a couple of sleeping tablets. Or Valium. Anything to calm the terrible fluttery anxiety about Luke that so tormented me. It was inhumane to expect me to get through such heartache without chemicals to ease my pain, I thought in anger. *No one* should be expected to suffer this way. In the real world no one *would* put themselves through this. Abstinence had gone too far in the Cloisters.

I knew it wasn't fair to ask the poor addicts to do without when people like me who *didn't* have a problem were imbibing freely. It wouldn't be right to wave temptation under their noses. But all the same . . .

I could hear bangs and thumps and screams and laughter as the others played their musical chairs in the room below me.

When Chaquie came up to bed she was flushed and happy-looking.

Briefly.

'I didn't see you at Mass this evening,' she said, purse-lipped.

(A priest came every Saturday to say Mass for those who were interested.)

'That's right, you didn't,' I said cheerfully.

She glared and I grinned brazenly.

Then she started on another of her hobby-horses. This time it was the evil of mothers who work. I made a great show of pulling the covers over my head and saying 'Goodnight'. But it made no difference. Chaquie had some things to get off her chest and she didn't care who knew it.

' . . . And the husband comes home after a long day in the office – or the beauty salon . . .' she allowed herself a little tinkle at this '. . . And the house is a shambles, the kids are screaming . . .'

'There's no dinner on the table,' I interrupted from under my blankets, deciding to beat her to it.

'That's right, Rachel,' she sounded pleasantly surprised, 'There's no dinner on the table.'

'His shirts aren't ironed,' I called up to her.

'That's ri . . .'

'The children come home from school to an empty, cold house . . .'

'That's ri . . .'

'They eat crisps and biscuits instead of a hot, nourishing meal . . .'

'Exac . . .'

'They watch pornography on the telly, they indulge in incest, the house burns down and their mother isn't there to stop it and they all die!'

A silence followed that and eventually I peeped out from under my blankets.

Chaquie was staring at me in confusion. She strongly suspected that I was taking the piss, but she couldn't be sure.

I had thought I hated her before that, but then I knew that I really, *really* hated her.

Fascist cow, I thought to myself. I knew her sort. She was a member of Right-wing Catholic Mothers Against Pleasure, or whatever they were called.

Shortly after that, in grim silence, Chaquie turned off the light and got into bed.

Mercifully, due to great exhaustion, I fell asleep.

20

Sunday. Visiting day!

Except not for me. I would have loved some contact with the outside world. I'd even have been glad to see my mother. But I hadn't been in for the required week yet, although I already felt as if I'd been there for several years.

The first thing I thought of when I was woken by Monica's flashlight, was Luke. I was tormented by thoughts of what he might have got up to the night before. Might *still* be getting up to. After all, it was only three a.m. where he was. Saturday night was only getting going.

I wanted to ring him. I wanted to ring him so badly it was almost unbearable. But he probably wasn't even home yet. Unless he was in bed with someone. Perhaps he's in bed with some girl right now, I thought, frantically. Maybe he's just this very second having an orgasm with another woman. I realized that this was how people go mad. That I really *would* need to go to a loony bin if I didn't watch myself.

I had to talk to him, I decided. I'd have to ring him. But I did a quick sum and realized I'd have to wait until at least three o'clock, when it would be ten in the morning in New York. *Oh, why can't I do it now? Fecking time difference!* Bitterly, I cursed the curvature of the earth.

In my heart of hearts I knew ten on a Sunday morning was probably still too early, probably by several days. But I didn't care. It would do.

After breakfast ended, Chaquie launched into frantic preparations for Dermot's arrival. To my surprise she asked me to help her to choose what to wear. That touched me so much I forgot I hated her.

And I was wildly grateful to have something to do. I didn't stop thinking about Luke, but it reduced the agony to a background-noise type of ache. It wasn't as bad, just omnipresent.

Chaquie had her entire, very large wardrobe spread around the very small room. Which reminded me that I really must get round to asking her would she mind making room for some of my stuff which was still in my suitcase on the floor.

'What do you think, Rachel?' she asked. 'The Jaeger suit with the Hermès scarf?'

'Er, maybe something a little less formal,' I suggested tentatively. 'Have you any jeans?'

'JEANS!' she hooted with laughter. 'Sacred Heart! I do not! Durm't would die if he saw me in jeans.' She gave at the knees to see herself in the (tiny, age-spotted) mirror and bobbed her hand around her perfect hair.

'Jeezus, Mary and holy Saint Joseph,' she declared, rolling her eyes. 'I'm like the wreck of the Hesperus.'

Of course, she was nothing of the sort. She looked immaculate.

'It's very important to look good for your husband,' she confided, as she put on a tailored skirt and a cardigan with beads and things appliquéd to the front. Awful stuff.

With jerky movements she back-combed her hair. She was nervous, *really* nervous about Dermot's visit.

'You look lovely,' I said, even though I thought she looked a right state.

I looked at my watch – midday. Only three more hours

and I'd be talking to Luke! 'When Dermot comes, would you like me, to, er ... you know?' I magnanimously offered Chaquie, as I made vamoosing type movements with my hands.

'What?'

'Would you like to have the room to yourselves so that you can, ahem, you know ...?'

She looked disgusted. 'What? Have intercourse, do you mean?'

'That's one way of putting it.' The language of romance.

'Sacred Heart, no!' she said. 'The only good thing about being in here is not being pestered by him and his flute when I'm trying to read my book in bed. Anyway, we're not allowed to have visitors up to our rooms.'

'Not allowed to have people up to our rooms?' It was my turn to look disgusted. 'Surely even in *prison* people are allowed their conjugals?'

Chaquie kept going to the window and eventually at half past one she said 'Here he is.'

It was almost impossible to describe her tone of voice. Admiration, relief and hatred in equal measures.

'Where?' I rushed to the window to get a look at him.

'There, getting out of the new Volvo.'

I stared down in fascination, hoping he'd be horrible. But from a distance he didn't look too bad. With his deep, deep tan and suspiciously black hair, he could be described as the kind of man 'who looks after himself'. He was wearing a denim shirt, a blouson leather jacket and a pair of chinos with the waistband up almost around his chest, one of the tricks tubby men use in a pointless attempt to hide their big stomachs. From the look of Dermot, Chaquie wasn't the only one to enjoy a Bacardi and coke from time to time.

As I stared at him, searching for faults, I noticed that he had small hands and, worse again, small feet. You could barely see his shoes under the cuffs of his trousers. I hated men with small hands and feet. It made them seem very unmanly, like imps or gnomes. Helen used to insist that men with small hands were her favourite, but that was only because she had a really small chest, and the smaller a man's hands were, the bigger her tits in comparison.

Chaquie hurriedly sprayed herself with almost an entire bottle of White Linen, then, smoothing her skirt and her hair, left the room to greet him.

I didn't know what to do. I didn't want to be alone, so I decided to go downstairs to see what was happening. I bumped into Mike on the landing. He was gloomily looking out the window the way Chaquie had been a few minutes ago.

'Hello,' I said, keen to talk. 'What are you doing?'

'Come here,' he said, and pointed out the window.

A woman and three children straggled up the drive, through the rain. They looked exhausted and frozen.

'That's my wife and kids.' His tone of voice was weird. First Chaquie, now Mike, they were all at it.

Mike's wife had a holdall over her shoulder.

'See that bag,' muttered Mike, pointing at it.

I nodded.

'That's for me,' he said.

I nodded again.

'Full of fucking biscuits,' he said bitterly. And off he went.

'What use are biscuits to me?' he roared back over his shoulder.

'I don't know,' I said nervously.

A while later I made for the dining-room. The corridor was full of happy children hurting each other and breaking things.

To my horror, I tripped on a My Little Pony and went flying. But, like a video of a dynamited tower block being run in reverse, I managed to spring back up before my knees had barely glanced off the floor. I looked around furtively to make sure that neither Chris nor Misty O'Malley had seen me. Two revolting, freckled little boys pointed at me and laughed until they cried.

As I went into the dining-room, Misty O'Malley was on her way out and she rudely pushed past me. It wasn't just a brief brush, but more like a hefty shove. She didn't apologize. I stared after her and even though I couldn't see her face, I knew she was smirking. Having a good laugh at me.

Tears filled my eyes. What had I ever done to her?

The dining-room was packed with the inmates and their visitors. Apparently when the weather was good, they could all walk around the grounds. But on wet days like today, they had to crowd, ten-deep, into the dining-room and watch the windows steam up.

I found Chaquie and Dermot and brazenly sat down near them, so that Chaquie was forced to introduce me. Dermot made eye contact and gave me the once over automatically. Not because he found me attractive, but because he wondered what *I* thought of *him*. Up close, you could see hundreds of broken capillaries lurking beneath his sunbed tan. I could understand why Chaquie was so keen to escape the attentions of Dermot and his flute. He was vile. And the obvious care he took of his appearance made him even more vile. He kept touching his hair, which, as well as being dyed to within an inch of its life, was blowdried, flicked and rigid with spray. It had so much fullness it was nearly like a beehive.

I watched him with blatant amusement. I knew his sort. A frequenter of wine bars, a buyer of drinks, the kind of man who, shortly after he had introduced himself would ask 'What age do you think I am? No, go on, tell me. Another drink?'

The funniest thing was seeing Dermot and his ilk trying to dance. And they always seemed to drink girly things like Campari and soda or Bacardi and coke. Sweet, fizzy, *undemanding* drinks. Brigit and I had met his like countless times. They'd buy us drinks all evening, then at closing time we ran away on them. Memories of the pair of us roaring, laughing, hiding round corners, saying 'You'd better get off with him', 'No, fuck off, *you'd* better', came rushing back.

You could tell just by looking at him that Dermot was the kind of man who lied about being married. (Probably even to his wife.) The kind of man who gave some elaborate excuse to get out of inviting you back to his flat. The kind of man that I would end up being grateful to snag if I didn't step on it, I thought, sunk into sudden gloom.

Chaquie turned her back on me and engaged Dermot in a low, muttered conversation. Not that that indicated discord or anything. The room was full of people having low, muttered conversations. They had no choice. Next week when Mum and Dad came to visit, we too would sit at the table and have a low, muttered conversation. The air was so full of the sounds of low, muttered conversations that I began to feel sleepy. The only thing that kept me from nodding off was the sounds of people tripping in the corridor and Mike occasionally shouting 'Willy, you little bastard, knock off trying to kill everyone with Michelle's Little Pony yoke!'

I felt better that Chaquie's husband was so awful. Until I looked round the room and saw Misty O'Malley leaning against the radiators, having a low, muttered conversation with a tall, blond, sickeningly gorgeous man and I felt lonely and jealous. I hated that there was such injustice in the world. Millions of men were mad about Misty and she was such a rude, unpleasant little bitch, and not even that beautiful, really, if you thought about it. While I was so nice and hadn't anyone.

I mooned around, killing time until three o'clock, trying to radiate orphanhood. I hoped to catch someone's eye so that I could smile bravely. I wanted everyone to wonder why I had no visitors and nudge each other and say 'Who's that poor child? Give her some chocolate.' But no one had any interest in me. Neil was sitting with a plain-looking woman and two little girls. He looked up and gave me a lovely, warm smile, then went back to his wife. They looked as if they were discussing dampproofing the garage.

When I eavesdropped on the third conversation involving a man pleading to his wife 'It'll be different this time, I promise,' I had to get out of there.

I went to the front door and half-heartedly stood on the front steps in the rain, and looked out at the mournful, dripping trees. I had meant to go round the grounds and find the gym and do an hour or so of body sculpting, but I just couldn't be arsed. Oh, now, now, I berated myself, this won't get the thighs narrowed.

So I screwed up my will-power and my resolve and determination, I squared my shoulders, set my jaw and swore, promised, *vowed* – I could almost hear the celestial trumpets and see the sun break through the clouds – 'I'll start tomorrow!'

Back I went to the dining-room and in my head rehearsed what I'd say to Luke. ('Hiiiii! Great! How are yooouuu?')

I saw Chris sitting with two people who looked like his parents. They were about the same age as mine and seeing the three of them sitting huddled together, awkwardly trying to make conversation, filled me with a strange grief. I couldn't help but notice the absence of a girlfriend-type figure hanging round him.

Good.

Stalin dragged me over to meet his Rita, a husky-voiced chain-smoker. She looked like a man in drag and more likely to break Stalin's ribs than the other way round. I was comforted by that.

At ten to three, I couldn't wait anymore so I found the counsellor on duty – the Sour Kraut – and asked her if I could make a call. She stared at me, as if I'd asked her for the loan of a thousand quid, then in silence led me towards the office. We passed Bubbly in reception. How manky to have to work on a Sunday. From Bubbly's resentful expression it looked like she agreed with me.

'Gif me the number,' Sour Kraut said.

'Em, it's a number in New York,' I said nervously. 'Is that OK?'

She glared at me through her John Lennon glasses, but she didn't say it wasn't.

'It's ringing,' she said, and handed me the phone.

Heart pounding, scalp tingling with sweat, I took the phone.

I'd practised my speech all day. I had decided to be breezy and chatty, rather than whingey and condemnatory. But my lips trembled so much I wasn't sure if I'd be able to compress them and actually speak when the time came.

I heard a click and my heart plummeted with acute disappointment – the answering machine. I decided to leave a message, anyway. Maybe someone would pick up the phone when they heard my voice. Patiently, I waited to hear the first verse of 'Smoke on the Water'.

But it wasn't 'Smoke on the Water'!

They'd changed their message to some Led Zeppelin song.

When Robert Plant started shrieking something about red-hot mommas and what he was planning to do to them as soon as he got home, I became seized with fear, convinced that the new message was symbolic. That Luke was trying to tell me 'Out with the old, in with the new'. It hit home with devastating force that life in New York was going on without me. What *else* had happened that I didn't know about?

I listened to the mad, energetic gee-tar break and as it neared an end I tried to stop shaking and poised myself to speak. But no! There was a second verse. And Mr Plant was off again, yelling and screeching and promising hot love left, right and centre. Then there was more frantic guitar playing. Finally Shake's voice said 'Do the message thing, man.' But I completely lost my nerve. I remembered how angry Luke was with me, how deeply nasty he'd been. He wouldn't want to talk to me, so I leant over and hung up.

'Machine,' I muttered at the Sour Kraut, who had been sitting there all along.

'You haf used vun off your two calls even though you did not speak.'

By five o'clock all the visitors had left. Everyone was subdued and sullen. Except me.

I was suicidal.

After tea, I opened the dining-room cupboard, foraging for chocolate I'd seen earlier in the day, and was nearly brained as an avalanche of biscuits, cakes, buns and chocolate fell out on top of me.

'Jesus!' I complained, as a bag of mini-Mars bars nearly took my eye out. 'What's all this about?'

'Guilt money,' said Mike. 'They always bring sackloads of sweets. Except for that yoke of Chaquie's. He just gave her a bag of mandarins. Did you clock his rug?'

'Dermot?' I asked in astonishment. 'He wears a wig?'

'How could you miss it?' laughed Mike. 'It was like a badger asleep on his scalp.'

'And what do you mean, "guilt money"?' I asked. That made me feel unaccountably anxious.

'Our families feel guilty for putting us in here.'

'But why would they feel guilty?' I asked. 'Isn't it for your good?'

'Is that what you really think?' Mike asked, his eyes narrowed.

'Of course,' I said, nervously. 'If you're an alcoholic, or a drug addict, then coming here is the best thing for you.'

'Do you think it's the best thing for *you*?'

What could I say? I decided to be honest.

'Look,' I said, conspiratorially, 'I shouldn't be here at all. My father just overreacted. I only came here to please my parents.'

Mike's face dissolved and he laughed and laughed.

'What's so funny?' I was annoyed.

'Because that's just what I said,' he grinned. 'I came here to please my wife, Chaquie's in to get her husband off her back, Don because of his mother, Davy so that he wouldn't lose his job, Eamonn because of his sister, John Joe's here because of his niece. We're all in here to please someone.'

I didn't know what to say. I couldn't help it if all of them were in denial.

21

It was Monday morning.

I'd had a terrible night's sleep, constantly dreaming of Luke, then waking up sweating and heartbroken. We were just about to go into group and apparently Neil's ISO, whatever that was, was coming.

'It stands for Involved Significant Other,' Mike said. 'Someone like your wife or your friends or your parents. They come along and tell the group how bad you were when you were drunk or stoned or eating them out of house and home.'

'Really?' I had a throb of voyeuristic anticipation.

A real life Irish Oprah. I should try and get Mum and Helen along for a session, they'd appreciate it.

'And who are your ISOs?' Mike asked drily.

'I haven't got any,' I said in surprise.

'No one ever saw you when you were on drugs?' he said. He sounded sarcastic.

I felt despair. How could I ever get these eejits to understand that taking recreational drugs was normal? That if any ISO of mine came to group they'd have nothing to report other than 'She enjoyed herself.'

'I've lived away from home for the last eight years,' I said. 'And I hardly think my flatmate's going to jump on a plane from New York.'

Mike gave another knowing laugh.

'Neil's wife is his ISO,' he said. 'ISOs are usually wives.'

'Well, I don't know what Neil's wife is doing coming here,' I said. 'He's not an alcoholic.'

'Is that right?' asked Mike. I detected scorn. 'How do you know that?'

'Because he told me.'

'Did he indeed?'

Neil and his wife were already in the Abbot's Quarter, as were the others – Misty, John Joe, Vincent, Chaquie and Clarence.

Neil looked as sweet and neat as a little boy who'd just made his Confirmation. I gave him a reassuring smile, not that he needed it. He gave me a kind of downturned clown's smile back. I knew it would be a very dull session and I was slightly disappointed. I'd been so looking forward to finding out about John Joe shagging a sheep.

Neil's wife, Emer, looked even duller and plainer than she had the day before. I automatically despised her because she'd kicked up such a fuss about Neil's drinking, or lack of. I couldn't bear killjoys. I was prepared to bet she was another member of Right-wing Catholic Mothers Against Pleasure, just like Chaquie. She was damn lucky Neil hadn't told her to feck off for herself.

Josephine came in and made us all introduce ourselves. Then she thanked Emer for coming, and started asking her questions.

'Would you like to tell the group about Neil's drinking?'

I sighed, four pints on a Saturday night wasn't much of a story. Josephine looked at me. I was afraid.

'Well,' Emer said in a quivery voice, 'he wasn't that bad, I suppose.' She looked at the lap of her skirt as she spoke.

He wasn't bad, *at all*, you stupid cow, I thought. I gave her a dirty look.

'Was he often drunk?' asked Josephine.

Emer gave Josephine a big, rabbit-caught-in-the-head-lights stare. 'No,' she said, her voice wavering. 'Hardly ever.'

She shot Neil a look, then went back to her skirt.

My contempt for her increased.

'Did he behave badly to you and your children?'

'No, never.'

'Did he ever disappear for days at a time?'

'No.'

'Did he ever keep you short of money?'

'No.'

'Did he ever verbally abuse you?'

'No.'

'Did he ever hit you?'

'No!'

'Was he ever unfaithful to you?'

'No.'

I started to sigh to convey my boredom with what Emer wasn't saying, then remembered Josephine and thought better of it.

Josephine spoke again. 'He must have been bad some-times, otherwise he wouldn't be in here.'

Emer shrugged her bony shoulders and didn't look up.

'Are you afraid of your husband?'

'No.'

'I'm just going to read something out for the group,' said Josephine. 'The questionnaire you filled out when Neil first came in.'

'Don't!' Emer exclaimed.

'Why not?' Josephine was gentle.

'Because . . . because it's not true!'

'So it's not true that Neil . . .' Josephine picked up a

sheet of paper '. . . that he broke your nose on three occasions, broke your jaw, fractured your arm, burnt you with cigarettes, put your fingers in the joint of a door and slammed it, threw your youngest child down the stairs where she went through the glass panel of the front door and had to have forty-eight stitches . . .'

'DON'T!' she screamed, her hands up to her eyes.

I couldn't believe what I was hearing. It was one thing to lie about how much he drank, but I was shaken by the horrors she had accused him of.

Neil glared at Emer as she sat sobbing.

Everyone looked as shocked as I felt.

I shifted uncomfortably in my seat – not just because I'd chosen one of the crappy ones – but because I didn't like the psychotherapy game so much any more. It had been such fun to start with, but it had become serious and frightening.

'What do you have to say to this, Neil?' Josephine asked quietly.

I breathed out. Thank God Neil was getting a chance to defend himself.

'She's a lying bitch,' he said slowly and thickly. He didn't sound like such a nice man, the way he said it.

'Are you?' Josephine asked Emer conversationally.

There was another silence which stretched on and on unpleasantly. I could hear my own ragged breathing.

'Are you?' Josephine asked again.

'Yes,' Emer said. Her voice was shaking so much she could hardly talk. 'None of what I wrote on that thing is true.'

'Still protecting him?' said Josephine. 'You'd rather put him ahead of yourself?' I wished Josephine would shut up. Emer had said none of it was true and I wanted it left there.

I yearned for group to be over so we could do something nice and normal like go for a cup of tea.

'Ahead of your children?' Josephine said softly, as Emer sat hunched over in her chair.

Another of those lengthy, excruciating silences. My shoulders were almost up around my ears with tension.

'No,' came the muffled reply.

My heart sank.

'What's that Emer?' said Josephine kindly.

Emer looked up. Her face was red and wet.

'No,' she said tearfully. 'Not ahead of my children. He can belt me but I want him to leave the kids out of it.'

I looked at Neil and his face was suffused with rage. He was unrecognizable as the friendly, twinkly man he'd been twenty minutes before.

'So, it *is* true, isn't it?' Josephine asked with infinite compassion. 'Neil did all those things you said on the questionnaire?'

'Yes.' The word came out as a wail.

'I quite agree,' said Josephine. 'And I have police and hospital reports here to back it all up.'

She turned to Neil. 'Perhaps you'd like to have a look at them, Neil?' she said pleasantly. 'Maybe you'd like to refresh your memory about what you did to your wife and children.'

My head snapped from Emer to Neil while I tried to figure out who was telling the truth. I was no longer so sure it was Neil. If Josephine said she had police reports, then it probably was true.

Neil was on his feet, swaying around like someone

with mad cow disease. 'Look at her,' he shouted and slurred. 'You'd hit her too, married to a stupid bitch like that.'

'Sit. Down. Neil.' Josephine was like a blade of steel. 'And how dare you use language like that in my presence.'

He wavered. Then he sat down heavily.

Josephine turned to Neil. 'Why did you hit your wife?'

'It wasn't my fault,' he shouted. 'I was drunk.'

Then he looked stunned at what he'd said, as if he hadn't meant to say it.

'When you were admitted here,' Josephine rustled another piece of paper, 'you told Dr Billings you drank an average of four pints a week . . .'

We all jumped as a strange noise came from Emer. A shocked snort.

'It has become clear today that you drank much more than that. Tell the group about it, please.'

'That's all I drank,' Neil swaggered. 'Four pints.'

Josephine looked steadily at Neil with a don't-push-your-luck expression.

'Maybe a bit more,' he mumbled hastily.

Josephine said nothing, just kept giving him that look.

'All right, all right,' Neil said resentfully. And in mumbly fits and starts, he told us how he drank four pints a night, then in response to Josephine's scorn said it was a bottle of vodka a week, then eventually admitted it was half a bottle of vodka a day.

'A whole one,' interrupted Emer, a lot braver now, 'a litre bottle. *And* wine and beer and whatever cocaine he could get his hands on.'

Cocaine, I thought in shock. *Him?* To look at him you'd think he wouldn't even know what cocaine was. I must ask him where you could buy it in Dublin.

'OK, Neil,' said Josephine, with the patience of a woman who had done this sort of thing many times before, 'let's start again. Tell the group how much you really drink.'

Reluctantly Neil reiterated what Emer had just said.

'Thank you, Neil,' said Josephine. 'Now will you please tell the group how much you *really* drink.'

'But I just . . .'

'Not at all.' Josephine smiled. 'You've only told us about the drinking Emer knows about. What about the bottles you keep in your car, the drink you have in your office?'

Neil stared at her, with a what-do-you-want?-blood? expression.

His eyes were sunk in his head and he looked exhausted.

'Because your business partner is coming in on Friday and he'll tell us then,' she said nicely. 'And,' she added, 'your girlfriend is coming later this week.'

Shortly afterwards group ended. Josephine said to Neil 'Stay with the feelings', whatever that meant. Then she and one of the nurses took Emer away. The inmates and I were left in the Abbot's Quarter, looking uncomfortably at each other. Chaquie and Clarence disappeared, muttering something about laying the table.

Neil sat with his head resting on the arm of his chair. He looked up, straight at me, with a beseeching expression on his face. I threw him a glare of scorn and disgust and turned away.

'Are you all right, Neil?' I was astonished to hear Vincent ask him.

Fuck Neil, I thought in a rage. Fuck Neil the piss-head, the wife-beater, the liar. I thought back to how he had tried to manipulate me into thinking that his wife was mad and that Josephine was a brainwasher and that he was such a nice guy.

At Vincent's question, Neil proceeded to have a hairy fit. He thumped the arm of his chair and started to bawl. But it was tears of rage, not tears of shame. 'I can't believe what that bitch wife of mine just did! I just can't believe it!' he screamed, tears pouring down his contorted face. 'What the fuck did she have to say all those things for? Why? Oh, Jesus Christ, WHY?'

'Come on for a cup of tea,' Mike suggested gently.

'She's making it up, you know, the fucking bitch,' Neil insisted. 'And to see her sitting there,' he gestured wildly at the chair that Emer had just vacated, 'looking like butter wouldn't melt in her mouth, well, I'm telling you that that woman has made my life hell for the past fourteen years. But it's always me, Neil did this, Neil did that . . .'

He became more and more incoherent. I threw my eyes to heaven while Mike, Vincent and *Misty*, of all people, made soothing noises. Even John Joe hovered awkwardly, looking as if he'd like to say something nice, if only he knew the words.

'What's *happened* to my life?' Neil demanded. 'Why has it all gone so wrong? And how did she know about Mandy? Can you believe she's had the nerve to meet up with her? I bet they talked about me, the pair of bitches.'

'Come on to the dining-room,' Mike suggested again. I didn't know why everyone was being so nice to Neil.

'I can't,' Neil muttered. 'I can't face anyone.'

'Yes, you can,' urged Mike gently. 'You're among friends.'

'Sure, it's happened to us all,' said Vincent, in a strange, unaggressive way. 'And we hated it too.'

'Yeah.' Misty giggled in a sweet way at Neil. 'It's par for the fucking course in here.'

Not *my* fucking course, I thought grimly.

'And it was good for us, it worked. Look at how well and normal we are *now*.' Misty gestured at herself, Vincent and Mike. (She swept her arm almost as far as John Joe, then hesitated and let it drop.) All of them burst out laughing, even Neil, between his sniffles.

I was baffled.

'Seriously,' said Mike, 'you'll look back at this day and you'll be glad. That's what someone told me the day my wife made shit of me in here. That having to face the truth was the start of my recovery.'

'But it's not the truth,' Neil said. 'She's a lying bitch.'

I wanted to drive my fist into his face. But no one even rebuked him.

Mike, Vincent, Misty and John Joe helped Neil up and led him gently from the room.

22

I had promised myself that Monday would be the day I'd get organized and start exercising. Once I was making myself skinny and beautiful I'd feel more hopeful about winning Luke back.

I decided to ask Chris to show me the gym. There are some women, who, when heart-broken, have no interest whatsoever in other men. I wasn't one of them. On the contrary, I yearned for male approval as a form of restoration. Call me shallow, call me needy, call me whatever you like so long as you call me.

After lunch, for once, Chris wasn't deep in conversation with a brown jumper. He was reading, his foot up on his opposite knee, deliberately looking sexy just to scare me away.

He wore an impressive pair of boots – black, square-toed, lizard-skin chelsea boots that would have given him the freedom of trendy New York City. While I was thrilled to be in close contact with such a well-shod man, it had the double-edged effect of scaring me away. I was so in awe of his footwear that I feared I wasn't worthy to talk to him.

I was afraid the other inmates would deduce that I fancied Chris. Luckily their attention was elsewhere, as Neil loudly held court, a circle of sympathetic nodding dogs around him. But I still couldn't get off my arse and approach Chris.

Just get up, I urged myself, walk four paces across the room and speak to him.

Right you are, I replied with conviction. But I remained superglued to the chair.

I'll count to five, I bargained. And then I'll do it.

I counted to five.

Ten! I've changed my mind. I'll count to ten and then I'll talk to him.

Just as I felt my bum lift off the chair to begin my cross-room odyssey, I froze with fear. My make-up! I hadn't checked it since that morning. I scurried along to my room and brushed my hair and retouched my make-up in a fierce, mascara-blobbing, lipstick-swerving hurry.

If he's still there when I get back, I swear to God I'll speak to him, I promised myself.

When I got back down, he was exactly where he'd been, still unencumbered by middle-aged men. I had no excuse.

Just pretend he's hideous, I advised myself. Try to imagine him with no teeth and one eye.

So, shaking slightly, I found myself making my way across the floor to him.

'Er, Chris,' I said. The words surprised me by sounding normal. And not an adolescent boy's voice-breaking soprano.

'Rachel.' He put his book down and looked up at me, his the-sun's-too-bright, blue eyes burning. His beautiful mouth was turned up in a slight smile. 'How's it going? Sit down.'

I was so thrilled that he hadn't slammed his book down on the table and thundered 'What?!' that I beamed at him.

'Will you show me something?' I asked.

'Wehay.' He gave a little laugh. 'My luck is in.'

Flustered and flushed, I couldn't think of anything witty to say, so I just said 'Er, no . . . I mean, I didn't mean . . . will you show me the sauna?' I felt safest asking to see the sauna, because I knew for sure there really *was* one.

'Certainly,' he replied. 'Do you want to get your stuff?'

'Not yet, I just want to see it, for the moment.'

'Right,' he said, putting down his book. 'Off we go!'

'Mind them lovely boots, Chris,' Mike called in a camp voice. 'You don't want to get them muddy.'

'Peasants,' I clicked, with a heavenward roll of my eyes. But Chris just laughed.

'John Joe wanted to know where I got them,' he grinned. 'He thought they'd do for milking the cows.'

Out we went into the freezing weather. The trees were swaying in the high winds and my hair whipped round my face. As we skidded across a fifty-yard patch of muddy grass I wondered about faking a slip and, when Chris went to help me up, pulling him down on top of me and . . . Before I got my chance we arrived at a little out-house.

In I burst, Chris right behind me. Then he slammed the door behind us to keep out the wind and the rain.

We were in a tiny, little room that was lovely and warm. It had a washing-machine and a spin dryer in it, both of which were hopping around doing their thing. The noise was intense, as it echoed off the stone walls and floor. I looked expectantly at Chris, waiting for him to lead me on further.

'Ready when you are.' I smiled, but it was tinged with anxiety because there didn't seem to be any doors other than the one we had just come in.

'You shouldn't say things like that to a man in my condition.' He laughed.

I tried to smile, but found I couldn't. He put his cold hands on top of the vibrating washing-machine, then ran his hands through his fair hair.

'Phew,' he said. 'You can see why they call it the sauna.'

'This is the sauna?' I asked, my voice trembling.

'Yes.'

I looked around. But where were the Swedish pine walls, the Swedish pine benches, the big fluffy towels, the pores that were opening and detoxifying? There was just this little room with exposed breeze blocks, a concrete floor and a couple of red plastic laundry baskets.

'It doesn't look much like a sauna,' I managed.

'The sauna is only its nickname,' said Chris, looking carefully at me. 'Because it gets so hot in here when we're doing our washing and drying. See?'

'*Is* there an actual sauna?' I asked, holding my breath.

And there was a pause that seemed to go on for ever before the answer came. 'No.'

Everything inside me slumped. But it was dull despair I felt rather than outrage. I had known. At some level, I already knew. There was no sauna. Maybe there wasn't even a gym. Or massage.

At that thought, I became gripped with panic.

'Can we go back over to the dining-room?' I asked, in a quavery, high-pitched voice. 'Can I ask you some questions about our timetable?'

'Sure.'

I grabbed him by the sweatshirt and broke into a run as I dragged him through the gale. This time there were no fantasies about tripping. I reached the timetable on the wall in the main house almost before Chris left the outhouse.

'OK,' I gasped, as my stomach churned. 'See all these things here, group therapy and more group therapy and A A meetings and even more group therapy . . . well, is there anything else we do that isn't on this list?'

I was aware that the rest of the inmates were looking up from their Neil enclave with interest.

'Like what?'

I didn't want to say straight out, 'Is there a gym?' just in case there wasn't. So I said, more obliquely, 'Does anyone ever do any exercise?'

'Well, I do some press-ups now and again,' he said. 'But I couldn't speak for the rest of them.

'I wouldn't have thought so, though,' he added, sounding doubtful.

'Where?' I demanded breathlessly. 'Where do you do your press-ups?'

'In the bedroom, on the floor.'

I slumped down another notch, but I still had a little bit of hope. Maybe there wasn't a gym, but perhaps they had other treatments. I sensed compassion emanating from Chris, a desire to be nice even though he was puzzled by me, so I took a risk.

'Are there any . . .?' I forced myself to say it. Go on, go on! 'Sunbeds?'

First Chris looked as if he was going to laugh. Then his face changed to infinite pity and wisdom and he gently shook his head. 'No, Rachel, no sunbeds.'

'No massage?' I managed to whisper.

'No massage,' Chris agreed.

I didn't bother going into the long list that I had in

my head. If there was no massage, which was fairly rudimentary, I was sure there was no seaweed treatment, no mudwraps, no funny stuff with algae.

'No . . . no swimming pool?' I forced myself to ask.

His mouth twitched slightly at that, but he just said 'No swimming pool.'

'So what do you do?' I finally managed to ask.

'It's all on this list here,' said Chris, bringing my attention back to the notice board.

I had another look and it was still just lots of group therapy, with the occasional A A meeting thrown in for variety. As I stared at it I noticed that the dining-room was billed as The Dining Hall. Dining *Hall*, my arse! More like the dining *hut*, I thought.

No, how about, the dining *shack*.

No, wait, the dining *tenement*.

No, better still, the dining *condemned building*, I thought with mounting hysteria.

I caught Chris's eye.

I had one other question.

'Er, Chris, you know all the people that are here in this building?'

'Yes.'

'Well, is that *all* of you? There isn't another wing in some other part of the grounds?'

He looked mystified by that. 'No,' he said. 'Of course not.'

I see, I thought. No fucking pop stars, either. That does it. That really poxing-well does it.

'Come on Rachel, you've group now,' he said gently.

I ignored him and walked away.

'Where are you going?' he called after me.

'Home,' I answered.

*

It was the worst day of my life.

I decided to leave immediately. I would go to Dublin, do a shitload of drugs, get the first flight back to New York and be reunited with Luke.

I wouldn't stay in this shabby, run-down madhouse a moment longer. I wanted nothing further to do with the place or its inmates. I had just about been able to put up with them while they were part of a luxury package. But there was no luxury package.

I was embarrassed, humiliated, foolish, tainted by association and desperate to leave. Mad keen to put as much ground between me and those alcoholics and drug addicts as possible.

I recoiled from the Cloisters as if I'd been burnt, as though I'd been cooing and patting a cute baby, only to find, to my horror, that it was a rat.

I marched up to tell Dr Billings I was leaving. But when I got to the door that led into the office area, it was locked. Locked!

Fear came to life in my veins. I was imprisoned in this awful place. I'd be here for all eternity drinking tea.

I rattled at the doorhandle, the way they do in black-and-white B movies. Next I'd be jiggling the telephone connection up and down, shouting 'Operator, operator!'

'Can I help you, Rachel?' asked a voice.

It was the Sour Kraut.

'I want to see Dr Billings, but the door is LOCKED,' I said, wild-eyed.

'You are turning the handle the wrong vay,' she pointed out coldly.

'Oh, ah, right, thanks,' I said, stumbling gratefully into Reception.

I ignored Bubbly the receptionist as she frantically

tried to tell me I couldn't see Dr Billings without an appointment.

'Watch me,' I sneered, as I marched in on top of him.

23

'I'm afraid you can't leave,' said Dr Billings.

'Says who?' I asked with a curled lip.

'Says you, actually,' he said smoothly, waving a piece of paper at me. 'You signed a legal and binding contract that you would stay here for three weeks.'

'So sue me,' I swaggered. I hadn't lived in New York for nothing.

'I'll get an injunction issued against you,' he riposted, 'which will force you by law to stay here until your three weeks are up. *And* I'll sue you for every penny you haven't got.'

He picked up another piece of paper and waved that at me. 'Your bank statement, you've let your financial affairs get into a bit of a mess, haven't you?'

'How did you get that?' I gasped.

'You authorized me to,' he said. 'On the same piece of paper in which you said you'd stay for three weeks. Now, have I made myself clear? I'm quite happy to get an injunction to stop you from leaving.'

'You can't do that.' I was full of impotent rage.

'I can and I will, I would be failing in my duty if I didn't.'

'I'll run away, I'll escape,' I said wildly. 'There's nothing to stop me from just walking out the gate now.'

'There's plenty to stop you, I think you'll find. Not least the high walls and locked gate.'

'Look, you power-mad bast ... pig,' I pleaded, alternating between rage and despair, 'there's nothing wrong with me! I only came here for the saunas and the massage, I shouldn't be here *at all*.'

'That's what they all say.'

What a liar he was! He had a nerve expecting me to believe that even one of the inmates wouldn't admit to being an alcoholic. It was as plain as the red bulbous noses on their broken-veined faces. But something was telling me that if I didn't calm down and speak rationally to him, I would get nowhere.

'Please listen,' I said, in a much less hysterical tone of voice. 'There's no need for us to fall out over this. But I only agreed to come here because I thought it was like a health farm.'

He nodded. Encouraged, I continued.

'And it's not like a health farm, at all. When I signed that contract saying I'd stay for three weeks, I signed under false pretences, do you see? I should have told you that I wasn't a drug addict, I can see that now.' I pleaded at him. 'And it was wrong of me to come just for the gym and stuff, but we all make mistakes.'

There was silence and I stared hopefully at him.

He finally spoke. 'Rachel,' he said, 'contrary to what you think, it is my opinion and the opinion of other people that you, in fact, *are* an addict.'

The Birmingham Six flashed into my head. *The Trial* by Kafka. My life was taking on the appearance of a nightmare. I was being convicted without due process of law for a crime that I didn't commit.

'What other people?' I asked.

Dr Billings waved yet another piece of paper. 'This was faxed from New York half an hour ago. It's from a ...'

he paused and looked at the page '. . . a Mr Luke Costello, I believe you know him?'

My first thought was delight. Luke had faxed me! He was in contact, that must mean that he still loved me, that he'd changed his mind.

'Can I see it?' I held out my hand, my eyes shining.

'Not yet.'

'But it's for me. Give me my letter.'

'It's not for you,' said Dr Billings. 'It's for Josephine, your counsellor.'

'What are you fucking talking about?' I spluttered. 'Why would Luke be writing to Josephine?'

'It's Mr Costello's replies to a questionnaire we faxed to him on Friday.'

'What kind of questionnaire?' My heart was pounding.

'A questionnaire about you and your drug usage.'

'*My* drug usage!' I was hot and shaky. 'What about *his* fucking drug usage? Did you ask him about that? Well did you?'

'Please sit down, Rachel,' said Billings, in a monotone.

'He takes loads of drugs!' I shrieked, even though he didn't.

'The thing is, Rachel – no, please sit down – the thing is, Rachel, is that Mr Costello isn't the one in a treatment centre for drug addiction.'

He paused. 'And *you* are.'

'But I shouldn't fucking B E H E R E !' I was in despair. 'It was a F U C K I N G M I S T A K E.'

'It most certainly wasn't a mistake,' said Billings. 'Haven't you given any thought to the fact that you nearly died when you took that overdose?'

'I didn't nearly die,' I scoffed.

'You did.'

Did I?

'It. Is. Not. Normal. Behaviour,' he spelt out. 'To find yourself in hospital having your stomach pumped because you took a life-threatening amount of drugs.'

'It was an accident,' I shot back at him, barely able to believe how dense he was.

'What does it say about your life?' he asked. 'What does it say about your self-respect? When you find yourself in that position? Because you did it, Rachel, remember. You put those pills in your mouth, no one forced you.'

I sighed. It was pointless trying to argue with him.

'And these replies from Mr Costello confirm what we already knew. That you have a chronic drug problem.'

'Oh please.' I tossed my head. 'Lighten up, for God's sake.'

'According to this you often took cocaine before you went to work in the morning, is that right?'

I felt myself shrink, and mad anger rushed through me at Luke. The fucking bastard! How could he betray me like this? How could he hurt me so? He used to love me, why had it all gone so wrong? My nose began to quiver with the onset of tears.

'I'm not going to answer that question,' I managed. 'You know nothing about my life, about how hard my job was.'

'Rachel,' he said gently. 'No one *has* to take drugs, no one's job is that bad.'

I should have been thumping the table and standing up for myself, but I wasn't able. I was too devastated by Luke's betrayal. Later the anger would return, and I would vow over and over again to get him back. I'd put his limited edition Led Zeppelin *Houses of the Holy* into the microwave where it would warp into Daliesque uselessness, I promised. I'd tear up the napkin that Dave Gilmour from Pink Floyd once signed for him. I'd throw his biker boots into the Hudson. While he was still wearing them.

But for the time being, I was a limp rag.

In a good cop/bad cop move, Billings sent for Celine, the nurse. And she took me into the nurses' room and made me a cup of sweet tea, which I didn't dash back into her face and which, to my surprise, I drank and felt comforted by.

24

'You see, Luke isn't a very nice person,' I was saying. 'He was always shallow and disloyal. Quite *evil*, actually.'

It was later in the day of the joint Questionnaire/No Gym disaster, and I was in the dining-room surrounded by inmates who hung on my every word. I was bitterly glad to have a platform to trash Luke on. And trash him I did.

I didn't so much *imply* that Luke was a thief, as just plain say it. What did it matter? None of these people would ever meet him anyway. Of course, Luke hadn't really stolen the money from his six-year-old niece's money box. The money she'd been saving up to buy a puppy. In fact, Luke didn't even have any nieces. Or nephews. But who cared?

I went too far, though, when I said he'd stolen a blind man's fiddle. The lads looked at me suspiciously and gave each other sidelong glances. 'He stole a blind man's fiddle?' Mike asked. 'Are you sure? Didn't that Irish saint fella do that? What was that his name was . . .?'

'Matt Talbot,' someone supplied.

'That's right,' said Mike. 'Matt Talbot. He stole a blind man's fiddle to get money for drink when he was still on the piss.'

'Er, that's right,' I backtracked hastily. 'I meant to say Luke stole *from* The Blind Man's Fiddle, a bar on West 60th Street where he worked.'

'Aaaahhh,' they breathed. '*From* The Blind Man's Fiddle.'

A close run thing. They turned to each other and nodded reassuringly, '*From* the Blind Man's Fiddle. *From.*'

I had spent the afternoon with Celine, in the cosy nurses' room. Despite the cosiness of the room, the benign, motherly presence of Celine and the staggering array of chocolate biscuits, I was almost hysterical with agitation. Suffering the agonies of the damned as I wondered what *else* Luke had put on the questionnaire. He knew far too much about me.

'Have you seen it?' I asked Celine, as my heart banged in my chest.

'No.' She smiled.

I didn't know whether or not to believe her.

'If you have seen it, please, *please* tell me what he's written,' I implored. 'It's important, this is my *life* we're talking about.'

'I haven't seen it,' she said mildly.

She doesn't understand, I thought in mute frustration. She has no idea how important this is.

'What do people normally put in them?' I asked tremulously. 'Is it usually terrible stuff?'

'Sometimes,' she said. 'If the client has done terrible things.'

Despair and nausea filled me.

'Cheer up,' she said. 'It can't be that bad, have you murdered anyone?'

'No,' I snorted.

'Well then.' She smiled.

'When will I be allowed to see it?' I asked.

'That's a decision for Josephine. If she thinks it's pertinent to your recovery she may read it out in group and . . .'

'Read it out in GROUP?' I shrieked. 'In front of the others?'

'It wouldn't be much of a group if it was only you, now, would it?' Celine said with another of her warm, yet completely impartial, smiles.

Panic bubbled up and fizzed over.

No bloody way would I be sticking around to be subjected to such treatment!

But I remembered that Dr Billings had said the gates were locked. It was true. The day I'd arrived Dad had had to introduce himself over an intercom before they opened them. And the walls were high. Far too high for a clumsy lump like me to climb.

How, in the name of Jesus, did I end up in this situation? I wondered. This must be just how Brian Keenan and John McCarthy felt when they found themselves chained to a radiator in a concrete basement in an unfashionable part of Beirut.

'It's not that bad,' Celine said, as if she really believed it. She gave a comforting smile that did nothing to comfort me.

'What do you mean?' I almost shouted. 'This is the worst thing that has ever happened to me!'

'Aren't you lucky then that you've had such a worry-free life?' Celine said.

I couldn't get it through to her how truly catastrophic this was.

My skin goosepimpled every time I thought of the questionnaire being read aloud to the other people in group. I would have given anything to know what Luke had written.

Or would I?

Did I really want to hear Luke condemning me?

I couldn't win. It was agonizing not knowing, but it would be excruciating if I did. I knew I'd read it with my face almost turned away, wincing with each cruel word.

I would have killed for a mood alterer. *Anything*. It didn't have to be Valium. A bottle of brandy would have done.

In mad agitation, I made to get up and go to confront Dr Billings and *insist* that he read it to me.

'Sit down,' Celine ordered, suddenly very firm.

'Wha . . . at?'

'Sit down, this time you won't be able to bully your way into getting what you want,' she said.

I was dazed by the implication that I'd been a bully on other occasions.

'You're too used to instant gratification,' she went on. 'It'll do you good to wait.'

'So you *have* seen this questionnaire?'

'No, I haven't.'

'Well, why are you talking about me and instant gratification?'

'Everyone who comes in here has spent most of their adult life seeking instant gratification,' she said, reverting to her mild, motherly manner again. 'It's a fundamental part of the addict's personality. You're no different. Although I know you'd like to think you are.'

Fucking, smug bitch, I thought, with a flash of hatred. I'll make her sorry. Before I leave here, I'll have her on her knees apologizing for being so mean to me.

'But by the time you leave you'll be agreeing,' she smiled.

I stared sullenly at my lap.

'Have another cup of tea,' she offered. 'And some biscuits.'

In silence I accepted them. I wanted to show her how disgusted I was by not eating a thing, but a chocolate biscuit is a chocolate biscuit.

'How are you now?' Celine asked after a while.

'I'm cold,' I said.

'It's the shock,' said Celine.

I was pleased with that. It meant it was OK to feel as dreadful as I did.

'I'm sleepy,' I said a while later.

'It's the shock,' Celine repeated.

Again, I nodded with satisfaction. Correct answer.

'It's your body trying to cope with something unpleasant,' she continued. 'Normally you'd use a drug to get you through the pain.'

Sorry, I thought, I'll have to deduct points for that.

But I didn't react because I reckoned it was her job to say it. For a few minutes, I ate my HobNobs and drank my tea and I thought I'd reached a plateau of calm. But as I finished the last biscuit the churning anguish returned as bad as ever. I was baffled by Luke's cruelty. It stung like a slap on sunburnt skin. First he ditched me, then he got me into tons of trouble. Why?

And that wasn't all I had to contend with, I realized, shifting my focus to the first shock I'd had. That the Cloisters wasn't the celebrity-packed, luxury hotel I'd expected. In the great horror of the Luke questionnaire drama, I'd briefly forgotten about it.

I was in a dirty, shabby dump of a treatment centre full of ugly, fat, rough alcoholics and drug addicts. There was no longer any celebrity sheen, no gymnasium gloss to distract from what the Cloisters really was.

Then my rage at Luke came back. I was angrier than ever.

'Luke Costello is a lying bastard,' I spat in tearful fury.

Celine laughed.

But in a kindly way.

Just to confuse me

'What's so funny?' I demanded.

'Rachel, it's my experience that what people say on those forms is true,' Celine supplied. 'I've worked here for seventeen years and not once has someone lied in them.'

'There's always a first time,' I quipped.

'Have you thought about what an ordeal it must have been for Luke to write what he did?'

'Why would it be an ordeal?' I said in surprise.

'Because if he knows enough about you to be able to comment on your addiction, he knows you well enough to care about you. He must have known his revelations would hurt you. No one is comfortable doing that to someone they love.'

'You don't know him.' I was beginning to gather steam. 'He's a nasty piece of work. It's not just the question-naire. He's always been a liar.'

Has he? a part of me wondered in surprise.

Who cares? another bit of my brain replied. He is now, OK?

'You didn't make a very wise choice of boyfriend,' Celine said, with another of those plump, housewifey, bread-bakery smiles.

That threw me. For a moment I didn't know what to say. Then I rallied. When in doubt, flatter.

'I know I didn't,' I said earnestly. 'You're absolutely right, Celine, I can see that now.'

'Or maybe he's not a bad person, at all,' she said mildly. 'Maybe you just want to believe he is, so that you can discount any information he gives about your addiction.'

Why did she think she knew so much about it? I wondered. She was only a bloody nurse. All she was good for was sticking thermometers up people's bums!

25

My consumption of Celine's last Club Milk coincided with the others being let out of group. Time to return to my own planet.

When I got to the dining-room, sleepy from shock and sugar, I felt as though I'd been away a long time.

Neil the wanker was still the centre of attention. Surrounded by a circle of people, nodding sympathetically and making murmury, agreeing noises. I concluded that they were all wife-beating, lying drunks as well. Even the women. I could hear him complaining 'I feel so betrayed, I can't believe what she's done to me, and she's bonkers, you know, *she* should be in a mental home, not me . . .'

I took a quick pause from hating Luke so that I could hate Neil instead. Anyway, his seconds as the most interesting thing in the dining-room were numbered. I had a disaster, a *real* disaster, which would blow his one right out of the water. His disaster wasn't worthy to touch the hem of the garment of my disaster!

Trying to exude beauty and tragedy, I stood in the doorway.

Right on cue, Chris looked up.

'I thought you were going home,' he said, with a wink and elbow smile.

My wistful-heroine look wobbled uncertainly. He'd been nice to me earlier, why wasn't he being nice to me now?

'Cheer up,' he twinkled. 'I'm sure some of the lads would be delighted to give you a massage, one of those mutual full body ones. They can ask Sadie for some chip oil.'

'They can ask, but they won't get,' called Sadie, who happened to be bustling lumpily past.

I winced with embarrassment, as I wondered if everyone was laughing at me for thinking the Cloisters was a health farm.

'It's not that,' I said, hurt. 'Something else has happened.'

I was almost glad that Luke had stitched me up so viciously. It would knock the unwelcome flippancy out of Chris good and proper. How dare he? Chip oil indeed! This was *serious*.

'A questionnaire has arrived?' He quirked an eyebrow at me.

Instantly on the defensive, I jerked my head up at him. 'How do you know?'

'One usually comes when you've been here a couple of days,' Chris said, his face serious. To my relief he seemed to have stopped laughing at me. 'And the shit hits the fan. At least the first instalment does. Who's it from?'

'My boyfriend.' My eyes filled with tears. 'My ex-boyfriend, I mean.

'You wouldn't believe what he said,' I said, pleased by the fat tears rolling down my face. I was counting on them to elicit sympathy and lots of comforting, physical contact from Chris.

Sure enough, he gently led me to a chair and pulled another up close, kindness on his face, our knees almost touching.

Bingo!

'I probably *would* believe what he said, you know,' Chris said. He stroked his hand along my forearm with an intimacy that embarrassed, yet pleased me. 'I've been here two weeks, and I've heard a lot of questionnaires. I'm sure you're no worse than any of the rest of us.'

I was slightly mesmerized by his closeness to me, the heat of his big man's hand along my sleeve, but I came out of my trance to protest tearfully. 'You don't understand, I'm only here because I thought this kip was a health farm. There's nothing the matter with me at all!'

I half-expected him to disagree, but he just made general, soothing-type noises, the sort a vet might make to a cow in labour.

I was relieved.

And impressed. So many men go to flustery pieces at a woman's tears. Which, of course is *no bad thing*, either. It can be very handy sometimes. But Chris was totally in control.

If he's this in charge just when I'm crying, what must he be like in bed, I found myself wondering.

'So what exactly did your boyfriend say?' Chris asked, hauling my imagination back from where it had been traipsing around in the place where people don't wear any clothes.

'Ex-boyfriend,' I said hastily. Lest there be any confusion.

As I turned my attention to what Luke had said on the form, I suddenly remembered how sweet he once used to be to me. A wave of excruciating nostalgia washed over me and a fresh batch of tears arrived.

'I've only been told about one of the things Luke said,' I sobbed. 'And that was a LIE!'

It wasn't a lie, as such, not *technically* a lie. But it gave a misleading picture of me, made me sound as if I wasn't a nice person. So in a way, it was a lie. And best kept from Chris.

'That's terrible,' Chris murmured. 'Your boyfriend lying about you like that.'

Something in his tone made me suspect he was making fun of me again. But when I shot him a sharp glare, his face was empty and smooth. Back to the crying.

'Luke Costello is a complete bastard,' I wept. 'I must have been out of my mind ever to have gone out with him.'

I turned to put my head down on the table. The move jostled my lycraed thighs against Chris's denim ones.

Oh, it's an ill wind . . .

Chris rubbed my back for a while as I lay bent over the table. I stayed there longer than was strictly necessary because his hand on my bra-fastener felt so nice. When I finally sat up again we had another tantalizing thigh jostle. How fortunate I was wearing such a short skirt.

From the far end of the table, heads looked at us with interest. If Neil didn't watch himself he was in danger of losing his captive audience. I clenched my teeth and sent powerful thought rays out to all the brown jumpers. *Go away. If any of you come near me now, I'll kill you.*

But strangely enough, apart from when Fergus, the acid casualty, passed me down a box of tissues, the others did leave us alone.

Chris made more soothing noises. His attention was calamine lotion on the stings of Luke's rejection, the antidote to Luke's poison.

'I don't understand why he had to lie to Dr Billings about me,' I told Chris mournfully. The more of a victim

I acted, the better. I'd bind Chris to me with ropes of sympathy.

I was vaguely aware that I'd lost sight of my true pain. Yes, I was devastated at what Luke had said. Not because he was lying about me – because it was *true*. But I couldn't tell Chris that. Honesty was a luxury that I couldn't afford.

Instead I tailored my pain in the hope of making Chris like me. Brave heroine remains dignified, although baffled by cruel boyfriend's lies, that kind of thing.

'What exactly did Luke say?' Chris asked.

'I'm so unlucky,' I said, sidestepping his question. A new crop of tears arrived. 'Nothing but bad things ever seem to happen to me. Do you know what I mean?'

Chris nodded, and his face was grim, in a way that made me nervous. Had I annoyed him?

At the moment I became convinced he knew I'd made it up about Luke lying, Chris suddenly pulled his chair closer to me. I jumped from both the abrupt movement and my own guilty fear. He'd moved so close his right thigh was wedged between both of mine. Practically up under my skirt, I noted with alarm. What was he doing?

I followed his movements with fear as he brought his hand to my face and lay his fingers along my jawbone. *Was he going to hit me?* For a second that stretched on for hours my face rested in the cradle of his hand. *Or was he going to kiss me?* When he moved his face nearer and it seemed that he was, I went into a mad panic about how we could do it without the tableful of brown jumpers seeing us. But he neither hit nor kissed me. Instead he moved his thumb along my cheek and rubbed away one of my tears. It was done efficiently but with strange tenderness.

'Poor Rachel,' he said, doing the other tear with his

other thumb. There was no mistaking the compassion in his voice. Passion, even? Maybe . . .

'Poor Rachel,' he said again. But even as he did so, Misty O'Malley brushed past us and, to my great surprise, I heard her laugh. She wasn't supposed to laugh. Everyone was supposed to feel sorry for me.

Poor me! Chris had said so.

She eyed me, an expression of excoriating scorn on her green-eyed little face. As I filled with rage and hard-done-by-ness, I looked at Chris, ready to take my cue from him. When he compressed his beautiful mouth, I eagerly waited for him to say 'Shut up, Misty, you little bitch.' But he didn't, he said nothing at all. And neither, reluctantly, did I.

Misty swaggered away and, without meeting my eyes, Chris slowly and thoughtfully said 'I've a suggestion to make.'

One involving me, him, no clothes and a condom? I wondered hopefully.

'You mightn't like it,' he warned.

He didn't want to wear a condom? OK, we could sort something else out.

'I know you feel lousy now,' he said carefully. 'You're hurt. But maybe you owe it to yourself to have a think about what this Luke said, because you might find that it isn't actually a lie at all . . .'

I stared at him open-mouthed, while inside me a voice whimpered *I thought you were my friend*. He stared back, deepest sympathy in his eyes.

What was going on?

Just then Misty O'Malley marched back into the room and said 'I need a big, strong man.' As the stampede of middle-aged porkers began, like feeding-time in the pigsty, she held up her hand and said 'But, in the absence of that, you'll have to do.' She reached out, gave me a special all-of-my-own smirk that no one else could see, and grabbed Chris by his hand.

He went! He stood up, brushed past my knees, sending a brief tingle through me, said 'I'll catch up with you later,' then left.

I almost burst into tears again. I hated Misty O'Malley for her ability to make me feel like the village idiot. I hated Chris for choosing Misty over me. Worse again, I was mortified beyond belief that Chris had known I was lying about Luke. And what I *really* didn't understand was why he was so nice about it.

But when the other inmates came to talk to me I realized I might as well be honest about what Luke had written. It wasn't as if it was even that bad, I reminded myself.

First to arrive at my side was Mike who, like Chris, knew before I told him that a questionnaire had arrived.

'S'obvious.' He grinned, puffing out his barrel chest. 'When you've been here three weeks you'll know the signs. Anyway, what did me-laddo have to say for himself?'

'He said that I sometimes took cocaine in the mornings before going to work.' As I said it out loud for the first time, the impact of Luke's treachery hit me with renewed force. Bitter rage at his betrayal of me welled up.

'And did you?' Mike asked.

The word 'No' hovered on my mouth, but I forced myself to swallow it.

'Now and then,' I said impatiently, annoyed at having to explain such things to this unsophisticated farmer.

'It's no big deal,' I said hotly. 'Lots of people do it in New York, it's different from here, you see. Highly pressured. It's no different from having a cup of coffee in the mornings. You wouldn't understand.'

Bit by bit, Neil lost the ratings war as the inmates flocked to my side. I took advantage of each new arrival to voice my grievances afresh.

I wanted soothing hands laid on my fevered feelings. And, because Luke had made me feel so worthless, I wanted to even up the balance by reducing him to nothingness.

The inmates didn't have Celine's objections to tearing Luke apart. And they joined in with stories of their own, 'Great questionnaires I have known'. We gorged ourselves on terrible tales of bastard friends and relations who had stabbed us in the back in many a Cloisters' questionnaire. I almost enjoyed myself. I didn't mind making common cause with the others because I needed *someone* to talk to, even if we were as similar as people from different planets. Sitting in the thick of a tableful of people who had nothing but sympathy and bars of chocolate for me was nice.

Several people offered to beat Luke up. Which touched me deeply. Especially as one of them was Chaquie.

They were more than happy to believe every terrible thing I told them about Luke. Except, of course, for the bit about the blind man's fiddle. But I smoothed over it and soon we were back to dishing Luke's dirt.

'Luke Costello couldn't tell the truth about anything!' I declared. 'You know, he'd lie if you asked him his favourite *colour*.'

The more I blackened his name, the better I felt. By the end I really did believe he was as awful as I professed.

Chris didn't reappear. I kept watching the door wondering where he was gone with Misty. And what they were doing.

Fuckers.

But I didn't have a chance to become morose because Mike and the gang were very interested in the high-pressured life I lived in New York.

'And would you be very busy at work?' Eddie asked. They all moved closer to me, their eyes bright with interest.

'You wouldn't believe it,' I told them. 'Eighteen-hour days wouldn't be unusual. And you could lose your job like THAT.' I snapped my fingers to demonstrate how easy it was. 'And there's no dole in New York.'

They oooohhhed with shock.

'You could end up on the streets in a matter of days,' I said darkly. 'And it's much colder in New York than it is here.'

'Colder than Leitrim?' asked Clarence.

'Much colder.'

'Colder than Cork?' asked Don.

'Much colder.'

'Colder than Cav . . .?' began John Joe.

'Colder than anywhere in Ireland,' I interrupted, slightly irritated.

'God, it sounds like an awful place, altogether,' said Mike. 'Why did you ever go there?'

I gave him a sad-girl smile and said 'Why indeed?'

'And this cocaine stuff is just like coffee?' asked Peter.

'No different. In fact I think they're from the same plant.'

'And how long were you going with this Luke character?' someone else asked.

'About six months.'

'And he owes you money?'

'Loads.'

'That's shocking.'

'And he's made me feel so humiliated,' I sniffed, with a twinge of genuine grief.

'No one can make us feel anything,' interrupted Clarence. 'Our feelings are our own responsibility.'

A silence fell and all the others swivelled round and stared at him in shock.

'WHAT?' Eddie demanded, his red face so scrunched up in annoyance and disbelief, he looked constipated.

'Our feelings are ou . . .' Clarence repeated, parrot-fashion.

'You fucking *eejit*,' roared Vincent. 'You're talking shite. Are you trying to get a job here?'

'I'm only saying!' protested Clarence. 'That's what they said to me when my brothers humbled me. No one can make us feel any way unless we let them.'

'We're trying to cheer up RACHEL,' Don hooted. 'The child is UPSET!'

'I'm trying to cheer her up too,' Clarence insisted. 'If she can detach from this Luke fella . . .'

'AH, SHUT UP,' chorused several voices.

'When you've been here five weeks, you'll know what I mean,' Clarence said loftily.

26

When I went to bed that night I was confused.

Luke's not that bad, a little voice pointed out. *You lied about him to get everyone on your side.*

He is that bad, another voice insisted. *Just look at what he's done to you. He's humiliated you, he's got you into loads of trouble, he's turned against you. He rejected you before you left New York and he reiterated it with that bloody questionnaire thing. So, yes, he is that bad. Maybe not in the exact way that you told everyone downstairs tonight. But he is that bad.* Satisfied, I turned over to go to sleep.

But I couldn't stop thinking about him.

I supposed, looking back, he'd always been madly uptight about me taking drugs.

I had never forgotten the way he had behaved at my party. The cheek of him considering he hadn't even been invited!

Brigit and I had held the party about two weeks after the Rickshaw Rooms débâcle.

Throwing a party had actually been my idea. I was so fed up with not being invited to the cool East Village and SoHo parties that I decided to throw a party myself and invite every good-looking, well-connected, groovily employed person I could pretend to know. That way, when they had a party, they'd *have* to invite me.

Brigit and I selected carefully and strategically.

'What about Nadia . . .?'

'No-bum Nadia? What about her?'

'She works at Donna Karan. Does the word *discount* mean anything to you?'

'Can't we just invite fat, ugly girls . . .?'

'No. There aren't any. Now, what about Fineas?'

'But he's only a barman.'

'Yes, but think long-term here. If he's our pal he'll give us a drink when we're broke. Which, correct me if I'm wrong, is all the time.'

'OK, Fineas is in. Carvela?'

'No way! Andrew the ad-man was mine until she came on the scene with her pierced tongue.'

'But she knows Madonna.'

'Giving a person a french manicure once doesn't amount to knowing them. She's not coming, OK? We need straight men, we're very short of those.'

'Whenever weren't we?'

'Helenka and Jessica?'

'Of course. If they'll come. Snotty bitches.'

We didn't invite the Real Men. It didn't even occur to us.

On the night of the party, we sellotaped three balloons to our front door, covered our living-room lamp with red crêpe paper and opened six bags of crisps. Although we already had three compact discs, we borrowed two more in honour of the occasion. Then we sat back and waited for the glittering event to unfold.

I had thought all a good party needed was truckloads of drink and drugs. Although we hadn't actually bought any drugs for our guests, we had ensured plenty would be available by franchising out the provision to Wayne, our friendly neighbourhood dealer. And we had a heroic amount of drink packed into the kitchenette. But still our apartment didn't look anything like a party.

I was baffled. As I sat in my empty, echoey living-room that Saturday night, I wondered what I'd done wrong.

'It'll be great when it's full of people,' Brigit promised me, then bit her knuckle and gave a muffled, anguished wail.

'We're ruined, aren't we, Bridge?' I asked, as the extent of my folly revealed itself to me. How had I ever thought I was worthy to hold a party and invite people who worked at Calvin Klein? 'We'll never eat lunch in this town again.'

The invitations had told everyone to come at about ten o'clock. But at midnight the flat was still like a graveyard. Brigit and I were suicidal.

'Everyone hates us,' I said, swigging wine straight from the bottle.

'Whose stupid fucking idea was this?' Brigit demanded tearfully. 'I would have thought at least Gina and them would have come, they *swore* they would. People are so *false* in New York.'

We sat for a while longer, trashing everyone we knew, even those we hadn't invited. We drank heavily.

In the absence of anyone else, Brigit and I turned on each other.

'Did you invite Dara?' she demanded.

'No,' I said defensively. 'I thought you were going to. Did you invite Candide?'

'No,' she snarled. 'I thought you were going to.

'And where's that fucking Cuban Heel?' she added viciously.

At the time Brigit, with her great fondness for the Hispanic lads, was having on-off-on-again dealings with a Cuban. When he was nice to her she called him Our Man in Havana. When he was horrible, which was most of the time, she called him The Cuban Heel. His name was Carlos and I called him The Gyrater. He thought he was an amazing dancer and performed with the least provocation. It was enough to make you lose your lunch, the way he carried on, doing all manner of exaggerated swerve action with his tiny hips. On the days that I didn't call him The Gyrater, I called him The Stomach-Turner, still in keeping with the rotation theme.

'And where's Wayne?' I demanded. 'There'll be no point in anyone else getting here if he doesn't.'

It was Wayne's absence that was making me more jumpy than anything else.

'Turn on some music.'

'No, because we won't be able to hear the door.'

'Put on some music! We don't want people to think they're at a wake.'

'A wake might be more fun! Remind me again whose idea this was.'

The bell rang shrilly, interrupting our bitter sniping.

Thank God, I thought passionately. But it was only the Cuban Heel and a few of his equally tiny friends. They looked doubtfully at the balloons, the crisps and the empty, silent, rosy-lit room.

While Carlos put on some music and Brigit gave out shite to him, Carlos's little friends undressed me with their limpid brown eyes.

I couldn't see the appeal, I really couldn't.

Brigit said that Carlos was amazing in the scratcher and that he had a ginormous willy. She would have loved it if I had got off with one of his friends but I would rather have rented out my vagina to a swallow to build a nest in it.

Music burst out, incongruously loud in the empty room, drowning out Carlos's, 'Sorry *enamorada*'s, and 'It wasn't my fault, *querida*'s.

'Here,' I thrust a cereal bowl at Miguel, 'have a crisp and stop looking at me like that.'

The music Carlos had put on was that South American, terminally up-beat, twenty-man trumpet band type. It was violently cheerful, conjuring up sun and sand and Rio and girls from Ipanema and brown boys with shining eyes. Men with frilly-sleeved shirts, big straw hats and bootlace ties, shaking maracas. The kind of music that's described as 'infectious'. It certainly made *me* feel sick. I hated it.

The bell rang again and this time it really was a guest.

The doorbell rang again and another ten people trooped in, bottles under their arms.

I got cornered by Miguel. To my surprise I couldn't duck past him. What he lacked in size he made up for in nimbleness. His eyes were about level with my nipples and there they remained for most of our conversation.

'Rachel,' he sang to me, with a flashing, olive-skinned smile, 'there are two stars missing from the sky, they are in your eyes.'

'Miguel . . .' I began.

'Tomas,' he beamed.

'. . . OK, Tomas, whatever,' I said. 'There are two teeth missing from your mouth, they are in my fist. At least they will be if you don't leave me alone.'

'Rachel, Rachel.' Doleful eyes. 'Don't you want a little Latin in you?'

'If the little Latin in question is you, then no, I don't.'

'But why not? Your friend Breeegeeet likes Carlos.'

'Brigit isn't well in the head. And apart from anything else, you're too small, I'd flatten you.'

'Oh no,' he breathed. 'We Cubans are skilled in the love-making arts, you and I will explore many things and there is no danger that you will flat . . .'

'Please.' I held up a hand. 'Stop.'

'But you're a Goddess, in my country you would be worshipped.'

'And you're a gouger, in my country you'd work in a chipper.'

He got a bit haughty at that, but unfortunately I still hadn't annoyed him enough to make him go away.

Then I had a bright idea. 'One minute, you're Cuban, right? Have you any coke on you?'

That, luckily, was the wrong thing to say. It turned out that Tomas's uncle Paco had recently come a ferocious cropper when the US Coastguard had discovered him in charge of a yacht crammed full of marching powder. Paco was currently languishing in a Miami prison and Tomas was outraged by my routine enquiry.

'I didn't *say* you were a criminal,' I protested. 'I just thought I'd *ask*, seeing as Wayne hasn't got here yet.'

Tomas went on a bit more about family honour and similar shite before he gave me another melting gaze and said 'Let us not quarrel.'

'No, it's fine,' I reassured him. 'I don't mind if we do.'

He reached up and took my hand. 'Rachel,' he stared meaningfully into my eyes, 'dance with me.'

'Tomas,' I said, 'don't make me hurt you.'

Then, mercifully, Wayne arrived.

I nearly got trampled in the stampede for him but I exercised my right as hostess to get first go of him. I loved having cocaine at a party. It was so much better than anything else for enhancing my confidence and giving me the courage to talk to men. I loved the feeling of invincibility it fired me with.

Because, in a way, at some deep level, I knew I was attractive. But it was only after I'd done a line or two that

that knowledge came to the surface. Drink would suffice. But cocaine was so much nicer.

And it wasn't just me, but everyone *else* was so much nicer when I was coked-up. Better-looking, funnier, more interesting, sexier.

Brigit and I bought a gram between us. The pleasure from the hit began long before I actually snorted anything. Just effecting the transaction with Wayne was enough to get my adrenalin rushing. The dollars that I paid him were crisper and greener than usual. I parted with them joyously. I loved the feel of the little packet in the palm of my hand. I bounced it up and down, feeling the magic, dense weight of it.

The least fun bit about doing coke was the queueing to get into the ladies' in the bar or club or wherever to take it. So the great thing about having a party in my flat was that there was no wait involved. Straight to my bedroom with Brigit to clear a little space on my dressing table.

Brigit wanted to discuss the Cuban Crisis.

'I can't bear it,' she said. 'He treats me like shite.'

'Why don't you break it off with him?' I suggested. 'He's got no respect.'

Also I felt it reflected badly on me to have a flatmate who had dealings with someone as uncool as Carlos.

'I'm his slave,' Brigit sighed. 'I can't resist him. And do you know something, I don't even *like* him.'

'Neither do I,' I said.

A mistake. Never agree with your friends when they're going through a bad patch with their fella. Because the minute they've made it up, she turns nasty on you and says 'What's all this about you not liking Padraig/Elliot/Miguel?' Then she tells *him* and they both hate you and rewrite history, saying that you tried to split them up.

And they give you the silent treatment whenever you're in the same room. They don't offer you a slice of their pizza anymore, even though they've loads, far too much for just two and you're starving and haven't had any dinner. And they make you feel paranoid and you worry that they're going to move in together and not tell you until the last minute and you'll end up having to pay both lots of rent until you find someone new.

'Ah, sure, he's grand,' I said hastily. Then forgot all about it because we'd chopped out two gorgeous, plump, white lines.

I went first, and while Brigit was doing hers, I felt the tingling start in my face and melt the numbness that came from the initial hit. I turned to my mirror and smiled at myself. God, I was looking well tonight. Radiant. Look at how clear my skin was. See how shiny my hair was. Look at how warm my smile was. How impish, how *sexy*. And my two little eye teeth that stuck out and that I usually hated, I suddenly realized how much they *suited* me. They actually added to my charm. I smiled lazily at Brigit.

'You look beautiful,' I said.

'So do you,' she said.

Then we said in unison, 'Not bad for a pair of heifers.'

And off we went and moved amongst our guests.

27

In no time at all the place was packed. There was a queue a mile long for the bathroom, of people who had shopped at the WayneMarket and who were still too inhibited to snort coke in public. Such decorum never lasted longer than the first line.

The music had gone to hell entirely during my brief absence. I tried to change it, but Carlos had hidden all the other discs. Brigit was no help as I frantically raced around trying to find where he'd put them. She was too busy trying to keep up with Carlos's gyrating hips. I feared for our few ornaments. After an unusually violent swerve, I began to worry about our light fittings.

Then all four of the Cubans were dancing, nimble little feet, treble-jointed hips, giving every woman in the place the glad eye. I had to turn away.

More and more people kept arriving. I knew nobody except Brigit and the Cubans. The buzzer went again and another army of people waltzed in. The only good thing about them was that they were male.

'Yo, girlfren', what's up?' They were about fourteen, with lots of hats and trainers and baggy clothes and skateboards and surfing terminology. Until then I had thought I was pretty cool. But my euphoria dipped briefly, bringing a feeling of middle-agedness. They were punctuating their sentences with funny hand gestures – all the fingers hidden except the little one and the thumb. They said 'Bitchin'' a lot. Their accents came straight from Harlem. Nothing wrong there. Except *they* had come straight from New Jersey. In a stretch limo. Suburban gougers trying to be cool. And they were at my party. Not good.

'Hello Rachel,' said a voice. I nearly fell to the floor in an 'I'm not worthy' pose. It was Helenka. I was deeply in awe of Helenka. I described her as a friend, but that was just wishful thinking.

Although we were both Irish she had made a much more significant success of her life in New York than I had. She was beautiful and had fantastic clothes and knew Bono and Sinead O'Connor and did PR for the Irish Trade Board and had been on the Kennedys' yacht and never spoke well of anyone. I was honoured she'd come to my party, it had put the stamp of success on it.

The fact that she was wearing a floor-length chiffon coat that was in that month's *Vogue* could only enhance the general feel-good factor.

'So this is your little apartment?' she asked.

'Mine and Brigit's.' I smiled graciously.

'*Two* of you live here?' She sounded astonished.

I didn't mind. I felt fantastic and nothing could upset me.

'What's this I hear about you getting off with one of those heavy-metaller boys?' Helenka asked.

'Me? Get off with one of them?' I barked with forced laughter.

'Yes, Jessica said she saw you at the Rickshaw Rooms practically having sex with him.'

Jessica was Helenka's right-hand woman. She wasn't as beautiful or as well-dressed or as gainfully employed or as well-connected as Helenka. The one area in which she held her own was the character-assassination one.

I cringed as I wondered what she'd said.

'Did, er, she?' was all I could come up with.

'I've always kind of thought one of those boys was sexy in a mad, animal kind of way,' Helenka said thoughtfully. 'You know?' She turned her emerald stare on me. She's just wearing green contact lenses, I told myself, as I tried to stop myself quivering in awe of her beauty.

'Luke,' she said. 'That's the one. He's got a great bod on him.'

'Actually,' I said, tripping over myself with pride, 'Luke was the one I got off with.'

'Or maybe it was Shake,' she said absently. 'Either way I'd never actually do anything about it.'

She gave me a scathing look and moved away. It looked as if I hadn't made much progress on my project of being Helenka's best friend.

As I stood by the door, I thought I must surely be imagining it when I saw a big, heavy, booted foot appear around the landing. Followed by nine more of them.

Five giants marched towards me, be-denimed and hairy; bedecked and bestrewn with six-packs – the Real Men had arrived.

Who had invited them? How had they known? I was ruined.

Paralysed by panic, there was a split-second when I could have slammed the door shut and denied all knowledge of any party but Joey had already made eye-contact.

'Get up the yard, yeh girl, yeh!' he greeted me.

What the hell, I thought. I felt invincible. Strong, dazzling, confident. Able to meet any challenges head-on. I could survive this heavy-metal lowering of the tone.

In they trooped, acting as if they had every right to be there. Out of the corner of my eye I could see Brigit's appalled face look from Joey to Carlos, then back to Joey again. She seemed to be trying not to scream.

As I politely greeted the boys, Helenka stared at me with her Wicked Stepmother look. I flushed but kept my head high. I was not afraid.

Luke was the last one in. 'Howya.' He grinned. 'How are you?'

Jesus, I thought, my loins instantly afire, he's looking well.

'Hello,' I purred, holding his gaze for what seemed like a day and a half.

Had he done something to himself? I wondered in a daze. Because, surely he was never that good-looking before? A head transplant, maybe? Perhaps he got the loan of Gabriel Byrne's face for the evening?

I found I had stood up straight and had thrust my chest at him, saucy-temptress-fashion. My nipples had gone hard just from looking at him.

'I'm sorry I didn't want to go out with you,' I said brazenly.

I would never have broached the subject if I hadn't had a couple of lines. But I had and I felt compassionate and bountiful.

'It's OK.' He looked amused.

'No, it's not,' I insisted

'It is.' He looked even more amused.

'Do you want to talk about it?' I asked, with gentle anxiety.

He was silent for a moment then he laughed.

'What?' My invincibility was rocked slightly.

'Rachel,' he said, 'I thought you were very nice. I would have liked to see you again. You didn't want to. End of story.'

'Is that all you thought of me?' I asked sulkily.

He shrugged and looked puzzled. 'What do you want me to say?'

'Well, didn't you fancy me?'

'Of course I fancied you.' He smiled. 'Who wouldn't?' That was more what I wanted to hear.

'Yes,' he said. 'I thought you were beautiful. And very nice. But I respect your decision. Now I'll leave you to it and I'll go and mingle.'

'Thought?' I grabbed the back of his jacket and pouted.

He turned to me in surprise.

'Thought?' I said again. 'You *thought* I was beautiful. Past tense?'

He shrugged, as if in confusion.

'Rachel, you didn't want to go out with me. Why are you asking me this?'

Silently I stepped close to him and, while he gazed at me in surprise, I hooked my index finger into the waistband of his jeans. And, holding his startled look, in one fluid motion I pulled him towards me.

I nearly laughed out loud with pleasure. I felt so *empowered* by my unusually raunchy behaviour – I was a woman in touch with her sensuality, who knew what she wanted and knew how to get it. His chest was against mine, his thighs were against mine, I could feel his breath on my upturned face. As I waited for him to kiss me, I was already planning how to get everyone out of my bedroom. There was no key for the door, but I'd put a chair under the handle. And wasn't it uncanny that I'd had my legs waxed just the day before?

The spark between Luke and me was undeniable. Not for the first time I regretted that he was so uncool. But maybe if he had his hair cut and bought new clothes and . . .

Anytime you like with the kiss, Luke.

Anytime at all.

But he didn't kiss me.

I waited impatiently. It wasn't going according to plan, what was wrong with him?

'Jesus.' He shook his head and, with a small push, moved away from me. Where was he going? He was mad about me and I was very attractive, very sexy. So what was going on?

'The arrogance of you,' he said with a little laugh.

I didn't understand him. I was being an assertive woman. I was a sister doing it for herself. Just like the magazines were always telling me to. I couldn't understand why it had backfired so unexpectedly.

'Tell me, Rachel,' he asked confidentially, 'what were you sniffing earlier?'

What had *that* got to do with anything? I wondered.

'I see,' he said. 'Well, get back to me when your ego has returned to earth.'

And he walked away!

My confidence was shaken. As if the lights had dimmed briefly, the party ceased to be a glittering social occasion. And was just a scrum of piss-heads and liggers crammed into an unfeasibly tiny New York apartment with three balloons sellotaped to the front door.

And then I squared my shoulders. It was just about time for another line. There was a great selection of attractive men standing in my front room. There was even a chance that some of them weren't gay.

Luke Costello could feck off for himself!

28

I got lucky that night. I got off with a bloke called Daryl who was someone important at a publishing house. He said he knew Jay McInerney and had been to his ranch in Texas.

'Oh,' I breathed, impressed. 'He has *two* ranches?'

'I'm sorry?' said Daryl.

'Yes,' I said. 'I knew he had a ranch in Connecticut, but I didn't know he had one in Texas too.' Daryl looked a bit taken aback.

I realized I was talking too much.

When we couldn't get into my bedroom for a shag we left the party and went to Daryl's apartment. Unfortunately things took a turn for the very weird soon after we got there.

We finished the rest of my coke. But right about the stage we should have been clambering into bed together, out-invincibling each other, he curled up into a ball and started to rock backwards and forwards, saying over and over again in a baby voice 'Mama. Ma. Ma. Mam. Mah. Mama.'

At first I thought he was joking, so I joined in and did a bit of mamaing myself. Until I realized that this was no joke and that I was nothing but a fucking eejit.

I straightened myself up, cleared my throat and tried to talk sense to him, but he was beyond hearing or seeing me.

By then, the sun had come up. I stood in the beautiful, airy, white-walled loft on West Ninth Street, staring at a grown man rolling around like a toddler on his varnished, cherry-wood floor. And I felt alone with such intensity, it was as though I was hollow. I watched the dust motes dancing in the early-morning light and felt as if I had a hotline to the centre of the universe and that too was hollow, empty and alone. I contained the emptiness of all of creation in the area that was once my stomach. Who would think that one human being could contain so much nothingness? I was an emotional Tardis, containing impossibly vast deserts of abandoned emptiness, weeks' worth of walking through a sandy isolated vacuum.

Emptiness around me. Emptiness within me.

I looked down at Daryl. He had gone to sleep with his thumb in his mouth.

I thought about lying down beside him, but somehow I didn't think he'd be too pleased to find me there when he woke up.

I hovered uncertainly, not knowing what to do. So I tore a page out of my notebook and wrote my number on it and then put 'Ring me!' and signed it 'Rachel'. I worried about whether I should put 'Love, Rachel' or just 'Rachel'. I thought 'Rachel' was safer, but less friendly. Then at the bottom I wrote, 'The girl from the party', just in case he didn't remember me. I toyed with drawing a picture of myself but managed to get a grip. Then I wondered if the exclamation mark in 'Ring me!' was too pushy. Perhaps I should have written 'Give me a call . . .?' instead.

I knew I was being silly. But when he didn't ring me, as he undoubtedly wouldn't, I would torment myself with what I had or hadn't done. (Maybe the note was too cold

– perhaps he wouldn't think I really wanted him to ring. He could be sitting at home this very minute, *dying* to ring me, but he thinks I don't want him to. Or maybe it was too aggressive – he might have realized how desperate I am. I should have played hard to get by writing '*Don't ring me*', etc, etc.) I put the note under his hand, then went to look in his fridge. I liked to see the fridges of stylish people. There was nothing except a slice of pizza and a round of Brie. I put the cheese in my bag and went home.

I tried to force myself to walk back through the sunlit morning to Avenue A because I believed exercise was a great way to normal out.

But I couldn't do it. The streets were menacing and threatening. Science-fiction land. I felt the few people that were out at that time – six o'clock on a Sunday morning – were turning and staring after me. I sensed every eye in New York on me, hating me, wishing me ill.

I found myself walking faster and faster, almost running.

When I saw a cab approaching, I nearly fell to my knees in gratitude. In I clambered, my palms slick with sweat, just about able to tell the driver my address.

And then I wanted to get out. I didn't trust him. He kept looking at me through his rear-view mirror.

With horror, the realization hit me that nobody knew where I was. Or who I was with. Everyone knew New York cab-drivers were total psychopaths. This cabbie could take me to a deserted warehouse and kill me and not a single person would know.

No one had seen me leave the party with Darren, Daryl, whatever his name was.

Except Luke Costello, I realized, with relief laced with

something unpleasant – he'd seen me and made some smart remark. What was it?

With a belly-flop sensation, I suddenly remembered the my-finger-in-waistband-of-Luke's-jeans episode and I wanted to vomit with shame. Please God, I begged, make it not have happened. I'll give next week's wages to the poor if you'll only erase it.

What had I been thinking of? I wondered in horror. Him, of all people? And the worst part of it was that he'd turned me down, he'd rejected me!

I returned to the present with a jolt as I felt the taxi-driver's eyes on me. I was so scared I decided to jump out at the next lights.

But then – mercifully – I realized that I was probably only imagining the sense of menace in the car. I nearly always got paranoid after a good session and I went weak with relief when I remembered that. There was nothing to be frightened of.

Then the man spoke to me and, even though *logically* I knew there was nothing to worry about, the fear flared up again.

'Been out partying?' he asked, meeting my eyes in the rear-view.

'I stayed in my friend's apartment,' I said, my mouth dry. 'A girlfriend's,' I emphasized. 'And my room-mate is expecting me around now.

'I called to tell her I was on my way,' I added.

He said nothing but he nodded. If the back of someone's head can look menacing, then his did.

'If I'm not home in ten minutes, she's going to ring the police,' I told him. That made me feel better.

Briefly.

Surely he was going the wrong way?

I followed our route with my heart in my mouth.

Yes, he was. He *was*. We were going uptown and we should have been going downtown.

Once again I wanted to jump out. But every traffic light was green. And we were going too fast for me to signal to anyone but, in any case, the streets were empty.

Irresistibly drawn back to the mirror, I found he was still staring at me.

I was fucking done for, I realized with calm acceptance.

A few seconds later terror burst into flames within me.

Unable to bear any more, I rooted around in my bag for the Valium. Making sure he didn't know what I was doing, I surreptitiously snapped back the lid and took out a couple. While I pretended to rub my face I got them into my mouth. And waited for the fear to leave me.

'What number do you want?' I heard my murderer say. When I looked out I realized I was nearly home. I was giddy with relief; he wasn't going to murder me, after all!

'Just here,' I said.

'We hadta go the long way round 'coz they're digging the street on Fifth,' he said. 'So take a coupla dollars off the meter.'

I thrust the full price at him, plus tip. (I wasn't *that* strung out.) And I gratefully exited.

'Hey, I know you,' he exclaimed.

Oh oh. Whenever someone said that I was afraid. They usually remembered me because I'd made a show of myself. I never remembered them for exactly the same reason.

'You woik in the Old Shillayleagh Hotel, right?'

'Right.' I nodded nervously.

'Yeah, I knoo I knoo ya when ya got in, and I kept looking atcha, but I couldn't remember from where. I see ya when I come in to the hotel to pick up a fare.' He was all smiles. 'You Irish? You sure look it with your black hair and your freckles. A proper colleen.'

'Yes.' I tried to force my rigid face to look pleasant.

'Me thoo. My great-great-grand-daddy was from Cork. From Bantry Bay. You know it?'

'Yes.'

'McCarthy's the name. Harvey McCarthy.'

'Actually,' I said in surprise. 'McCarthy *is* a Cork name.'

'So how you doin'?' He was all set for a chat.

'Fine,' I mumbled. 'But my room-mate, you know, I'd better . . .'

'Yeah, sure, but take good care now, you heah!'

The apartment was like a scene from a rockumentary. Cans and bottles and overflowing ashtrays everywhere. A couple of people I didn't know were asleep on the sofa. Another body was thrown on the floor. None of them stirred as I let myself in.

When I opened the fridge to put the cheese in, an avalanche of beer cans fell out around the kitchen floor making a ferocious racket. One of the sleeping bodies jerked and mumbled something that sounded like 'Parsnips on the internet', then all was quiet once more.

The Valium hadn't made any impact on my paranoia so I spilled a few more into my hand and washed them down with a can of beer. I sat on the kitchen floor and waited to feel normal.

Eventually I thought I could face going to bed. When the emptiness took hold I hated going to bed alone. I opened another can of beer and went into my room. Where to my surprise there were two, no wait, three. No, one minute, *four* people already in my bed. I didn't know any of them.

They were all men, but none of them looked attractive enough for me to bother climbing in with. Then I realized that they were the 'Yo' girlfren', what's up?' crew. Little bastards, I thought. The bloody cheek of them.

I tried pushing and poking to wake them up and get them out. But nothing doing.

So I crept into Brigit's room. It smelt of alcohol and smoke. Sunlight was sneaking under the blinds and the room was already warm.

'Hello,' I whispered, sliding into bed beside her, 'I stole you some cheese.'

'Where did you go to with the coke?' she murmured. 'And you shouldn't have left me to deal with this on my own.'

'But I met a man,' I explained quietly.

'It's not on, Rachel,' she said, her eyes still closed. 'Half that gram was mine. It wasn't yours to take.'

My fear ripped wide open again. Brigit was cross with me. My free-floating paranoia had something concrete to hang on. I wished fiercely that I hadn't left. Especially considering how fruitless the whole mission had been.

Mama.

Mama indeed.

Fucking headcase, I thought dismissively.

I hope he rings.

Brigit turned over and went on sleeping. But I could feel her anger. I didn't want to be in her bed anymore, but I had no place else to go.

29

I was nearly sick with fear that the questionnaire might be read out in that morning's group. Please God, I prayed. I'll do anything you want, just let this cup pass from my lips.

The only thing was that the inmates seemed to be on my side, most of them anyway. When I went down to make the breakfasts, Don shouted 'What do we WANT?' And Stalin replied 'Luke Costello's bollix for earrings.'

Then Don shouted, his eyes bursting from his skull, 'When do we want IT?' And Stalin replied, 'Now!'

And there were energetic variations of the theme all through breakfast. Among the things wanted were Luke Costello's kneecaps for ashtrays, Luke Costello's arse for a doormat, Luke Costello's willy for a bracelet and, of course, Luke Costello's bollix in an eggcup, for target practice, for golf-balls, to juggle with, to play marbles with and for gobstoppers.

I was deeply touched by their support. Of course, not everyone joined in. Mike didn't, he just wore an unreadable expression on his granite-ugly face. Most of the older people who'd been there for more than a month looked on with mouths pursed in disapproval. Frederick, who had attained the grand age of six weeks, tutted and tisked and said 'You shouldn't be blaming anyone else, you should be looking to see what your part in all of this is.' Then everyone who was on my side – Fergus, Chaquie, Vincent, John Joe, Eddie, Stalin, Peter, Davy the gambler,

Eamonn and Barry the child all shouted 'Ah, shut up.' Even Neil did, although I was happy to do without his support.

I carefully watched Chris, desperate for a sign that he was still my friend, and I felt hurt when he didn't say he wanted Luke's balls for anything. But to my relief he didn't seem to be allying himself with the self-righteous oldtimers either. And just as we were on our way to group – me feeling like I was going to face a firing squad – he grabbed me.

'Morning,' he said. 'Can I have a quick word?'

'Sure,' I said, desperate to please him, wondering if he still liked me even though he knew I was a liar.

'How are you feeling today?' He looked lovely, the pale blue of his chambray shirt enhancing the colour of his eyes.

'OK,' I said cautiously.

'Can I make a suggestion?' he asked.

'OK,' I said, even more cautiously. I really didn't think this was going to be one of those me, him, no clothes and a condom ones.

'Well,' he went on, 'I know you don't think you need to be here, but why don't you try and get the best out of the place.'

'In what way?' I asked carefully.

'You know the life story thing they make you write when you've been here a while?'

'Yes,' I said, thinking of what John Joe had read in my first session of group.

'Well, even if you're not an addict,' said Chris, 'it can be very helpful.'

'How?'

'You know how it is,' he said, with a wry smile that

made my insides feel funny, 'we can all benefit from some kind of psychotherapy.'

'Can we?' I hooted in surprise. 'Even you?'

He laughed, but in a sad way that made me shift uncomfortably.

'Yes,' he said, with a ten-mile stare that took him far away from me. 'We can all do with help being happy.'

'Happy?'

'Yes,' he said. 'Happy. Are you happy?'

'God, yes,' I said confidently. 'I have a lot of fun.'

'No, *happy*,' he repeated. 'You know, content, serene, at peace with yourself.'

I wasn't that sure what he was talking about. I couldn't imagine feeling content or serene, but more importantly, I didn't *want* to feel that way. It sounded frighteningly dull.

'I'm fine,' I said slowly. 'I'm perfectly happy except for some things in my life that need to be changed . . .'

Like just about everything, the thought forcibly struck me. My love-life, my career, my weight, my finances, my face, my body, my height, my teeth. My past. My present. My future. But other than that . . .

'Think about doing your life story,' Chris suggested. 'What harm can it do?'

'OK,' I said reluctantly.

'With your ex-boyfriend's questionnaire, that's two things you have to think about.' He flashed me a smile. And then he was gone.

I stood looking after him in confusion. I couldn't understand what was going on. I mean, did he fancy me or didn't he?

I sat down – I'd missed the good chairs – and tried to see from Josephine's face whether I was for it or not. But, in the wake of Emer's visit, the focus was on Neil. I was deeply satisfied when the group addressed some of the glaring discrepancies between what Emer had told us about Neil and what Neil had told us about Neil.

Neil was still saying that, if they lived with Emer, they'd beat the crap out of her too. And, while none of the others were as mean as I would have liked, they kept trying to point out to Neil that what he was saying was wrong. On and on through the morning they laboured, Mike, Misty, Vincent, Chaquie, Clarence. Even John Joe managed a couple of words about how he'd never raised his hand to a calf.

But Neil steadfastly refused to admit to anything.

'You're disgusting,' I eventually burst out, unable to help myself. 'You big bully.'

To my surprise, there wasn't the expected chorus of agreement from the others. They just turned the same compassionate faces on me that they already had on Neil.

'Is that right, Rachel?' Josephine asked. I instantly wished I hadn't said anything. 'You don't like the bullying side of Neil?'

I said nothing.

'Well, Rachel,' she said. I could feel something unpleasant approaching. 'The things we dislike most in others are the characteristics we like least in ourselves. This is a good opportunity to examine the bully within you.'

You couldn't *fart* in this place without a laughable interpretation being placed on it, I thought in disgust. And she was wrong. I was the most unbullying person I knew.

To my great relief, the spotlight was on Neil again in the afternoon. Still no mention of my questionnaire.

Josephine had decided the inmates had been given enough of a chance to help Neil and that now it was time to send in the heavy guns – her.

It was fascinating. Josephine referred back to Neil's life story, which he'd read in a session before I'd arrived. With spot-on accuracy, she unravelled his life, as if she'd just pulled a loose thread in a jumper.

'You said almost nothing about your father,' she said agreeably. 'I find that omission very interesting.'

'I don't want to talk about him,' Neil blurted.

'That's perfectly obvious,' she replied. 'Which is exactly why we *should* talk about him.'

'I don't want to talk about him,' Neil said again, louder this time.

'Why not?' Josephine had got that dog-with-a-bone light in her eyes.

'I don't know,' said Neil. 'I just don't.'

'Let's find out, will we?' Josephine said, with fake comradeship, ' *Why* you don't want to.'

'NO!' Neil insisted. 'Let it be.'

'Oh no,' she insisted. 'Letting it be is the last thing we should do.'

'There's nothing to tell.' Neil's face had darkened.

'There's obviously plenty to tell,' Josephine said. 'Why else are you so upset? Tell me now, did your father drink?'

Neil nodded warily.

'A lot?'

Another wary nod.

'That's a rather important detail to omit from a life story, isn't it?' Josephine said shrewdly.

Neil shrugged nervously.

'When did he start drinking heavily?'

There was a long pause.

'When?' she barked again.

Neil jumped and said, 'I don't know. Always.'

'So it's something you grew up with?'

Neil assented.

'And your mother?' Josephine prompted. 'You seem very fond of her?'

Grief dragged his face. 'I am,' he said in a hoarse, emotional voice that surprised me. I had thought the only person Neil loved was himself. That he probably shouted his own name when he was coming.

'Did she drink?'

'No.'

'Not with your father?'

'No, it wasn't like that. She tried to stop him.'

A deep hush had fallen on the room.

'And what happened when she tried to stop him?'

There was a horrible, tense silence.

'What happened?' Josephine asked again.

'He hit her,' he said thickly, tears in his voice.

How does she know? I wondered, amazed. How did Josephine know to ask such questions?

'Did this happen often?'

There was a tortuous absence of sound until Neil blurted 'Yes, it happened always.'

I got the same sick feeling I'd had the day before when I found out about Neil beating Emer.

'You're the eldest child in the family,' Josephine said to Neil. 'Did you try to protect your mother?'

Neil's eyes were faraway, in a frightening place in the past. 'I tried, but I was too small to do any good. You'd hear it downstairs . . . you know? The thumps. The slaps, the cracks . . .' He paused and opened his mouth as if he was going to puke.

He placed the palm of his hand across his open mouth and we all stared at him, bug-eyed with horror.

'And she'd try not to scream, you know?' he managed, with a twisted half-smile. 'So that it wouldn't upset us, upstairs.'

I shuddered.

'And I'd try and distract the others, so that they wouldn't know what was happening, but it made no difference. Even if you couldn't hear anything, you could feel the fear.'

My forehead was sweaty.

'It always happened on a Friday night, so as each day in the week passed we got more and more scared. And I swore that when I was big enough I'd kill the bastard, I'd make him beg for mercy the way he made her.'

'And did you?'

'No,' Neil struggled to say. 'The fucker had a stroke. And now he sits in a chair all day long, with my mother dancing attendance on him. And I keep telling her to leave and she won't and it drives me mad.'

'How do you feel about your father now?' Josephine asked.

'I still hate him.'

'And how does it make you feel that you've turned out exactly like him?' Josephine asked, the mildness of her manner not hiding the apocalyptic nature of the question.

Neil stared, then gave a shaky smile. 'What do you mean?'

'I mean, Neil,' Josephine said with emphasis, 'that you are exactly like your father.'

'Not at all,' Neil stammered. 'I'm nothing like him. I always swore I'd be completely different from him.'

I was stunned at Neil's complete indifference to the truth.

'But you're just like him,' Josephine pointed out. 'You behave *exactly* like him. You drink too much, you terrorize your wife and children and you're creating a future generation of alcoholics in your own children.'

'NO,' Neil howled. 'I don't! I am the opposite kind of man from my father.'

'You beat your wife the way your father beat your mother.' Josephine was relentless. 'And Gemma – she's your eldest? – probably tries to shield Courtney's ears from the sounds of it, the way you did with your brothers and sisters.'

Neil was nearly hysterical. He pressed himself back into his chair, terror on his face as if he was up against a wall, surrounded by savage, barking, baying pitbulls.

'No!' he wailed. 'It's not true!'

His eyes were horrified. And as I watched him, I had the shocking realization that Neil really did believe it wasn't true.

There and then, for the first time in my life, I truly understood that fashionable, bandied-about, over-used word – denial. It made my intestines cold with fear. Neil couldn't see it, he honestly, really couldn't, and it wasn't his fault.

A glimmer of compassion sparked to life in me. We sat in silence, the only sound Neil's sobs.

Eventually Josephine spoke again.

'Neil,' she said matter-of-factly, 'I appreciate that you're in tremendous pain at the moment. Stay with those feelings. And I'd ask you to bear in mind some things. We learn behaviour patterns from our parents. Even if we hate those parents and their way of behaving. From your

237

father, you learnt how a man is supposed to behave, even if on one level you abhorred it.'

'I'm different!' Neil howled. 'It's not the same for me.'

'You were a damaged child,' Josephine continued. 'And in some ways, still are. It doesn't excuse what you've done to Emer and your children and Mandy, but it does *explain* it. You can learn from this, you can heal the damage in your marriage and in your children, and most importantly of all, in yourself. This is a lot to take on board, especially considering the extent of your denial, but luckily you're here for another six weeks.

'And the rest of you.' She threw a glance round the room. 'Not all of you are from alcoholic homes but I'd advise you not to use that as an excuse to deny *your* alcoholism or addiction.'

30

We limped back to the dining-room, drained after all the emotion of the session.

Every afternoon, after group, two of the more senior inmates went to the sweetshop in the village and brought back lorryloads of cigarettes and chocolate. The placing of the orders was a lively affair.

'I want chocolate, so I do,' said Eddie, to Frederick who was writing down orders on an A4 pad of paper. Frederick had the biggest, reddest nose I'd ever seen. 'Name me out something nice.'

'Turkish Delight,' he suggested.

'No, too small, gone in one bite.'

'Aero?'

'No, I'm not paying good money to eat holes.'

At this there was a shout of 'Ah, ye tight-fishted bollix,' from Mike, Stalin and Peter, who were passionately discussing the merits of ice-cream Mars bars over ordinary Mars bars. ('The ice-cream ones are three times the price.' 'But they're miles nicer.' 'Three times nicer?' 'Well, I don't know about that.')

'Curly Wurly?' Chris suggested.

'Didn't I just say I'm not paying good money to eat holes.'

'And the chocolate always falls off,' Clarence added.

'Double-Decker?' Nancy said. Nancy was the fiftyish housewife who was addicted to tranquillizers, and this was the first time I'd ever heard her speak. Talk of chocolate had cut through to that twilight world she seemed to inhabit.

'No.'

'Fry's Chocolate Creme?' suggested Sadie the sadist, who happened to be present.

'No.'

'Toffee Crisp?' From Barry the child.

'No.'

'But they're lov . . .'

'Minstrels!' Mike offered.

'Topic? A hazelnut in every bite?' From Vincent.

'Walnut WHIP?' Don hooted. 'Lose yourself in a Walnut Whip DREAM?'

'Milky Way?' Peter.

'Bounty?' Stalin.

'Caramel?' Misty.

'Revellers.' Fergus the acid casualty.

'Revels.' Clarence corrected him.

'Fuck off.' Fergus was annoyed.

'A Picnic,' Chaquie said.

'A Lion Bar?' Eamonn.

'I think Picnics and Lion Bars are actually the same thing,' Chaquie said.

'No they're not,' fatso Eamonn insisted. 'They're quite different. The Lion Bar has peanuts in it but the Picnic has raisins. They're superficially the same because they're both wafer-based.'

'All right,' Chaquie conceded.

Eamonn smirked.

'You'd know if anyone would,' she added.

Eamonn tossed his head haughtily and his jowls wobbled like a bowl of jelly.

The suggestions continued to pour in. 'A Fuse?'

'A Galaxy?'

'A Marathon?'

'Wait!' Eddie shouted. 'Wait, back up a bit, a *what*?'

'A Fuse?' asked Eamonn.

'Yes,' Eddie declared, his face redder than ever with joy. 'A Fuse. Are they new?'

Everyone looked at Eamonn. 'New*ish*,' he said thoughtfully. 'They were introduced to the Irish market over a year ago and have sold consistently well, appealing to people who want relatively uncomplicated confectionery but without the traditional eight-square format. They're an interesting blend – a *fuse*, if you will – of raisins, crispy cereal, fudge pieces and, of course . . .' he delivered a winning smile around the table '. . . chocolate.'

Everyone nearly stood up and applauded.

'He's great, isn't he?' Don murmured. 'Really knows his stuff.'

'OK,' said Eddie, sold. 'I'll have seven of them.'

'So will I,' Mike shouted.

'Put me down for five,' yelled Stalin.

'Me too.'

'Six.'

'Eight.'

'Three,' I found myself saying, even though I hadn't intended to order anything. Such was Eamonn's oratorial power.

Then everyone ordered a hundred cigarettes each, a few tabloids, and off Don and Frederick went into the cold evening, down to the village.

After tea, as we loitered in the dining-room, Davy looked up from his paper and exclaimed. 'Look! Look!

Here's a picture of Snorter out on the razz.' There was a mad surge as everyone gathered round to look.

'Looks like he's back on the sauce,' said Mike sadly.

'He didn't last long, did he?' said Oliver.

They all shook their head despairingly and seemed very, very upset.

'I thought he was going to be OK,' murmured Barry.

'He said he was really going to try this time,' said Misty.

'I suppose in his line of work – groupies, cocaine, Jack Daniels . . .' Fergus said wistfully. 'What can you expect?'

A pall had settled over the table.

'Is this Snorter out of Killer?' I asked cautiously. Killer was a crappy heavy-metal band, that, despite their crappiness, were very popular. Luke probably had all their records.

'That's the fella,' said Mike.

'How do you know him?' I asked, nonchalantly. I didn't want to make a fool of myself by jumping to any conclusions.

'Because he was HERE!' Don screeched, his goitrey eyes almost bursting from his head. 'In here. With UZZ!'

'Is that right?' I murmured, my heart doing a little flutter of hope. 'And what was he like?'

There was a chorus of approval for Snorter.

'Lovely fella,' said Mike.

'Sound man,' agreed Stalin.

'Grand head of hair on him,' said Clarence.

'Awful tight trousers, the way you could see his goose-pimples,' said John Joe.

'Awful tight trousers, the way if he doesn't watch himself he won't father any children,' roared Peter, then convulsed with laughter.

However, if the tabloids were to be believed, Snorter

had no problems in that department, having already been taken to court several times by women on the receiving end of his overworked gonads.

'And where did he . . . er . . . *stay*?' I tried to be diplomatic. But I found it hard to believe he could have stayed in one of the crammed bedrooms. Snorter was no stranger to first-class hotels.

'He stayed in with us, of course,' said Mike. 'He had the bed between me and young Christy here.'

Well, well, well, I thought. So the occasional famous person really did stay at the Cloisters. But the knowledge brought me no joy. Not much brought me joy, as I lived in the shadow of the questionnaire.

The three Fuses helped, though.

31

The following morning in group my relief was almost hysterical when it became clear that John Joe was to be centre stage.

Josephine started in on him immediately. 'Last Friday, we were looking at your romantic and sexual history,' she said. 'Perhaps you've had some time to think about it since then.'

He shrugged. I could have predicted that.

'You've had what, viewed from the outside, at least, seems like a very lonely life. Would you agree with that?'

'I suppose,' he mumbled obligingly.

'Why didn't you ever marry?' she asked, as she had asked on Friday.

He looked bewildered, as if he really hadn't a clue. 'Maybe, er . . . you know, the right woman didn't happen along?' He attempted bravely.

'Is that what you really think, John Joe?' she asked with a horrible smirk.

He let his hands fall in a gesture of helplessness. ' 'Tis, I suppose.'

'I don't think so, John Joe,' she said. 'Now, I asked you on Friday if you had ever lost your virginity. Are you prepared to answer that?'

He just looked at his boots, not even peeping up from under his bushy eyebrows.

It was clear that Josephine wasn't going to have the

same kind of success with John Joe that she'd enjoyed the previous day with Neil. I suspected that there wasn't anything to discover about John Joe.

Wrong.

'Tell me about your childhood,' she suggested cheerfully.

Jaysus, I thought, what a cliché.

John Joe looked blank.

'What was your father like?' she asked.

'Ahhh, 'tis a long time since he kicked the bucket . . .'

'Tell us what you remember,' she said firmly. 'What did he look like?'

'A fine big man,' he said slowly. 'As tall as the dresser. And he could carry a bullock under each oxter.'

'What's your earliest memory of him?'

John Joe thought long and hard, staring far back into the past.

I was very surprised when he actually began to speak.

'I was a gossur of three or four,' he said. 'It must have been September, because the hay was in, and standing in little ricks in the field below, and there was the harvest smell in the air. I was making sport on the flagstones, firing a stick around, with one of the pigs.'

I listened in amazement at John Joe's lyrical description. Who would have thought he had it in him?

'And for a bit of crack, I got the notion in me head to land the pig a belt of the stick. So I did and, didn't I get the suck-in when I kilt it shtone dead . . .'

And who would have thought this frail old man had it in him to kill a pig?

'PJ started crying like a woman and went running in, "You're after killing the pig, I'm going to tell Dada on you" . . .'

'Who's PJ?' Josephine asked.

'The brother.'

'And were you frightened?'

'I suppose I was. I suppose I knew 'twasn't advisable to be going round killing pigs. But when Dada came out, he took a look and the next thing, he's scarthing laughing and says "By the living jingo, but it takes a big man to kill a pig!"'

'So your father wasn't angry?'

'No, indeed he was not. He was proud of me.'

'Did you like it when your father was proud of you?'

'I did. 'Twas powerful.'

John Joe was positively animated.

I reluctantly began to admire Josephine, she certainly knew what people's triggers were. Even if I wasn't sure where she was going with this John Joe/father thing.

'Give me one word to describe how your father made you feel,' she told him. 'It can be anything. Happy, sad, weak, clever, strong, stupid, anything at all. Think about it for a few minutes.'

John Joe thought long and hard, breathing through his mouth in a very annoying fashion.

Finally he spoke. 'Safe,' he said firmly.

'You're sure?'

He nodded.

Josephine seemed pleased.

'Now, you referred to PJ "crying like a woman",' she said. 'That sounds quite contemptuous of women. What I mean is, it sounds like you haven't much resp . . .'

'I know what contemptuous means,' John Joe interrupted. His slow, heavy voice carried pride and irritation.

I could feel the rest of us sit up in our chairs in surprise.

'*Are* you contemptuous of women?' she asked.

'I am!' He astonished us all by answering immediately. 'With their whingeing and their crying, always needing to be minded.'

'Hmmm.' A knowing smile played on Josephine's un-lipsticked mouth. 'And who does the minding?'

'Men do.'

'Why's that?'

'Because men are strong. Men have to mind the others.'

'But you're in a difficult position, aren't you, John Joe?' she asked, a strange light gleaming in her eyes. 'Because even though you're a man, and supposed to do the mind-ing, you like to be minded yourself. You like to feel *safe*.'

He nodded warily.

'But women can't take care of you, that's what you think. To be properly *safe* a man would have to take care of you.'

For a few moments she let all kinds of questions and answers hang in the air.

What's she getting at? I wondered frantically. Surely, she couldn't mean . . . ? She wasn't implying . . . ? That John Joe is . . . ?

'Gay.'

'Or "homosexual" is a word you may be more familiar with,' she said briskly.

John Joe's face had gone grey. But, as I watched in jaw-dropped amazement, there wasn't the flurry of furious, drooling denial that I expected. ('Who are you calling queer? Just because you're an oul' dyke of a nun who hasn't ever seen hide nor hair of a man's naked lad . . .' etc., etc.)

John Joe looked *resigned*, more than anything else.

'You knew this about yourself, didn't you?' Josephine looked closely at him.

To my further astonishment John Joe shrugged wearily and said 'Yerra, I did and I didn't. What good would it done me?'

'You could have become a priest,' I almost said, 'and had your pick of the boys.'

'You're sixty-six years of age,' Josephine said. 'What a very lonely life you must have had until now.'

He looked exhausted and heartbroken.

'It's about time you started to live your life properly and honestly,' she went on.

'It's too late,' he said heavily.

'No, it's not,' Josephine said.

Visions of John Joe swapping his antique, black, shiny suit for 501s, a white T-shirt and a shaved head swam before me. Or John Joe in a check shirt, leather chaps and a handlebar moustache having exchanged milking cows for dancing to The Village People and The Communards.

'John Joe,' Josephine said, in a return to schoolmarm fashion, 'understand one thing. You're as sick as your secrets; as long as you live a lie, you will continue to drink. And if you continue to drink you will die. Soon.'

Scary stuff.

'There's a lot of work to be done, John Joe, on how you've lived your life, but we've broken through a big barrier here today. Stay with the feelings.

'And as for the rest of you, I know not all of you are latent homosexuals or lesbians. But don't think that just because you're not, that you can't still be alcoholics and addicts.'

Later that day a new inmate arrived. I first got wind of it when Chaquie rushed into the dining-room after lunch and screeched 'We've a new girl! I saw her when I was doing the hoovering.'

I wasn't happy when I heard the new arrival was a girl. I had competition enough from Misty O'Bloody Malley for Chris's attention.

Luckily the new girl was possibly the fattest woman I'd ever seen in real life. I'd seen some people as ginormous as her on *Geraldo* but I didn't believe they actually existed. She was sitting in the dining-room when we returned from afternoon group. Dr Billings introduced her as Angela, then went off.

Chris sidled up to me.

My heart leapt, then he said 'Rachel, why don't you go and talk to Angela?'

'Me?' I said. 'Why me?'

'Why not? Go on,' he urged. 'She'll probably be more comfortable talking to women just now. Go on. Remember how frightened you were on your first day.'

I started to say 'But it was different for me,' but I wanted to please him. So I stuck a smile on and went over to her. Mike joined me and we attempted to have a chat.

Neither of us asked her what she was in for, although we suspected it might have something to do with food and eating too much of it.

She looked scared and miserable and I found myself saying 'Don't worry, my first day was awful but it gets better,' even though I didn't mean it.

Don and Eddie were shouting at each other across the table because Don had spilt a drop of tea on Eddie's paper. Eddie was insisting that Don pay for a new one but Don was adamantly insisting that he wouldn't. I knew how harmless the row was, but Angela looked horrified by it. So Mike and I tried to cheer her up about it.

'Eddie's furious.' I laughed. 'Although a *fat* lot of . . . er . . . good it'll do him.'

As I said 'fat' I found that I'd made eye-contact with Angela and the moment went on for ever. I hated myself. I was always putting my foot in things. Always.

'But Don's such a little Hitler, it's about time someone cut him down to . . .' Mike froze, then forced himself to finish, 'size,' he muttered.

'It's only a newspaper, after all,' I said, with forced jollity. 'Not some huge, weighty matter. It's no big deal.' To my horror, 'weighty' and 'big' came out much louder than I had intended.

I could feel beads of sweat on my upper lip.

Did I see Angela flinch?

Then Fergus, who had been trying to adjudicate the Don/Eddie scrap, lurched over to us.

'How's it goin'?' He nodded at Angela and sat down.

'Man.' He shook his head in disbelief. 'Really heavy.'

We all tensed. Rigor mortis nearly set in.

'Don and Eddie, do you mean?' I asked, anxiously trying to smooth things over.

'Yeah,' sighed oblivious Fergus. 'Like Eddie really thinks he'll get money out of Don? FAT CHANCE.'

'You'd think Don would display a little . . . largesse . . .' I faltered. 'I mean, generosity.'

I was sweating buckets by then.

'It's a huge waste,' Eddie shouted at Don. To Mike and me, it sounded more like 'HUGE WAIST'.

'Oh look,' Stalin shouted. 'Look at the BIG ARSE . . . Mumble, mumble.'

It transpired he was looking at the football pages and Arsenal had had a big win, but it didn't sound like that.

I was a limp rag.

Next, Peter came over and sat down with us. I breathed a huge sigh of relief.

'Hello,' he said to Angela, 'I'm Peter.'

'Angela.' She smiled nervously.

'Well,' he barked with a fake laugh, 'there's no need to ask you why you're here.'

I nearly passed out.

'Maybe Angela and Eamonn will fall in love,' Don suggested later, his hands clasped, his eyes aglow. 'Wouldn't that be lovely? And they'd have lots of lovely, bouncing babies.'

'You can't say that,' tutted Vincent.

'Why not?' Don demanded. 'Didn't Liz Taylor and Larry Foreskinsky meet at a treatment centre? Love stories *can* happen, dreams *can* come true.'

I wondered if Don's homosexuality was still too latent for him to have discovered Judy Garland. If so, I really must bring her to his attention.

Twice a day, for the rest of the week, I sweated terror-stricken buckets in case Josephine read out the question-naire in group. But she didn't and I tentatively began to hope that she mightn't at all. Despite being saved, it didn't stop me from completely burning up whenever I thought of Luke. Which was most of the time. I lurched from boiling rage where I planned terrible vengeance to whimpering confusion as I wondered why he'd been so cruel to me.

Being with the other inmates gave me a strange, unexpected comfort. They were nearly all wildly enthusiastic in their condemnation of Luke and very affectionate to me.

However, I liked to think that whenever Chris hugged

me it meant *more*. Because we weren't in the same group, I only saw him at meal times and in the evenings. But he always took care to come and sit beside me after dinner. I looked forward to seeing him, to us having a special, private little chat. At times, I was almost able to convince myself that being trapped in the Cloisters wasn't an entirely bad thing. Such close proximity to each other was bound to help our budding relationship along.

The week carried on.

On Wednesday, Chaquie read her life story, which was mild and tame.

On Thursday, one of Clarence's brothers came as his Involved Significant Other but, as Clarence was no longer in denial about his alcoholism, there were no surprises. In fact, Clarence kept beating his brother to the punchlines of each horror story.

On Friday, Neil's girlfriend, Mandy, came. For some reason I had expected a dolly-bird in a short skirt and heavy eyeliner. But Mandy could have been Emer's older, dowdier sister. It seemed to me that Neil was looking for a mother-figure. Mandy confirmed what everyone already knew. That Neil drank an awful lot and was fond of giving his women a slap and breaking the occasional bone.

Thursday night was Narcotics Anonymous night.

When I'd looked at the notice board the first day, there had seemed to be millions of meetings. But in actuality there was only one a week. As it was my first meeting, I was curious. Almost excited. But it was just mad stuff.

What happened was, me, Vincent, Chris, Fergus, Nancy the housewife, Neil and two or three others trooped off to the Library. Where a beautiful, blonde woman with a Cork accent sat with us and tried to pretend that she'd been a heroin addict until seven years before.

She was called Nola, at least that's what she *said* her name was. But she was so poised and glamorous that just by looking at her I could tell she'd never had a day's debauchery in her life. She must have been an actress that the Cloisters used to try and convince the druggies that they could get better. But she didn't fool me.

She asked me if I'd like to say anything and, startled, I mumbled that I wouldn't. I was afraid she'd be cross with me. But she gave me such a beautiful dazzling smile that I wanted to climb into her pocket and stay with her. I thought she was *gorgeous*.

Two nice things happened that week, in the midst of my Luke-induced rage and confusion. First, I came to the end of my week on breakfasts and was now on Clarence's lunch team, which meant lie-ins and no eggs. Secondly, I was weighed by Margot, one of the nurses, and I was under eight-and-a-half stone, which I had fantasized about for most of my life.

But when she said 'Good, you've put on a couple of pounds,' I was mystified.

'Since when?' I asked.

'Since the day you arrived.'

'How do you know how heavy I was then?'

'Because we weighed you.' She looked interested and pulled a white card towards her. 'Don't you remember?'

'No.' I was really puzzled.

'Not to worry,' she smiled, writing on the card. 'Most people are in such a chemical fog the day they arrive here that they don't know which end is up. It takes a while for the mists to clear.'

'Haven't the others been commenting on how thin you are?' she asked.

They had, at times. How had she known?

'Yes,' I faltered, 'but I didn't believe them, I just thought because they were farmers and the like, they wanted a fine hoult of a woman, as they say, with calf-bearing hips and the strength to walk four miles with a sheep under each arm and cook up a field full of spuds for the tea each evening and . . .'

You couldn't make a joke about *anything*. As I said all that, Margot wrote furiously on the white card.

'It's a *joke*,' I said scornfully, and looked meaningfully at the card.

Margot smiled conspiratorially at me. 'Rachel, even jokes tell us plenty.'

There was no full-length mirror for me to verify Margot's findings against. But as I tentatively felt my hipbones and ribs I realized I *must* have lost weight – the hipbones hadn't been so clear of blubber since I was ten. While this truly elated me, I had no idea how it had happened. Years of attendance at the gym hadn't made any impact before. Maybe I had been lucky enough to come by a tapeworm.

One thing was for sure, though, I promised fiercely, now that I had lost it, I was determined not to put it on again. No more Pringles, no more biscuits, no more eating between meals. No more eating *at* meals, for that matter. That should take care of things.

And before I knew it, we had reached the end of the week, raced through the cookery class and games of Saturday, and suddenly it was Sunday again.

32

On this Sunday, I was allowed visitors. What I was hoping was that Anna would come to visit with a narcotic or two about her person. I was no longer worried about drugs showing up in a random blood test. On the contrary, if they threw me out I'd be delighted.

In the unpleasant event of Anna not coming, I had a letter already written for her, for Dad or someone to ferry back, requesting that she hotfoot it out to Wicklow with a bag of drugs under her oxter for me.

While I was looking forward to some visitors, I was worried about a couple of things. First I was dreading the great mirth that would issue forth from Helen when she learned that there was no gym, swimming pool or massages. And that there were no celebrities currently in residence.

But, worse than that, I was afraid of my mother. I was dreading seeing her disappointed, martyred eyes.

Maybe she won't come, I thought. There was a brief flare of hope before I realized that if she didn't come, it would be far worse than if she did.

Finally, my nerves stretched to screaming point, I saw our car turn into the drive. I could hardly believe it when I saw Mum sitting in the front seat beside Dad. I would have expected her to be lying in the back covered by a blanket in case someone saw her and put two and two together. But instead there she was as bold as brass, sitting upright, without even dark glasses, a balaclava or a wide-brimmed hat. My spirits rallied until I noticed I could only see one person in the back of the car. I prayed for it to be Anna. Anna and lots of drugs.

But as the car door opened, even from my window I could hear the voices raised in argument. With acute disappointment, I realized the person was Helen.

'Why do you have to drive so slowly?' she was shouting, as she got out of the car. She was wearing a long coat and a furry hat, Dr Zhivago style. She looked stunning.

'Because the shagging roads are icy!' Dad shouted back, red-faced and flustered. 'Feck off and let me drive the car my way.'

'Stopit, stopit,' hissed Mum, laden down with bags. 'What'll they think of us?'

'Who cares?' Helen's voice carried on the cold air. 'Pissheads, the lot of them.'

'STOP!' Mum hit Helen on the shoulder.

Helen hit her back. 'Get off! What are you so narky for? Just because your daughter is a pisshead too.'

'She is *not* a pisshead,' I heard Mum say.

'Ooooooohhhh, language,' Helen sang. 'That's a sin, you'll have to say that in confession.

'Anyway, you're right,' Helen continued triumphantly. 'She's not a pisshead, she's a cokehead!'

Mum and Dad's faces went blank and they both bowed their heads.

I watched from the window, immobile with unexpected grief. I wanted to kill Helen. I wanted to kill my parents. I wanted to kill myself.

We hugged awkwardly, the only way we knew how, and smiled. My eyes filled with tears.

Helen greeted me by saying 'KERR-IST, I'm fro-zened.' Mum greeted me by pushing Helen and saying 'Don't be taking the Lord's name in vain.'

Dad greeted me by saying 'Howdy.' At the time I didn't pay too much attention to it.

Before a conversational lull could occur, Mum thrust a bag into my hand. 'We brought up some things.'

'Lovely,' I said, sifting through it. 'Tayto and Tayto and . . . more Tayto. Thanks.'

'And Bounties,' said Mum. 'There should be a ten-pack of Bounties.'

I looked again. 'I don't think so.'

'I put them in,' said Mum. 'I remember doing it this morning, I'm certain of it.'

'Ah, Mum,' said Helen sympathetically, her little cat face the picture of innocence, 'your memory isn't what it once was.'

'Helen!' Mum said sharply, 'give them back.'

Sulkily Helen opened her bag. 'Why can't I have any?'

'You know why,' said Mum.

'Because I'm not a junkie,' said Helen. We all winced.

'Well,' she threatened, 'it can be arranged.'

'Have one,' I offered, as she sullenly handed them over. 'Three?'

I showed them around, proud, shy. Ashamed only when they said things like 'This place could do with a coat of paint, it's nearly as bad as our house.' I saved Mum from tripping on Michelle's My Little Pony.

'Anyone famous here?' Helen murmured at me.

'Not at the moment,' I said airily. And to my great relief she simply declared 'For fuck's sake!' and left it at that.

I led the three of them into the dining-room. It was

packed to the rafters and looked like the Day of Judgement. We managed to squash onto the end of a bench.

'Waaaalll,' said Dad in a strange voice, 'it's all mad purt.'

'It's what, Dad?'

'Mad purt.'

I turned to Mum. 'What's he saying?'

'He's saying it's all mighty pretty,' she explained.

'But why are you talking in such a stupid voice?' I asked him. 'And anyway it's not. It's far from mad purt.'

'*Oklahoma*,' Mum whispered. 'He's got a small part in the Blackrock Players' production of it. He's practising his accent. Aren't you, Jack?'

'Sure ay-am.' Dad flicked the brim of an imaginary hat.

'May-am,' he added.

'He has us driven demented,' added Mum. 'If I have to hear the corn is as high as an elephant's eye one more time, I'm going to shoot the elephant.'

'Get off your horse,' Dad drawled, 'and drink your milk.'

'And that's not *Oklahoma*, so it isn't,' Mum scolded. 'That's that other fella, go on punk, make my day – what's his name?'

'Sylvester Stallone?' Dad said. 'But that's not . . . ah now. I'm forgetting to practise.'

He turned to me. 'Method acting, you see. I have to live, eat and breathe my part.'

'He's had baked beans for his tea every night for a week,' Helen said.

Out of the blue it occurred to me that perhaps it was not surprising I was in a treatment centre.

'Jeeee-zus!' Helen exclaimed. 'Who's yer man?'

We followed her gaze. She was looking at Chris.

'Not bad! I wouldn't kick him out of bed for farti . . .
OW!

'What did you hit me for?' she demanded of Mum.

'I'll give you bed where you'll feel it,' Mum threatened.
Then she noticed a few people were looking at her, so
she gave them a bright papering-over-the-cracks smile
that fooled no one.

'It's his legs, isn't it?' Helen said thoughtfully. 'Does
he play football?'

'I don't know.'

'Find out,' she ordered.

We sat in awkward silence, the initial surge of joy at
our meeting gone. I was ashamed that we weren't even
having the low, muttered conversations that everyone else
was having.

Now and then one of us tried to kick-start a chat by
saying something like 'So, are they feeding you all right?'
or 'February is a desperate month, isn't it?'

All the while, Mum was looking sidelong at Chaquie,
at her golden hair, her perfect make-up, her plentiful
jewellery, her expensive clothes. Eventually, she nudged
me and, in a stage-whisper they probably heard in Norway,
hissed 'What's up with her?'

'A bit louder and we could dance to it,' I replied.

She glared at me.

Suddenly her face went white and she ducked her head.
'Sacred heart of Jesus,' she intoned.

'What?' We all twisted and stretched to see what she
was looking at.

'Don't look,' she hissed. 'Keep your heads down.'

'Wha-*at*? Whooooo?'

She turned to Dad, 'It's Philomena and Ted Hutchinson. What are they doing here? What if they see us?'

'Who are they?' Helen and I clamoured.

'Folks your Maw and Paw know,' said Dad.

'How do you know them?'

'From the golf-club,' said Mum. 'Saints preserve us, I'm mortified.'

'Waall, that's not how we first met 'um,' drawled Dad. 'It's lak thee-yus. Their dog . . . ah mean . . . their dawg, ran away and we'all found the critter and . . .'

'Oh God, they're coming over,' said Mum. She looked fit to pass out.

I was not feeling good. If she was so ashamed about me being here, I wanted to know why she had made me come in the first place.

From the terrifying saccharine smile she suddenly plastered across her face, I deduced she had made eye contact. 'Oh hello, Philomena,' she simpered.

I turned around. It was the woman I'd seen sitting with Chris last Sunday. His mother, I assumed. She was handling things with much more aplomb than Mum was.

'Mary,' she boomed, 'I'd never have taken you for an alcoholic.'

Mum forced herself to laugh.

'What are you in for, Philomena? The horses?'

More forced hernia-inducing cackles, as if they were at a cocktail party. Davy, the gambler, was at the other end of the table. I saw the bleak expression on his face and felt a rush of protectiveness.

'Our son is in here,' said Philomena. 'Where's he gone? Christopher?'

Definitely Chris's mother. Good. It was no harm at all if his parents knew my parents. It might come in handy just in case he didn't ring me when we got out. I could use the excuse of dropping a tupperware container up to Mrs Hutchinson, to see him. Mum was bound to need a tupperware container dropped up to Mrs Hutchinson within a day of me getting out. Mum and her friends *constantly* dropped tupperware containers up to each other. Gateau Diane, coleslaw, that kind of thing. They seemed to do little else.

Mum attempted to do some introductions.

'Our daughters, Claire . . .' She gestured at me.

'Rachel,' I corrected.

'. . . and Anna, no, the other one . . . Helen.'

Helen politely excused herself by saying conspiratorially to Mr and Mrs Hutchinson 'Janey, I'm bursting to make my wees,' and sidled off. A while later I went after her. It wasn't that I didn't trust her, it was just that I didn't . . . trust her.

She was sitting on the stairs literally surrounded by men. The dining-room must have been full of abandoned wives and children. One of the men was Chris. It didn't surprise me, and it certainly didn't make me happy.

She was regaling her captive audience with stories of her heavy drinking. 'Very often I'd wake up and not remember how I got home,' she boasted.

No one topped her boast by saying 'That's nothing. Very often I'd wake up and not remember whether I was dead or alive,' which they would have been perfectly entitled to do.

Instead, they were tripping over themselves with enthusiastic suggestions. That she check into the Cloisters, there was room for a woman at the moment, there was an empty bed in Nancy and Misty's room . . .

'You can always share my bed if you're stuck,' Mike suggested. And I felt a surge of fury. His poor, downtrodden, biscuit-bearing wife was only a few feet away.

Clarence tried to stroke Helen's hair.

'Stop that now,' she said sharply. 'Not unless you pay me a tenner.'

Clarence made a move to rummage round in his pocket, but Mike restrained him by putting his hand on his arm and saying 'She's joking.'

'No, I'm not,' Helen replied.

While all this furore was taking place, I jealously watched Chris's face. I wanted to see how he reacted to Helen. Well, what I really wanted to see was that he *didn't* react to Helen.

But a couple of glances passed between the two of them that I didn't like the look of. They seemed loaded and meaningful.

I felt sick and I hated myself for always fading into insignificance around any of my sisters. Even my mother sometimes outshone me.

Like a fool, I'd thought I might have made enough of an impact on Chris not to disappear under the onslaught of Helen's charms. But once again, I'd been wrong. I got that terrible, but oh-so-familiar feeling of 'Who are you trying to kid?'

I stood among the men, forcing myself to join in the laughter, feeling non-existent and elephantine, simul-taneously.

I was so upset that, when she was leaving, I forgot to give Helen the letter for Anna, telling Anna to come and visit me with lots of drugs. And later, when I asked Celine for a stamp she said 'Certainly. Bring me the letter and, when I've read it, I'll let you know if you're allowed to post it.'

I was so pissed-off that I marched straight over to the

confectionery cupboard, flung wide the door and waited to be concussed by the Sunday evening avalanche of chocolate. I wavered momentarily, trying to lay my hands on some will-power. But then Chris said 'God, that sister of yours is a gas woman,' and I was awash with the same old agony that I was me. And not Helen. Or somebody else. *Anyone* else, anyone other than me.

Chocolate, I thought, sick and miserable. That'll make me feel better, seeing as there's no drugs available.

'She's great, isn't she,' I managed to say.

I caught Celine smirking to herself, as she pretended to busy herself with the tapestry thing she always had in her hand when she was spying on us.

Unable to help myself, I picked up a bar of fruit-and-nut so massive you could sail to America on it. 'Who owns this?' I called.

'I do,' said Mike. 'But work away.'

I finished it in about twenty seconds.

'Crisps,' I shouted out to the room. 'I need something salty.'

I could have eaten the Tayto that Mum had brought me, but I wanted attention and looking after as much as a savoury snack.

Don rushed to my side with a six-pack of Monster Munch, Peter called 'I can do you some Ritz biccies', Barry the child said 'If it's a real emergency I can spare a bag of Kettle Crisps' and Mike muttered in an undertone that I was supposed to hear and that Celine wasn't, 'I've got something nice and salty in my pants you can suck on.'

I waited for Chris to offer me something, to let me know that he knew I still existed, but he said nothing at all.

33

They say the path of true love never runs smooth. Well, Luke and my true love's path didn't run at all, it limped along in new boots that were chafing its heels. Blistered and cut, red and raw, every hopping, lopsided step, a little slice of agony.

In the week after the party I thought of him a lot. I was so ashamed every time I remembered how badly I'd behaved. At the time I'd thought I was a *femme fatale*, but afterwards I felt more like a prostitute. I couldn't stop thinking about it, the way you can't help probing a sore tooth with your tongue.

Even though I hoped I would never clap eyes on him again, he intrigued me. His rejection had sparked an interest that I hadn't previously felt.

Fair play to him, a part of me thought. A man with principles.

Then another part of me screamed *No, wait a minute, he rejected me.*

It was the Thursday night after our party and Brigit and I were as bad-tempered as a sackful of weasels.

I'd had a heavy session the night before and the come-down had been particularly severe because I was out of Valium to take the edge off it. And I hadn't any money to restock until I got paid. I'd felt so depressed all day that I hadn't been able to go to work. Listlessly lying on the couch, vaguely in the horrors, feeling the slowness of my heart beating, wishing I had the energy to open my veins, was all I'd been able for.

Carlos had done another disappearing act on Brigit after he had somehow sussed at the party that Brigit had had carnal knowledge of Joey. (It might have had something to do with Gaz coming up to her with tearful respect, and saying in Carlos's earshot 'Jays, you're some woman, Joey says you gave him the best blow-job of his life.')

Brigit was distraught and I wasn't much better. Darren or Daryl the publishing mogul, best friend of Jay McInerney, hadn't rung me.

'If I only knew where he was,' Brigit whispered in agony. 'If I just knew that he wasn't with someone else I might at least get some sleep. I haven't slept in three nights, you know.'

I made soothing noises along the lines of 'You're far too good for that despicable little gouger.'

'Would you ring him,' begged Brigit. 'Please, just ring him and see if he answers, then quickly hang up.'

'But how will I know? Him and his friends all sound exactly the same to me.'

'OK, OK,' she said, pacing up and down, breathing deeply. 'Ask to speak to him and if it's him, hang up.'

'But he'll recognize my voice.'

'Disguise it, put on a Russian accent, breathe some helium or something. And if it's not him, but they say he's there, just hang up as well.'

So I rang, but all I got was the answering machine and its awful samba music.

'Oh Jesus.' She had her fingers in her mouth as she destroyed her good new nylon nails. 'He's only doing this to punish me, you know.'

I suspected that Carlos wasn't really put out by Brigit sleeping with Joey, but had just been looking for an excuse to ditch her yet again. But I murmured 'Louser' to let her know she had my support.

'And it's not like he hasn't shagged other people,' she anguished.

'And pig-face Daryl hasn't rung me either,' I said, keen not to be outdone. 'Please God, if you make him ring I'll give all my money to the poor.'

I always said that because it was safe; *I* was the poor, so all I had to do was keep the few bob that I had and I was still keeping my bargain with God.

On into the night we fretted, doing all the usual things. Picking up the receiver to make sure the phone was working, ringing Ed and getting him to ring us back just to make sure we could get incoming calls, saying 'I'm going to split this pack of cards and if the first one I see is a King, he'll ring.' (It was a seven.) Then saying 'Best out of three, if the next one I pick is a King, he'll ring.' (It was another seven.) Then saying 'OK, best out of five, if . . .'

'SHUT UP!' Brigit shouted.

'Sorry.'

Finally Brigit put her finger to her lips and said 'Ssshhh, listen.'

'What?' I choked excitedly.

'Can't you hear it?'

'Hear what?'

'The sound of the phone not ringing.' Then, to my surprise, she laughed, as if a cloud had just lifted from her.

'Come on.' She grinned. 'I can't bear it, this fecking vigil, let's do something nice instead.'

The terrible depression that I'd been suffocating under all day stirred slightly.

'Let's get dressed up,' I said eagerly. 'Let's go out.' I hated being at home in the evening because of what I might be missing. That was the great thing about coke. Something glamorous always happened when you took some. You either met a man or went to someone's party or *something*. Coke kickstarted my life. And the more I took, the more exciting the results.

'You're broke,' Brigit reminded me.

She was right, I realized in disappointment. No chance of being able to afford to buy drugs that evening. I thought briefly about asking Brigit if I could borrow some more money from her, then thought again.

'I've enough for a drink and a tip,' I said instead.

'When are you going to pay back that money you owe me?'

'Soon,' I said uncomfortably. Brigit had become strangely stingy of late.

'That's what you keep saying,' she muttered.

'Oh, please,' I begged, 'stop being such a miserable killjoy and let's go out. I've had enough for one week of playing "Let's pretend I've just met the man for me".' Usually when Brigit and I were poor and needed entertaining, she detailed a fantasy in which I met the man of my dreams, then I'd do the same for her. It was a game we rarely tired of.

'What am I wearing?' I'd ask.

'That Donna Karan wrap-around dress that we saw.'

'What colour, black?'

'Dark green.'

'Even better. Thank you, Brigit. Can I be really skinny?'

'Oh, yes. Eight and a half stone do you?'

'A bit lighter.'

'Eight?'

'Thanks,' I'd say. 'And how? Liposuction?'

'No,' she'd say. 'You've had amoebic dysentery and the fat just fell off you without you having to do anything.'

'But how did I get amoebic dysentery? Isn't it an exotic kind of disease? You can't get *that* over the counter.'

'OK, you met this man who'd been on holiday in India . . . but, look it doesn't matter how you caught it! This is a *fantasy.*'

'OK, sorry. Do I look fragile and big-eyed and mysterious?'

'Like a well-dressed gazelle.'

To counteract our low self-esteem, we both wore our good dresses. Brigit's Joseph shift that she'd got in the thrift shop on Fifth Avenue that nice, rich people gave their old clothes to. And I wore my short, black Alaia dress, that came from the same thrift shop. Plus my fake Prada bag that I'd got in Canal Street for ten dollars.

I might not have looked quite a million dollars but I was good for at least twenty-seven or twenty-eight of them.

As usual, I agonized about wearing my high, black, snakeskin, ankle-strap shoes in case they made me too tall.

'Ah, go on,' said Brigit. 'What's the point in buying them if you never wear them?'

And off we went, me teetering slightly in the unfamiliar heels, to the Llama Lounge.

The Llama Lounge was a sixties-style reproduction

cocktail bar: mad halogen lamps and peculiar metal chairs and general space-age jiggery-pokery. Very, very stylish.

Brigit gingerly sat on an inflated, transparent, plastic sofa. 'I'm not sure this thing can hold my weight,' she said anxiously.

'No!' I tried to sit beside her but she was having none of it. 'Between the two of us we're bound to burst it,' she explained.

'Oh, cripes,' she said, when she was finally installed.

'What?'

'This thing is see-through and you know the way everything spreads when you sit down? Everyone behind me will think I've fifty-inch hips.

'Go round and see, will you?' she said in a low, desperate voice. 'Don't make it look like you're checking, just be casual.'

Feeling foolish, I circled the sofa.

'You're OK,' I said when I returned, then took my place on a silver bucket chair that had my bum almost on the floor and my knees several inches higher. It reminded me unpleasantly of having a smear test.

'I'm so sawry,' interrupted a gentle, nasal voice. 'Can I just ask you . . . ?'

From my prone position, I looked up at a groovy youth. Seventeen at the most. Too young.

'Is that, like, something, you know . . . *mystical*, that you just did?'

'What did I just do?'

'The encircling of your seating place.' He was ridiculously pretty. I was really glad he wasn't a girl, there was enough competition.

'Oh, the encircling?' I felt a bout of devilment upon me. 'It was indeed. An ancient Irish . . .'

'Chinese!' Brigit said at the same time.

'It has been observed in both the Chinese and Hibernian cultures,' I said smoothly. 'It brings . . .'

'Good luck?' Girlie-boy interrupted eagerly.

'The very thing.'

'Thank you.'

'You're more than welcome.'

'You'd think he could have bought us a drink,' said Brigit bitterly.

We watched him go back to his group of equally youthful friends and enthusiastically explain something to them. He drew several circles on the table with his finger. Then, he paused, looked anxious and drew them in the opposite direction. A worried look appeared on his face and he stood up and made a move towards us again.

'Clockwise,' I called to him.

He beamed and sat back down and went on explaining.

After a few minutes we saw all five of them get up and walk, in reverential single file, around their chairs. When they got back to where they started from they shook hands and hugged each other emotionally.

A few minutes later a girl from another table came and asked them something. Girlie-boy spoke to them and pointed at Brigit and me a lot and drew a few more circles in the air. Shortly after that, the girl went back to her friends and then they all got up and walked around their seats. More hugging and kissing. Then someone went over to *their* table . . . And so it went on. It was like watching a very slow Mexican wave.

It was hot. We sat on our uncomfortable chairs and sipped our elaborate drinks. Great frosting and adorning with food went on with the drinks at the Llama Lounge. And you couldn't look within a six-foot radius of a barman without having an ultra-stylish little dish of pistachio nuts pressed on you.

I began to normal out and not just because of the half bottle of tequila I'd imbibed since lunchtime.

Brigit and I felt better than we had in days. Our morale had lifted slightly because someone was being nice to us, even if it was only ourselves.

Then Brigit decreed that it was my turn to get a go on the see-through seat. Which was all very well, in a back-of-bare-thighs-sweating-against-the-vinyl kind of way.

Until it was time for me to get up to go to the loo.

Because I couldn't.

'I can't get up,' I said in alarm. 'I'm stuck to this fecking couch.'

'Of course you're not,' Brigit said. 'Just push yourself forward and out you come.'

But I couldn't get my hands to grip the sweaty plastic. And my thighs were stuck fast to it.

'Jesus Christ,' muttered Brigit, as she stood up and grabbed me by the arm. 'Is it too much to ask to come out for a quiet drink and . . .'

She heaved, but still I couldn't budge.

Brigit bent her knees and crouched like someone doing a tug-of-war and gave another huge pull.

Painfully, a layer of skin being left behind – it was a shame that I'd recently wasted fifty dollars having my legs waxed when this would have done just as well – I began to separate from the sofa. With a great, slow sucking noise that had everyone in the place looking up from their drinks in astonishment, Brigit managed to peel me off.

And just as I popped out, with a final slurp that sent

Brigit flying, who did I come face to face with, only Luke bloody Costello.

He arched an eyebrow in a way that managed to ooze contempt, and said 'Hi Rachel,' in knowing, humiliating tones.

Then he smiled, with a glint in his eye that frightened me.

34

'Take off your dress,' Luke said softly.

Badly startled, I flicked a lightning-quick look at him to see if I was hearing things. We were standing in my kitchen, me at the sink, Luke leaning with his back against the opposite counter, his arms folded. Allegedly about to have a cup of coffee.

Instead, unless I was having audio hallucinations, he had just told me to take my dress off.

I blurted, 'What did you say?'

And he gave a slow, lazy, sexy smile that scared me.

'You heard,' he said.

Luke Costello has just told me to take my dress off, I thought, panic and outrage jostling for supremacy. The fecking nerve of him. But what will I do?

The obvious thing was to just tell him to leave my apartment. Instead I croaked 'But we haven't even been introduced,' in an attempt to laugh my way out of it.

He wasn't amused.

'Go on,' he said, in a tone that I found frighteningly compelling. 'Take it off.'

My throat tightened with fear. I wasn't coked-up or drunk enough for this kind of thing. The only reason Luke was in my flat *at all* was because Brigit abandoned me to his mercy in the Llama Lounge. Nadia told her that the Cuban Heel had been sighted in Z Bar, so she joyously left to flush him out.

273

I had tried hard to leave with her but she wouldn't let me. 'You stay here,' she said wickedly, suddenly in great humour. She winked, nodded her head at Luke and said 'But watch that fella, keep your hand on your ha'penny.' And off she danced, thinking she was great, leaving me staring bitterly after her.

A few minutes later, I tried again to escape, but Luke insisted with very firm gallantry that he would buy me a drink and then walk me home. And, when we got to my apartment and he invited himself in for coffee, I tried to refuse but couldn't.

'The dress,' he said, again. 'Take it off.'

I put down the kettle that I'd been filling. He meant business, I could hear it in his voice.

'Open the top button,' he said.

That's when I should have shown him the door. This wasn't a game, this was grown-up stuff and I was afraid.

But, instead, I lifted my hand to my neckline . . . then wavered . . . and stopped.

To hell with this, I thought, I'm not standing in my kitchen and taking my dress off for Luke Costello.

'Or I'll come over there and do it for you,' he said, with quiet menace.

Quickly, fearfully, I found myself fumbling with the button and I opened it, unable to believe what I was doing.

Something was wrong with my Outrage switch – why wasn't I picking up the phone and calling the cops? Instead of just feeling relieved to be wearing the short, sexy Alaia dress?

'Now the next one,' he said softly. He was watching me with half-closed eyes.

I could feel excitement churn in my stomach. With shaking fingers I opened the next button.

'Keep going,' he said, with another scary, sexy smile.

With him watching me intently, I couldn't stop myself from slowly undoing the buttons one by one until they were all open. Mortified, I clutched the dress closed across my stomach. 'Take it off,' he said.

I didn't move.

'I said,' he threatened softly. 'Take. It. Off.'

The pause dragged on for a long, silent time. Until, embarrassed, defiant, but unable to stop myself, I shook the dress off my shoulders and arms, and held it out to him.

For once I was wearing a decent bra; a nice black lace one that had only one small hole. I'd never have taken the dress off otherwise. And, although my knickers were a different pattern from the bra, at least they were black lace too. I dipped my head so that as much of my hair as possible fell forward to cover my shoulders and breasts. Too late, I realized that the small hole in my bra was quite a big one and that it had fitted itself neatly around my nipple. A do-it-yourself peep-hole bra.

Luke reached out and took the dress, not letting his hand touch mine, and threw it on the counter behind him. Our eyes met and something flickered across his face that made me shiver. Even though the night was warm, I had goosepimples.

'Now, what will I do with you?' He looked at me appraisingly, as if I was a prize cow. I wanted to squirm and hide but I forced myself to stand straight, hold my stomach in and stick my chest out. I even thought about putting one hand on a hip, but found I couldn't be that brazen.

'What will I get you to take off next?'

Laughably enough, my first fear was for my shoes; I didn't want to lose them because they were high and made my legs look long and slim. Well, not as fat as they usually looked, in any case.

'OK, take off your bra.'

'Oh no!'

'Oh, yes, I'm afraid.' He gave a lazy, mocking smile.

We stared across the kitchen at each other, me flushed with shame and arousal. I suddenly caught sight of the tell-tale bulge in his jeans and found my hands reaching round my back to open the clasp.

But after I'd unclipped it I became paralysed, I couldn't do any more about taking it off.

'Go on,' he said authoritatively, when he noticed I'd come to a halt.

'I can't,' I said.

'OK,' he said, suddenly compassionate. 'Just move one of the straps down your arm.'

Mesmerized by his unexpected gentleness, I did what he told me.

'Now the other one,' he said.

Once again, I found myself obeying.

'Now give it to me,' he ordered.

As I held out my arm to hand him the bra, my breasts wobbled and I caught him looking at them. I had a brief flare of awareness of how much he wanted me.

Then it was back to feeling that mixture of humiliation and sick excitement.

'Now come here and do what you did to me at your party,' he ordered.

I felt a wash of shame and didn't move.

'Come here,' he said again.

Automaton-like, I walked towards him, my eyes lowered.

'You see, you and I,' he said, taking my hand roughly

and moving it towards his groin, 'have some unfinished business.'

I squirmed and turned. 'Now, now,' he chided, as I tried to pull my hand away.

'No,' I said again, looking at the floor.

'You're starting to repeat yourself,' he mocked.

His fingers were on my wrist, my nipples swung against the rough fabric of his shirt, but that was the only contact between our two bodies. He seemed to be deliberately holding himself away from me. And I was far too frightened of this big, strange man to lean against him. I couldn't even look at him.

'Go on,' he said, as he tried to move my bunched-up fist against the long bulge of his erection. 'Finish what you started last Saturday.'

I cringed with embarrassment and felt queasy with arousal. I didn't want to touch his penis, I didn't want to stroke his erection through his jeans.

'Bet you *Daryl* didn't have one of these,' he said nastily, still moving my hand against him.

I was mortified. I'd forgotten that Luke had seen me with Daryl. I realized he must think I was a right whore so I tried to pull away.

'Oh no,' Luke laughed unpleasantly. 'No more playing games. *Men* don't like it when you tease.'

I got the impression he wouldn't include Daryl under the heading of 'men'.

As my skin flushed and prickled, I forced myself to put a few fingers on the buckle of his belt. Then found I couldn't go any further. I could feel something building within me and I had to stop before I became overwhelmed by it.

This time, Luke didn't tell or force me to do anything.

I could hear the hoarse sound of his breathing above me and I could feel the warmth of his breath on my scalp.

We were both marking time, waiting, for I don't know what. I had the sensation that we were both in a kind of siding, holding on for something to pass. Then he slid one of his arms around my waist in an oddly protective gesture. The feel of the skin of his arm on the skin of my back made me jump.

Slowly, unable to look at him, I began to undo his belt. His thick, black leather belt – even *that* seemed grown-up-man-scary – slid out with a faint, evocative slapping sound. And hung, the heavy buckle on one side of his flies, the length of leather on the other.

I could hear him trying to keep his breathing normal but I knew he was struggling hard.

Then it was time to start on the buttons of his jeans. *I can't, I can't*, I thought, gripped with panic.

'Rachel,' I heard Luke say, hoarsely. 'Don't stop . . .'

Holding my breath, I popped open the first button. Then the next one. Then the next.

When they were all done I stood still, waiting for him to tell me what to do next.

'Look at me,' he said.

Reluctantly, I lifted my eyes and when we finally looked at each other something burst open within me, something I could see mirrored in his face.

I stared at him in fear and wonder, longing for him. For his touch, his tenderness, his kisses, the rasp of his jaw on my cheek, the scent of his skin in my face. I lifted a trembling hand and lightly touched his silky hair.

The moment I touched him, the dam burst. This time we didn't wait for the madness to pass. We fell on each other, pulling, tearing, kissing, scratching.

Panting, I tore at his shirt, trying to get it off him so that I could smooth my hands over the silky skin of his back, the line of hair on his stomach.

His arms were around me, he was caressing me, biting me. He tangled his fingers up in my hair and pulled my head back and kissed me so hard it hurt.

'I want you,' he panted.

His jeans were around his knees, his shirt was open but he was still wearing it. We were on the floor, the tiles cold against my back. He was on top of me, his weight forcing me down. I was on top of him, pulling his jeans off, then sliding his boxers down so slowly he groaned and said 'Jesus, Rachel, just do it, for fuck's sake!'

I greedily watched his eyes that were dilated dark with desire.

His jeans were off, my knickers were halfway down my thighs, my nipples were raw from where he'd bitten me, my shoes were still on, we were both panting as if we'd been running.

I couldn't wait anymore.

'Condom,' I murmured feverishly.

'OK,' he gasped, rummaging round in his jacket.

'Here,' he handed the little foil packet to me. 'I want you to do it.'

Frustrated that my shaking hands wouldn't move faster, I tore it open and put it on the glistening tip.

Then reverentially – while he gave a moan – I smoothed it the long, hard length.

'Oh God,' I panted. 'You're so sexy.'

He paused for a moment and gave me an unexpected grin that nearly made me come.

'That, Rachel Walsh,' he smiled, 'is fine talk coming from you.'

*

I didn't want him to leave. I wanted to go to sleep in my own bed with Luke's arms around me. I didn't know what it was about him. Was it because I hadn't had a boyfriend since I came to New York? I wondered. Maybe, I thought doubtfully. After all, a woman has needs.

But it wasn't just that. In all the seduction/rejection fracas I'd forgotten how entertaining he'd been that first night in the Rickshaw Rooms. And so he was again.

'OK, babe,' he said, the minute he got into my bedroom. 'What does this room tell me about Rachel Walsh?

'First off, I can tell you're not what they call an anal retentive, are you?' he said, surveying my bomb-site boudoir. 'You've been mercifully spared a terrible neurotic obsession with tidiness.'

'If I'd known you were coming I'd have redecorated,' I said good-humouredly, as I lay on my bed, resplendent in Brigit's good dressing-gown.

'Now, that's nice,' he said, taking in a poster advertising the Kandinsky exhibition at the Guggenheim.

'Fond of the visual arts, are you?'

'No,' I said, surprised to hear someone like Luke saying words like 'visual arts'. 'I stole it from work. It's covering a hole in the wall where a load of plaster fell off.'

'Fair enough,' he said, equably. 'Just as long as I know. Give us a look at your books,' he said, bearing down on them. Luckily he'd wrapped a towel around his dangly bits so I wasn't too distracted by him moving around the room. 'What kind of person are you really? Good, there's your *Collected Works of Patrick Kavanagh*, just like you told me the first night I met you; nice to know the girl doesn't tell lies.'

'Come away from them,' I ordered. 'Leave them alone,

they're not used to visitors, you'll upset them and they won't lay for weeks.'

I was embarrassed by my book 'collection' – eight books don't really amount to a collection. But the thing was I didn't need any more. I rarely found a book that spoke to me and even when I did it took me about a year to read it. And then I reread it. And then I read it again. Then I read another of the ones I'd already read a million times. And then I came back to the first one. And read it again. I knew this wasn't the usual approach to literature, but I couldn't help it.

'*The Bell Jar, Fear and Loathing in Las Vegas, The Trial, Alice in Wonderland, Collected Works of PG Wodehouse* and not one but *two* Dostoyevsky books.'

He smiled at me admiringly. 'You're no eejit, are you, babe?'

I wondered if he was being sarcastic, and couldn't decide. So I just shrugged vaguely.

I was especially mortified by my Dostoyevsky books. 'What's wrong with John Grisham?' Brigit demanded every time she caught me with them. 'Why do you read all that up-its-own-bum stuff?'

I didn't know why, except that I found it very comforting. Especially because I could just open it on any page I liked and I knew exactly where I was. I didn't have to bother with all that tedium of finding where I'd left off and remembering who was who and all the other problems that assail someone of less than average intelligence with a criminally short attention span.

'You had a right nerve telling me to take my dress off the way you did,' I said teasingly, as we lay on my bed. 'What made you so sure that I would? I might have been going out with someone else.'

'Like who?' He laughed. 'Daryl? That thick-looking eejit.'

'He's not a thick-looking eejit,' I said haughtily. 'He's really nice and has a great job.'

'You could say the same about Mother Teresa,' Luke scoffed, 'but I still wouldn't want to go home with her.'

I was glad that Luke was jealous of me being with Daryl, but I was slightly ashamed of the whole incident. So I tried to change the subject.

'I wouldn't have thought that the Llama Lounge was your kind of place,' I said.

'It's not.'

'What were you doing there?'

He laughed and said 'I shouldn't tell you this but I had scouts on the lookout for you.'

I had a simultaneous ego rush and a surge of contempt for him.

'What do you mean?' I wasn't sure I wanted to know, except for the huge part of me that wanted to know everything.

'You know Anya?' he asked.

'God, yeah.' Anya was a model and I wanted to be her.

'I told Anya about you and she rang me and said that you were in the Llama.'

'How do you know Anya?' I asked.

'I work with her.'

'Doing what?'

'Number-crunching, babe.'

'What's that?'

'Accounts work. At Anya's agency.'

'Are you an accountant?' I asked in astonishment.

'No. Just a lowly clerk.'

'Thank God for that,' I breathed. 'My sister Margaret's

husband, Paul, is like an accountant, only worse. You know the things I mean, what's that they're called?'

'Auditors?'

'That's right. So tell us, what's Anya like? Is she nice? Has she any vacancies for friends?'

'She's a great girl,' he said. 'One of the best.'

As his eyes closed and his speech became faint and mumbly, he lay on his side. I lay myself against the smooth skin of his back and put my arms around him, sneaking a feel to see if his stomach did that lean-to action that mine did. It didn't.

But after he went to sleep I suddenly became fixated by the condom he'd had in his jacket pocket. I couldn't sleep for thinking about it. Even though I knew it was a responsible thing to do, it made me jealous. Jealous of the unknown woman he'd have used it on, if it hadn't been used on me. And what did it tell me about Luke? I wondered angrily. That he was always on the look-out for a shag? Anytime, anyplace, anywhere? Ever-ready, his trusty condom poised to be called into active service? Mad-for-it-me Costello. How many more of them did he have in his pocket, ready to be used at a moment's notice? On Anya, probably, if he got half a chance, not that she'd have anything to do with a fool like Luke.

I looked at him as he lay sleeping and decided I didn't like him anymore.

I woke in the middle of the night with sickening period pains.

'What's up, babe?' Luke murmured, as I writhed in cramping agony.

I paused. How could I say it?

'I am becursed'? Maybe he wouldn't understand.

'I'm blobbing'? Helen said that. Even to men.

I decided on 'I've my period.' Snappy, to the point, no room for confusion, yet not as clinical as 'I'm menstruating.'

'Great!' Luke exclaimed. 'No need for condoms for the next five days.'

'Stop it,' I groaned. 'I'm in agony. Bring me drugs, look in the drawer over there.'

'OK.' He hopped out of bed and, even though I didn't like him anymore, there was no denying that he had a fine body on him. In the dark, I watched the silver from the street-lights glint on the hard length of his leg, that lovely line that runs sideways along a well-muscled thigh. Not that I'd know.

He rummaged round in a drawer while I admired the view of him from the side. What a gorgeous bum he had, I thought, dizzy with pain. I loved the hollow at the side of it. I'd love a couple of them myself.

He came back with my big container of industrial-strength pain-killers.

'Dihydracodeine?' He read from the label. 'Heavy gear. You can only get them on prescription.'

'That's right.' No need to tell him I *bought* the prescription from Digby the smack-head doc.

'OK,' he said, reading slowly from the label. 'Two now and none again for six hours . . .'

'Can you get me some water?' I interrupted. Two, my foot. Ten would be more like it.

While he was in the kitchen, I crammed a handful of tablets into my mouth. Then when he came back I let him give me two, with the glass of water.

'Manks,' I mumbled, barely able to speak because my mouth was so full. But I knew I'd got away with it.

35

Naturally I couldn't go to work the next day. Liberated from guilt because, for once, I really *was* sick, I took another handful of pills and set about enjoying my day off.

And it was a good one.

Pleasantly floaty from the painkillers and the humidity, I watched *Geraldo*, then I watched *Jerry Springer*, then I watched *Oprah*, then I watched *Sally Jessy Raphael*. I ate a carton of ice cream and a family-sized bag of tortilla chips. Then it was time for a little sleep.

When Brigit came home from work I was lying on the couch, wearing track-pants and a bra-top, eating Cinnamon Toast Flakes straight out of the box. Because as everyone knows, cereal eaten straight from the packet – like broken Club Milks and any food eaten standing up – has no calories.

'Did you skip work again?' were her first words.

'I was sick,' I said defensively.

'Oh, Rachel,' she said.

'I really *was* sick this time.' I was annoyed. Who needs a mother when you've got Brigit?

'You'll lose your job if you keep doing that.'

God knows why she was cross with me. Many was the time, in the past, that Brigit had begged me to ring in dead for her.

Anyway, it was too hot to fight.

'Shut up,' I said awkwardly. 'And tell me how you got on last night with Our Man in Havana.'

'*Madre de Dios!*' she declared, all that she remembered from the Spanish lessons she had gone to in an attempt to win the heart of the unfair Carlos. 'High drama or what! Turn off that telly and turn on the fan, till I tell you.'

'The fan is on.'

'God, and it's only June.' She sighed. 'Anyway, wait till you hear.'

Her face darkened with anger as she related how she'd legged it to Z Bar and Carlos had left. So she went to his apartment, but Miguel was guarding the door and wouldn't let her in. But she got as far as the hall and saw a little Hispanic babe, about three foot high, with snapping brown eyes and a don't-fuck-with-me-or-my-brothers-will-flick-knife-you air.

'And the minute I saw her, I just *knew*, d'you know what I mean, Rachel, I just *knew* that she was something to do with Carlos.'

'Women's intuition,' I murmured. Although maybe I should have said 'Women's neurosis'.

'And was she?' I asked. 'Something to Carlos?'

'His new girlfriend, according to her, and she made me come in and she kept screeching in Spanish at Carlos, then she said to me, "Steeck to joor own kind".'

'Steeck to joor own kind?' I was shocked. 'Like in *West Side Story*?'

'Exactly,' said Brigit, her face a study of fury. 'And I don't want to steeck to my own kind, Irish men are the pits. And wait till you hear the worst bit, she called me a *gringa*. Those exact words, "Joo are a *gringa*." And Carlos let her, he just sat there like he couldn't speak for himself anymore!

'BASTARD,' she shouted, throwing my can of deodorant across the room, where it bounced off the far wall. 'The dirty, lousy little bollocks. I ask you, a *gringa*, what an insult.'

'But, wait a minute,' I said, anxiously. '*Gringa* isn't really an insult.'

'Oh, right,' Brigit said hotly. 'So being called a prostitute isn't really an insult. Thanks very much, Rach . . .'

'*Gringa* doesn't mean prostitute,' I said loudly. You had to talk loudly to get through to Brigit when she was in this kind of mood. 'It just means white person.'

There was a stunned silence.

'So what *is* Cuban for prostitute?'

'I don't know, you're the one who did the Spanish lessons.'

'You know,' Brigit looked a bit mortified, 'I thought she seemed a bit confused when I said that I was no *gringa* and the only *gringa* round there was *her*.'

'So is that the end of Carlos?' I asked. Until the next time in any case. 'Are you devvo?'

'Devvo,' she confirmed. 'We'll have to get jarred tonight.'

'Right you are. Or maybe I could ring Wayne and . . .'

'NO,' she shouted. 'I'm sick of you . . .'

'What?' I stared in fear at her.

'Nothing,' she muttered. 'Nothing. I just want to get pissed and maudlin and cry. You can't feel miserable with coke.

'Not if it's you that's taking it, anyway,' she added cryptically. 'I'm going to get changed.'

'*Prostituta*,' Brigit called from her room.

'You're not exactly a saint yourself,' I spluttered.

'No,' I could hear the laugh in her voice. 'I've looked it up, that's the Spanish for prostitute.'

'Ah, right.'

'I want to make sure I'm insulting her properly in the letter.'

'What letter?' I asked slowly.

'The letter I'm writing to that Spik chick.'

Oh no.

'Cheeky hoor,' Brigit's voice continued. 'Who does she think she is to be rude to me? Isn't that good? Spik chick? And because we're Irish, we're Mick chicks. Let's see if we can think of any more.'

'Would you not be better off writing a letter to Carlos?' I suggested tentatively.

I could hear her muttering 'Bick, cick, dick, eick, fick, gick, hick . . . No.'

'Why not?'

'Because then he'd know I cared about him.

'You know,' she added, 'if your woman is going to last as Carlos's girl she'll need to be good at two things.'

'What are they?'

'Blow-jobs and forgiveness.'

The phone rang. Both of us dived headlong onto it, me in the living-room, Brigit in her bedroom. Brigit got there first. Even as a child she'd always had marvellous reflexes. Many was the happy hour we'd spent thumping each other just below the kneecap, with the edge of a ruler, shouting 'It moved!'

'It's for me,' she called.

About seven seconds later she ran back into the living-room and gasped. 'Guess who that was.'

'Carlos.'

'How did you know? Anyway, he wants to apologize to me. So, er . . . he's coming round this evening.'

I said nothing. Who was I to judge?

'So, come on, let's tidy this place up, he'll be here in half-an-hour.'

I half-heartedly crumpled up empty tortilla bags and beer cans and dragged my duvet back to my bedroom.

Carlos didn't come in half-an-hour. Or in an hour. Or in an hour-and-a-half. Or two hours. Or three hours.

Brigit disintegrated over the course of the evening, just fell apart in slow motion.

'I don't believe he's doing this to me again,' she whispered. 'After the last time, he promised he wouldn't torture me like this.'

At an hour-and-a-half, she cracked and made me ring him. There was no answer. Which pleased her because she thought it meant he was en route. But when he hadn't arrived twenty minutes later she had to give up on that idea.

'He's with her, the little girl Spik,' she moaned. 'I can just *feel* it. I know it, I'm a witch, my feelings are always right.'

There was a small, horrible nugget of gladness in me. I wanted him to be so manky to her that she'd eventually have to give up on him. But I was ashamed of it.

At the three-hour mark she stood up and said 'Right, I'm going round there.'

'No, Brigit,' I begged. 'Please . . . your dignity . . . your self-respect . . . a pig . . . *bay* of pigs . . . not worth pissing on . . . what's the point . . . sit down . . .'

Just then the bell rang. It was as if the entire apartment had exhaled with relief.

'At the eleventh hour,' Brigit murmured.

I decided not to mention we'd said goodbye to the eleventh hour some time ago and that we were now at the sixteenth or seventeenth hour.

A strange light appeared in Brigit's eyes.

'Watch this,' she said, through a clenched jaw, and sauntered towards the entryphone. She picked it up and took a deep breath. And in the loudest voice I had ever heard she bellowed 'FUCK OFF!'

Then she turned away and started to shake with laughter. 'That'll show him, the gouger.'

'Can I've a go?' I asked eagerly.

'Be my guest.' She was in fits.

'Ahem.' I cleared my throat. 'OK, here goes. YEAH, FUCK OFF!'

Then the pair of us were in each other's arms, crying with laughter.

The bell rang once more, long and shrill, knocking us into momentary silence.

'Ignore it,' I gasped.

'I can't,' she snorted. Then we both exploded again.

She had to wait until she was able to speak before she picked up the phone and said 'Come in, you fat, hairy pig,' and pressed the 'open' button.

He looked wary and hurt. And well he might.

Because it was Daryl, not Carlos. Daryl! So dreams do come true.

It was hard to believe that he'd just walked over our threshold. In all honesty, I'd given him up for dead. He must have lost my phone number, I realized, but remembered the address from the night of the party. I was so happy I nearly went into spasm.

It was funny now that things had worked out, how silly my fears seemed.

'Hey, Rebecca,' he said vaguely.

'Rachel,' I corrected him, embarrassed.

'No, *Daryl*,' he said. 'My name is Daryl.'

He didn't seem to be as good-looking as I remembered him being on Saturday night, but I didn't care. He had great clothes and knew Jay McInerney and my heart was set on him.

'So, Rebecca,' he said, not really focusing on me. 'I'm loo . . .'

'Sorry,' I forced myself to say. 'But my name is Rachel.'

Then I felt guilty, in case he thought I was criticizing him.

'But it doesn't matter,' I added.

I nearly said 'Call me Rebecca if you want.'

'How come you guys told me to fuck off?' he asked, and gave a deep sniff that explained the dancey, unfocused state of his eyes.

Brigit had been struck dumb with disappointment and disbelief, so I had to answer.

'We thought you were somebody else . . .'

The bell rang again and Brigit became very animated, very quickly. She ran to the door, picked up the entryphone and started screeching an incoherent tirade, where only one in every ten words was audible. 'FUCKERBAS-TARDLATEWANKBETTERTHINGSTODO FUCKERSHITHEADBURNINHELL.'

She finished by saying 'Come in, you wanker,' and pressed the button.

Then she seemed to notice Daryl properly. 'MAMA Mia,' she said darkly and gave a strange little laugh.

'MAMA Mia. MAMA MAMA Mia. Har Har.'

I should never have told her about my time with Daryl, I realized fearfully. Now that she had gone bonkers, such knowledge could be very incendiary.

She stuck her thumb in her mouth and put her face very close – too close – to Daryl's, before saying again, very meaningfully, 'Mama'. She gave another odd, evil laugh and moved towards the door. All the better to beat the shit out of Carlos when he arrived.

So when Luke ambled in, two huge cartons of Ben & Jerry ice cream in his arms, Brigit looked as if she had died.

'Howya, Brigit,' he deadpanned. 'The heat getting to you?'

She stared at him with hollow, shell-shocked eyes. 'Luke,' she mumbled. 'Was that you who rang . . .?'

''Fraid so,' he said. 'What's up? The Cuban gone AWOL again?'

She assented mutely.

'Would you not give it up as a bad job and walk out with a nice Irish lad instead?' he suggested.

She stared at him, her eyes two disused tunnels.

'Would some ice cream make you feel any better?' he asked kindly.

This is a man who knows women, I found myself thinking, even though I too had gone into shock at his unexpected arrival. Particularly his unexpected arrival with Daryl on the premises.

Brigit nodded jerkily and stretched out her hand. When Luke held out a tub of ice cream towards her, she hesitated, then quickly snatched it from him, like a child who was afraid it would be taken away. 'All . . . for . . . mmme?' she just about managed to ask. I'd seen her catatonic from disappointment before, but never so bad.

Luke nodded.

'All for Brigit,' she said thickly, her arm cradled around it.

Everyone watched her anxiously.

'Good,' she slurred. 'All for poor Brigit.'

In silence, we watched her attempt to walk.

'Spoon,' she mumbled, stumbling towards the kitchen. 'Eat. Feel better.'

Then she lurched to a halt, 'No, no need. Eat anyway. No spoon.'

All eyes were on her until she managed to reach her bedroom. When she slammed the door, Luke turned to me. 'Rachel,' he said, in a different voice from the one he'd been coaxing Brigit with.

It was a meaningful voice that made my stomach feel as if I'd already eaten some of the ice cream he'd brought for me. But I couldn't savour the sensation because I was too aware of Daryl hovering and sniffing.

'Ah, hello, Luke,' I said, uncomfortably. 'We weren't expecting you.'

As soon as the words were out of my mouth, I wished I hadn't said them because they sounded unwelcoming. So I quickly said 'But I'm delighted to see you.' Then I wished I hadn't said *that* because it sounded patronizing and false.

My skin was twitching. Oh, why had Luke come when Daryl was here? And why did Daryl have to be there when Luke arrived?

It never rains but it fecking well pours and I was afraid I'd be washed away in the deluge.

I was afraid that Daryl would think badly of me for knowing someone who wore a *Lord of the Rings* T-shirt.

But, and this surprised me, I was also planking it because Luke obviously thought that Daryl was some kind of shallow disco-bunny.

I like Luke, I realized, not one bit happy with the discovery.

Then Luke focused on Daryl and his face changed.

'Darren,' he nodded grimly.

'Daryl,' Daryl corrected.

'I know,' said Luke.

'Would anyone like a drink?' I asked shrilly, before a fight broke out.

Luke followed me into the kitchen.

'Rachel,' he crooned softly, his big sexy body nearly touching mine, 'you don't remember, do you?'

'What?' I got a faint hint of his smell, and it made me want to bite him.

'You asked me to come round tonight.'

'Did I? When?'

'This morning as I was leaving.'

My heart was seized by the cold hand of fear because I had no recollection of doing so. And it wasn't the first time something like that had happened.

'Oh, God,' I giggled nervously, 'I mustn't have been awake.' Although I'd been awake enough to get him to ring in sick for me.

'Pretend you're my brother,' I remembered saying to him.

'In that case,' Luke said, his face stony, putting the remaining carton down on the counter, 'I'll leave you to it, then.'

Bleakly, aware of how badly I had handled everything, aware that it was all my fault, I watched him leave.

I wanted to stop him, but every part of me except my brain was paralysed, as if I'd just woken up while under general anaesthetic.

Come back, my head shouted, but my voice wouldn't cooperate.

Go after him and grab him, my head ordered, but my arms and legs were having a power-failure.

As the door slammed behind him, I heard Daryl sniff and say 'Hey, you know, that guy is rilly hostill.'

Wearily, I turned my attention to Daryl, as I decided to salvage what I could from the situation.

36

'Jesus, it's nearly nine o'clock!' Chris declared. A great stampede out of the dining-room began for Monday morning group. Sour Kraut's group on their way to the Library, Chris at its head. Barry Grant's group off to the Sanctuary and Josephine's group to the Abbot's Quarter.

Pushing and shoving, we raced down the corridor. In we crowded, good-naturedly clamouring about getting the best seats. Chaquie and I wrestled as we tried to get on the same one. With a hefty shove she heaved me onto the floor and bounced triumphantly onto the chair. We were both in hysterics. Mike got the other good chair. Then Misty sat on top of him, wriggled around and said 'I want it. Give it to me,' she smirked, double-entendring like there was no tomorrow. Mike went grey and limped away to the worst chair, where the spring could draw blood from a buttock if it was a long session.

Josephine kicked off by saying 'Rachel, we've been neglecting you a bit this past week, haven't we?'

My bowels turned to water.

Questionnaire time. How could I ever have thought I'd escape it? That'd teach me for having a laugh with Chaquie. My high spirits had tempted fate.

'Haven't we?' Josephine asked again.

'I don't mind,' I mumbled.

'I know you don't mind,' Josephine said jovially. 'Which

is precisely why we're going to make you the centre of attention.'

My heart pounded and helpless rage battled round inside me. I wanted to overturn chairs, punch smug-arse Josephine, run out the gates and all the way back to New York and kill Luke.

It struck me forcibly how mad it was that I was there and had to endure such humiliation and pain.

Josephine rustled some sheets of paper in her hand and I stared in mute anguish. Don't do it, please don't do it.

'I'd like you to write your life story,' she said, holding out a piece of paper towards me. 'Here are the questions I want addressed when you're doing it.'

It took me a short while to realize that I'd been saved, that she wasn't going to read out Luke's betrayal. All she wanted me to do was write a stupid life story. No problem!

'No need to look so frightened,' she said with a knowing leer.

I smiled weakly.

Shakily, I sneaked a quick glance at the sheet of paper she had given me. All it was, was a list of questions that were to serve as guidelines for writing my life story. 'What is your earliest memory?' 'Who was your favourite person when you were three years old?' 'What do you remember about being five years old?' 'Ten?' 'Fifteen?' 'Twenty?'

I'd thought doing this would be a difficult, creative exercise, as I tried to dredge up random memories of my earlier life. Instead it would be as simple as filling out an insurance claim form. Good.

That morning's session was devoted to Clarence who, at over six weeks, would be getting out fairly shortly.

'You realize that if you want to stay away from drink,'

Josephine said to him, 'you'll need to change your life when you get back outside.'

'I've changed already, though,' Clarence said eagerly. 'I know things about myself that I'd never seen before in all my fifty-one years. I've had the courage to listen to my family telling their stories about my drinking. And I can see that I was selfish and irresponsible.'

It was strange to hear someone as odd as Clarence speaking so knowledgeably and authoritatively.

'I grant you that, Clarence,' Josephine said, with a smile that for once wasn't ironic. 'You've come a long way. But I'm talking about the practical changes you have to make.'

'But I've hardly thought of drink while I've been in here,' Clarence insisted. 'Only when the bad stuff happened.'

'Exactly,' said Josephine. 'And bad stuff will happen out there as well, because that's the nature of life. But you'll be in a position to get your hands on alcohol then.

'What can you suggest?' She threw the question open to the floor.

'What about psychotherapy?' Vincent demanded. 'Surely we don't learn enough about ourselves in the two months we're here to last us the rest of our lives?'

'Good point, Vincent.' Josephine beamed. 'Well observed. Each one of you will have to change a lifetime's behaviour when you go back out into the real world. On-going psychotherapy, either group or one-to-one, is vital.'

'Stay away from pubs,' Misty interjected passionately. 'And stay away from the people you used to drink with, because you'll have nothing in common with them. That was my downfall.'

'Take it from Misty,' Josephine said. 'Unless you want to end up back in here in six months' time.'

'Go to lots of AA meetings,' Mike suggested.

'Thank you, Mike.' Josephine tilted her head. 'You'll all find AA or NA a great support when you get out.'

'You could take up lots of new hobbies,' suggested Chaquie, 'to fill the time.'

I was enjoying this session. It was exciting helping a person plan their new life.

'Thank you, Chaquie,' Josephine said. 'Have a think about what you'd like to do, Clarence.'

'Well . . .' he said shyly. 'I've always . . .'

'Go on.'

'I've always wanted . . . to learn to drive. I kept saying I'd start soon, but I never got anything done because when it came down to it, I always preferred to drink than to do anything else.' Clarence looked surprised at what he'd just said.

'That!' Josephine hissed, her face aglow, 'is the most perceptive thing you've said in all your time here. You've recognized a fundamental feature of an addict's life. Maintaining your habit is so important you've no real interest in anything else.'

Just as I felt smug about having loads of interests – parties, going out, clothes, enjoying myself – Josephine said 'And I'd like you all to remember that celebrations and going to pubs, nightclubs and parties are not interests in their own right. They're merely peripheral to feeding your addiction.'

She looked directly at me when she said that, her intelligent, blue eyes merry and shrewd. And I hated her as I had never hated anyone. And, believe me, I had hated plenty.

'Is something wrong, Rachel?' She asked.

'I see,' I spluttered, gripped with fury. 'So going to a party makes you an addict?'

'I didn't say that.'

'Yes, you did, you said . . .'

'Rachel,' she was suddenly very firm, 'for a normal person, a trip to a party is just that. A trip to a party. But for an addict, it's a situation where their drug of choice, whether it be alcohol or cocaine, is available. It's interesting that you heard it the way you did . . .'

'And I *hate* that word,' I ejaculated.

'What word?'

'*Normal*. So if you're an addict you're *abnormal*?'

'Yes, your responses to commonplace life situations are abnormal. An addict uses their drug instead of dealing with life, whether it's good or bad.'

'But I don't want to be *abnormal*,' I burst out. What the . . .? I thought in surprise. I hadn't meant to say that.

'No one wants to be abnormal,' Josephine said, looking at me with cherishing eyes. 'That's why an addict's denial is usually so powerful. But here in the Cloisters you'll learn new responses, normal ones.'

Shocked and confused, I opened my mouth to set the record straight, but she'd moved on.

Logically I knew she was a stupid bitch and that there was nothing at all wrong with having a healthy social life, but emotionally I felt beleaguered. I was worn-out. I constantly seemed to be explaining or apologizing simply for being me and living my life my way.

Usually I just shrugged off any of the Cloisters' codology that allegedly pertained to me, but that day I couldn't locate the strength. Careful, I warned myself, with a premonition of fear. Don't leave yourself open, they'll break you down if you let them.

*

As I sat in the dining-room that evening to write my life story I felt strange. At home, as if I belonged. How I had the temerity to feel almost OK, I'll never know. Between being ditched and stitched by Luke, with the dreaded questionnaire yet to come, things were grim. But like people who managed to live fulfilled and happy lives on the side of a volcano, I sometimes managed to switch off from my unviable situation. I had to. I'd go mad if I didn't.

Misty wasn't there, which helped. She always made me feel edgy and angry.

I sucked the end of my pen and looked at Chris, especially at his thighs. God, he was delicious. While I had the pen in my mouth I willed him to look at me. I reckoned it was a fairly provocative pose. But he didn't look. Then the end of my tongue went numb from the taste of ink. Yuk! Anxiously, I wondered if my teeth had turned blue.

Since the previous day I'd watched Chris closely to see if Helen had supplanted me in his affections. He hadn't been *un*friendly, the usual banter and the occasional gift of physical contact. But was I imagining an infinitesimal slipping away of his interest in me? So small as not to be visible to the naked eye. Perhaps I was simply extremely paranoid, I soothed myself.

I tried to focus on my life story but couldn't help being drawn back to look at Chris again. He was playing Trivial Pursuit with some of the other inmates. Or at least trying to. Arguments kept erupting because Vincent suspected Stalin of learning off all the answers. He swore he'd seen him going through the cards and studying them.

Davy the gambler was begging them to play for money. Matchsticks even.

The bickering reminded me of my family. Except the inmates weren't as vicious, of course.

It had started to snow; we left the curtains open so we could see the soft flakes fluttering against the window.

Barry the child was dancing round the room, doing Tai Chi, his slow, graceful movements soothing to watch. He was really beautiful, like a dark-haired cherub. And he always seemed upbeat and happy, in a trancey world of his own. I wondered what age he was.

Eamonn waddled in and nearly tripped over Barry.

'What's going on?' he demanded. 'That's dangerous, you shouldn't be doing that.'

'Let the lad do his chow mein,' Mike protested.

Then Chaquie arrived, complaining loudly about something she'd read in the papers about unmarried mothers being given free condoms to stop them expanding their families.

'It's disgraceful,' she fumed. 'Why should the tax-payers' money be spent giving them free french letters? They shouldn't need anything at all.'

'Do you know what the best contraceptive is?' she demanded.

Barry screwed up his forehead in thought. 'Your face?'

Chaquie ignored him. 'The word "no"! It's as simple as that, just two little letters, n and o. No. If they had any morals at all they wouldn't need . . .'

'AH, SHUT UP!' Everyone roared as one.

Things quietened down briefly until John Joe asked Barry to demonstrate the rudiments of Tai Chi to him, and Barry, sweet child that he was, obliged.

'See, you slide your leg along the floor here. No, *slide*.'

Instead of sliding gracefully, John Joe simply picked up a heavy-booted foot and planted it clumsily on another part of the floor.

'Slide, see, like this.'

'Show me again,' John Joe asked, moving closer to Barry.

All of us who were in John Joe's group stiffened, thinking the same thing. 'He fancies Barry. Oh God, he fancies Barry!'

'And gently raise your arm.' Barry lifted his arm as gracefully as a ballerina. John Joe thrust his out, as if he was punching someone.

'Now kind of tilt your hips.'

John Joe complied with enthusiasm.

Another babel of voices broke out because Stalin knew the capital of Papua New Guinea. '*How* did you know it?' Vincent demanded. '*How* would a gobshite like you know something like that?'

'Because I'm not a thick eejit, like some I could mention,' Stalin insisted.

'Not at all.' Vincent laughed darkly. 'Not. At. All. It's because you've been swotting up on them answers, that's why. Capital of Papua New Guinea, me arse, sure you hardly know the capital of Ireland, even though you live in it. If you weren't an alcoholic you'd never have been out of Clanbrassil Street, you're hardly what you might call *well-travelled* . . .'

'Shush, would you, I'm trying to write my life story,' I said good-naturedly.

'Why don't you go to the Reading Room?' Chris said. 'You'll get more peace there.'

I was torn between wanting to be able to sit and admire him, and wanting to show gratitude for his suggestion.

'Go on,' he urged with a smile. 'You'll get lots done there.'

No more needed to be said.

But as soon as I tried to write my life story, I mean

really write it, as opposed to just sitting with it in front of me, I suddenly understood why, the first night I'd been there, everyone in the Reading Room had been slapping the desks with the palms of their hands, crumpling up balls of paper, throwing them at the wall in despair and shouting 'I can't do this!'

Faced with the questions, I found I deeply didn't want to answer them.

37

What was my earliest memory? I wondered, looking at the empty page in front of me. Any one of many. The time that Margaret and Claire put me in the crolly doll's pram and pushed me round in it at high speed. I still remembered being squashed into the too-small pram, blinded by the summer sun and Margaret's and Claire's laughing faces beneath the brown, pudding-bowl haircuts we all had. I remembered how much I hated my hair and wished fiercely for long, golden ringlets like Angela Kilfeather's.

Or running after Margaret and Claire on my chunky, little legs, trying to keep up. Only to be told 'Go home, you can't come, you're too small.'

Or coveting Claire's powder-blue patent sandals, which had a strap across the toe and another around the ankle and – the best part of all – a white, patent flower on the bit across the toe.

My earliest memory could have been of the time I ate Margaret's Easter egg and we all got locked out.

Instantly, it was as if the lights in the Reading Room had dimmed. Oh dear, I still felt peculiar even twenty-three years later, as I recalled that day. It certainly didn't *feel* like twenty-three years, it felt like yesterday.

It was a Beano Easter egg, I remembered clearly. I don't think they make Beanos anymore, I thought, trying to distract myself from the painful memory. As I recalled, Beanos became extinct some time in the seventies. I supposed I could always check with Eamonn. They were lovely, like Smarties, but in much brighter, groovier colours.

Margaret had saved the Easter egg from April and it was then about September. That was the kind of sister Margaret was. I was *tormented* by her ability to hoard.

I was the total opposite. When we got our Sunday packet of Cadbury's éclairs, I could hardly wait to get the paper off before shoving them into my mouth. And when I'd finished, hers were still untouched. Then, of course, I was sorry I hadn't saved mine and I wanted hers.

For months, the Easter egg stood on top of our wardrobe, winking and dazzling me with its glittery red paper. I coveted it incessantly with every inch of my plump little body. I was obsessed with it.

'When do you think you'll eat it?' I'd ask, trying to pretend that I didn't care. Trying to pretend I didn't feel I would die if it wasn't in the next five minutes.

'Oh, I don't know,' she said airily, control-freak that she was.

'Really?' I said, with grim nonchalance. It was vitally important never to let anyone know what it was that you really wanted. Because if they knew, they deliberately wouldn't give it to you. If you ask, you don't get, was my experience.

'I might never eat it,' she mused. 'I might just throw it out.'

'Well,' I said carefully, holding my breath at the thought of clinching the deal and getting what I wanted, 'there's no need to throw it out, I'll eat it for you.'

'Do you *want* to eat it?'

'Yes,' I said, forgetting to dissemble.

'Aha! So you want to eat it.'

'No! I . . .'

'You do, it's obvious. And Holy God says that, because you've asked, it makes you unworthy. You weren't humble, see?'

At the age of five and a quarter, Margaret was an authority on God.

I knew very little about Him except that He was a right old meanie and behaved the way the rest of the people in my world did. If you wanted something and asked for it, you were automatically disqualified from getting it. It seemed to me that the only safe way to live your life with God around, was to want things you didn't want.

The God I grew up with was a cruel one.

The sister I grew up with was a cruel one.

I was confused by her self-control, confused by my own weakness. How come I wanted her Easter egg so badly and she didn't seem bothered at all?

The day I finally cracked, I didn't *intend* to eat it.

Not all of it, in any case.

I only meant to scoff the little cellophane bag of Beanos in the middle. The plan was to rewrap the Easter egg in its red tinfoil and cardboard box and replace it on top of the wardrobe, as good as new. And, if Margaret ever came to eat it, and found her little bag of sweets missing, she'd just think she got a dud one from the factory. I might even say that I didn't get any Beanos in the middle of *mine* either, I thought, pleased with my cunning. That claim would certainly add authenticity.

The notion of stealing it gestated slowly and resentfully. I chose my time carefully.

Claire and Margaret were at school; Margaret's teacher said she'd never met such a well-behaved little girl in her thirty-eight years of teaching. Smelly-bum Anna was asleep in her cot, and Mum was out at the clothes-line, a trip that usually meant an absence of several hours as she stood at the garden wall talking to Mrs Kilfeather, mother of Angela of the angelic, golden ringlets.

I dragged a yellow wicker chair over to the big, heavy, brown wardrobe (sleek, white, jerry-built, plastic-looking fitted wardrobes were still in our future. Such wardrobes were 'mod-cons' and our house had no 'mod-cons'.)

I clambered up on the chair and stood on my tippy-toes, stretching hard to reach. I told myself over and over again that it was obvious that Margaret didn't want the Easter egg. I nearly had myself convinced I was doing her a favour. Finally, I tipped it with my hand and it tumbled down on top of me.

I carried the box and lay on the floor between my bed and the wall, so that if Mum came in, I wouldn't get caught.

There was a moment of fear before I pulled at the cardboard. But I was beyond resisting by then. My mouth watered, my heart pounded, my adrenalin pumped. I wanted chocolate and I was going to have it.

Opening the box wasn't easy. Margaret still had the *sellotape* on it, for Janey's sake. That meant, I realized in disgust, she hadn't opened it, even to *lick* it.

Carefully, fat little hands sweating, I lifted the sellotape. But it was no good, the cardboard came with it. But I decided I was too excited to care and that I'd worry about that later.

Reverentially, I lifted the red, shiny ball of chocolate from the box and the smell hit me. Desperate to start cramming chunks of chocolate into my mouth, instead I forced myself to carefully peel away the tinfoil. Once off, the two halves fell apart, exposing the rustly cellophane bag of Beanos nestling within. Like Little Baby Jesus in the manger, I thought excitedly.

I had genuinely only planned to eat the Beanos but, once I'd finished them, I wanted more. *More.* LOTS MORE!

Why not? I asked myself. There's plenty. Anyway, she doesn't even *want* it.

I can't, I realized, she'll kill me.

You can, I coaxed, she won't even notice.

OK, I thought, a compromise quickly forming, I could eat one half of it, then cover the other half again with the red paper, stick it back on top of the wardrobe with the good side facing out and Margaret will never know.

Happily convinced, proud of how clever I'd been, I took one half of Margaret's Easter egg in my hand and, panting slightly from fear and anticipation, snapped it in half. Joyously, blood racing from fulfilment, I stuffed it into my mouth, barely tasting the chocolate before I swallowed it.

The frenzy was brief.

At about the time the last mouthful disappeared, the shame arrived. Guiltily, rapidly, I covered the remaining half with the tinfoil. I didn't want to look at it anymore.

No matter how hard I tried, I couldn't stop the shiny paper from looking puckered and wrinkled. But when I tried to smooth it out with my fingernail, I ripped it! My lust for sugar and chocolate had been sated. Fear, which couldn't coexist with such lust, reappeared.

With deep regret, I wished I hadn't touched anything. I wished I'd never even heard of Easter eggs. Margaret would know. And, even if Margaret didn't, God knew. I'd go to Hell. I'd burn and sizzle like the chips Mum made for us every Friday.

Sick with chocolate overload and nostalgia for ten minutes previously when the chocolate was still unconsumed, I rearranged the paper, and put the remaining half of the Easter egg back into the box. But it wouldn't stay upright because the other half wasn't there to support it against the back part of the box.

And now that the sellotape had half the box attached to it, it was no longer sticky.

Then I was really afraid. Really, really afraid. I would have given anything to put time back, before I'd eaten it. *Anything.*

Please God, help me, I prayed. I'll be good, I'll never do anything like this ever again. I'll give her my Easter egg next year. I'll give her my Cadbury's éclairs every Sunday, just don't let me get caught.

Eventually, I managed to jam the remains of the Easter egg into the front hole of the box. I closed it up and put it back on top of the wardrobe.

I convinced myself it looked fine. The front bit was perfect, you'd never know that the back bit no longer existed. Margaret's Easter egg was just like the man they found down in O'Leary's swamp who'd had his skull beaten in, I realized, not displeased with the image. The discovery had caused great excitement along our road and in at least four other roads either side of us. But our road was the centre of all the fuss because one of our citizens, Dan Bourke's father, found the corpse. At first, he thought the man was just having a little lie-down because his face looked normal. But when Mr Bourke lifted him up, his brains spilled all down his back. Dan Bourke said it was so disgusting that his dad got sick.

We weren't supposed to know about it, I heard Mum say, 'Ssshh, walls have ears,' and jiggle her eyebrows at us. But Dan Bourke, who had the inside track, told us everything. He said it happened with a poker and I subsequently took a great interest in our poker and wondered if that too could make a man's brains spill down his back. I asked my mother and she said, no, that our poker was a nice person's poker.

That didn't stop us playing 'Dead man in O'Leary's swamp' with it, for part of the summer. There was very little to it. One of us would pretend to hit the other on the head with the poker, then the one who'd been hit had to lie down for ages, then someone else had to be Mr Bourke and come along and pretend to puke. Once, Claire did the puking bit so well, she really *did* throw up.

That was great.

When Mum found out about our game, she took the poker away and we had to use a wooden spoon instead which wasn't half as authentic.

As it happened, the removal of the poker coincided with the Shaws getting a paddling pool and Hilda Shaw suddenly being inundated with invitations from wannabe new best friends.

Claire, Margaret and I all tendered bids. As usual, I wasn't even shortlisted. Claire and Margaret got as far as the second interview, then received the manila envelope telling them they'd been among the successful applicants.

So while they swanned off in their pink togs that had three rows of little frills around the bum bit, I had to stay at home in the back garden, odd-man-out as always, and play Annoy-The-Mother.

('Mummy, why is the sky?'

'Why is the sky *what*, Rachel?'

'No, just why is the sky?'

'You can't just ask why is the sky, it doesn't make sense.'

'Why?'

'It just doesn't.'

'Why?'

'Stop saying why, Rachel, you're annoying me.'

'Why?'

'Go and play with Claire and Margaret.'

'Can't, they're in Hilda Shaw's paddling pool.'

Pause.

'Mummy, why is the grass?'

'Why is the grass *what*, Rach . . .')

Anyway, Margaret's rearranged Easter egg looked fine on the wardrobe, so I thought. Reassured, I went to check on my mother. She was still out in the garden, talking to Mrs Nagle, on the other side. What do they talk about? I wondered. And how can they do it for so long? Grown-up people were funny. Especially the way they never wanted to *break* things. Or pinch people.

I loitered, hanging onto my mother's skirt, leaning against her. I thought she'd never leave, so to speed things up and get some attention I complained 'Mummy, I need to do a poo,' even though I didn't.

'Oh, blast!' she exclaimed to Mrs Nagle. 'I can't call my soul my own round here. Come on!' But as soon as we got inside she busied herself with Anna. I *still* didn't have her attention.

Who or what would I play with? And unbidden, the thought shimmered to me of the remaining half of Margaret's Easter egg. Just up the stairs. A few minutes' walk away. So near. It would be so easy to just . . .

No! I mustn't, I reminded myself.

But why not? Another voice wheedled. Go on, she won't mind.

So back I went to the scene of the crime. Over to

the wardrobe, up on the chair and down with the Easter egg.

This time I ate it all and there was none left to put in the box as a façade. The terror and shame returned, but worse, far, *far* worse than the last time.

Too late, I realized I was done for.

Heart thumping with fear, I knew I couldn't just leave the empty box sitting on the wardrobe. I looked around for places to dispose of the evidence while I wished I'd never been born. Under the bed? No way, most of our games took place under there. Behind the couch in the good room? No, when I'd hid Claire's Sindy doll there after I cut all its hair off, they'd found it alarmingly quickly. I finally decided on the coal-hole because it was no longer used. (I was still too young to make the connection between warm weather and no fires.)

And then I agonized about what I'd say when Margaret noticed the absence of her prize piece of confectionery.

Naturally, I had no intention of owning up. On the contrary. If I could have blamed anyone else I would have. But that didn't usually work either. When I'd tried to frame Jennifer Nagle for pulling the head off Margaret's crolly doll, it had all gone horribly wrong.

I'd suggest it had been stolen by a man, I decided. A scary man in a black cape who went round stealing Easter eggs.

'What are you doing out there?' Mum's voice made me jump and the pitter-pattering of my heart went into overdrive. 'Come on, Anna's in her go-car, if you don't get in here right now we'll be late collecting them from school.'

I prayed – although not with any great faith – that when

we got to the school, Margaret might have broken her leg or died or something handy like that.

No chance.

So on the way back I prayed that *I* might break my leg or die. I often prayed to break my leg, actually. You got loads of sweets and everyone had to be nice to you.

But I reached home, alive, with full bodily integrity, and almost gibbering with terror.

There was a brief moment when I thought I was saved – my mother couldn't open the back door. She jiggled and fiddled the key and still nothing happened. She pulled the handle towards her and tried again, but the door remained closed.

And a trickle of ominous fear began in me.

The grim muttering that Mum had been doing under her breath grew louder and less muttery and more shouty.

'What's wrong, Mummy?' I asked, anxiously.

'The lock seems to be fecking well broken,' she said.

Then I was really afraid! My mother never said 'fecking'. She gave out to Daddy when he did and told him to say 'flipping' instead. Things must be bad.

With a deep, abiding certainty, I knew that this was all my fault. It had something to do with me eating Margaret's Easter egg. I'd done a bad sin, it might even be a mortal one, although I wasn't really sure what that was, and now I was being punished. Me and my family.

I waited for the sky to darken the way it did in the pictures of Good Friday I'd seen, after Baby Jesus died.

'Isn't this desperate, Rachel?' Claire asked slyly. 'We'll never see the inside of our lovely house again.'

At that I burst into noisy, terrified, guilty tears.

'Stop it,' Mum hissed at Claire. 'She's bad enough as it is.'

'We'll get a man to fix the lock,' Mum told me impatiently. 'Stay here, mind Anna, while I run over to Mrs Evans to ring someone.'

As soon as she was gone, Margaret and Claire regaled me with horror stories of girls in their class in school who'd had the lock on *their* house broken and never got back into their homes.

'She had to go and live in the dump,' Claire said. 'And wear torn clothes.'

'And she had a cornflakes box for her pillow,' Margaret added.

'And her only toy was a piece of paper that she had to make into shapes, even though she'd had piles of dolls and fuzzy felt in her house.'

I wept terrified tears, appalled at what I'd destroyed. I was single-handedly responsible for depriving my family of a home. All for being a little pig.

'Can't we get another house?' I begged.

'Oh no.' They both shook their heads. 'Houses cost a lot of money.'

'But I've got money in my tin,' I offered. I would have given my life, let alone the fifty new pence I had in the red post-box tin that Auntie Julia had given me.

'But the tin is locked in the house,' Claire pointed out and the pair of them collapsed with malicious laughter.

Mum came back and said that we had to sit round the front so that the man would see us when he arrived. Neighbours offered us sanctuary and tea, but Mum said we'd better stay where we were. So Mrs Evans sent over a plate of banana sandwiches, which Claire and Margaret ate with gusto, while sitting on the grass. I couldn't eat a thing. I would never eat again. Especially not Easter eggs.

People passing up and down the road looked at us with interest, as they made their way home from school or work for their early-seventies-style repast. Hurrying past us for their instant mash, followed by instant whip, humming a David Cassidy song, resplendent in their acrylic tanktops, waiting for the Vietnam war to end and the oil crisis to kick in.

Normally, I would have been mortified by the state of our family sitting in the front garden eating banana sandwiches in September. It was OK in summer but once everyone had gone back to school, it was no longer appropriate. I always had a keen sense of what other people thought of me. But this time I didn't care. I didn't give a feck.

Hollow-eyed, racked with despair, I stared at the passers-by.

'Will the man really be able to let us back into our house?' I asked Mum again and again.

'Yesss! For Pete's sake, Rachel, yesssss!'

'And we won't have to go and live in the dump?'

'Where did you get this notion about the dump?'

'Do you really think the man will come?'

'Of course he will.'

But the man didn't come. And afternoon moved into evening, the shadows lengthened and the temperature dropped. And I knew what I had to do.

I had to confess.

Dad arrived home before the man did. It turned out there was nothing wrong with the lock, Mum had just been using the wrong key. By then, of course, it was too late. I'd spilled my guts in an attempt to right the imbalance I'd wrought in the universe.

38

I decided not to use the Easter egg story. I feared that it didn't paint me in a flattering enough light. So when group rolled around the following morning, I'd almost none of my life story written. Josephine was cross.

'I'm sorry,' I apologized, feeling as if I was back at school and hadn't done my homework. 'But I found it hard.'

Big mistake. Big, huge, enormous mistake with a double chin, thunder thighs and love-handles.

Josephine's eyes glinted as if she was a tiger moving in for the kill.

'Because there was so much noise in the dining-room,' I cried. 'I meant *that* kind of hard, not the other kind. I'll do it tonight.'

But she was having none of it.

'We'll wing it now,' she said. 'You needn't write anything, just tell us things in your own words.'

Shite.

'It might be better if I had a think about it and then wrote it,' I protested. I knew my protest was shoving me closer to having to do it, but I couldn't stop myself. If I'd had any sense at all, I'd have pretended to be delighted about the impromptu suggestion. Because then she wouldn't let me do it.

'No time like the present.' She smiled, knives in her eyes.

'Right,' she began. 'Your sister was in to see you on Sunday, is that right?'

I nodded, and clocked my body language. At the mention of Helen, I'd closed up. My arms folded tightly around my body, my legs crossed and curled. This wouldn't do. Josephine would draw all kinds of imaginary conclusions from the way I sat.

I peeled my arms off me and let them hang loosely by my side. I uncrossed my legs and opened them in such a relaxed way that Mike thought his luck was in. Hurriedly, uncomfortably aware that he'd had a good look at my gusset, I brought my knees firmly together.

'By all accounts this sister of yours caused a bit of a stir on Sunday,' said Josephine.

'She always does,' I said conversationally.

I shouldn't have. You could *smell* Josephine's excitement.

'Is that right?' she squeaked. 'And I hear she's a very attractive young woman.'

I winced. I couldn't help it. It wasn't that I minded Helen or any of my sisters being miles better looking than me, it was people's *pity* that got me down.

'And what's the age difference between the two of you?'

'Six years, she's nearly twenty-one,' I said, trying to keep any tone whatsoever out of my voice, so that nothing could be inferred.

'You sound very flat,' said Josephine. 'Does her youth upset you?'

I couldn't help but give a wry smile. It didn't matter what I did, *something* negative would be read into it.

Josephine looked questioningly at my smile.

'I'm just putting a brave face on it,' I joked.

'I know,' she said, deadly serious.

'No! Look, it's a joke . . .'

'You must have been very jealous when Helen was born,' Josephine interrupted.

'Actually, I wasn't,' I said, surprised. Surprised because Josephine was off-target. That she hadn't reduced me to a gibbering, crying wreck the way I'd seen her do to Neil and John Joe.

Nah haaaa. Hope she's good at dealing with failure.

'I can hardly remember when Helen was born,' I told her honestly.

'OK then, tell us what it was like when Anna was born,' she suggested. 'What age were you?'

All of a sudden, I wasn't so sure of myself. I didn't want to talk about when Anna came.

'What age?' Josephine asked again. I was annoyed with myself because, by not answering straight away, I'd let my feelings show.

'Three and a half,' I said, lightly.

'And you were the youngest until Anna came?'

'Um.'

'And were you jealous of Anna when she was born?'

'No!' How did she know? I'd forgotten she'd asked me the same about Helen, that her method was hit-and-miss rather than omniscience.

'So you didn't pinch Anna? Or try to make her cry?'

I stared at her, appalled. How on earth did she know? And why did she have to tell everyone in the room?

Everyone sat up. Even Mike had taken a break from trying to make eye-contact with my knickers.

'I suppose you hated Anna for taking attention away from you?' she suggested.

'No, I didn't.'

'Yes, you did.'

I was hot and sweaty. Squirmy with embarrassment and anger. Raging at being pitched back into that frightening world where my actions had had catastrophic results. I'd nearly have preferred the questionnaire to this.

I did *not* want to remember.

Even though it was always kind of there, half-remembered.

'Rachel, you were three years old, an age that child psychologists recognize as a very difficult one to cope with a new addition to the household. Your jealousy was *natural*.' Josephine had gone all gentle on me.

'What are you feeling?' she asked.

And instead of telling her to get lost, my mouth opened and the words, 'I'm ashamed,' tearfully sidled out.

'And why didn't you tell your mother how you felt?'

'I couldn't,' I said in surprise. New sisters were things I was supposed to get excited about, not resent.

'Anyway,' I added. 'Mummy was gone funny.'

I could feel everyone's interest move up a notch.

'She stayed in bed crying a lot.'

'Why was that?'

'Because I was mean to Anna,' I said slowly. My spirit shrivelled as I forced myself to say it. I'd made my mother go to bed and cry for six months because I'd been bold.

'So what did you do to Anna that was so terrible?'

I paused. How could I tell her and all the other people there how I'd pinched a tiny, defenceless baby, how I'd prayed for her to die, how I'd fantasized about throwing her in the bin.

'OK,' Josephine said, when it became clear I wasn't going to answer. 'Did you try to kill her?'

'Noooo!' I nearly laughed. 'Of course I didn't.'

'Well, you can't have been so bad, in that case.'

'But I was,' I insisted. 'I made Daddy go away.'

'To where?'

'Manchester.'

'Why did he go to Manchester?'

How could she ask? I wondered in shame and pain. Wasn't it perfectly obvious? That he'd gone away because of me.

'It was all my fault,' I blurted. 'If I hadn't hated Anna, Mummy wouldn't have cried and gone to bed, and Daddy wouldn't have got fed up with all of us and gone away.' And with that I horrified myself completely by bursting into tears.

I only cried briefly before saying 'Sorry,' and straightening myself up.

'Did it ever occur to you that your mother might have been suffering from post-natal depression?' Josephine said.

'Oh no, I don't think so,' I said, firmly. 'It wasn't anything like that, it was because of me.'

'That's very arrogant of you,' Josephine said. 'You were only a child, you couldn't possibly have been that important.'

'How dare you! I *was* important.'

'Well, well,' she murmured. 'So you think you're important?'

'No, I don't!' I interrupted, furious. That hadn't been what I'd meant at all. 'I never feel better than anyone else.'

'That's certainly not the impression you gave when you arrived at the Cloisters,' she said mildly.

'But that's because they're farmers and alcoholics,' I exploded, before I realized that I had said anything.

I could have cut my vocal cords out with a potato-peeler. 'I think you'll grant me that point.' She smiled graciously. 'You have the over-developed sense of self-importance that a lot of addictive personalities seem to have, *plus* the massively low self-esteem.'

'That's stupid,' I muttered. 'It doesn't make sense.'

'But that's the way it is. It's a recognized fact that people who become addicts often have a very similar personality type.'

'I see, so you're *born* an addict?' I said scornfully. 'Well, what chance do people have in that case?'

'That's one school of thought. In the Cloisters we see it slightly differently. We think it's a combination of the type of person you are and the life experiences you have. Take your case – you were less . . . *robust*, emotionally, shall we say, than others might have been. Not your fault, some people are born with, for example, bad eyesight, others are born with sensitive emotions. And you were traumatized by the arrival of a new sister at an age where you were easily damaged . . .'

'I see, so everyone with a younger sister becomes a cocaine addict?' I said angrily. 'In fact, I have *two* younger sisters. What do you make of that? Shouldn't I be a heroin addict as well as a cokehead? Good job I haven't got *three* younger sisters, isn't it?'

'Rachel, you're being facetious. But that's just a defence mechanism . . .'

She came to a halt as I howled like a hungry prairie dog.

'No more!' I screamed. 'I can't bear it, it's all such, such . . . CRAP!'

'We've touched on a deep well of pain here, Rachel,' she said calmly, as I nearly frothed at the mouth. 'Try and stay with those feelings instead of running away from them as you've always done in the past.

'We have a lot of work to do where you forgive the three-year-old Rachel.'

I moaned with despair. But at least she hadn't said those terrible, cringe-inducing words, 'inner child'.

'And as for the rest of you,' she finished, 'don't think that just because *you're* not carrying a huge burden of distorted childhood pain around with you, that you're not alcoholics or addicts.'

All through lunch I cried and cried and cried and cried. Proper crying, that disfigured and blotched my face. Not the fake, girly tears I'd produced for Chris the day I heard Luke had shopped me. But unstoppable, heaving sobbing. I couldn't catch my breath and my head felt light. I hadn't cried like that since I was a teenager.

I was filled with grief. Sorrow that went way beyond the heartbreak Luke had caused me. Sadness, deep, pure and ancient, had me helpless in its grip.

The others were really nice to me, giving me tissues and shoulders to roar on, but I was barely aware of them. I didn't care, even about Chris. I was in another place where all the raw poignancy that had ever existed was being pumped into me. I expanded to accommodate it, the more that came, the more I felt it.

'What's wrong?' a voice cherished. It might have been Mike. It might even have been Chris.

'I don't know,' I wept.

I didn't even say 'Sorry,' the way most people do when they're overcome with emotion in public. I felt loss, waste, irretrievability. Something was gone for ever and even if I didn't know what it was, it broke my heart.

A cup of tea appeared on the table in front of me and the tenderness of that gesture multiplied my grief tenfold. I sobbed louder and harder and felt like puking.

'Hob NOB?' Someone, who could only have been Don, screeched right into my ear.

'No.'

'God, she *is* in a bad way,' I heard someone murmur.

And, mercifully, I found myself sniggering.

'Who said that?' I gasped, through the tears.

It was Barry the child, and I laughed and cried and cried and laughed, and someone stroked my hair (probably Clarence who knew an opportunity when he saw one) and someone else circled their palm on my back, as if I was a baby who needed to break wind.

'It's nearly time for group,' someone said. 'Are you up to it?'

I nodded because I was afraid to be on my own.

'In that case . . .' Chaquie said, and swept me up to our room and produced all kinds of mad stuff, like Beauty Flash and Three Minute Repair to mend my disfigured face. It was rather counter-productive because the feel of her gentle fingers on my skin set the tears flowing again in a river that washed away the expensive creams as soon as they were smoothed on.

In the dining-room, after group, Chris pushed through the sympathetic throng around me. I was glad that Chaquie and the others made way for him so unquestioningly. It showed they knew Chris and I had a special bond. He smiled a smile that was only for me and raised his eyebrows in an 'Are you OK?' way. From the concern in his pale blue eyes, I'd clearly been imagining any lessening of his interest in me.

He sat down, his thigh against mine. Then tentatively, nervously slid his arm along my back and around my shoulder. Very different from the quick casual hugs he usually gave me. The downy hairs on the back of my neck stood on end. My heart quickened. This was the most intimate contact we'd had since the day he'd wiped my tears away with his thumbs.

I desperately wanted to put my head on his shoulder. But I sat rigid, unable to pluck up the nerve. *Go on*, I urged myself. I'd begun to sweat slightly with desire for him.

Eventually, as butterflies came to life in my stomach, I managed to lean my head against him, savouring the clean, detergent smell of his chambray shirt. He didn't smell like Luke, I thought idly. Then felt a short brief throb of loss before I remembered that Chris was just as delicious as Luke. We sat quietly and still, Chris's arm tight around me. I closed my eyes and, for a few moments, let myself pretend it was a perfect world and he was my boyfriend.

It reminded me of an earlier, more innocent age, when the most a boyfriend did was put his arm around you and – if your luck was in – kissed you. The enforced decorum demanded by the Cloisters was sweet and romantic. It touched, rather than frustrated me.

I could sense his heartbeat and it was going faster than usual. So was mine.

Mike walked past and leered. Misty ambled after Mike and, when she caught sight of me and Chris, glared with such venom it almost removed the top layer of skin from my face.

As embarrassed as if we'd been caught *in flagrante delicto*, I wriggled away from Chris. Deprived of his clean, male, scent and the feel of his big shoulder and arm through the soft fabric of his shirt, I felt bereft. I hated Misty with a passion.

'So tell me,' Chris said, seemingly unaware of the condemnatory glares, 'why were you so upset earlier?'

'Josephine was asking me in group about my childhood.' I shrugged. 'I don't know why I got so upset. I hope I'm not going mad.'

'Not at all,' Chris protested. 'It's perfectly normal. Think about it. For years you've suppressed all your emotions with drugs. Now that the suppressants have been taken away, *decades*' worth of grief and anger and all kinds of stuff will resurface.

'That's all it was,' he finished kindly.

I rolled my eyes. I couldn't help it. Chris saw me.

'Oh no, I forgot.' He laughed. 'You don't have a problem with drugs.'

He got up to leave. *Please don't*, I wanted to say.

'Funny though,' his voice drifted back to me, 'that you're acting just like someone who has.'

39

After tea that evening, we were given a talk. We often had talks, usually given by one of the counsellors or Dr Billings. But I never listened. That night was the first time I'd ever paid attention, happy to be distracted from the deep grief I'd been swamped with.

The talk was about teeth and it was given by Barry Grant, the snappy, pretty little Liverpudlian woman who called people 'divvys' a lot.

'All rice,' she ordered, in a booming voice that didn't fit with the rest of her. 'Keeyalm jown, keeyalm jown.'

We calmed down because we were afraid she'd head-butt us. She began her lecture which I found very interesting. For a while at least.

Apparently people with drug and food disorders often had terrible teeth. Partly because of their debauched lives – ecstasy-takers ground their teeth into nothingness; and bulimics, who rinsed their teeth with hydrochloric acid every time they puked, were lucky to have a tooth left in their head; as were any alcoholics who did a fair bit of throwing up.

As well as the debauchery, Barry Grant said, they all neglected to go to the dentist. (Apart from the inmates on the other end of the scale, who went to the doctor, dentist and hospitals *far too much*, on all manner of trumped-up charges.)

There were lots of reasons why addicts didn't attend the dentist, Barry Grant went on to explain.

Lack of self-respect was one; they didn't think they were worth looking after.

Fear of spending money was another. Addicts prioritized their spending so that most of it went on drugs or food or whatever it was they were keen on.

Fear itself was the biggest reason, she said. Everyone was afraid of going to the dentist but addicts never faced up to it. The way they never faced up to *anything* frightening, she said. Whenever they felt afraid they drank a bottle of whiskey or ate a lorry-load of cheesecake or put their month's wages on a dead cert.

All fascinating stuff that had me nodding and 'hmmm'ing. If I wore glasses I would have taken them off and swung them knowledgeably by the arm. Until out of the blue it occurred to me that I hadn't been to the dentist for about fifteen years.

More, probably.

About nine seconds after that I got a twinge in one of my back teeth.

By bedtime I was demented with pain.

'Ache' came nowhere near describing the metallic, hot, electric sparks of screaming torment that shot up into my skull and down into my jaw. It was horrible.

I kept leaping up to grab my jar of dihydrocodeine and cram my head full of precious, soothing painkillers. Then stumbling back in confusion as I realized there weren't any to take. That all those gorgeous little removers of pain were sitting in the top drawer of my dressing-table in New York. Always assuming that it *was* still my dressing-table, that Brigit hadn't brought in a new flatmate and thrown my stuff out on the street.

That was far too unpleasant to contemplate. Luckily my toothache was so phenomenally awful that I couldn't think about anything else for long, anyway.

I tried to bear the pain. I managed a good five minutes before I shouted 'Has anyone got any painkillers?' to the dining-room at large.

It took me a moment to figure out why everyone guffawed with laughter.

I went, almost on my knees, to Celine, who was the nurse on duty that night.

'I've got a terrible pain in my tooth,' I whimpered, my hand cradling my jaw. 'Can I have something for the pain?

'Some heroin would do nicely,' I added.

'No.'

I was stunned.

'I didn't mean it about the heroin.'

'I know. But you still can't have any drugs.'

'They're not *drugs*, they're just things to kill pain, you know that!'

'Listen to yourself.'

I was bewildered. 'But it hurts.'

'Learn to live with it.'

'But . . . but this is barbaric.'

'You could say that life is barbaric, Rachel. Regard this as an opportunity to coexist with pain.'

'Oh God . . .' I spluttered, 'I'm not in group now.'

'It doesn't matter. When you leave here you won't be in group anymore and you'll still have pain in your life. And you'll find out that it won't kill you.'

'Of course it won't kill me, but it hurts.'

She shrugged. 'Being alive hurts, but you don't use painkillers for that.

'Oh no, I forgot,' she added. 'You always have, haven't you?'

The pain was so bad that I thought I was going mad. I couldn't sleep with it and for the first time in my life, I cried with pain. *Physical* pain, that is.

In the middle of the night, Chaquie could take no more of me tossing around and scratching my pillow in frantic torment and she marched me downstairs to the nurses' station.

'Do something with her,' she said, loudly. 'She's in agony and she's keeping me awake. And I've Dermot coming tomorrow to be my Involved Significant Other. I'm finding it hard enough to sleep.'

Celine reluctantly gave me two paracetamol, which didn't even make a dent in the pain and said 'You'd better go to the dentist in the morning.'

The fear was nearly as great as the pain.

'I don't want to go to the dentist,' I stammered.

'I bet you don't.' She smirked. 'Were you at the lecture earlier this evening?'

'No,' I said, sourly. 'I decided to skip it and went for a few pints down in the village instead.'

She widened her eyes. She wasn't pleased.

'Of course I was at it! Where else would I be?'

'Why don't you regard going to the dentist as the first grown-up thing you've ever done,' she suggested. 'The first frightening thing you've ever managed to do without drugs.'

'Oh, for God's sake,' I muttered under my breath.

Even though one of the nurses, Margot, went with me, I was the envy of the inmates.

'Will you try to ESCAPE?' Don wanted to know.

'Of course,' I mumbled, my hand to my swollen cheek.

'They'll set the leopards looking for you,' Mike reminded me.

'Yes, but if she hides in the river they'll lose the scent,' Barry pointed out.

Davy sidled up to me and discreetly asked me to put a both-ways on the two-thirty at Sandown Park.

And on the three o'clock.

And on the three-thirty.

And on the four o'clock.

'I don't know if I'll be near a bookie's,' I explained, feeling guilty. Anyway, I wouldn't have known what to do, I'd never been in a bookie's in my life.

'Will you be handcuffing me?' I asked Margot, as we got into the car.

She just threw me a disdainful look and I cringed. Humourless hoor.

To my alarm, as soon as the car left the grounds, I started to shake. The real world was strange and scary and I felt I'd been away for a very long time. That annoyed me. I hadn't been at the Cloisters for even two weeks and already I was institutionalized.

We went to the nearest town, to Dentist O'Dowd, the dentist the Cloisters used whenever an inmate's teeth started playing up. Which, according to Margot, happened all the time.

On the walk from the car to the surgery, I felt that everyone in the entire town was looking at me. As if I was a maximum-security prisoner who'd been released for the morning to attend his father's funeral. I felt different, alien. They'd know, simply by looking at me, where I'd just come from.

I clocked a couple of youths standing on a corner. I

bet they sell drugs, I thought, adrenalin starting up in my veins as I wondered how I could lose Margot.

No chance.

She frogmarched me along to the dentist, where, from the air of contained excitement, I gathered I was expected. The fourteen-year-old receptionist couldn't take her fascinated little eyes off me. I could see what she was thinking. I was a weirdo, a misfit, someone from life's margins. Bitterly, I supposed she'd been elbowing the nurses all morning, saying 'What'll she be like, the *drug addict*?'

I felt deeply misunderstood. She was passing judgement on me because I was at the Cloisters, but she'd got it all wrong, I wasn't one of *them*.

As she sniggered none-too-discreetly, she got me to fill out a form.

'And the bill will be sent to the, er, CLOISTERS?' she asked with pretend discretion. All the people in the waiting-room jerked awake with sudden interest.

'Yes,' I mumbled. Although I felt like saying, 'Could you make that a bit louder. I don't think the people in Waterford quite heard it.'

I felt old and jaded, annoyed by the idealism of the young receptionist. She probably thought that she'd never, ever, in a million years end up in the Cloisters and that I was really thick to let it happen to me. But I'd been like her once. Young and stupid. I'd thought I was invulnerable to life's tragedies. I'd thought I was too smart to let anything bad happen to me.

I took my seat and settled in for a long wait. It might have been several lifetimes since I'd been to the dentist, but I knew the routine.

Margot and I sat in silence reading torn copies of the

Catholic Messenger, the only available reading material. I tried to cheer myself up by reading the 'Intentions offered' page, where people pray for whatever bad thing they're experiencing to pass.

To know that other people were miserable always helped.

Now and then another spasm of toothache took hold and I would press my tormented face into my hand, keen softly and yearn for drugs.

Whenever I looked up, all the eyes in the place were fastened onto me.

Of course, as soon as the receptionist said 'Dentist O'Dowd will see you now,' the pain went away. That always happened to me. I created a big song and dance about pains, injuries etc. But the minute I got to the doctor all symptoms disappeared, leaving everyone thinking I had Munchausen's Syndrome.

I slunk into the surgery. The smell alone was enough to make me feel faint with fear.

Luckily Dentist O'Dowd was a plump jolly man who was all smiles, instead of the Doctor Death figure I'd imagined.

'Clamber up there, good girl,' he urged, 'and let's have a look.'

I clambered. He looked.

While he banged around in my mouth with a spiky little metal thing and a mirror, he began a conversation that was supposed to put me at my ease.

'So you're from the Cloisters?' he asked.

'Aaarr,' I tried to nod.

'Alcohol?'

'Go.' I tried to indicate a negative with wriggles of my eyebrows. 'Grugs.'

'Oh, drugs, is it?' I was relieved he didn't sound disapproving.

'I often wonder how you know you're an alcoholic,' he said.

I tried to say 'Well, no point in asking me,' but it came out sounding 'Ell, oh oi i akn ee.'

'Obviously, if you end up in the Cloisters, then you *know* you're an alcoholic, that tooth is on its last legs.'

I tried to sit up in alarm, but he didn't notice my distress.

'It's not as if I drink every day,' he said. 'If we do a root canal we might be able to save it. And no time like the present.'

A root canal! Oh no! I didn't know what a root canal was but from the way other people carried on when they had to have one, I was led to believe that it was something to fear.

'Not every *day*, as such,' he carried on. 'Most evenings, though, ha ha.'

I nodded miserably.

'But never when I need a steady hand with the drill the next day. Ha ha.'

I looked longingly at the door.

'But once I start I can't stop, do you know what I mean?'

I nodded fearfully. Best to agree with him.

Please don't hurt me.

'And at some stage in the evening, I find I can't get drunk anymore. D'you know what I mean?'

He didn't need any confirmation from me.

'And the depression *afterwards*. Sure, don't *talk* to me.' He was passionate. 'I often wish I was dead.'

He had stopped his banging and scraping, but left the mirror and the spiky thing in my open mouth. He rested his hand against my face, in thoughtful mode. He was a man settling in for a long conversation.

'I've actually thought about suicide after a hard night,' he confided. I felt saliva slowly make its way down my chin, but was afraid I'd seem unsympathetic if I wiped it. 'Dentists are the profession with the highest rate of suicide, would you believe?'

With wriggles of my eyebrows and flashes of my eyes I tried to convey compassion.

'Sure, it's a lonely kind of an oul' life, looking at the inside of people's mouths, day-in-day-out.' The saliva had turned into a veritable niagara. 'Day-in-day-feckin'-out.'

He affected a whiny voice, ' "My tooth hurts, can you fix it, I've a pain in my tooth, do something about it." That's all I hear, teeth, teeth, teeth!'

Yikes, a looper.

'I went to a couple of A A meetings, just to see, you know.' He looked appealingly at me. I looked appealingly back.

Please let me go.

'But it wasn't for me,' he explained. 'Like I said, I don't drink every day. And never in the mornings. Except when the shakes are very bad, of course.'

'Aaar,' I said encouragingly.

Talk to your captor, build a relationship, try to get him on your side.

'My wife has threatened to leave if I don't lay off the sauce,' he went on. 'But, if I did that, I feel there'd be nothing left for me, that my life would be over. I might as well be dead. D'you know what I mean?'

Then he seemed to come to.

And he regretted unburdening himself, sorry that he had weakened himself in my eyes.

He quickly sought to redress the balance.

'Now I'm just going to give you a little injection, but you'd know all about them, wouldn't you?' he chortled nastily. 'I love getting you drug addicts here, most people are terrified of needles! Ha, ha, ha.

'Here, do you want to do it yourself? Ha, ha, ha.

'Did you bring your tourniquet? Ha, ha, ha.

'At least you won't have to share your needle with anyone else, ahahahahaha!'

I sweated with dreadful fear because he was wrong, I was terrified of needles. And terrified of the horrors that lay ahead.

My whole body went rigid as he lifted up my lip and pricked the sharp point of the needle into the tender skin of my gum. As the cold liquid flooded into my flesh my hair stood on end in revulsion. The pain from the needle puncture intensified the longer he held it in my gum. I thought it would never end.

I'll wait five more seconds, I willed. But if he hasn't finished by then, I'll have to make him.

Just as the pain reaching screaming point, he stopped.

But by then I had realized I was too much of a coward to have any more dental interference in my mouth, that I'd rather take my chances with the toothache.

However, just as I was about to push past him and run out, a gorgeous tingly numbness crept through my lip and one side of my face, radiating outwards with soothing fingers.

I had a rush of elation. I *loved* that feeling. Relaxing back into the chair, I savoured it. What a wonderful thing novocaine was. I only wished it could be applied to my entire body. And my emotions.

The rush didn't last long, though. I couldn't help

remembering all kinds of awful stories I'd been told about dentists. How Fidelma Higgins went into hospital to have her four wisdom teeth taken out under general anaesthetic. Not only did they not take out the four offending teeth, but they removed her perfectly healthy spleen instead. Or once, when Claire had to have an extraction, the roots of the tooth were so strong she swore the dentist had the sole of his shoe resting on her chest before he got good enough leverage to wrest it out. And of course, every dentist phobic's favourite – the scene from *Marathon Man*. I hadn't even seen *Marathon Man*, but it didn't matter. I'd heard enough about it to feel sick to the stomach at my vulnerability to excruciating pain at the hands and drill of this very scary man.

'Right, that mouth should be frozen by now.' Dentist O'Dowd interrupted the horror film playing in my head. 'We might as well get going.'

'Wh . . . what exactly is a root canal?' I'd rather know what was happening to me.

'We take the inside of the tooth out. Nerve, tissue, lock, stock and barrel!' he said cheerily. And with that he started drilling with the gusto of a man putting up shelves.

Knowing what he was about to do made my shoulders clench to my temples with horror. It would hurt something ferocious. And there would be a hole right through to my brain, I thought with a pit-of-my-stomach kick of queasiness.

A short time later the nerves in all my other teeth began singing and jumping. I forced myself to wait until I couldn't bear it any longer – about four seconds – before waving my hand to flag him down.

'All my other teeth are hurting now,' I managed to mumble.

'Already?' he asked. 'It's amazing how fast you drug addicts metabolize painkillers.'

'Do they?' I was surprised.

'You do.'

He gave me another injection. Which hurt more than the first one, the tender skin already bruised and broken. Then he revved up his drill as if it was a chainsaw and off he went again.

It took hours.

Twice I had to ask him to stop because the pain was so awful. But twice I squared my shoulders, looked him in the eye and said 'I'm OK now, carry on.'

When I finally stumbled back into the waiting-room to Margot, my mouth felt as if it had been run over by a truck, but the toothache had gone and I was triumphant.

I had done it, I had survived and I thought I was great.

'I wonder why my teeth flared up now?' I mumbled thoughtfully on the drive back.

Margot looked at me carefully. 'I'm sure it's no coincidence,' she said.

'Isn't it?' I said in surprise.

'Think about it,' she said. 'I believe you had a bit of a breakthrough in group yesterday . . .'

Had I?

'. . . but your body is trying to divert you from facing your emotional pain by giving you physical pain instead. Physical pain, being, of course, far easier to deal with.'

'Are you saying I'm putting this on?' I demanded hotly. 'You go back and just ask that dentist and he'll tell you . . .'

'I'm not saying you're faking it.'

'But then wha . . .?'

'I'm saying that your desire to avoid looking at yourself

and your past is so powerful that your body is colluding with you by giving you something else to worry about.'

For the love of Jayzis.

'I'm *sick* of so much being read into everything,' I said viciously. 'I had a toothache, that's all, no big banana.'

'You were the one who questioned the timing in the first place,' Margot reminded me mildly.

We drove the rest of the way in silence.

On our return to the Cloisters I was greeted as if I'd been away for several years. Nearly everyone jumped up from their lunch, although Eamonn and Angela weren't among their number, and shouted things like 'She's BACK' and 'Nice one, Rachel, we've missed you.'

In honour of my mutilated mouth, Clarence absolved me from my team pot-washing duties. Which felt as wonderful as the time we were all sent home from school because the pipes had burst. But even not having to scrub pots didn't compare with the rush I got when Chris threw his arms around me.

'Welcome home,' he croaked. 'We'd given you up for dead.'

A little warm bubble of happiness went 'pop!' in my stomach. He must have forgiven me for rolling my eyes at his advice yesterday.

I was inundated with questions.

'What's the world like out there?' Stalin wanted to know.

'Is Richard Nixon still president?' Chris asked.

'Richard Nixon is president?' Mike demanded. 'That young whippersnapper? When I arrived here he was still only a senator.'

'*What* are you talking about?' Chaquie's face was

340

scrunched up in disgust. 'That Nixon chap is long gone. It's years since he was . . .'

She paused. Barry the child was semaphoring her.

'It's a joke,' he said. 'You know, a *joke*? Ha. Ha. Look it up in the dictionary, you dozy wagon.'

'Oh,' said Chaquie, dazedly. 'Nixon. What am I thinking of? But with Dermot coming this afternoon I'm not really myself . . .'

To everyone's alarm she looked as if she was going to cry.

'Relax the head, missus,' said Barry, hastily moving away. 'You're not really a dozy wagon.'

The room held its collective breath for a few tense moments until Chaquie's face brightened.

As soon as we had the all-clear I regaled everyone with great tales of being under the knife.

'Root canals?' I scoffed. 'No bother.'

'But didn't it HURT?' Don wanted to know.

'Nothing to it,' I boasted, electing to draw a veil over the scenario of me crying tears of agony while in the chair.

'And weren't you ascared?' John Joe asked.

'I couldn't afford to be scared,' I said primly. 'It had to be done and that was that.'

Which was almost true, I realized in surprise.

'How much did it cost?' Eddie asked the question that mattered most to him.

'God, I don't know,' I said. 'Not very much, I'm sure.'

Eddie laughed darkly. 'What shower did you come down in? You must have been born yesterday. Those dentists and doctors won't even give you the time of day without charging through the nose for it.'

'Eddie,' I decided to take a risk, 'do you know something? You're a bit neurotic about money.'

40

And so to group.

Down the hall we charged, Eddie shouting after me 'Just because I know the value of money . . .!'

Dermot and his wig were already there. Now that I knew he had one, I couldn't take my eyes off it. It was so *obvious*. And big enough to deserve a chair of its own.

Dermot had dressed up in honour of being Chaquie's ISO. He wore a double-breasted suit that tried and failed to bring his enormous stomach to heel. From the side, he looked like a big letter 'D'.

Chaquie was perfumed and immaculately made-up, even more than usual.

I was curious and sceptical about what Dermot would have to say for himself. I believed Chaquie when she said that all she drank was a Bacardi and coke now and then with the girls. Chaquie was not Neil, and I was sure she hadn't deliberately misled me about the extent of her alcohol problem the way he had.

In fact, I suspected that Chaquie, irritating and all as she was with her in-your-face right-wing views, had led a fairly blameless life.

I was surprised to find my attitude had changed since I'd first met Chaquie. I now had a strange grudging fondness for her.

Josephine arrived and we all straightened up and calmed down.

She thanked Dermot for coming and said 'Perhaps you'd like to tell us a bit about Chaquie's drinking.'

Idly, I stuck my tongue into my tooth. I couldn't stop doing that. I was extremely proud of myself and my root canal.

'She was always fond of drink,' Dermot said, having none of Emer's reticence.

Chaquie looked dismayed.

'She was always giving me guff about having to have whiskey for a cold or port and brandy for an upset stomach or . . .'

'Can I help it if I'm often not well?' Chaquie interrupted, her accent posher than ever.

Josephine glared and Chaquie subsided.

'As I said,' Dermot sighed, 'she was always fond of it, but she hid how bad things were until she'd got the ring on her finger. And then she started making a show of me.'

Chaquie exclaimed. Josephine silenced her with a frown.

'What kind of show?'

'I work very hard,' Dermot said. 'Very hard. I'm a self-made man and I built the business up from nothing . . .'

'And you did that all by yourself, did you?' Chaquie interrupted, her voice unexpectedly shrill. 'Well, you couldn't have done it without me. It was my idea, getting the upright sunbeds.'

'It was not!' Dermot said irritably. 'I read about them in a catalogue long before you ever saw them in that place in London.'

'You didn't! That's a pure lie. You didn't even know how they worked.'

'I'm telling you,' Dermot emphasized each word with a chop of his midgety hand, 'I read about them.'

'Perhaps we could come back to this,' Josephine murmured. 'We're here to talk about Chaquie's drink problem.'

'We could be here all week in that case,' Dermot said with a bitter snort.

'Fair enough. Please carry on,' Josephine invited. He needed no second bidding.

'I didn't know how bad it was for a long time because she was drinking on the sly,' he said. 'Hiding bottles and saying she had a migraine when she was really going to bed with a bottle of drink.'

Chaquie's face was bright red.

'And feeding me a pack of lies. I found about twenty empty bottles of Bacardi at the end of the garden and she said she knew nothing about it and blamed it on some lads from the corporation estate.

'And we had the bank manager and his wife over for dinner one night. I was trying to get a loan off him to extend the premises and Chaquie starts singing, "Happy birthday, Mr President, coocoocachoo," like she's Marilyn Monroe, wiggling her backside and giving him a faceful of cleavage . . .'

I flicked a glance at Chaquie. Her face was a picture of horror. I felt a shameful mixture of pity and glee.

'. . . she'd been drinking all afternoon. But when I asked her about it, she lied and said she was stone-cold sober. When a child could have seen she was drunk. Then she went out to the kitchen to serve the smoked salmon roulade and never came back. We waited for hours, and I was highly embarrassed and trying to keep the conversation going with Mr O'Higgins. And when I went looking for her, where did I find her, only in bed, out cold . . .'

'I wasn't well,' Chaquie mumbled.

'Needless to say,' Dermot said with satisfaction, 'I didn't get the loan. After that her drinking got worse so that she was langers every night of the week and most of the days too. I couldn't depend on her for anything.'

'You'll never let me forget that business with the loan, will you?' Chaquie exclaimed. 'And it had nothing to do with me not being well. It was because the figures didn't add up and I told you that before you ever went to O'Higgins with your stupid proposals.'

Dermot ignored her.

'And all the time I was building up the business,' he continued. 'Working night and day to have the premier beauty salon [pronounced 'premeer beauty salong'] in South County Dublin.'

'I worked night and day too,' Chaquie exclaimed. 'And I was the brains behind most of the ideas. I thought up the idea of the special offers.'

'You did in your . . .!' Dermot paused. 'You did not.

'We do special offers, d'you see.' He looked at Misty and me as he said this. 'A whole day's pampering, the works. An aromatherapy session, a mud-wrap, a go in the sauna, a pedicure or manicure, and a complementary danish pastry, all for fifty quid. A saving of fifteen pounds if you have the manicure or eighteen if you opt for the pedicure.'

Josephine opened her mouth, but she was too late.

'We also cater for male clients [pronounced 'clee-yongs'].' Dermot was off with more of his salesman's patter. 'We've found that the Irish man is far more discerning about his appearance and, while in the past a man might be considered a nancy-boy if he took care of his skin, nowadays it's the done thing, really. I myself . . .'

he placed a tiny, pudgy hand on a broken-veined cheek '. . . use skin-care products and feel the better for it.'

Clarence, Mike, Vincent and Neil stared at Dermot stonily. John Joe, however, looked interested.

'Dermot,' Josephine said sharply, 'we're here to discuss Chaquie's drinking.'

'He's always at that,' Chaquie interrupted, looking at Dermot with hatred. 'It's so embarrassing. Once, at Mass, when he was offering the woman next to him the sign of peace, he looked at her nails and said she'd benefit from a manicure. In the Lord's house! Did you ever?'

'I've a living to make,' Dermot said hotly. 'If we were relying on you, we'd have gone bust a long time ago.'

'Why is that?' Josephine asked, guiding the conversation back to Chaquie's failings.

'I had to stop her working in the salong because she was jarred on the job and upsetting the clee-yongs. And getting things arseways and booking people in for sunbeds straight after leg waxes and everyone knows you can't do that and that you're running the risk of being sued and once you get a bad name, sure you're sunk . . .'

'Is that true?' Josephine interrupted. 'Were you drunk at work, Chaquie?'

'Indeed, I wasn't.' She folded her arms and pushed her face onto her neck, which gave her a double-chinned look of sanctimonious outrage.

'Ask any of the girls who work there,' Dermot interrupted passionately.

'Ask any of the girls who work there,' Chaquie mimicked nastily. 'Or one girl in particular, isn't that right?'

You could feel everyone's interest expand dramatically.

'I know exactly what you're doing, Dermot Hopkins,'

Chaquie went on. 'Make me out to be an alcoholic, deny that I ever contributed to the business, get your *girlfriend* in to agree with you and leave me with nothing.'

She turned to the room at large. 'We weren't even married for a year before he started having affairs. He hired the girls in the salon not on their abilities but on . . .'

Dermot was trying to shout her down, but she shouted even louder. '. . . BUT ON THE SIZE OF THEIR CHESTS. And if they wouldn't sleep with him he sacked them.'

'You lying bitch.' Dermot was shouting at the same time as she was.

'And now he's decided he's in love with one of them, a little nineteen-year-old called Sharon with her eye on the main chance.' Chaquie's face was flushed and her eyes were glittery with pain and rage. She took another deep breath and shrieked 'And you needn't think she's in love with you, Dermot Hopkins. She's just looking for a cushy number. She'll make a bloody eejit of you.'

Chaquie's accent had changed. The surburban tones had disappeared and a rough Dublin accent had appeared in its place.

'And what about your carry-on?' Dermot's voice was sopranoesque with rage.

'What carry-on?' Chaquie screeched back at him.

Josephine was trying to calm things down but she hadn't a hope.

'I know about you and the fella that put down the new carpet.'

Things got a bit confused after that because Chaquie leapt up and tried to smack Dermot. But from what we could gather, Dermot was implying that the new carpet wasn't the only thing that got laid. Chaquie hotly contested his version of events and it was impossible to know who was telling the truth.

In disarray, the session ended.

And the first person to reach Chaquie and put their arms around her and ferry her off for tea was me.

41

Over the next couple of group sessions, in a scenario that I now recognized, Josephine delved into Chaquie's psyche and pulled all kinds of rabbits out of the hat.

It became clear that Dermot, unpleasant and all as he was, hadn't been lying.

Josephine pressed Chaquie and pressed her until finally she came clean about how much she drank. When she finally owned up to drinking a bottle of Bacardi a day, Josephine questioned her further until she admitted supplementing the Bacardi with brandy and Valium.

Then Josephine searched for reasons.

She worried away at two things – Chaquie's obsession with her appearance, and her insistence that she was a good, respectable, upper-middle-class citizen. And, as usual, Josephine's instincts were spot-on.

It all came out. Chaquie's dirt-poor origins in an over-crowded corporation flat in a neglected area in Dublin. Her lack of education, the fact that she had cut off all contact with her family because she was afraid they'd show her up in front of her new-found middle-class friends and her terrible fear that she'd have to go back to that background of deprivation. It became clear that she had nothing except Dermot.

She relied on him totally and resented him bitterly for it.

Chaquie admitted that she had never felt at ease with

her friends, that she was afraid they'd realize that she was the fraud she felt she was.

I looked at her, at her lovely skin and her golden hair and her perfect nails and was in awe of how successfully she had reinvented herself. I would never have believed there was so much pain and insecurity rampaging about below her sleek, glamorous surface.

Then Josephine questioned her about the carpet-man. And eventually, after a question and answer session that I found excruciatingly painful to listen to, Chaquie admitted that she had indeed christened her new carpet by having sex on it with the carpet-layer.

The details weren't salacious and fascinating, they were simply sordid. She said she'd only done it because she'd been drunk and desperate for affection.

My heart bled with pity. I expected people my age to behave that way. It seemed far more pathetic and shocking for someone like her, of her age and station, to do it. With passionate force it struck me that I didn't want to end up like Chaquie.

This could be you, my head said.

How? another part of me asked.

I don't know, the first voice said in confusion. *I just know it could be.*

'I wanted to die with the shame when I sobered up,' Chaquie choked.

Not content with that, Josephine needled away until Chaquie admitted having lots of anonymous sex with anyone she could get her hands on, particularly tradesmen.

It was astonishing, especially in light of the judgemental, Catholic stance Chaquie had always taken. But then again, I realized, as I began to get the hang of this whole Cloisters thing, maybe it wasn't astonishing at all. She desperately papered over the cracks of her shame by pretending to be the well-behaved, respectable person she wished she was.

I was staggered by it all.

On Friday evening, I noticed the awful grief that I'd had earlier in the week had lifted. Because it had returned.

'The tooth didn't distract you for too long, did it?' Margot smiled at me as I sat at the dinner table crying buckets.

I should have thrown my plate of bacon and cabbage at her, but I just cried even more.

I wasn't alone.

Neil was sobbing terribly. That afternoon in group Josephine had finally broken through his denial. Suddenly he saw what everyone else in the whole world could see. That he was an alcoholic who could rival his much-hated father in the atrocity stakes. 'I hate myself,' he sobbed into his hands. 'I hate myself.'

Vincent was also in floods due to the examination of his childhood Josephine had subjected him to in morning group. And Stalin was bawling his eyes out because he'd got a letter from Rita saying that, when he got out of the Cloisters, he wasn't to come home. She'd applied for a divorce.

The dining-room had so many weeping people in it, it was like a crèche.

'She's met someone else,' Stalin bawled. 'Someone else to . . .'

'To break her ribs,' Angela interrupted, her tiny, cupid's bow mouth pursed even smaller in her fat face.

Oh dear. Angela had been stricken by a dose of *NIJ* – New Inmate's Judgementalness. Just wait until she had an

Involved Significant Other who would tell her group about how she had broken her mother's arm with a karate chop to stop her reaching for the last slice of Viennetta, or something like that. Then she wouldn't be so self-righteouser-than-thou.

I felt sorry for her.

On Friday evening, as usual, the new list of team duties went up on the notice board. The minute Frederick secured it to the cork with a red thumbtack, we all surged at it, desperate to see our fate, as if it was a list of war dead. When I saw that I was on Vincent's team and, worse again, that that meant breakfasts, I was very, very upset. OK, so I was upset *anyway*, but now I was *really* upset. So upset that I didn't want to shout at anyone, I just wanted to go to bed and not wake up.

Chris approached me with a box of tissues.

'Tell me things,' I gave him a watery smile, 'distract me.'

'I shouldn't really,' he said, 'you should *stay with the pain* and . . .'

I lifted my cup of tea threateningly.

'Easy.' He smiled. 'Only having a laugh. So what's up?'

'I'm on Vincent's team,' I said, telling him the one tangible piece of misery I knew. 'And I'm afraid of him, he's so aggressive.'

'Is he?' Chris looked over at Vincent who was still sobbing his eyes out at the far end of the table. 'He doesn't look very aggressive to me.'

'Well he used to be,' I said doubtfully. 'The first day I came here . . .'

'That was two weeks ago,' Chris pointed out. 'A week is a long time in psychotherapy.'

'Oo-oh,' I said slowly, 'you mean you think he's different now . . .

'But he was *so* threatening,' I felt I should remind Chris.

'People change in here,' he replied equably. 'That's what the Cloisters is about.'

That irritated me.

'Tell me how you ended up in this madhouse.' I'd always been curious about Chris and his past and wished I was in his group so I'd know more about him. But I'd never before had the courage to ask him something so brazen.

To my surprise, a look of pain skittered across Chris's face, like a breeze blowing over a field of corn. I was so used to thinking of him as totally in control and omniscient that his vulnerability scared me.

'This isn't my first time in here, you know,' he said, pulling a chair close to me.

'I didn't know,' I said. That shocked me. It meant his drug habit must be very advanced.

'Yeah, I was in here four years ago and I didn't listen to anything. But this time I'm doing it properly and I'm going to get my life back together.'

'Were you very bad?' I asked nervously. I liked him too much to want to hear stories of him rolling round in puke, a needle stuck in his arm.

'It depends on what you mean by "bad",' he said with a twisted little smile. 'While my life wasn't exactly *Trainspotting*, with me shooting up smack and living in a squat, it wasn't a fulfilled, useful life either.'

'What, er, drugs did you take?'

'I mostly smoked hash.'

I waited for him to continue with a long list: crack, angel dust, heroin, jellies . . . But he didn't.

'Just hash?' I croaked.

'Believe me,' he grinned, 'it was enough.'

I hadn't thought you could be a drug addict without using needles. Nervously, I asked another question.

'How did you manage for money?' I hoped he'd say he'd dealt drugs or been a pimp.

'I had a job.' He seemed surprised.

'But . . .' I was confused. 'You don't sound like a drug addict to me.'

He opened his mouth and reeled off 'I spent nearly every night on my own, off my head. Most days in work I was unable to perform. I was forever preoccupied with where the next smoke was coming from. I never wanted to do anything like go to the pictures or go for a meal because it might take time away from being stoned.'

He paused and said lightly 'Is that bad enough for you?'

'No.' I was still confused.

'OK,' he took a deep breath, 'I owed money to everyone, I was a friend to no one. And it wasn't just that I lived my life badly. What went on in my head wasn't good either. I always felt on the edge of things, not good enough, you know?'

I nodded cautiously.

'I got into the wrong kind of relationships with the wrong kind of people. I didn't care about anyone except myself. And I didn't care much about me either.'

Anxiously, I wondered what kind of relationships he was alluding to. 'I've used drugs to deal with every unpleasant thing that life has ever thrown at me. When I came in here they told me that I had the emotions of a twelve-year-old.'

'How do they know?' What kind of measuring process did they use?

'Because that's when I began using drugs. You only grow up by living through the shit that life throws at you. But, whenever life threw problems at me, I just got out of it. So my emotions stayed stopped at twelve.'

'I can't see what's wrong with being twelve, actually.' I gave a little laugh to let him know I was having a joke.

He wasn't amused.

'It means I've never had a sense of responsibility. I've let people down, I've stood people up . . .'

I was beginning to dislike him, he was far too uptight and humourless.

'I've told millions and millions of lies to protect my own skin, so that people wouldn't be annoyed with me.'

That *really* put me off him. How weak!

'What age did you start using drugs at?' he surprised me by asking.

Me?

'I was about fifteen,' I said stumbling over my words. 'But I was only ever a social user. I certainly never did any of those things that you described, taking drugs on my own, owing money, being irresponsible . . .'

'Didn't you?' he asked, with a face-splitting grin.

'What's so funny?' I was annoyed.

'Nothing.'

I decided to change the subject. 'What will you do when you get out of here?' I asked.

'Who knows? Get a job, behave myself. You never know.' He gave me a wink. 'I might even go to New York.

And while I'm there, see this Luke bloke and sort him out.'

Stars filled my eyes and I disappeared on a wild fantasy. A vision of me arriving back to New York with Chris on my arm, going into the Cute Hoor with him, both of us hysterically in love, Chris no longer with the emotions of a twelve-year-old, the pair of us mad keen to party. A handsome, well-matched couple.

Naturally we would lie about where we had met.

More visions flitted past. Luke puking with grief. Luke begging me to take him back. Luke going bonkers with jealousy and trying to hit Chris . . . it usually came back to Luke trying to hit Chris. One of my favourites.

42

The night Luke stormed out of my kitchen – oh yes, even though he'd done it with cold control, he'd *stormed* nevertheless – the course of our true love stopped running at all and actually came to a complete standstill. It spent over two weeks doing nothing but loitering on a street corner, waiting for dole day, half-heartedly whistling at local girls coming home from their shifts at the factory.

And of course Daryl was no compensation.

When he'd arrived so unexpectedly on my doorstep and scared Luke off, he hadn't even come to see me. He was only there because his dealer had been busted. He was doing the rounds of everyone he knew on the island of Manhattan as he looked for an alternative source of drugs. Once upon a time, people used to recommend hair-dressers to each other. Or plumbers. Or even personal trainers. Now it's dealers. In different circumstances I might have thought this was charming.

Good-neighbours-New-York-close-of-Millennium style. Instead of dropping by to borrow a cup of sugar, they come to borrow a couple of grams of coke. But in the wake of Luke's departure I thought little was charming.

And of course I didn't have hide nor hair of a drug to give to Daryl.

But I knew a man who did.

As it happened, due to the feelings of wretchedness engendered by Luke's leaving, I was keen to see Wayne

357

myself. So, I cynically used Daryl's desperation to my own advantage. Daryl had money for drugs, but didn't know where to get them; I knew where to get them, but didn't have the wherewithal to do so.

We needed each other.

I placed a phonecall to Wayne, then Daryl and I sat back and waited. I even managed to cheer up slightly. OK, so Luke hated me again, but Daryl was wearing really nice clothes. A pair of ultra-groovy purple velvet flairs that were at the cutting edge of attractive menswear.

It wasn't his fault they made him sweat so much.

But he *did* have a very glamorous job.

'Apart from Jay McInerney, do you know any other authors?' I asked, leaning forward and hoping he was a tit-man, it was the best I could offer him.

'Um yeah,' he sniffed, his eyes sliding away from mine. 'I know lots.'

'How does it work?' I asked, ducking and diving my head, trying to follow his escaping glance. 'Do you have authors specifically assigned to you?'

'Yeah,' he said, with a furtive little look, that gave me a crick in my neck as I tried to meet it. 'That's what happens.'

'So who are yours?' I asked, despairing of making proper eye contact with him. *What was his problem?* 'What have your most successful books been?'

'Let's see,' he said thoughtfully. At his words I suddenly felt a rush of pleasurable anticipation. It was great to be talking to someone who knew famous people.

He didn't disappoint me.

'You've heard of the writer, Lois Fitzgerald-Schmidt?' he asked, in a tone that implied that of course I had.

'Yes!' I said enthusiastically.

Who?

'You have?' Daryl asked enthusiastically back.

'Of course,' I said, glad to have achieved an air of animation. It seemed to please him.

'I was in a key position for the marketing of her book, *Gardening for Ballerinas*, which made the *New York Times* list in the spring.'

'Oh yes, I've heard of it.' In fact, as I remembered, it had won novel of the year award, or something similar. I smiled across at Daryl, proud to be with someone who had such an interesting and successful career.

Thinking fast, I wondered if I should pretend I'd read the book. I could throw in a few vague sentences like 'Wonderful lyrical use of language', and 'Marvellous strong imagery'. But, on balance, I was afraid I wouldn't be able to sustain an entire conversation like that.

All the same, in New York it was very important to read the books that were currently fashionable. Or at least to pretend to. I'd even heard of people offering a service where they would read the book for you then present you with a résumé of it. And for an extra charge they would give some recommended phrases to throw around at glamorous dinner parties ('Derivative plagiarism' and 'Yes, but is it *art*?' and 'I liked the cucumber scene').

So I said apologetically to Daryl 'I haven't got round to reading it yet. I've bought it, of course, and it's in a pile by my bed that I keep trying to work my way through. It's hard when you're as busy as I am . . .'

Naturally, there wasn't a single syllable of truth in that sentence. The only book beside my bed was *The Bell Jar*, which I was reading for the umpteenth time.

'I'm going to start as soon as I've finished *Primary Colors*,' I promised him, as I wondered if *Primary Colors* was still happening. It wouldn't do to get such a thing wrong.

'So tell me,' I smiled winningly at him. '*Gardening for Ballerinas*, will it change my life? What's it about?'

'Er,' said Daryl awkwardly. 'You know . . .?'

I moved closer to him, wondering at his reticence. It was obviously a controversial book addressing what? Incest? Satanism? Cannibalism?

'It's about . . . well . . . *gardening*. For, em, ahem, ballerinas. Well, not just ballerinas, obviously,' he added hurriedly. 'The bending and squatting could apply to *all* dancers really. We're a non-élitist publishing house.'

My mouth made shapes as if I was enunciating vowels. A, then O, then A again, then O.

'You mean it's not a novel?' I finally managed.

'No.'

'It's a gardening manual?'

'Yes.'

'And what number did it get to in the *New York Times* best-seller list?'

'Sixty-nine.'

'And what form did the work you did in your key marketing position take?'

'I packaged up the books and sent them to the shops.'

'Goodbye, Daryl.'

43

Not as such. I didn't actually, there and then, utter the words 'Goodbye, Daryl'. Not to *him*. But I said them to myself. Especially as he let slip that the lovely loft apartment he'd taken me to after my party wasn't even his.

So, even though we spent the night together, and most of the next morning, I didn't hold out any hopes that Daryl and I would be shortly applying for a joint mortgage. I only put up with him, and all the crap he talked, for my share of the drugs.

Of course the stingy creep didn't look too pleased when it became obvious that he wasn't going to make his escape from me with his full two grams intact.

But I just thought 'Tough, you owe me.'

At a very late stage in the evening, it dawned on me like a punch in the face that I'd been thinking of *Boating for Beginners,* not *Gardening for fecking Ballerinas.*

In the days that followed I heard nothing from Luke. My head kept saying soothingly *he'll call.* But he didn't.

Poor Brigit was forced to come out with me every night, as I scoured the city looking for him. Everywhere we went, even if it was only down to the grocery store for ten tubes of Pringles, I was in a state of constant alert and full make-up.

I shouldn't have let him escape, I reiterated frantically, over and over. I've made a terrible mistake.

We never saw him. Which wasn't fair because in the days when I didn't give a damn about him I could hardly put a foot outside my front door without tripping over him or one of his hairy friends.

In the end I had no choice but to co-opt a select few, a *very* select few, friends to assist with the search. But still no luck. If I met, say, Ed, at the Cute Hoor and he told me he'd seen Luke not ten minutes previously at Tadgh's Boghole and Brigit and I tore at breakneck speed to the Boghole, all that would be there when we arrived would be an empty glass of JD, a smoking ashtray and a still-warm seat with a Luke's-arse-shaped indentation in it.

Very frustrating.

I finally ran into him on the day I like to call Black Tuesday. That was the day I got sacked and Brigit got promoted.

I'd known for ages that my days were numbered at the Old Shillayleagh, and I found it hard to give a damn. I hated working there more than life itself. And ever since I'd cut out an article on impotency cures and sellotaped it onto my boss's locker, with a Post-it saying 'I thought you might find this helpful,' I'd felt the unemployment line moving several steps closer.

All the same, being sacked wasn't nice.

It became even less nice when I got home and found Brigit dancing jigs round the apartment because her salary had been doubled and she'd been given a new office and a new title. Assistant deputy vice-president of her department. 'I only used to be *junior* assistant deputy vice-president, look at how far I've come,' she said with glee.

'Lovely,' I said bitterly. 'I suppose now you'll go all

New York and macho, getting to the office to start work at four in the morning, working till midnight, bringing files home with you, skipping holidays, thinking you're great.'

'I'm glad you're so happy for me, Rachel,' she said quietly. Then she went into her bedroom and slammed the door so hard, the front wall nearly fell off the apartment block. I stared bitterly after her. What was *her* problem, I wondered self-righteously. *She* wasn't the one who'd just been sacked! Talk about salt being rubbed into my wound. I threw myself onto the sofa, savouring my well-deserved self-pity.

I'd always felt that there was only a finite amount of good fortune in the universe to go round. And Brigit had just hogged our apartment's entire quota, leaving none for me, not a single atom.

Selfish bitch, I thought angrily, as I scoured the place looking for a drink or a drug. Just look at poor me, poor *unemployed* me, who'll probably have to get a job in McDonald's, if she's lucky. Well, I just hope Brigit's not able for the job and that she has a nervous breakdown. That'll show her, the smug cow.

I opened all the cupboards as I searched for a bottle of rum that I was sure I'd seen somewhere, but then I remembered I'd drunk it the previous night.

Ah shite, I thought, savouring my misfortune.

In the absence of artificial mood-enhancers, I tried to console myself by thinking that Brigit would have no life, that they'd work her into the ground, that there was a high price to be paid for a successful career. Then terrible insecurity snatched me in its claws. What if Brigit leaves me? I thought, in panic. What if Brigit moved into a lovely, mid-town apartment that had air-conditioning and an in-house gym? Then what would I do? Then where would I go? I couldn't afford to keep up with that kind of rent.

In that moment, I had a St Paul on the road to Damascus style revelation. I suddenly saw what side my bread was buttered on.

I got off the couch, swallowed my misgivings and gently knocked on Brigit's bedroom door.

'I'm sorry, Brigit,' I pleaded, 'I'm a selfish hoor, I'm really sorry.'

A wall of silence.

'I'm sorry,' I said again, 'It's just that I was sacked myself this afternoon and I felt a bit, you know . . .'

Still no response.

'Come out, Brigit, *please*,' I begged. 'I'm sorry, I really am.'

The door was flung open and Brigit stood there, her face raw from crying.

'Oh Rachel,' she sighed. And I couldn't place her tone. Forgiveness? Exasperation? Pity? Weariness? It could have been any of them, but I hoped it was forgiveness.

'Let me take you out and buy you champagne to celebrate,' I offered.

She hung her head and traced a pattern on the floor with her toe.

'I don't know . . .'

'Oh go on,' I urged.

'OK,' she conceded.

'Just one prob,' I said talking very quickly. 'I'mkindof-skintatthemoment,butifyouloanmesomemoneyI'llpayyou backassoonasIcan.'

Quietly, a bit too quietly for my liking, actually, she sighed and agreed.

I insisted we went to the Llama Lounge.

'We must, Brigit,' I said. 'It's not every day one of us gets promoted. Certainly not if it's me, hahaha.'

At the Llama Lounge the management had put up a sign beside the inflated sofa that said 'People with bare legs sit here at their own risk.' Brigit and I both took one look at it and said in unison, 'We're not sitting there!' I hoped this of-one-mindness meant Brigit had forgiven me. But conversation remained stilted. I strove hard, overstrove, probably, to let her know how happy I was about her good fortune, but it was an uphill battle.

In the middle of me telling her again how pleased I was for her, she looked at the door and murmured 'Here's your fella.'

Please God, let it be Luke, I prayed, my innards atremble. And God obliged, but with a rider clause. It was indeed Luke.

However, he was accompanied by none other than the exquisite Anya, skinny, tanned, almond-eyed Anya.

The first thought that jumped into my head was, if he's good enough for Anya, he's good enough for me.

Not that I was being given the choice, of course. Luke threw a non-committal nod over at Brigit and me, but didn't come any closer.

My world bellyflopped while Brigit wondered aloud 'What's up with Cool-Arse Luke?'

Luke and Anya looked very intimate. Like they'd just clambered out of bed. Surely I was imagining it? I wondered anxiously. But their faces were very close together, turned into each other. Then their thighs touched. As I watched aghast, he slid his arm along the back of her chair, lightly touching her slim, yet muscular shoulders.

I'd known he fancied Anya, all along, I thought resentfully. I'd just bloody well known it. And him giving me all that crap about what a nice girl she was.

'Stop staring,' Brigit hissed.

I jerked and kind of came to.

'Swop places with me,' Brigit ordered. 'You're to sit with your back to him. And take that starving baby look off your face. And put your tongue back in, it's banging off your knees.'

I did what I was told and then wished I hadn't. So I tried to get Brigit to stare by proxy for me.

'What's he doing now?' I asked her.

She flicked a glance at them. 'He's holding her hand.'

I moaned softly.

'Still?' I asked a few seconds later.

'Still what?'

'Is he still holding her hand?'

'Yes.'

'Oh Christ.' I could have cried. 'What does he look like?'

'About six one, dark hair . . .'

'No! What does his *face* look like? I mean, does he look happy, does he look like he's mad about her?'

'Suck that down,' Brigit curtly indicated my drink. 'We're leaving.'

'No,' I protested in a low fierce voice. 'I want to stay. I have to stay and watch them . . .'

'No.' Brigit was very firm. 'No way, it does no one any good. And let this be a lesson to you. The next time you meet a man as sexy and nice as Luke Costello, maybe you won't shag it up.'

'Do you think he's sexy and nice?' I asked, in huge surprise.

366

'Oh course I do,' she said, astonished.

'Well, why didn't you say?'

'Why? Do you need me to endorse everything for you before you'll let yourself like it?' she asked.

Stupid wagon, I thought, annoyed. She'd only been promoted a matter of hours and already she was acting like she was someone's boss.

I mourned him for some days. I felt the loss acutely. But I didn't hold out any hope because I knew I couldn't compete with Anya. No way. I knew my limitations.

I devoted my time to glancing around for a job. The effort I put into it wasn't deserving of the word 'looking'.

With my poor employment history and lack of higher education my options were strictly limited. However, I managed to stumble over a job in another hotel. Not as nice as the Old Shillayleagh, not of course that the Old Shillayleagh *was* nice. My new place of work was called the Barbados Motel. I had no idea why. It was nothing like Barbados, unless people pay for their time in Barbados by the hour.

My boss, Eric, was one of the fattest men I'd ever seen, and was called The Head Hauncho on account of his colossal love-handles. Most of the other staff were illegal immigrants because of the management's penchant for paying below the minimum wage.

However, it was a job.

In other words, hard labour, misery and tedium all rolled into one.

After my first day there I staggered home, exhausted and depressed, and as I got in the phone was ringing.

'Yes?' I demanded, none-too-civil, keen to work off my filthy humour on whoever was on the other end.

There was a brief – loaded – pause, then Luke's voice, like a caress, said 'Rachel?' And my charcoal world sparked into blazing light.

Instinctively I knew that this was no enquiries phone call along the lines of 'I can't find my Beavis and Butthead jocks and I'm wondering if I left them at your place. Any chance you'd give them a wash and drop them round to me?'

On the contrary.

From the tone of his voice, just from the way he'd said 'Rachel?' – as if he was stroking me – I knew everything was going to be all right.

Better than all right.

I'd been certain I'd never hear from him again. I almost wept with relief, with joy, with deliverance, with gratitude for my second chance.

'Luke?' I said. See the way I didn't go 'Daryl?' or 'Frederick?' or 'Beelzebub?' or some other man's name, the way I would have if I'd still been playing games with him?

'How are you?' he asked.

Call me babe, I yearned.

'Fine,' I said. 'Well, I was sacked from my job and I've got a new one but it's in a horrible place and I think it's used by prostitutes and the money is poxy, but I'm fine. And how are you?'

He gave a little laugh, a warm, friendly, I-think-you're-great laugh and I felt as if I loved him.

'Any chance I could take you out for dinner?' he asked.

Take you out for dinner. *Take* you for dinner. So much is conveyed with that one word. It means, I like you. I'll take care of you. And, most importantly of all, I'll *pay* for you.

I wanted to say, 'But what about Anya?' and for once in my self-destructive life I managed to do the right thing and kept my fool mouth shut. 'When?' I asked. *Now, now, now!*

'Tonight?'

I suppose I should have pretended I was busy. Isn't that one of the golden rules to make sure you snare your man? But I had no intention of letting him slip through the net again.

'Tonight would be lovely,' I said sweetly.

'Oh, and sorry I didn't come over to you and Brigit the other night,' he added. 'Anya's fella had just ditched her and I was trying to cheer her up.'

My cup spilleth over.

44

It was a date, a proper one.

He said he'd collect me at eight-thirty and take me to a French restaurant. I felt a slight frisson of alarm at his talk of French restaurants because only hicks and out-of-towners went to French restaurants and Turkmenistanian was the thing to impress a girl. But then I thought, so what.

I got ready slowly and calmly. The kind of churning excitement that I usually associated with Luke was absent. Instead a steady quiet anticipation hummed within me.

I had butterflies in my stomach, but they were asleep. They stretched and turned occasionally, just to remind me that they were there.

Of course, I reminded myself, Luke could be stringing along me and Anya and God knows how many others. But I just *knew* he wasn't. I didn't know where such deep abiding certainty came from, but I didn't doubt it.

We'd gone through so many twists and turns; sleeping with each other after the Rickshaw Rooms, him asking me out, me refusing, me coming onto him at my party, *him* refusing, him looking out for me everywhere, meeting him in the Llama Lounge, having mind-blowing sex, Daryl arriving and Luke leaving in a huff. After all of that, the mutual overtures and rejections, for him to still want to take me out and for me to still want to go, it meant there was some little glimmer of understanding.

We'd arrived at a plateau, where we both knew enough about the other, even the bad bits, *especially* the bad bits, and still wanted to proceed.

In preparation for my free French meal, I dressed demurely.

On the outside at least.

I wore what I called my grown-up dress. I called it that because it wasn't black, it wasn't made of lycra and you couldn't see the line of my knickers under it. It was a dark grey, nun-like shift. Because of these qualities I'd thought it was a total waste, but Brigit had bullied me into buying it. She'd said it would come in very handy one day. I'd said I wasn't planning on dying, entering a convent or being up in court on a murder charge. But, as I admired my demure, yet strangely unrevolting reflection, I admitted she'd been right.

It got better. I wore high heels *and* I put my hair up. Normally I could only do one or the other, not both, not unless I enjoyed towering over people like the Incredible Hulk. But Luke was man enough for me at my zenith.

Underneath my cassock I had struggled into black stockings and a suspender belt. A sure sign that I was mad about Luke. Because surely no one could wear such underwear if they weren't planning on taking it off very shortly? Uncomfortable and unnatural, that's what it was. I felt as ridiculous as a drag artist.

Eight-thirty arrived and so did Luke. I took one look at him, dark-eyed, clean-shaven and citrus-fragranced, and my butterflies woke up en masse and started bickering over whose turn it was to make the coffee.

He looked a lot sleeker than I'd ever seen him before. Acres less hair and denim than was usually in evidence. I realized it meant he was taking me seriously and I brimmed with pleasure.

As he crossed the threshold, I braced myself to be snogged to within an inch of my life. But, to my surprise, he didn't kiss me. Momentarily startled, I rallied gamely and declined to descend into the pit of depression that beckoned so warmly. I didn't think, *He doesn't fancy me*. I knew he fancied me, I would have staked my life on it.

He politely sat on the sofa and politely didn't push me to the floor and ravish me. How strange it felt to be in the same room as each other for more than five seconds and still be wearing clothes!

'I'll be ready in a minute,' I promised him.

'Relax,' he said.

I could feel his eyes following me as I bumped awkwardly round the flat looking for my keys. Here a hipbone crunched against the counter, there an elbow skinned on the doorhandle. Nothing like the feeling of being watched by a man I desire to bring on my incipient clumsy oafness. Eventually I turned and demanded in contrived exasperation, 'What?'

I knew it'd be good, see.

'You look . . .' he paused, '. . . beautiful.'

Correct answer.

I didn't know the restaurant he took me to, hadn't even heard of it. But it was lovely. Thick carpets, lighting subdued to the point of sulkiness, and humble, murmuring waiters with French accents so exaggerated that they couldn't even understand each other.

Luke and I barely spoke all evening.

But this didn't indicate discord. In fact, I'd never felt so close to anyone, ever. We couldn't stop smiling at each other. Huge, face-splitting, glowing smiles right into each other's eyes.

He continued with the polite, not-wrestling-me-up-against-a-wall behaviour that he'd kicked the evening off with. Instead, we had more cab-paying and door-opening and non-contact-ushering than you could shake a stick at. And with every gesture, we grinned out loud.

When he politely held my hand and helped me into the cab, we both beamed our heads off. Then after we'd arrived at La Bonne Chère (The Good and Dear) he deferentially helped me out of the cab and we gave each other dazzling smiles that rushed up from our toes. A brief pause while he paid the cab, then we turned to each other, crinkling our eyes so much we could barely see.

He said 'Are you right?' – the Irish version of 'Shall we?' – extended his elbow for me to hook, and off we swung into the restaurant. Where we were greeted enthusi-astically, if indecipherably, by the waiters. And *that* made us catch each other's eyes and smirk.

We were led to a table that was so discreet and dimly lit that I could barely see Luke. 'This do for you, babe?' he murmured. I nodded gleefully and beamed my assent. Anything would have been wonderful.

There was a brief moment of awkwardness when we sat down opposite each other, because after all, we'd never been in such a situation before. There's only one thing more shy-making than the first time you go to bed with a man and that's the first time you go to dinner with a man. Luke attempted conversation with a cheery 'Well?' And I thought about replying, but then that joyous feeling filled me up and spilled out at my mouth, forcing it to burst into another ecstatic grin, and I realized there was no need to say anything. Luke replied to my smile by

373

return of post and we both dazzled each other like a pair of village idiots. And so we remained, smiling and glazed, until the frog waiter arrived and unctuously proffered the menus.

'I suppose we'd better . . .' Luke indicated the menu.

'Oh right,' I said, and tried to concentrate.

After a few seconds I looked up and found Luke staring at me and we both burst into smiles again. Slightly embarrassed, I dropped my eyes. But I couldn't stop myself looking up at him once more and he was still staring at me, so we both had another smile for our trouble.

Again, I felt delighted, yet embarrassed, and murmured 'Stop.'

And he murmured back 'Sorry, can't help it, you're so . . .'

Then we both had a lovely, warm little chuckle and he reindicated the menu and said 'We'd really better . . .'

And I said 'We really should . . .'

I felt as if I would burst with the happiness of being with him. I was sure I must bear some resemblance to a bull-frog, puffed-up to the max with joy.

He ordered champagne.

'Why?' I asked.

'Because . . .' he paused, looking at me speculatively.

'Because . . .' he said again, a smile in his eyes. I held my breath because I was certain he was going to say he loved me.

'Because you're worth it,' he finally said.

I gave a secret little smile. I'd seen his face, I knew how he felt about me. And he knew that I knew.

All night I felt quite calm on the surface. But under that I was pleasurably breathless. Every part of me. I felt like my lungs were barely managing to inhale, my heart just sustained a beat, my blood dragged itself sensuously through my veins. I'd slowed into a different rhythm, drugged by what I felt for him.

All my sensations were heightened. My nerves were raw, exposed, on the outside. Mine was the Pompidou Centre of central nervous systems.

I took pleasure in each breath that I drew. I savoured every bump of my heart in my chest, every flutter in my stomach.

Each breath felt like a victory, as my chest rose and fell, then after an infinitesimally-too-long pause, rose and fell again. Like conquering a small hill. And then another. And then another.

'That nice?' He nodded at my *pomme au fenêtre* or whatever it was.

'Yairs, lovely,' I murmured, managing to swallow a good two or three atoms of it.

There was a lot of picking up our forks and letting them hover over the food – which probably was delicious, but neither of us seemed to be able to eat – then smiling at each other like two morons. Then putting our forks down and catching each other's look before exploding into wreaths of smiles again.

Apart from the sensation that my stomach and oesophagus had been filled with quick-setting concrete, I felt floaty and elated.

We both seemed to know that what we felt for each other was a fragile, precious thing that had to be carried carefully and kept very still. We couldn't disturb it or unsettle it, but despite its lack of activity we were both completely aware of it. Aware of little else.

There was no need to outdo each other with funny stories because we both knew we could tell funny stories.

There was no need to lep on each other and tear our clothes off, that would happen all in the fullness of time.

The only rockyish patch in the whole night occurred when Luke said 'How's Daryl?'

'Look,' I said awkwardly, electing to put some of my cards on the table, 'nothing happened with me and Daryl.'

'I'm sure it didn't,' he said.

'How?' I said, a small bit miffed.

'Because he's *gay*,' Luke laughed.

'Get lost!' I was the colour of a tomato. Although, once I thought about it, it would explain a lot.

Except shouldn't it have been 'Dada', rather than 'Mama'?

'But he devotes too much of his energy to his drug habit,' Luke said in disgust, 'for him to have *any* kind of sexuality.'

'Oh right,' I said, not quite sure what to say, but fairly sure I should say something.

All evening a quiet stream of desire had gently sparkled over the bedrock of certainty we felt for each other. As Luke paid the bill (See? *See?* Didn't I say? I'll *take* you.) some of the winter snows melted and the torrent increased.

When we got outside into the humid night, Luke asked politely 'Would you like to walk or get a cab?'

'Walk,' I said, all the better to build more anticipation.

On the way, he didn't even hold my hand, just did the kind of hovery action with his hand over the small of my back, which I thought was very cute. The enforced separation, the so-near-and-yet-so-farness of being next to him, but not touching, served to heighten my longing for him.

As we commenced our final descent to the front door

of my apartment block, I had a surge of relief. About bloody time, I thought. The lack of physical contact with him had put a greater strain on me than I'd realized. Joyfully, I geared up for the 'Will you come in for coffee, f 'naar, f 'naar?' scenario.

I speeded up my steps and was all set to burst into the building and start running up the stairs, when he slowed down. Then stopped. He pulled me in out of the way of passing pedestrians and kissed me on the cheek. I was dying to grab him by the crotch, but it had been such a lovely, *contained* date that I forced myself to wait a few minutes longer.

'Thank you for a wonderful evening,' he murmured at me.

'You're welcome,' I said. 'Thank you.'

I smiled politely, but I was thinking impatiently, enough of the messing, let's hurry upstairs so you can dash me to the floor and stick your hand up my skirt, like you usually do.

'I'll see you soon?' he asked. 'Give you a ring tomorrow?'

'Fine,' I said, but my elation had started to drain away, as if a plug had been pulled. He couldn't seriously be going to call it a night, could he? The decorum of the evening had been all fine and dandy, but only because I hadn't for a second thought it was real. And had I really gone to all the time and effort of putting on stockings and a suspender belt for me to be the person to remove them?

'Goodnight,' he said, then he leant down and gave me a very brief kiss on the mouth. His lips lingered just long enough for it to feel like a sacred moment. Then he pulled away and my head was full of dizziness and stars.

'Oh, before I forget,' he said, and handed me a little parcel that seemed to have appeared out of nowhere. Then without further ado – or more appropriately a*don't* – he turned on his heel and strode off down the street, leaving me staring slack-jawed after him.

For Christ's sake, I thought in disbelief. I mean, for *Christ's* sake.

I gave him a few minutes to turn around and grin and say 'Ha ha, only joking, do you want to see my knob?' But he just kept walking.

All I could see was his back getting further and further away from me and the sound of his boots becoming fainter. Then he turned the corner and I couldn't see or hear anything.

Still I waited, hoping to see his head appear back around the corner as if it was on a stick, but nothing doing.

When I finally accepted that I had no other option, I stamped up the stairs, disappointment bitter in my mouth. 'What was his game?' I muttered. Seriously, just what the hell was he up to?

Desperate for some clues as to Luke's motives, I tore open the little parcel he'd given me, far too agitated to appreciate the beautiful wrapping paper and the shiny little bow on it. But all it was was a book of Raymond Carver's poems.

'*Poems?*' I screeched, in disgust. 'I want a *ride*.' And I threw the book at the wall.

I slammed and banged things around the apartment. Brigit, the bitch, wasn't home, so I had no one to complain to.

Viciously, I ripped off the saucy underwear, berating myself for putting it on in the first place. I should have known I was tempting fate. I felt as if the lacy suspender belt and silky stockings and the little knickers were all having a good laugh at me. 'You'd think she'd have learnt by now,' they chuckled to each other. Bastards.

Eventually, at a completely loose end, I realized I had no option but to go to bed. Fully certain that I was too revved up to get even a minute's sleep, I threw my grown-up dress on the floor and kicked it round the room a bit. (I'd already hung it up, but I went back into the wardrobe and took it off the hanger, and kicked the crap out of it, as I searched for a scapegoat for my lone status.) In the middle of me breathlessly promising the dress that that was the last time it would ever see the light of day, the phone rang.

'Who the hell is that?' I wondered, hoping it would be a wrong number so I could shout at them.

'I'm not finished with you yet,' I threatened the grown-up dress, where it cringed against the wall, as I went to answer the phone.

'HELLO,' I roared aggressively into the mouthpiece.

'Er, is that you Rachel?' a man's voice asked.

'YES,' I admitted belligerently.

'It's Luke.'

'AND?'

'Sorry, I didn't mean to disturb you, I'll talk to you tomorrow,' he said humbly.

'No wait! Why are you ringing?'

'I was worried, you see, after tonight.'

I said nothing, but my heart was beating quickly with relief.

'I thought I was doing the right thing,' he said quickly. 'Trying to be a gentleman, I wanted to change the pattern with you and me, you know, to move things forward. But then after I got home I thought maybe I wasn't clear enough, and that you might just think I don't like you anymore when I'm mad about you, so I thought I'd ring you, then I thought it might be too late and you'd be asleep, maybe it *is* too late and you're asleep . . .'

'What are you trying to say?' By now I was very excited. I could feel his anxiety, his desire to do the right thing. Was a declaration of love on the cards? Was he going to ask me to be his girl?

Then he stopped being serious and the laugh reappeared in his voice. 'I suppose a ride is out of the question?'

Insulted to the core and bitterly disappointed, I slammed the phone down.

I gibbered with outrage. *Gibbered,* so I did. 'Can you *belie* . . .? Did you hear what he just *said*?' I demanded from the room at large and my grown-up dress in particular.

'The cheek of him; the *cheek* of him.'

I shook my head in disbelief. 'If he thinks I'll give him the time of day after that sort of behaviour, he has another think coming . . .'

I sighed in a more-in-sorrow-than-in-anger way and enjoyed another appalled shake of my head.

'*Honestly* . . .' I exhaled in disgust.

Six seconds later I found myself picking up the phone.

Of *course* a ride wasn't out of the question.

45

Another weekend. Two days free from the fear of the questionnaire.

Despite that relief, my emotions were still in complete disarray.

Terrible sadness came and went, came and went. I was actually glad when I was angry or heartbroken about Luke, because at least I could identify the feeling.

Saturday morning kicked off with cookery, as always.

And, of course, we had the usual scuffle involving Eamonn and a foodstuff, this time a tin of cocoa powder, which culminated in Eamonn being led away, as he invariably was on a Saturday morning.

We all covertly watched Angela, wondering if – *hoping*, really – she'd do something similiar. But Angela was nothing like Eamonn, she'd behaved herself beautifully at the previous week's session.

In fact, if it wasn't for her breathtaking girth, you'd never know she had a problem with nosh because she *never* seemed to eat. I had overheard her telling Misty that she had terrible trouble with her glands and a criminally slow metabolism. Which could have been true.

Either that or she locked herself in the bathroom three times a day and secretly ate the contents of a medium-sized supermarket. One or the other. I suspected the latter. I would have said that a lot of hard, dedicated work went into maintaining an arse as big as hers.

I was surprised that Misty didn't point that out, but Misty was very nice to her. Which made me wonder moodily why she couldn't be nice to me. The little bitch.

It took a while for Betty to get everyone organized with flour and sugar and mixing-bowls and sieves and all the rest.

Clarence kept putting his hand up and saying 'Teacher.'

And Betty kept saying 'Call me Betty.'

And Clarence kept saying 'OK, teacher.'

And then a peace descended on the room. Everyone was concentrating so hard, their brown jumpers covered with flour, that I became aware of a charged atmosphere in the room. A strange harmony that was spine-tingling. Almost as . . . almost as, as if *we were in the presence of the divine*, I was surprised to find myself thinking.

Then I was floored by massive embarrassment for thinking such new-age-wankology. Next I'd be reading *The Celestine Prophecy*, if I didn't watch myself!

But shortly afterwards, I had another attack of acute sentimentality. When the men took their lopsided, misshapen, burnt, raw-in-the-middle, flopped cakes out of the oven, the pride they had in their creations made my eyes well up. Each of these cakes was a little miracle, I thought, as I shed a discreet tear. These men are alcoholics and some have done terrible things, but they have made a cake all by themselves . . .

Then I *cringed*.

I couldn't believe what I'd just been thinking.

Thank *Christ* there's no one here who can read minds, I reassured myself.

I found Saturday nights the hardest in the Cloisters. Humiliated that the whole world was getting dressed up and going out. Everyone except me. But worse than that, I was tormented with worry about Luke. Saturday night was when he was most likely to meet another girl. It did my head in.

I completely forgot I was angry with him. Instead I ached, longed for him, while feeling crazed with jealousy and fear of losing him. Even though it was obvious that I'd already lost him. But if he met someone else, then I really *had* lost him.

I tried to take my mind off him with the usual Saturday night games. I'd played them the previous week, but half-heartedly. I'd been embarrassed by them, constantly imagining what people like Helenka and other glamorous New York people would say if they could see me. I'd kept casting my eyes to Heaven and tisking, just in case Helenka had psychic powers. So that she'd realize I was only doing it because I had to and that I certainly wasn't enjoying myself. *Games!* My whole demeanour cried. *How cringy!*

But this week, I was surprised to discover just how much fun it was. First, we split up into teams and played Red Rover, running the length of the freezing sitting-room and breaking through the barriers of other people's arms. It was alarmingly exhilarating.

Then someone produced a skipping rope.

I had a bad few minutes in the middle of the skipping, as everyone else was being 'called in' except me. Exactly the same thing had happened throughout my youth and I felt sulky and angry and left out.

I slunk over to the wall and threw myself down on a chair. Even if someone calls me in, I thought angrily. I'm not bloody going.

'Are you enjoying yourself?' Chris appeared at my side. The hairs stood up on my skin. God, I *fancied* him.

Those eyes, those thighs . . . One day, I thought longingly. Maybe one day me and him will be in New York together, majorly in love . . . Then Misty was called in to the skipping and my envy blotted out all else.

'They make me sick here,' I said bitterly. 'They really do. Making us remember our childhood like this.'

'That's not why we do this.' Chris sounded astonished. 'It's because we enjoy it, we let off a bit of steam. Anyway, what's wrong with remembering your childhood?'

I said nothing.

Chris looked concerned.

Vaguely, I could hear Misty, who was skipping like a dainty, little elf singing '. . . And I call Chri-is in . . .'

'If you find it that awful to remember, you'd better tell them in group,' Chris said.

'Oh God, it's my go!' he exclaimed and leapt up into the middle of the rope with Misty.

John Joe was turning the rope with Nancy, the housewife who was addicted to Valium. Even though everyone was clumsy and falling round the room, Nancy and John Joe were just that little bit *too* uncoordinated. In fact, Nancy was barely able to stand.

I watched Chris as he skipped. Ungainly and awkward, but very cute. His face was a picture of concentration as he tried hard to get it right.

I sat there feeling miserable, listening to them all chanting the skipping song, when I heard Chris singing the words '. . . And I caaallll *Rachel* in.'

Joyfully, I jumped up. I loved being called in and I never was. Never. It was always the bigger girls.

Or the smaller ones.

I leapt into the turning rope and skipped along with Chris for a few seconds, smiling shyly with the joy of being picked. Then Chris's lovely lizard-skin chelsea boots got tangled up in the rope, and I tripped and the pair of us fell sprawling onto the floor. There was a delicious second of lying next to him and then John Joe threw a little fit and said he was sick of turning the rope. In a surge of unexpected magnanimity, I found myself turning the rope with glassy-eyed Nancy. She was so lost in the tran-quillizer wilderness she terrified me.

After John Joe had almost broken every bone in his own and the bodies around him, it was time for musical chairs. Initially, I was afraid of being rough and pushing others off the chairs and onto the floor. Except for when it was Misty, of course. But, when I realized the whole idea was to be as vicious as possible, I really began to have a good time. Laughing and gasping, tussling and fighting, I felt I'd never enjoyed myself so much before. Without drugs, I mean.

And it wasn't until I was going to bed, and I thought of Luke in New York, probably just about to go out, that my happiness evaporated.

On Sunday morning every man in the Cloisters, including Chris, I was sorry to say, approached me and said 'Will that sister of yours be coming today?'

'I don't know,' I had to tell them. But, when visiting time rolled around, Helen appeared with Mum and Dad. No sign of Anna, unfortunately. Dad was still talking in his *Oklahoma* voice.

When I got Helen on her own – Mum and Dad were deep into a conversation with Chris's parents, I dreaded to think what they were talking about – I slipped her the letter requesting Anna to visit me bearing narcotics.

I said to Helen 'Would you give that to Anna?'

'But I won't see her,' said Helen. 'I've a job.'

'You've a job?' I was very surprised. Not only was Helen notoriously lazy, but, like me, she couldn't actually *do* anything. 'Since when?'

'Wednesday night.'

'Doing what?'

'Waitress.'

'Where?'

'In a fucking . . .' She paused as she searched for the right word. '. . . A fucking *abattoir* in Temple Bar called Club Mexxx.'

'That's with three xs,' she added. 'That should tell you something about it.'

'Well, er, congratulations,' I said. Although I wasn't at all sure they were appropriate. Like saying congratulations to your friend when she's just found out she's pregnant, but has no boyfriend to speak of.

'Look, it's not my fault that I was too short to be an air hostess!' she suddenly exclaimed.

'I didn't know you'd applied to be a trolley dolly,' I said, in surprise.

'Well, I did,' she said moodily. 'And I wouldn't mind, but it wasn't even a proper airline, it was one of those crappy charter ones, Air Paella, that'd employ *anyone*. Except me.'

I was in shock because her disappointment was so tangible. She'd always got exactly what she wanted. She put her face in her hands in a gesture of despair that frightened me. 'I wouldn't mind, Rachel, but I had everything else perfect, I looked just the part.'

'How d'you mean?'

'You know, the inch-thick tangerine foundation, the white neck, the scary, pretend smile, the visible panty line.

Not to mention the selective deafness. I would have been *brilliant*!

'I practised very hard, Rachel,' she said, her bottom lip trembling. 'I really did. I was horrible to every woman I met and slimed all over every man. I practised opening the freezer door and standing beside it and nodding and giving a fake smile and saying, "Thanksbyebyethanksthanksbyebye thanksthanksbye thanksthanks byebyebye", for *hours*, but they said I was too short. "What do I need to be tall for?" I asked them. And they said to put things in the overhead lockers. Well, that's a load of shite as anyone knows, because if you're an air hostess it's your *job* to ignore all the women and let them do everything themselves. And if it's a man who needs help, you just flash him your jugs and get him to do it himself too. And he'll be *glad* to do it. Thrilled.'

'Why the freezer door?'

'Because where they stand when the people are getting off is always cold, see?'

'Well, er, it was a good idea to practise,' I said awkwardly.

'Practise!' Mum had reappeared. 'I'll give her practise. She defrosted a freezer load of Magnums and crispy pancakes on me with her "Thanksbyebyethanks". Practise, indeed!'

'They were only mint Magnums,' said Helen. 'Not worth the space they took up, it was a mercy killing, the humane thing to do.'

Mum continued to make tutty, disapproving noises as if she was Skippy the bush kangaroo trying to convey that Bruce had fallen out of the seaplane, had fractured his arm in three places and needed rescuing from a swamp full of crocodiles.

'Anyway, yeah, like, thanks for all the support, Mum,'

Helen burst out, as though she was twelve. 'I suppose you just wish I never got a job.'

I waited for her to explode 'I never asked to be born,' and slam from the room.

But then we all remembered where we were and put a lid on it.

Mum moved away again. This time to bond with Misty O'Malley's parents. Dad was still knee-deep in conversation with Chris's father.

'So have you any stamps?' I turned to Helen. If she wouldn't give the letter to Anna, then I'd try and post the bloody thing. Slip it into the outgoing post without anyone knowing.

'Me?' Helen demanded. 'Stamps? Do I look like I'm married?'

'What are you talking about?'

'Only married people carry stamps around with them, *everyone* knows that.'

'Well, never mind,' I said. It had just occurred to me – how could I have ever forgotten? – that in five days, the three weeks I'd contracted to stay for would be up. I could freely leave. No bloody way would I elect to stay for the full two months like the rest of them. I'd be off like a shot. Then I could take as many drugs as I liked.

46

After the visitors left, Sunday Afternoon Suffocation suddenly descended on me. The bleak, dissatisfied sensation that if something didn't happen soon, if something didn't change, I would burst.

I roamed restlessly from the dining-room to the sitting-room to my bedroom and back again, unable to settle anywhere. I felt like a caged animal.

I yearned to be in the outside world where I could kickstart events by getting off my face. Springboard my emotions from the grey, misty depths of depression to the clear blue sky of happiness. But in the Cloisters there was nothing to ejector-seat me.

I consoled myself with the thought that it was my last Sunday afternoon in the kip. That in less than a week I wouldn't have to feel those feelings anymore.

But, with a throb of undiluted angst, I realized I'd felt such restlessness and emptiness in the past. Often. It usually kicked in at about four o'clock on a Sunday, but had arrived slightly late today, no doubt still on New York time.

Maybe it would follow me, when I left the Cloisters.

Maybe, I agreed. But at least then I'd be able to do something about it.

All the other inmates were getting on my nerves, with their bickering and bantering. Mike was in a right fouler, parading round, pawing the ground, looking more like a bull than ever. He remained tightlipped about the source of his bad humour, but Clarence told me that Mike's bratty son Willy had greeted his father by saying 'There's the alco-pop.'

'What???' Mike had demanded.

'Alco-pop,' sang Willie. 'You're me da, so you're my *pop*, and you're an alco. Put it together and you're an *alco-pop*!'

'He nearly brained the child,' Clarence intoned, far too close to my ear.

Vincent, on the other hand, was irritating me because he was in such a *good* mood. In flying form because he'd got his wife to bring in the Babyboomer Trivial Pursuit questions with her. He waved the red box around in Stalin's face. 'Now we'll see who's so great at getting the pieces of pie, so we will!' He crowed triumphantly. 'Now that you've had no chance to learn the new answers off.'

Stalin burst into tears. He'd been hoping that Rita would come and visit him and call off the divorce, but there had been no sign of her.

'Let him alone!' Neil turned on Vincent. When Neil realized he was an alcoholic, he spent a day or two crying, then took Vincent's place as Mr Angry. He raged against himself for being an alcoholic, but he also raged against everyone and everything else. Josephine said his anger was to be expected, that no one wants to be an alcoholic, but that he'd come to terms with it soon. We couldn't wait. In the meantime we were all terrified of him.

'The poor fecker is in bits about his wife,' Neil roared into Vincent's face. 'So don't be tormenting him any further.'

'Sorry.' Vincent looked mortified. 'I wasn't, it was only a joke . . .'

'You're very aggressive, so you are,' Neil bellowed.

'I know,' Vincent mumbled humbly. 'But I've been trying hard . . .'

'Not hard enough!' Neil slammed his fist down on the table.

Everyone started heading for the door at high speed.

'Sorry,' Vincent muttered.

Everyone paused and began to return.

Things quietened down briefly until Barry the child raced into the dining-room, all of a dither. Apparently great ructions were in progress upstairs because Celine had found Davy reading the racing pages. As Davy was a compulsive gambler, that was as bad as someone like Neil being found distilling homebrew under his bed.

According to Barry, Davy had gone ballistic. So much so that Finbar the gardener, handy man and all-round, general half-wit had to be called upon to restrain him. With that, there was a surge from the dining-room, Barry the bringer of glad tidings at its head, as everyone ran for ringside seats at the mêlée.

I didn't go.

I was too narky to be bothered.

But, when the dust had settled, I perked up to discover I was alone in the dining-room with Chris. Even bitch-face Misty had left.

'Are you OK?' he asked gently, coming to sit beside me.

I looked into his blue-water eyes and felt tingly from his beauty.

'No,' I shifted. 'I feel . . . I feel . . . I don't know, just fed-up.'

'Right, I see.' He thoughtfully ran his big square hand through his wheat-coloured hair, wearing a becomingly worried face while I breathed hopefully at him. Oh, how I *savoured* being the centre of his attention!

'What can we do to cheer Rachel up?' he said, as if he was just talking to himself. I positively squirmed with pleasure.

'Let's go for a walk,' he suggested brightly.

'Where?' I asked.

'Out there.' He nodded at the window.

'But it's dark,' I protested. 'And cold.'

'Come on,' he urged, with one of his special wry smiles. 'It's the best I can offer you.

'For the moment,' he added, tantalizingly.

I ran to get my coat and the two of us went out into the face-numbingly cold night and marched around the dark grounds together.

I didn't say much. Not by choice. I would have loved to talk to him, but I was nervous and my brain did what it always did when I was nervous. It turned into a lump of concrete; grey and heavy and empty.

He didn't strike up a conversation either. We walked for a long time in silence, the only sounds our breathing, as we blew out clouds of vapour in front of our faces, and the crunch of the grass under our boots.

It was too dark to see his face. So, when he said 'Hold it, hold it, stop a second!' and put his hand on my arm, I didn't know what he was up to. My down theres leapt with the anticipation of a furtive, sylvan grope. And I regretted wearing six layers of clothes.

But he was only linking arms with me.

'Give me your arm,' he said, crooking my elbow into his. 'OK, off we go again!'

'Off we go indeed!' I said, trying to pretend, with my excessive jolliness, that I wasn't at all bothered by my contact with him. That my breathing hadn't become shallow and ragged and that a thrill hadn't shot, like an express train, from my elbow straight through to my loins.

On and on we stamped, side by side, arms and shoulders touching. We're nearly the same height, I told myself, trying to turn it into a virtue. We're well matched.

Being so close to him made me feel better about Luke. It helped calm my fear that he'd met someone else. It soothed my raw emotions. Momentarily, at least, I was so filled with desire for Chris, it blocked out the awful memories of Luke.

I yearned for Chris to kiss me. Longing made my head light. Almost mental with desperation.

What wouldn't I give . . .

To my alarm, I found we were almost back at the house. *Already?*

The light from the windows shone near us, so that we could see each other in shadow.

'Look.' Chris turned to me, his face into my face, almost touching. Every nerve ending leapt onto full alert, certain that a clinch was coming.

'See that big bathroom there,' he pointed, his body tantalizingly almost touching mine.

'Yes,' I said thickly, following his outstretched arm, as it pointed up at a lighted window. He didn't move any closer to me, but he didn't move away either.

If I breathe out a lot, my stomach might touch his.

'Two people were caught having sex in there,' he said.

'When?' I could hardly speak, as he kept me there, hovering on the brink.

'A while back.'

'Who were they?' I forced myself to ask.

'Patients, clients, whatever we want to call ourselves. People like us.'

'Really,' I mumbled, wondering where all this was going.

'Yeah,' he chuckled. 'Two people like you and me were caught having sex in that very bathroom.'

It sounded as though he had deliberately structured that sentence for maximum provocativeness. But then he moved away from me and I felt like I'd fallen off a cliff.

'What do you think of that?' he asked.

'I don't believe you,' I said, my voice dull with disappointment. All that anticipation and nothing to show for it . . .

'Honestly,' he promised, his eyes flashing sincerity in the darkness.

'No way,' I said, finally able to fully concentrate on what he was saying. 'How could people be so . . . so . . . I mean, how could they break the rules like that?'

He laughed. 'You are so surprisingly innocent,' he drawled. 'And I thought you were a wild girl.'

Furious with myself, I spluttered 'Oh, but I am. Honestly.'

'Will we go back in?' He nodded at the house.

Confused and frustrated, I nodded. 'OK.'

47

On Monday morning in group Josephine turned her attention to Mike and humbled the living daylights out of him.

'Mike, I've been meaning to get back to you,' she said, sounding apologetic. 'It's about time we looked again at your alcoholism, isn't it?'

He declined to reply. Just stared as if he'd like to maim her.

Great, I thought gleefully. While someone else was in the hotseat, it meant there was no room for me.

Josephine turned to the room at large. 'Have you any questions for Mike?'

Do you perm your hair? I wondered. And if so, why?

No one said anything.

'OK,' sighed Josephine. 'I'll do it myself. You're the eldest of a family of twelve?'

'I am,' Mike agreed loudly.

'And your father died when you were fifteen?'

'He did,' Mike bellowed.

'That must have been hard?'

'We managed.'

'How?'

'By working hard.' Mike's ugly face was stonier than ever.

'On the land?'

'On the land.'

'Cattle?'

'Mostly arable.'

I hadn't a clue what they were on about.

'Long days?'

'Up in the dark and still working when the sun went down,' Mike said almost proudly. 'Seven days a week and no such thing as a holiday.'

'Very commendable,' Josephine murmured. 'Until your drinking got out of control and you disappeared on week-long binges and the work stopped getting done.'

'But . . .' Mike began.

'We've had your wife in here,' Josephine cut him off. 'We know all about it. You know we know.'

And off she went. All morning she worried away at him.

She tried to get him to admit that he kept himself so diverted trying to organize his entire family into a slick workforce, that he never got a chance to mourn his father.

'No, no, no,' he insisted, annoyed. 'We had to get a system going, otherwise we would have starved.'

'But why were you the one who had to do it?'

'I was the eldest,' he mumbled painfully. 'It was my sole responsibility.'

'It wasn't,' said Josephine. 'What about your mother?'

'My poor mother,' Mike stammered. 'I wouldn't want to worry her.'

'Why not?'

'I think the world of my mother,' Mike said quietly, as if Josephine should be ashamed for asking such a question.

'Yes,' Josephine said quietly. 'You've an odd attitude to women, haven't you? The Madonna/whore distinction is very marked in you.'

'Wha . . .?'

'Anyway, we'll come back to that some other time.'

Despite her intensive cross-examination, he wouldn't admit to anything.

After lunch my luck held because Misty was for it. A double blessing. Anything bad that happened to her cheered me up immensely. And while she was being humbled it meant I wasn't.

I'd got off fairly lightly, I realized. I was sure that they wouldn't bother with the questionnaire at such a late stage in my stay. Apart from that one day when she'd questioned me about my childhood, Josephine hadn't given me too hard a time. And only five days to go before I could leave. Five days to convince me I had a drug problem? Well, I didn't give much for their chances.

With that in mind, I was able to really enjoy Misty being trashed by Josephine without worrying that the same thing was in store for me.

And trash her she did. Josephine suspected that Misty had only relapsed as a publicity stunt.

Which Misty vigorously denied.

'This isn't a plug for *Tears before Bedtime*, my new book,' she insisted. 'I'm not in here just so that my new book *Tears before Bedtime* gets publicity.'

She looked fragile and delicate and beautiful. 'Really I'm not,' she insisted, her large eyes pleading don't-misunderstand-me.

I wanted to puke, but there was a shamed silence from everyone else.

Suckers, I thought, furious that they couldn't see how they were being manipulated.

'You couldn't be more wrong,' she protested, allowing a little quiver to appear on her bottom lip.

More shame. More silence. Josephine watched her with narrowed eyes.

'I'm actually looking for material for my *next* book,' Misty added, almost as an afterthought.

There was a stunned silence, before a clamour of questions broke out.

'Will I be in it?' John Joe asked excitedly.

'Will I?' Chaquie asked in alarm. 'You won't use my real name, will you?'

'Or mine,' Neil said anxiously.

'I'll be the hero, won't I?' Mike swaggered. 'The one who gets the girl?'

'What about me?' Clarence began.

'STOP IT!' Josephine roared.

Nice one, I thought smugly. Give her hell. I wondered if I could let this slip to Chris. It would be good for him to know what a shallow little hoor she was. Although, I thought doubtfully, I wasn't sure Chris was that interested in Misty's strength of character.

'This is your second time in this treatment centre,' Josephine raged. 'When are you going to take it seriously? For God's sake, you're an alcoholic!'

'Of course I'm an alcoholic,' Misty calmly insisted. 'I'm a *writer*!'

'Who do you think you are?' Josephine spat. 'Ernest Hemingway?'

I smirked with glee.

Great stuff.

Then Josephine tore strips off Misty for being such a flirt.

'You're deliberately and extremely provocative to many of the men here. I'd like to know why.'

Misty wouldn't cooperate, and Josephine got nastier and nastier.

The afternoon was a pleasure from start to finish. But at the end, as I was slipping out the door for the great tea-drinking, Josephine grabbed me by the sleeve. In a second I went from being relaxed and good-humoured to paralysed with terror.

'Tomorrow,' she said.

Oh no, my brain screamed. Oh no! Tomorrow is questionnaire day. How could I ever have thought I'd avoid it?

'Tomorrow,' she said. 'I thought it was only fair to warn you . . .'

I felt close to tears.

'To give you a bit of time to prepare yourself . . .'

Thoughts of suicide raised their heads like little buds in the early spring.

'. . . Your parents will be coming in as your Involved Significant Others.'

It took a second or two to absorb it. I was so focused on Luke and the horrible things he might have said about me that for a while I didn't know what parents were.

Parents? Do I have parents? But what do they have to do with Luke?

'Ah, right, so,' I said to Josephine. I walked to the dining-room, absorbing what she'd told me.

OK, I realized, thinking fast, the situation wasn't as catastrophic as it *could* have been because they knew very little about me. But all the same, I was frightened. I had to ring Mum and Dad and find out what they were planning to say.

The counsellor lurking in our midst was the small and cute-looking Barry Grant. When I asked her if I could make a phonecall, she complained loudly 'Orr ay, Rrachel gail, I'm 'avin' me sea.'

She kindly gestured at the cup of tea in front of her, so I had a vague notion of what she was saying.

I fidgeted and fidgeted until she finally stood up and led me to the office. As we passed through reception, I was surprised to see Mike perched up on Bubbly the receptionist's desk.

Is Bubbly a Madonna or a whore? I wondered.

'A lovely girl like you?' He was crooning and twinkling at her. 'I'd say you have to beat them off with a shitty stick.'

Whore, I think.

'Oi!' Barry Grant roared at him. 'Norr again! I'll 'ave you.'

Mike jumped several feet.

'Ah, good luck, I'll see you again,' he said hurriedly to Bubbly, and bolted for the door.

'Stay away from the gails,' Barry Grant bellowed after him.

'And stop encouraging him,' she barked at Bubbly. 'You're supposed to be a professional.

'Come on, you,' she shouted at me – I suppose she didn't want me to feel left out – 'What's the number?'

Dad answered the phone by saying 'El Rancho Walsho.' I could hear 'The Surrey with the Fringe on Top' playing in the background.

'Hello, Dad,' I said. 'How's the acting? The roar of the greasepaint, the smell of the crowd?'

I thought it politic to pretend we were friends. That way he might be nice about me the following day.

'Mad fan,' he said. 'And how's yourself?'

'Not so mad fan, actually, what's this I hear about you coming to be my ISO tomorrow?'

I heard an intake of breath so sharp he sounded as if he was being garrotted.

'I'll get your mother!' he squeaked. Then the phone clattered onto the table.

There followed ages of loud whispering, as Dad filled Mum in on the situation and they each tried to blame the other.

'Whisper whisper whisper,' went Mum anxiously.

'WHISPERWHISPERWHISPER!' Dad replied frantically.

'Well, whisper, *whisper.*'

'You're her whisper, whisper whisper whisper women's work!'

I caught the general gist. 'What'll I say?' Mum hissed.

'Just tell her the truth,' Dad hissed back.

Then Mum hissed 'Tell her the truth yourself.'

And Dad hissed 'You're her mother, that kind of a caper is women's work.'

Dad must have threatened to cut Mum's housekeeping because Mum eventually took the phone and in a shaky, fake-up-beat voice, she declared 'D'you know something, but the only good Surrey is a dead Surrey. He has me *tormented* with that *Okla-bloody-homa.* And, listen to this, you won't believe this, do you know what he asked me to get for him in Dunnes, grits! To have for his tea, as it were. Well, what are grits, sez I. Cowboy food, sez he. Sure, the only grit I know is the stuff you find in the bottom of a bird cage . . .'

When I eventually managed to get a word in, she reluctantly confirmed that, yes, she and Dad were coming in to make shite of me.

I found it hard to believe. Even though I was in a treatment centre and this kind of thing happened to people, it wasn't supposed to happen to me. I wasn't like the others. And that wasn't some sort of mad, addict's denial. I really *wasn't* like the others.

'Well, come if you must,' I sighed. 'But you'd better not be mean about me, or who knows what I might do.'

Barry Grant reached for a pen as soon as I said that.

'Of course we won't be mean about you,' Mum quavered. 'But we have to answer the woman's questions.'

Which was exactly what I was afraid of.

'Maybe, but you don't have to be *mean* about me.' Even to my own ears I sounded like a thirteen-year-old.

'Are you coming in the morning or afternoon?' I asked.

'Afternoon.'

That was slightly better because if they were coming in the morning there was a chance they might stay all day.

'And, Rachel love,' Mum sounded like she was going to cry, 'we're not going to be mean. We're only trying to help.'

'Good,' I said grimly.

'All rice?' Barry Grant asked, gimlet-eyed, when I hung up.

I nodded. The situation was under control and I *was* all rice.

Anyway, I reminded myself. Four more days. What harm can it do?

48

Brigit and I were both lying on her bed, barely able to move from the August heat. Enervated by the dazzling, white light of a New York summer, which reflected off the concrete sidewalks and the concrete buildings, throwing back a hundredfold more heat and bleachedness. It had gone beyond bright and was now almost something evil.

'. . . so the night he first claps eyes on you, you've never been so skinny, you're all ribs and cheekbones,' Brigit was saying.

'Thanks,' I said. 'But how? Surgery?'

'Noooo,' she twisted her mouth thoughtfully. 'That wouldn't work because the scars would show in the little Dolce and Gabbana chiffon frock that you're wearing when you spill your glass of champagne on him.'

'Cor,' I breathed. 'Dolce and Gabbana, that's very decent of you, thanks! And champagne. Nice one!'

'Let's see,' she said, and got a faraway look in her eyes. I watched in reverential silence as she sought to pad out my fantasy.

'OK, I know!' she announced. 'You've one of those worms that live in your intestine and eat all your food so that you don't get any of it and you lose tons of weight.'

'Inspired,' I declared.

Then a thought struck me. 'But how did the worm get into my intestines?'

'It was in some meat that wasn't cooked properly . . .'

'But I'm a vegetarian.'

'Look it doesn't *matter*,' she exploded. 'I keep telling you. This is make-believe.'

'Sorry.'

I was suitably humble for a moment and then I said 'And how did I afford the Dolce and Gabbana dress? Have I got a new job?'

'No,' she said shortly. 'You stole it.

'And you got caught nicking it,' she added. 'You're out on bail and due up in court the following Monday. And as soon as the dream man finds out you're a potential jail-bird he does a runner on you.'

Brigit appeared to be tired of playing the game.

'Anyway, you don't need me to do this for you anymore,' she said. 'You *have* a fella.'

'Don't,' I squirmed.

'But you do,' she said. 'What's Luke? He's a fella, there's no denying it.'

'Stop.'

'What's up with you?' she said in exasperation. 'I think he's lovely.'

'Why don't *you* go out with him then?'

'Rachel,' she said in a loud voice. 'Stop it. I said I liked him, I didn't say I fancied him. You'd really want to do something about that jealousy of yours.'

'I'm not jealous,' I objected hotly. I hated being called jealous.

'Well, you're something,' she said.

I didn't reply because she'd started me thinking about Luke. Even though I couldn't make up my mind what I felt about him, I always became mildly hypnotized at the mere mention of him. My brain kind of glazed over.

He was official*ish*, my boyfriend. Since the dinner in

404

The Good and Dear, I'd spent every weekend with him. But now that I was back in control with him, my previous ambivalence reared its head and I wasn't so sure I still wanted him.

Every Sunday I promised myself that the following Saturday I would do something different. Something glamorous that involved trendy people whose star couldn't have been more in the ascendant if it tried. *Not* Luke Costello. But every six days later I was powerless to resist when Luke said 'What do you want to do tonight, babe?'

'Right, now your turn,' I said, coming to. I was keen to change the subject. 'You've just had a really bad dose of the flu, no wait, food poisoning, because you ate some gone-off ice cream and you puked for a week.'

'Ice cream doesn't go off,' she interrupted.

'Doesn't it? I'm sure it does. Not that it ever gets the chance around me. Anyway, who cares, you got food poisoning and you're like a skeleton. So thin that people come up to you and say, "I think you've lost too much, Brigit, you'd really want to put some back on, you're like someone from a concentration camp."'

'Lovely.' Brigit drummed her heels on the bed with pleasure.

'Yes, people are muttering about you and you can hear them saying, "She looks absolutely wretched." So we go to a party and you haven't seen Carlos for ages, but he's there . . .'

'No,' she interrupted. 'Not Carlos.'

'Why not?' I hooted in surprise.

'Because I'm over him.'

'Are you?' I was even more surprised. 'But I didn't know you'd met someone else.'

'I haven't.'

'But then how can you be over him?'

'I don't know, I just am.'

'You're scaring me, Brigit.' I looked at her as if I'd never seen her before. 'You know what Claire always says, "The only way to get over one man is to get under another." And you haven't been riding anyone else, I'd have noticed.'

'Doesn't matter, I'm still over him.

'Aren't you glad for me?' Brigit asked. 'Aren't you glad I'm no longer in rag order?'

'Well, yes, of course I am. I'm just surprised, that's all.'

But I wasn't glad. I was unsettled and uncomfortable. And *confused*.

First her promotion, now this.

Brigit and I had always been so alike. Apart from our attitudes to our careers – in other words, Brigit *had* an attitude – our reactions to life were nearly always identical. In fact, the only other thing we didn't share was the same taste in men, which was probably why our friendship had lasted as long as it had. Nothing like a clash of interests along the lines of 'Here! I saw him first' to put the mockers on a friendship that had endured since junior school.

But now she'd gone all weird on me. I couldn't understand how she'd just turned around and ceased to care about Carlos. Because I'd never, under my own steam, got over a man. It was always a team effort. I needed a new man to come along and put his back into making me miserable before I could get over the grief caused by the previous one.

My reaction to rejection was to go out and seek immediate reassurance. Usually by sleeping with someone else. Or at least to give it my best shot; naturally I wasn't always successful.

I had always envied those women who said things like 'After Alex left me, I just shut down, I couldn't feel anything for another man for nearly a year.'

I would have *loved* to have had no feelings. Because men were mad about you if you felt nothing for them.

And now Brigit seemed to be turning into the very image of those spooky self-contained women.

How *dare* she be over Carlos without having met someone else?

'Go to the fridge,' she pushed me with her foot. 'Go to the fridge and find me something cold.'

'I didn't know Helenka lived in our fridge,' I japed and we both laughed limply and weakly.

'I can't, Brigit,' I apologized. 'I've no energy, I'd collapse.'

'You lazy, useless hoor,' she complained. 'You'd have energy aplenty if Luke seventies-throwback Costello arrived around here with his lad in his hand looking for some lurve action.'

I wished she hadn't said that, though, because a shock of desire for him passed through me, leaving me dissatisfied and fidgety. It was hours before I was due to see him and suddenly everything until then seemed pointless and boring.

'D'you want anything?' Brigit asked, hauling herself to her feet.

'Bring us a beer, why don't you,' I suggested.

'There's none left,' she called a few moments later, from the kitchen. From the tone of her voice I sensed great narkiness emanating from her.

Not again, I thought dispiritedly. She'd been so moody lately. What the hell was up with her?

A good ride, that's what she needed. It was what we *all*

needed. I might even start a petition and carry a placard saying, 'Ride Brigit Lenehan now!' and 'Ride the New York one.' And maybe I'd organize a march from the Cute Hoor to Tadhg's Boghole, me at its head, shouting into a megaphone 'WHAT DO WE WANT?'

And everyone else would have to shout back 'A RIDE FOR BRIGIT LENEHAN.'

And then I'd yell 'WHEN DO WE WANT IT?'

And everyone would reply 'NOW!'

'Yeah,' Brigit repeated nastily. 'No beer left. Who would have thought it?'

'I said I was sorry,' I called out to her.

Then I steeled myself and added 'How many more times do I have to say it.'

I was a lot braver than I would have been if Brigit had still been in the room. I was hopeless at face-to-face confrontations.

I had always found it easier to have arguments with people when they weren't actually there. In fact, I'd had some of my best rows with people who were in other countries at the time.

'I mean, for God's sake, Rachel,' she called back. 'We needed everything. Bread, diet coke, and that's diet coca *cola*, dear, not the coke you *usually* use to lose weight . . .'

I curled inwards with fear at the nastiness of her tone.

'. . . jack's roll, coffee, cheese. And what do you come back with? With bread? No. With cheese? No. With any of the things on the list? No. Instead she arrives back . . .'

I knew things had got pretty bad when she started to talk about me in the third person.

'. . . and what has she bought, what has she got with her except twenty-four cans of lager and a bag of Doritos. Which is all very well if it's her *own* money she's spending.

If it's her *own* money she's spending she can buy as much beer as she *likes*.'

Her voice was getting nearer, so I shrank back against the bed.

'And then for her to drink them all in a matter of hours.' She had appeared in the doorway and I wished I was in a North Korean logging camp, where they work the prisoners twenty-three hours a day. It had to be preferable to how Brigit was making me feel.

'Sorry,' I said, because it was all I *could* say.

She ignored me. When I couldn't bear the tension any longer I braved the silence by saying again, 'I'm sorry, Brigit.'

She looked at me. We locked eyes for ages.

I couldn't read her face, but I willed and willed her to forgive me. I tried to send thought messages from my head to hers.

Forgive Rachel, I vibed. Be her friend.

It must have worked because Brigit's face softened. Seizing my advantage, I said 'Sorry' again. I figured it couldn't do any harm and it might actually do some good.

'I know you are,' she eventually admitted.

I breathed out with relief.

'Although, really, come *on*,' she said, her voice a lot more normal. 'Twenty-four cans of beer.' She started to laugh and I felt elated with deliverance.

'Right,' I said, hauling myself off the bed, fighting through the thick air. 'I must get ready for Luke.'

'Where are you meeting him?'

'I'm calling round to Testosterone Central, and then we're going out. Coming?'

'Depends. Is this a date?'

'No, just going for a couple of drinks with him and forty-nine of his closest friends. Please come.'

'Well, all right, but I'm not going to sleep with Joey just to oblige you.'

'Aw, please, Brigit,' I begged. 'I'm sure he fancies you. It would be lovely, it would be so romantic.' I paused. 'It would be so *handy*.'

'You selfish bitch,' she exclaimed.

'I'm not,' I protested. 'I'm only saying that . . . well, you know, you and I live together and Luke and Joey live together and . . .'

'No!' she exclaimed. 'No way. We're *adults*, you and I . . .'

'Speak for yourself.'

'And as adults we don't have to do everything together. That means that we can go out with men who aren't friends with each other.'

'Fine,' I said sulkily.

We sat in silence for a few tense minutes.

'Well OK,' she sighed resignedly. 'I'll think about it.'

49

I was mad keen for Brigit to get off with Joey, because I was still slightly mortified to be going out with one of the Real Men. If I could have roped in a friend of mine to go out with another of them, I'd have felt a lot more comfortable.

I didn't like being the only one.

Of course I knew I was shallow and a horrible person and all that, but I couldn't help it.

Brigit and I had our showers, which was kind of pointless because five minutes later we were sweating like pigs again. We put on the minimum of clothes, then swam through the heavy humid air to Luke's.

I felt nervous and shy as I rang his bell. He always made me feel that way. A strange compulsive mix of lust and reluctance. Revulsion, nearly. A tiny little flicker of it playing around in the lining of my stomach.

We exited the lift slowly, too hot to go any faster. The door of the apartment was open and Luke was lying on the floor, wearing just a pair of denim cut-offs. His tanned chest and legs were bare and the fan whirred over him, blowing his long hair into his eyes. When I came face-to-face with him, his eyes darkened, then he smiled at me. Meaningfully, with a promise in his look and a bulge in his shorts. I felt a violent rush of desire and nausea.

'How's it going, seventies throw-back?' Brigit greeted Luke.

'Seventies sling-back,' Luke replied.

'Seventies bad-back,' Brigit riposted.

'Seventies out-back,' Luke managed.

'Seventies clutch-bag,' Brigit chanced.

'No,' Luke was firm. 'That's cheating.'

Luke and Brigit got on very well. Which sometimes pleased me.

And which sometimes didn't.

It's a narrow line. Well, but not *too* well.

Then I did what I did every time I went to Luke's apartment. I pretended to slip in a testosterone slick.

Luke obliged me by laughing. Then Brigit and I both wobbled around for a bit, windmilling our arms, shouting things like 'Mind out, there's another pool of it over there!'

'Jesus,' said Brigit, looking around the cluttered, macho apartment. 'This place gets worse. There's so many male hormones in the air that my balls will drop if I stay here too long. Any chance of a glass of iced coffee?'

'Oh God, I don't know,' Luke said, rubbing his stubble in a perplexed gesture that I found so sexy I wished Brigit would go away for a while and leave me and Luke to do some horizontal surfing. 'We don't do much home catering.

'I could run out to the corner and get a take-away for you,' he offered. 'Or how about a beer,' he offered eagerly. 'We've got lots of beer.'

'Why doesn't this surprise me?' Brigit asked drily. 'OK, a beer it is.

'Am I seeing things?' Brigit had picked up a leather jerkin that had 'Whitesnake' on the back of it. She shook her head almost sadly and said 'What year is it, Luke? Just tell me what year it is.'

This was only a matter of time. She did it every time she saw Luke.

'1972, of course,' Luke said.

'It's not, you know,' Brigit said briskly. 'It's 1997, actually.'

Luke looked horrified. 'What manner of rawmaysh are you talking, woman?'

'Pass me the paper, Rachel,' she ordered. 'Lookit here, you poor sad throw-back, see where it says the date . . .'

Luke did his usual reeling and clutching of his forehead and I decided I was tired of being left out.

'Where's the lads?' I enquired.

'Out,' Luke said. 'Back any minute.'

Just then there was a commotion at the door, noises of stumbling and shouting; instructions and exhortations and complaints. And an ashen-faced Gaz was half-led, half-dragged into the apartment by Joey and Shake.

'Not far more now, man,' Joey was saying to Gaz.

Each of them, in turn, tripped over a pair of biker boots that were thrown in the middle of the floor.

Each of them in turn muttered 'Jayzis'.

I wondered how they could wear so much denim in this heat. In fact, I wondered how they could wear so much *hair* in this heat.

'We're home, man,' Shake said.

'Thank fuck for that,' Gaz mumbled, then put the back of his hand to his forehead, just like a Victorian spinster who'd been flashed at and was about to swoon. His eyes fluttered closed and his knees buckled under him.

'He's going, he's going,' Shake declared, all drama, as Gaz crumpled and hit the deck.

Gaz had fainted! What a laugh.

Luke, Brigit and I raced over for a closer look and to find out what it was all about.

'Give the man some air, man,' Joey ordered.

'Come on, man.' He hunkered down beside Gaz. 'Keep breathing, man, come on, man, deep breaths.'

Gaz obliged by wheezing like an asthmatic.

'Loosen his stays,' I murmured.

'What's up?' Luke demanded.

I had thought it was just the heat that had Gaz in such a state but, when Joey said huffily 'Let the man have a bit of privacy,' it was obvious that something far more interesting had happened.

Joey was always a little bit uptight when Brigit was around. He acted as if Brigit was mad about him, actually hounding him, and trying to trap him into going out with her. The cheeky article. Just because she'd slept with him. But this particular time, it was clear that Joey's reticence had nothing to do with Brigit.

My blood quickened with anticipation. What had happened? Maybe Gaz had been knocked down. New York cyclists were vicious.

I cast my eye over his prone body looking for tell-tale injuries – perhaps the track of a bikewheel on his face – when I noticed there was something wrong with his left arm.

It was swollen and bloody. So bloody that it nearly obscured the word 'ASSS' inscribed in gothic lettering on his skin.

'What's wrong with his arm?' I demanded.

'Nothing,' Joey said defensively.

And suddenly I knew.

'He's had a tattoo done,' I exclaimed. 'Is that why he's fainted?'

What a girl, I thought with contempt.

Gaz's eyes fluttered open. 'That fucker was a butcher,' he croaked. 'He tortured me.'

I looked again – 'ASSS'.

'What were you getting done?' I asked.

'Only a tattoo of the best band in the known universe.'

'But ASSS?' Brigit asked, confused. 'A band called ASSS?'

'No,' Joey said testily, rolling his eyes at Brigit's alleged stupidity. 'They're called Assassin.'

'But where's the rest of the word?' I asked, baffled. 'It seems to me you're missing an A, an S, an I and an N. And how you're going to fit in an A between those two Ss, I don't know.'

'The tattoo-man couldn't spell,' Joey said shortly.

'Gaz couldn't take any more pain, man,' Shake said at the same time. 'He was begging like a dawg for the tattoo-man to stop . . .' Shake's voice trailed away when he noticed Joey frowning violently at him.

'He's going back to get it finished,' Joey said grimly. 'He's only home for a rest.'

'I'm not going back!' Gaz proceeded to throw a fit on the floor. 'Don't make me, don't make me, it was fucking agony, man. I'm telling you, I held out for as long as I could, man, but, man, the pain, man, I'M NOT GOING BACK . . .' He looked deranged with fear.

'But, listen, man,' Joey said in a low, don't-embarrass-yourself-in-front-of-the-girls voice. 'What about the rest of the name? You're going to look like a wanker if you don't get it finished.'

'I'll chop my arm off,' Gaz offered wildly. 'Then no one will know.'

'Shut up, man,' Joey threatened. 'We'll get you good and tanked up and then we'll go back.'

'NO!' Gaz shrieked.

'Yeah, listen, man,' Shake soothed. 'Bottle of JD, we'll have you flying, man, feeling no pain.'

'NO!'

'Man, do you remember the first time I ever met you,' Joey looked hard at Gaz who was still lying on the broad of his back on the floor. 'First of July 1985, Zeppelin Records? You told me you'd lay down your wife for the Axeman. What's up with you? What's *wrong* with you, man, that you won't go through a small amount of pain for the world's greatest band? After all they've done for you? I'm disappointed in you, man, you know?'

Gaz looked wretched. 'I can't do it. I'm sorry, man, to let you down like this, man, but I can't do it.'

'For fuck's sake,' Joey angrily sprang to his feet and aimed a kick at the sofa. He ran his hands through his hair, paused, then kicked the sofa again. Abruptly, he began rooting around in a drawer.

Me, Luke, Brigit, Shake and Gaz – especially Gaz – watched him anxiously. There was no telling what Joey might do, he was very upset.

Joey found what he was looking for. Something black and shiny. It was too small to be a gun, so it must be a knife.

I wondered if he was proposing to hold Gaz down and carry on from where the tattooist had left off.

From the look on everyone else's faces I wasn't the only one who was wondering that.

Joey approached with menace.

'Give me your arm,' he ordered Gaz.

'No, listen, man, there's no need for this . . .' Gaz protested.

'Give me your fucking arm. No mate of mine is going to be a laughing stock.'

Gaz began to scrabble to his feet. 'Get the knife off him,' he beseeched Luke.

'Give me the knife, man,' Luke stepped in front of the approaching Joey. I almost melted with lust at Luke's mastery.

'What knife?' Joey demanded.

'*That* knife.' Luke nodded at Joey's hand.

'It's not a knife,' Joey protested.

'Well, what is it so?'

'It's a MARKER, a magic MARKER,' he shouted. 'If he won't get the tattoo finished, I'm going to *draw* the rest of it on him.'

Relief rushed through the room. In fact we were all so delighted that Joey wasn't going to kill Gaz that we spent a good while practising writing A, I, S and N in gothic letters with him.

Next, Shake tentatively suggested a game of Scrabble. Shake *loved* Scrabble. And to look at him you'd think he was more likely to get his kicks throwing tellys out of hotel-room windows.

'One game,' I said obligingly. 'And then we're going out. It's Saturday night, you saddo.'

'Thanks,' Shake said gleefully. We broke out the beers and Shake, Luke, Joey, Brigit and I gathered round the board on the floor.

Gaz watched *Ren and Stimpy*. It was for the best, really. He'd done nothing but cause arguments the last time, insisting things like 'noize', 'chix', 'zitz' and 'Gaz' were words.

With noise and chatter, the game started. I was totally focused on it because I quite enjoyed Scrabble myself. But when I happened to glance up, Luke's eyes were on me, dark and meaningful. Something in his expression made me shy. I looked away, but my concentration was destroyed, and the only thing I could cobble together from my letters was 'hat'. While Brigit got 'joyful' and Shake got 'hijack'.

I found I was irresistibly drawn back to look at Luke. This time he held my gaze and smiled. It began slowly and spread out into a great, big warm beam. So admiring, so loving was it, I felt as if I had my own personal sun.

Shake intercepted the smile. 'What?' he asked anxiously, looking from me to Luke and back again. 'Don't tell me you've got "quincunx" again?'

50

Summer in New York moved into fall, a much more humane season. The killer heat abated, the air became crisp and the leaves on the trees turned every colour of red and gold. I continued to see Luke every weekend and most of the week too. While I still lived in fear of certain people's scorn, it was getting harder and harder to deny to both myself and others that he was my boyfriend. After all, wasn't he with me the historic day I bought my new fall coat, a chocolate-coloured, Diana Rigg-type, belted raincoat? Didn't I hold his hand in the street? (Although I let it drop when we went into Donna Karan.) And on the way home, didn't he insist on stopping in front of every shop, pointing things out in the windows and declaring 'Hey, Rachel, babe, that'd look *blinding* on you'?

I kept having to drag him away, while saying sternly, 'No, Luke. That's way too short. Even for me.'

But he continually protested, while trying to pull me into the shop, 'No such thing as too short, babe, not with your legs.'

In October Brigit met another little Hispanic, this time a Puerto Rican called José, who proved as elusive as Carlos ever had. Her new job ensured she didn't have as much spare time as she used to. But what little she had, she spent hanging around waiting for Josie (as Luke and I called him) to ring. *Plus ça change . . .*

419

'Why can't I ever meet someone nice?' she demanded tearfully of me one evening. 'Why can't me and Josie be like you and Luke? *José*, I mean. What's wrong with you and Costello, that you can't call Josie by his right name?

'*José*, I mean!' she shouted in exasperation.

I was delighted that Brigit was miserable. It meant that while she was pissed-off with Josie she'd forget to be pissed-off with me. It made a welcome change.

'What do you mean, "Me and Luke"?' I asked.

'You know.' She flailed around with her hands. 'In love.'

'Ah, *hardly*,' I protested, filled with warmth at the suggestion that Luke was in love with me. But I wasn't sure whether he was or not, although he was very generous with the 'I love you's. The trouble was he told *everyone* he loved them, even Benny the bagel man. Whenever I did something nice for him he said 'Thanks, babe, I love you.' And it didn't have to be a big something nice, something as small as making him a toasted cheese sandwich would do. If other people were there he'd stick out his arm, point at me and say 'I love this woman.' In fact, he sometimes did that when it was just the two of us.

Brigit watched my confused face. 'Are you seriously trying to tell me that you're not in love with Luke Costello?' she demanded. 'Are you still holding out on him?'

'I *like* him,' I defended myself. 'I *fancy* him. Isn't that enough for you?'

It was true. I *did* like him, I *did* fancy him. I just couldn't help thinking there was supposed to be *more*.

'What do you want? Some kind of celestial messenger to come along with a bugle and *tell* you you've fallen in love with him?' she demanded viciously.

'Easy, Brigit,' I said anxiously. 'Just because Josie's late ringing you, there's no need to humble me for not feeling the right way about Luke.'

'If it looks like a duck, walks like a duck, quacks like a duck, then the chances are it's a duck,' Brigit said darkly.

I looked blankly at her. Why was she calling Josie a duck?

'I mean,' she sighed, 'you like Luke, you fancy him, you keep buying new bras, you can't stay away from him. You come home here every evening and say "We're forcing ourselves to take a night off from each other tonight," then at five to nine you ring him, if he hasn't rung you first. Next thing you've put a toothbrush and a clean pair of knickers into your bag and you're off round to his place, like a hare out of a trap. *Don't* try telling me you're not in love with him.'

She paused. 'You haven't been taking your toothbrush lately, you scuzzy article. Don't you clean your teeth anymore?'

'I do.' I blushed.

'Aha!' she exclaimed. 'A H A ! All becomes clear. You've got a new toothbrush that lives in Luke's. A special *luurve* toothbrush.'

I shrugged, embarrassed. 'Maybe.'

'I bet.' Brigit shrewdly watched my reactions. 'I bet you've got a lovely new deodorant and a lovely new jar of face-cream over there too.

'I KNEW IT!' she bellowed triumphantly, when I couldn't deny it.

'Cotton wool?' she asked. 'Make-up remover?'

I shook my head.

'Not yet at the stage where you take off your make-up when you're with him,' she sighed. 'Ah, love's young dream.'

'You've cooked for him,' she continued. 'He's taken you away for a weekend, he rings you every day at work, you smile your head off each time you open the door to him, you haven't had a hair on either of your shins since last June. He's so thoughtful and romantic. DON'T try telling me you're not in love.'

'But . . .' I tried to protest.

'You're too contrary,' she complained. 'If he treated you like shite and broke it off with you, then you'd decide you were mad about him.'

I watched Brigit biting her nails and pacing up and down and tried to get a handle on how I felt about Luke.

I couldn't deny that most of the time with him it was wonderful. I fancied him violently. He was sexy and macho, sweet and handsome. Sometimes we spent entire days in bed. Not just having sex. But talking. I loved being with him because he was so funny, such a great entertainer. And he made me feel as if I was too. He asked me questions and got me to relate anecdotes and laughed at all the funny bits.

Brigit was right when she'd said he was thoughtful and romantic. For my birthday in August he took me to Puerto Rico for the weekend. (Brigit tried to stowaway in my holdall and when she couldn't fit she begged me to kidnap a youth for her. 'All I ask,' she'd pleaded, 'is that he's over the age of consent.')

And Luke *did* ring me every day at work. I now depended on him calling so I could take a break from messing up the reservations at the Barbados Motel to whinge to a sympathetic ear. 'Tell that Eric dude he'd better watch it, babe,' Luke threatened daily. 'If he upsets my woman he has me to answer to.'

And it was wonderful to stagger home to him from

a hard day, to find that he'd made Shake and Joey go out for the evening and had cooked me dinner. It didn't matter that the plates had been stolen from Pizza Hut, the napkins were McDonald's serviettes and the food was either takeaway or microwaved and the wine was actually beer. He had the important romantic things – candles, condoms and a whole chocolate cheesecake, all for me.

The phone rang, jolting me out of my Luke-induced reverie. Brigit threw herself bodily across the room and dove on the phone. It was Josie.

As she chattered extra-animatedly to him, I suddenly realized the main problem with Luke and me. It wasn't the most obvious thing, that I was ashamed of his terrible clothes. It was that we had *different priorities.* He had a surprisingly wide range of interests. Too wide, if you asked me. He often made me do things I didn't want to do, like go to the cinema, or the theatre. Whereas my main hobby was having fun in fashionable, glamorous places. I wanted to party a lot harder than he ever did. Of course, he enjoyed going out and getting jarred, but my favourite way of letting off a bit of steam was doing coke. And Luke had a real down on drugs. He had constant fights with Joey, because Joey insisted on keeping a stash of coke in the apartment. Which I *loved.* It was nice to know there was some handy if I was ever stuck.

Brigit got off the phone. 'That was Josie,' she beamed. 'His sister is in some play-type of installation thing in TriBeCa. I need you to come.'

'When?' I asked.

'Tonight.'

I hesitated. Brigit misread it.

'I'll pay,' she shrieked. 'I'll pay. But you've got to come. Please. I can't go on my own.'

'Luke'd probably like to come too,' I said casually. 'You know how he enjoys plays.'

'You sly hoor.' Brigit Lenehan was no eejit. 'Aren't you and him supposed to be taking a night off from each other?'

'We'd discussed it,' I said reasonably. 'But now that this unforeseen event has cropped up . . .'

'You're pathetic!' she declared. 'You can't even go one night without seeing him.'

'Not at all.' I said, my calm voice belying the delight I felt at the thought of seeing him. I hadn't known how I'd survive until the following evening. 'He'd be very sorry to miss a play. Especially when he knows the brother of one of the cast.'

The phone rang and Brigit devoured it.

'Hello,' she said eagerly. 'Oh, it's you. What do you want? Well, tell me what you want to say to her and I'll pass it on.'

She turned to me. 'It's Luke,' she said. 'He says to tell you he can't live without you, and can he come over.'

51

Lunch-time at the Cloisters. My parents were due in about half an hour as my Involved Significant Others. There was an awful lot of activity in the dining-room, which didn't succeed in distracting me from my stomach-churning anxiety.

We had a new inmate. A man. But of the tubby, brown-jumper-wearing variety. Barely a man at all, in other words. Not that it mattered, because I was, after all, promised to Chris. Even if Chris didn't know it yet.

The new brown jumper's name was Digger and the first thing he said to me was 'Are you famous?'

'No,' I assured him.

'No, I didn't think you were,' he said. 'But I thought I'd better check anyway.

'I'll give them two more days,' he added with menace, 'and if they haven't got anyone good in by then, I'm going to ask for a refund.'

I thought back. I'd wondered if there was a pop-star wing and, instead of labelling him a thick eejit, I smiled kindly.

'She's famous.' I indicated Misty. But Digger wasn't impressed with someone who'd written a book.

What he had in mind was a sports personality. Preferably a premier division football player.

Don had come to the end of his eight weeks and we were giving him a card and a bit of a send-off.

Frederick, who was leaving the following day, presented him with the card, then made a little speech.

'You annoyed the life out of me, with all your fussing and foostering . . .'

Lots of laughter greeted that.

'. . . but I was awful fond of you anyway. And everyone here wishes you all the best out there. And remember, *stay with the feelings*.'

More laughter. Followed by demands for a speech from Don.

He stood up, plump and short, blushing and smiling, smoothing his tank-top over his round stomach. Taking a deep breath, he launched into 'When I first came here I thought ye were all mad, I didn't want to be in with a crowd of alcoholics. I thought there was nothing wrong with me.'

I was surprised by the amount of knowing smiles and nods that were exchanged when he said that.

'I hated my poor mother for putting me in here. But I learnt the hard way how selfish I've been, and how I've been wasting my life. So, the best of luck to ye. Hang on, it gets better. And I'll tell you one thing. I'm not going to drink. And do you know why? Because I don't want to end up back here with you crowd of gob-shites!'

'Have a pint waiting for me in Flynns,' roared Mike. Everyone laughed, including me. Then there were lots of tearful hugs.

Some of them even for Don.

Suddenly the time came for group, and we reluctantly left him sitting alone in the empty dining-room, waiting for his lift. He looked longingly at us. And we moved away, already separate.

426

I won't let this session get to me, I vowed defiantly, as I marched down the corridor. Less than four more days and I'm out of here.

Mum and Dad were already sitting in the Abbot's Quarter, dressed as if they were going to a wedding. It wasn't every day they came to a rehabilitation centre to dissect the life of their middle child.

I nodded awkwardly at them and mumblingly introduced them to Mike, John Joe and the others.

Mum gave me a shaky, watery smile and to my alarm I felt tears start in my eyes.

Then Josephine, the MC, arrived.

'Thank you for coming,' she said. 'We're hoping you can shed light on Rachel and her drug-taking.'

I felt myself shrink and cringe and pull myself back into the chair, in an abortive attempt to disappear. I always hated hearing what people thought of me. My whole life had been an attempt to get people to like me and it was hard to listen to the extent of my failure.

Mum opened the bidding by bursting into tears. 'I can't believe Rachel is a drug addict.'

You're not the only one, I thought, trying to fight off terrible wretchedness.

Dad took charge. 'Rachel hasn't lived at home for the last eight years.' He'd dropped his Wild West accent for the session. 'So we'd know very little about drugs and the like.'

Big lie. Didn't they share a house with Anna?

'No problem,' Josephine said. 'There's plenty of other vital information you can give us. Particularly about Rachel's childhood.'

Mum, Dad and I stiffened as one. I didn't know why,

it wasn't as if they'd locked me in a cupboard and beat and starved me. We had nothing to hide.

'I'd like to ask you about a time she remembers as particularly traumatic,' Josephine said. 'She got very upset about it one day in group.'

'We didn't do anything to her,' Mum burst out, shooting me a furious look.

'I'm not suggesting you did,' Josephine soothed. 'But children often see the adult world in a distorted way.'

Mum glared at me.

'Did you ever suffer from post-natal depression?' Josephine asked.

'Post-natal depression!' Mum snorted. 'Indeed'n I did not! Post-natal depression wasn't invented in those days.'

My heart sank. Nice try, Josephine.

'Did anything happen to you or the family shortly after Anna arrived?' Josephine pressed.

I squirmed. I already knew the answers and I wanted it to stop.

'Well,' Mum said warily, 'two months after Anna was born, my father, Rachel's grandad, died.'

'And you were upset by this?'

Mum looked at Josephine as if she was mad. 'Of *course* I was upset by it. My own father! Of course I was upset.'

'And what form did this upset take?'

Mum threw me a filthy look. 'I cried a lot, I suppose. But my father had died, what was I *expected* to do!'

'What I'm trying to get at,' Josephine said, 'is did you have some sort of a breakdown? Rachel remembers it as a very painful period and it's important to get to the bottom of it.'

'Breakdown!' Mum's face was aghast. 'A breakdown!

428

I'd have *loved* a breakdown, but how could I, with a family of small children to rear?'

'Maybe "breakdown" is the wrong word. Did you ever at any stage take to your bed? Even for a short while?'

'Chance would have been a fine thing,' Mum sniffed.

And I felt small childish voices clamour inside my head. 'But you did! And it was all my fault.'

'Do you not remember those couple of weeks?' Dad interjected. 'When I was away on the course . . .'

'In Manchester?' Josephine asked.

'Yes,' he said, shocked. 'How do you know?'

'Rachel mentioned it. Carry on.'

'My wife was finding it hard to sleep, with me being away and it only a month since her father died. So her sister came to stay with us, and she was able to take to the bed for a while.'

'You see, Rachel,' Josephine said triumphantly. 'It wasn't your fault at all.'

'I remember it differently,' I muttered, finding it hard to accept this version of events as the truth . . .

'I know you do,' she agreed. 'And I think it's important for you to see how you *do* remember it. You exaggerated everything. The scale of the disaster, the length of time it went on for and most importantly of all, your part in it. In your version you played a starring role.'

'No,' I choked. 'Not a *starring* role. More like, more like . . .' I searched for the words to express how I felt. '. . . more like, the role of the baddy! The evil streak of the family.'

'Not at all,' Dad blustered. 'Evil! What did you do that was evil?'

'I pinched Anna,' I said in a little voice.

'So what! Anna pinched Helen when she arrived. And Claire did exactly the same to Margaret and Margaret did the same to you.'

'Margaret pinched me?' I blurted. I'd thought Margaret had never done a bad thing in her life. 'Are you sure?'

'I am, of course,' said Dad.

'Remember?' He turned to Mum.

'I can't say that I do,' she said stiffly.

'Indeed you can,' he exclaimed.

'If you say so,' she said, in a tone that let everyone know she was humouring her poor, deluded husband.

Josephine looked at Mum, then looked at me. Looked at Mum again, then gave a secret little smile.

Mum's face reddened. She suspected that Josephine was laughing at her, and she might have been for all I knew.

'The way I remember it,' Dad gave Mum a funny look, then turned to me, 'is that you were no worse and no better than any of your sisters.'

Mum muttered something that sounded like 'No better, certainly.'

I felt sick.

'Have you some kind of resentment against Rachel, Mrs Walsh?' Josephine asked.

I reeled from her brazenness.

So did Mum from the appalled look on her face. Then she rallied.

'No mother likes to have to come into a treatment centre because her daughter's a drug addict,' she said sanctimoniously.

'Is that the only thing you have against her?'

'That's all.' Mum looked murderous.

Josephine looked questioningly at Mum. And Mum tossed her head, her mouth pursed into a cat's bum.

'So, Rachel.' Josephine smiled at me. 'I hope you can see now that you've nothing to blame yourself for.'

Would Mum have done all that crying just because her father had died? I wondered tentatively. Had Dad left merely to go on a course?

But why would they lie? They'd no need to.

And with that I felt my past transform slightly, as if a part of it had been scrubbed clean.

Josephine turned to Mum and Dad and said 'Tell us about Rachel, in general terms.'

Mum and Dad exchanged doubtful looks.

'Anything at all,' she said cheerily. 'Everything helps us to get to know her better. Tell us about her good points.'

'Good points?' Mum and Dad were startled.

'Yes,' encouraged Josephine. 'Like, is she clever?'

'Ah no,' Dad laughed. 'Claire's the clever one, she has a degree in English, you know.'

'And Margaret's not bad, either,' Mum chipped in. 'She hasn't a degree, but I'd say if she'd gone to college, she'd have done well.'

'That's right,' Dad turned to Mum. 'She was such a good worker, that even though she wasn't as bright as Claire, she'd have probably made the grade.'

Mum nodded conversationally. 'Although she's done very well for herself *without* a degree, she has a load of responsibility in that job, more than some of the people who have degrees . . .'

Josephine loudly cleared her throat.

'Rachel.' She smiled graciously. 'That's who we're discussing.'

'Ah, right.' They nodded.

Josephine waited in silence until Dad blurted out,

'Average, Rachel's average. No eejit, but no rocket scientist either.

'Hahaha,' he added, half-heartedly.

'So what *are* her good points?' Josephine pressed.

Mum and Dad turned to each other, looked perplexed, shrugged and remained silent. I could sense the other inmates shift uncomfortably and I cringed. Why wouldn't my fucking parents make something up and spare me this shame?

'Was she popular with boys?' Josephine asked.

'No,' said Mum, definitively.

'You sound very sure?'

'It was her height, you see,' Mum explained. 'She was too tall for most of the lads her own age. I'd say she had a complex about it.

'It's hard for tall girls to land boyfriends,' she explained.

I watched Josephine look very pointedly at the top of my mother's head, then at the top of my father's head, a couple of inches lower. A gesture that was completely lost on Mum.

'But I suppose apart from her height, she can look attractive sometimes,' Mum added half-heartedly. She didn't believe a word of it. Neither did Dad because he interjected 'No, Helen and Anna are the good-looking ones of the family.

'Although . . .' he added jovially.

Say I am too, I begged silently. *Say I am, too.*

'. . . the pair of them are such minxes,' he continued, 'especially Helen, that you'd wonder why anyone bothers with either of them. They'd have you driven mad!'

He seemed to expect a burst of sympathetic laughter, but his words fell on silence. The other inmates were staring at their feet and I wished I was anywhere in the world other than that room. A Turkish jail would have been nice.

The time dragged by so slowly.

'She can sing,' Dad blurted, into the mortified quiet.

'No, she can't,' Mum muttered, giving him a shut-the-fuck-up look. 'That was a mistake.'

Naturally Josephine was all ears. So they had to tell her about the Saturday afternoon when I was seven and we were having a new kitchen fitted. The old one had been ripped out and, because I had no one to play with, I sat there on my own. In the absence of anything else to do, I sang songs. ('Seasons in the Sun', 'Rhinestone Cowboy' and other favourites of long car journeys.) Mum, who was upstairs in bed with the flu, heard me. And the combination of her delirium and the effect the empty, echoey kitchen had on my youthful voice – turning it into something high and clear and tuneful – convinced her she had a fledgling opera singer for a daughter.

Less than a week later, in a mood of high anticipation, I was despatched to a private singing coach. Who did her best with me for a couple of lessons until she felt she really couldn't swizz my parents any longer by taking their money under false pretences. 'It might work if all her singing could be done in kitchens that are being redecorated,' she explained to my outraged mother. 'But I'm not sure that could be guaranteed.'

Mum never forgave me. She seemed to think I'd deliberately conned her. 'Why didn't you tell me you couldn't sing?' she'd hissed at me. 'Think of the money we've wasted.'

'I did tell you,' I protested.

'You didn't.'

'I *did*.'

433

'You didn't.'

Then I stopped defending myself because I felt guilty about misleading them. While I had suspected that the whole thing was a big mistake, I had undeniably got caught up in the general thrill of it all. I had longed to be talented and special.

How I wished Dad hadn't brought it up.

Then, because there seemed to be nothing else to say, Josephine ended the session.

That night I began packing my bag. Not that I had ever unpacked it properly. It was still thrown on the floor by the side of my bed, tights and skirts and shoes and jeans all tangled higgledy-piggledy in it.

'Going somewhere?' Chaquie shouted at me, as I took my good jacket out of the wardrobe and threw it into the bag.

Like Neil, Chaquie had lost the run of herself entirely since she'd admitted she was an alcoholic. She rivalled Neil as the narkiest inmate in the Cloisters. She shouted and screeched at everyone and everybody, especially her old buddy, God. 'Why did you make me a fucking alcoholic?' she regularly shrieked, looking heavenward. 'Why me?'

Josephine kept assuring her that her anger was perfectly normal. That it was all part of the process. Which was scant comfort to me who had to share a room with Chaquie and got yelled at constantly.

'The three weeks that I'm legally bound to stay for are up on Friday,' I explained nervously to her.

'I'd planned to escape at the end of my first three weeks too,' she said through clenched teeth. 'But then they brought in that fucker I'm married to and opened up the whole can of worms. Next they threatened me with an injunction and now I have to stay for the duration.'

'Ah well,' I said awkwardly.

'I'll miss you,' I said, realizing that I really would.

'I'll miss you too,' she roared at me.

52

The following morning we had the usual stampede down the corridor to the Abbot's Quarter. We burst in the door, laughing and pushing, in our rush to get to the good chairs. To our surprise there were already two people sitting there.

Time came screeching to a halt for me as I realized in slow motion that I knew the man. I couldn't remember where I'd seen him before but there was something about the way he looked that . . .

The nano-seconds groaned by as I clocked his hair, his face, his clothes. Who was he? I knew I knew him.

Was it . . .?

Could it be . . .?

Oh, my God, it couldn't possibly be . . .

It was . . .

It was.

'Hello, Luke,' I heard myself say.

He stood up, taller and bigger than I remembered him. His hair was messy and his handsome face unshaven. So heartstoppingly *familiar*. I was suffused with delight for the briefest instant. Luke, *my* Luke, had come to get me! But even as a smile exploded on my face, it was already inching away in confusion. This was all wrong. He wasn't behaving like my Luke. His expression was granite-grim and he hadn't leapt on me, kissed me and swung me round the room.

Memories came rushing back of the terrible final scene when he'd broken it off with me. Then with scalp-crawling horror, I remembered the questionnaire. It had arrived in person. How could I have ever thought I'd avoid it?

'Rachel.' The unfriendly nod and the fact that he didn't call me 'Babe' indicated he hadn't come in peace. I shrank with rejection.

The instant where I turned to the tall blonde woman who stood next to him took about an hour. I knew her too. I'd definitely seen her before. Maybe not to talk to, but I knew the face.

Surely it wasn't . . .?

No, it couldn't be . . .?

What had I ever done to deserve this . . .?

'Hello, Brigit,' I said, my lips mumbly and numb.

She was as unfriendly as Luke, just giving me a brief 'Morning'. I *quailed.*

I turned to Mike and the others, foolishly feeling that I should introduce everyone. My knees trembled with shock and, after I introduced Mike to John Joe, and Chaquie to Misty, shakily sat down on the worst seat. Four or five springs set about gouging tunnels in my bum but I barely felt it.

Luke and Brigit also sat down, looking exhausted and miserable. You could *smell* the agog interest of Mike and the other inmates.

Meanwhile, I thought I had died and gone to hell. From Luke's and Brigit's hostility, I knew their visit indicated something bad. This can't be happening, I thought repeatedly. This cannot be happening. I was very shaken by both of them being there. But *more* shaken by Luke. We'd been so close, so easy with each other, and I was devastated by the coldness between us. Whenever we'd been together he'd been wildly, generously affectionate. But now Luke was sitting on the other side of the room from me, bristling with an invisible force field that warned me not to try and touch him under any circumstances.

'How's it going, Rachel?' He finally attempted conversation.

'Great!' I found myself saying.

'Good.' He nodded, miserably. I wasn't used to seeing him look miserable, he usually looked so alive. There were any number of things I desperately wanted to know. Have you a new girlfriend? Is she as nice as me? Have you missed me? But I was too stunned to manage anything.

I turned to Brigit. She looked the way she did when she had no make-up on, even though she was plastered in it. That was weird.

It was all weird.

The last time I'd seen or heard from her was in our apartment in New York, as I was leaving for the airport with Margaret and Paul. I'd hugged her, but she'd just stood like a plank of wood. 'I'll miss you,' I'd said.

'I won't miss you,' she'd replied.

And instead of getting upset about it, I'd totally wiped it from my mind. I'd just remembered.

Bitch, I thought.

Josephine arrived and said things about Luke and Brigit arriving unexpectedly from New York. 'We'd have warned you they were coming, Rachel,' she smiled, 'but we didn't know ourselves until this morning.'

She was lying. I could see it on her face. She'd known they were coming, but she'd kept it from me to cause maximum impact.

Without further ado, Josephine did the introductions and confirmed what I'd suspected. That Luke and Brigit had both come as my Involved Significant Others. Brigit hadn't done a questionnaire because what she wanted to convey was so important a personal visit was called for.

I felt sick with dread.

'Brigit, I realize how upset you are,' Josephine said. 'So we'll proceed gently.' It looked as if Brigit was going to be the warm-up act, with the main feature of Luke to follow.

I braced myself for her accusations, literally sweating with fear. This was the worst thing that could ever happen to me.

I wondered if people felt like this when they were taken into a sound-proofed cell to be tortured by the Inquisition. When they were aware of the horrors that awaited them, but still couldn't believe it was really about to happen. To them. Not their friend. Not their colleague. Not their brother. Not their daughter. But to them.

'You've known Rachel a long time?' Josephine asked Brigit.

'Since we were both ten.' Brigit's eyes flickered nervously over mine, then away.

'Can you tell us about Rachel's drug-taking.'

'I'll try.' She swallowed.

There was a horrible, loaded silence. Maybe she can't think of anything to say, I prayed fiercely.

But no.

Brigit spoke.

'We've tried to get her to stop for ages.' She looked at her lap, her hair hiding her face. 'Everyone has. Everyone knows she has a problem . . .'

I was so tense I was almost vibrating. I won't listen, I repeated, like a mantra. I won't listen. But bits of her damning indictment made their way to me, despite my best efforts to drown them out.

'. . . very aggressive when we tried to talk to her . . . getting worse and worse . . . took drugs on her own . . . stole other people's . . . and before going to work . . . always out of it . . . lost her job . . . always telling lies, not just about drugs, but about everything else . . .'

On and on she went. I was gobsmacked at how vicious she was about me. I sneaked a glance at Luke in the hope he'd be staring at Brigit, open-mouthed with astonishment and outrage at her accusations.

But to my horror he was nodding in agreement.

'. . . the most selfish person you ever met . . . very worrying . . . hanging around with dodgy people who take drugs . . . never any money . . . owes money to everyone . . . passed out in the hallway . . . could have been raped or murdered . . .'

And on. As I listened to her twist and distort my life, presenting something ordinary and harmless as sick, I began to get angry. She wasn't exactly squeaky-clean herself.

'. . . I was afraid to go home . . . hoped she wouldn't be there . . . extremely embarrassed by her . . . any time of the day or night . . . always off work . . . getting people to ring in sick . . .'

Suddenly I was shouting my head off. 'And what about you?' I howled. 'Since when were you such a goody two-shoes? It's only since you lickarsed your way into your new, think-you're-great promotion that you've gone all uptight about drugs.'

'Rachel, behave,' Josephine ordered.

'No, I won't,' I bawled. 'I'm not going to sit here and listen to this . . . this kangaroo court condemn me, when

I could tell you about some of the things that she's done . . .'

'Rachel,' Josephine menaced, 'shut up and at least have the manners to listen to someone who has come three thousand miles out of concern for you.'

I opened my mouth to say 'Concern? HAH!' But then I saw Luke's face. The mixture of pity and disgust on it derailed my fury. I was so used to seeing him look at me with admiration that, briefly, I felt dizzy with confusion. Humiliated, I shut up.

Brigit looked shaken, but started again.

'. . . mad paranoid . . . accusing me of flirting with Luke . . . more and more irrational . . . couldn't talk to her . . . not just cocaine . . . big jars of Valium . . . joints . . . tequila . . . never wanted to do anything that didn't involve drugs . . . stopped washing her hair . . . getting really thin . . . said she wasn't . . .'

A long time later she stopped. She hung her head and looked so abject it was obviously a ploy. She and Luke had probably rehearsed it on the plane.

'Happy now?' I sneered, overflowing with bitterness and bile.

'No,' she wailed, and, to my surprise, burst into tears.

What's she crying about? Surely that's my prerogative?

Josephine said really gently 'Can you tell the group why you're so upset.'

'I didn't want to do this,' she sobbed. 'I don't want to be mean. She was my best friend . . .'

Despite all the accusations she'd thrown at me, I suddenly got a lump in my throat.

'I'm only doing this to help her get better,' she cried. 'I know I was angry and I felt like I hated her . . .'

That appalled me. Surely not? Brigit hate me? Brigit

be angry with me? That couldn't be right. Why would she do that? Because I'd taken some of her coke once in a while? She'd want to lighten up, she really would.

'But that's not why I'm doing this. I just want her to sort her life out and go back to the way she used to be . . .'

Brigit burst into tears again and Luke silently placed his hand over Brigit's and gave her a firm grip.

As if they were a husband and wife whose child had meningitis and they were bravely waiting in the hospital corridor for news from the intensive care unit.

Nice touch, Luke, I thought scornfully.

I had to think scornful thoughts, because when I saw him holding another woman's hand, it stopped it from hurting as much.

That should be my hand he's holding, I thought miserably.

Thanks, no doubt, to the infusion of strength from Luke's firm grip, Brigit recovered her aplomb and was able to answer the multitude of questions Josephine was itching to ask.

'How long would you say Rachel's drug-taking has been a problem?'

'For a year at least,' Brigit answered, sniffing and dabbing at her eyes. 'It's hard to say because we all drank a fair bit and took drugs in a social context. But by last summer she was way out of control.

'. . . she kept saying she was sorry. Over and over again, it was the most over-used word in her vocabulary. Apart from "more".'

There were a few sniggers at that. I reddened with anger.

'. . . but she wouldn't actually change her behaviour, showing she wasn't sorry at all.

'. . . and I hated being her keeper, having to keep her in line. I'm the same age as her, in fact she's three months older than me, and I felt like I was her jailer or her parent. And she called me names, "killjoy" and "a miserable bitch". Which I wasn't.'

I was distracted from Brigit's litany by Luke shifting around in his chair, trying to get comfortable. He slouched low, almost horizontal, his long, hard thighs wide apart.

I dragged my attention back to Brigit, it was less painful.

'. . . I shouldn't have had to be her disciplinarian, it doesn't come naturally to me. And, as soon as she was forgiven for something, she just went out and did it again.

'. . . being narky isn't my way, I hated what she did to me, the way her behaviour changed me. I was always resentful. Or annoyed. I'm not like that, usually I'm very easygoing . . .'

I was alarmed to discover that for a minute I'd let myself get caught up in compassion for Brigit. I forgot, briefly, that it was *me* who was the baddy in Brigit's tale of woe.

Then I reminded myself what was going on. Brigit was simply trying to rewrite history in the light of her new, responsible job. She wanted to distance herself from her old druggy life in case her employers got wind of it. This wasn't about me, at all.

But the next thing she said, I nearly throttled her for. She said '. . . and she was horrible to Luke. She was ashamed of the way he looked because she thought he wasn't trendy enough . . .'

What did she have to say *that* for? I panicked. Things were bad enough with me and Luke, without her adding fuel to the fire. Quickly, I looked at Luke, desperately hoping he hadn't heard. But of course he had. Terrified,

I attempted a protest. 'That's not at all true,' I insisted.

'It is true,' Luke bit angrily. *Oh fuck*. I had no choice but to shut up and let Brigit continue.

'. . . and she kept trying to get me to go out with one of Luke's friends, *any* of Luke's friends, because she was afraid she wouldn't be able to stand up to people like Helenka, on her own. She didn't care that I wasn't suited to any of Luke's friends, she was too focused on herself. She just tried to play God with the lives of the people around her . . .

'. . . she even put on a New York accent when she was around people she wanted to impress. "Whatever", and "As if", and all that kind of thing . . .'

But I wasn't really listening. I was too shaken by Luke's anger. He was usually such a lovely person, especially to me. It was all weird and peculiar – he *looked* just like Luke Costello, the man who'd been my best friend, my lover for six months. But he was acting like a stranger. Worse, like an enemy.

'Let's look at another aspect of Rachel,' Josephine cut into my thoughts. She wanted to discuss my career. I had a wild urge to screech 'Do you want to know what colour my knickers are?'

'Rachel's bright,' Josephine said to Brigit. 'Why do you think she didn't have a job that used her abilities?'

'Maybe because it's hard to hang onto a decent job when your major occupation is taking drugs,' Brigit said. 'Besides, she thinks she's thick.'

'You've a good job, haven't you?' Josephine asked.

'Er, yes,' she admitted, startled.

'You've a degree, haven't you?'

'Yes.'

'In business studies?'

'Er, yes.'

'You've travelled to London, Edinburgh, Prague and New York doing work experience towards your degree and Rachel has basically *followed* you, isn't that right?' Josephine asked.

'I wouldn't say she *followed* me,' Brigit said. 'But, as I was going to those places, and she was bored with Dublin, she decided to come too.'

'And all the time you progressed in your career and Rachel achieved nothing?'

'I suppose,' Brigit admitted.

I felt worthless, like a stupid little lapdog.

'It's nice to be with someone who isn't as successful as oneself,' Josephine mused, as if she was just thinking out loud. 'The contrast is very heartening.'

'I . . . but . . .' Brigit looked confused and tried to say something, but Josephine had already moved on.

The session eventually dragged itself to its tortuous end. Josephine said Luke would be on after lunch, then ushered Luke and Brigit out to the staff dining-room. It humiliated me further that they were going to the 'normal person's' quarters. I deeply resented being marginalized, being treated like a looper.

As they left the room, I noticed Luke place his hand protectively in the small of Brigit's back. Although there was nothing small about Brigit's back, I thought, bitchiness keeping the agony at bay.

Once they'd disappeared from view, I was filled with a terrible bleakness. Where was Luke gone? Where could I find him? I wanted him to put his arms around me and pull me against his chest. I wanted comfort, the way it used to be.

I entertained a mad fantasy of breaking into the staff

rooms and engineering a meeting with him. Surely if we spoke calmly he'd see that he still cared about me? He'd cared so much about me once it was inconceivable it had entirely gone away. Then all this madness could stop.

For a moment it seemed entirely feasible, perfectly possible. Briefly the future seemed full of redemption. Then I came to my senses. It wasn't feasible at all.

The inmates swarmed over me, offering sympathy and compassion.

'Look,' I was desperate to defend myself, 'you've got to understand that what Brigit said wasn't really about me at all. She exaggerated it by miles because she's got this new job, see? They'd go mad if they knew she took drugs. And you'd want to see the amount of drugs she takes. She taught me everything I know.' I forced a laugh and waited for Mike and the others to join in. They didn't, just patted me and made soothing noises.

I couldn't eat a single thing at lunch. Instead, I prayed as I had never prayed before. I did all manner of frantic negotiating with God. A life in the missions if he would either visit a terrible calamity on Luke or, miles better, bring about a reunion with him. But I'd stitched God up in a couple of deals in the past and maybe he didn't want to do business with me.

About ten minutes before group kicked off for the afternoon's star attraction, a wave of nausea rolled over me, darkening my vision. Eagerly, I hoped that this presaged my imminent death.

I lurched along to the bathroom, hugging the wall because I could hardly see the floor for all the black patches swimming before my eyes. But as soon as I threw up, I felt OK again. Certainly not about to pass my expiry date. Bitter was my disappointment.

53

Before I knew it I was sitting in a chair in the Abbot's Quarter – I had been allowed one of the good seats out of sympathy for my predicament – and Luke was due any minute.

Maybe he wouldn't be mean to me, I thought with a blast of hope that nearly sent me into orbit. Maybe when it comes to it, he just won't be able to be cruel. After all, Luke had been my boyfriend, he'd been mad about me. Surely he still cared? Surely he wouldn't hurt me?

Wasn't this the man who had made hot-water bottles for me every month when I got my period, a man who hadn't been afraid to buy what we'd called my 'feminine hygiene products' for me?

Once again, for the merest split-second I fantasized about Luke and me getting back together. About us returning together to New York and closing the door on this horrible episode.

Then I remembered how terrible the Brigit session had been, that the vote from the Costello jury wasn't likely to be any better. I felt sick with dread again.

I prayed and prayed to be spared, but, at two o'clock on the dot, Luke, Brigit and Josephine all trooped in and sat down. When I saw Luke I got that infinitesimal rush of joy, the way I had in the morning. He was so sexy and handsome, big and *mine*. Then I saw his grim, cold expression and remembered that things were very different now.

The session started. I could sense the excited squirming of the other inmates. They'd probably knitted at the guillotine in a former life, I thought in disgust, omitting to remember that I'd been all agog when *their* ISOs had come abitching.

'Can you tell us your relationship to Rachel?' Josephine asked Luke.

'Boyfriend,' he mumbled. 'I mean, ex-boyfriend.'

'So you were ideally placed to witness her addiction?'

'Yeah.'

I took a crumb of comfort from Luke's apparent reluctance.

'A few weeks ago you took the trouble to fill out a questionnaire on Rachel's addiction. Is it all right with you if I read it out to the group?'

Luke shrugged uncomfortably and I felt as if my stomach had flopped down to my toes.

Any time you like with the earthquake, God, I begged silently. It's not too late.

But God, capricious creature that He was, was otherwise engaged. Visiting *my* earthquake on a remote area in China, where it benefited no one. When He could have been causing mayhem in County Wicklow and doing me a huge favour. I later discovered that the remote area was called the Wik Xla Province and felt a bit better. God hadn't deserted me, he was just a bit deaf.

To my alarm Josephine produced sheaves of paper. It looked like Luke had written a book.

'Right.' Josephine cleared her throat. 'The first question is "What drugs are you aware that Rachel uses?" and Luke has answered, "Cocaine, crack cocaine, ecstasy . . ."'

I wanted to die, my disappointment was that bitter. There would be no mercy. Luke, *my* Luke, had undeniably turned on me. There had been hope right until that second, but now it was gone.

'"speed, hash, grass, magic mushrooms, acid, heroin . . ."'

Someone gasped at the 'heroin' part. For God's sake, I thought angrily. I'd only *smoked* it.

'". . . Valium, Librium, prescription painkillers, anti-depressants, sleeping tablets, appetite suppressants and any kind of alcohol."'

She paused and took a breath. 'Luke has added a postscript to this. It says "If it's a drug, Rachel will have taken it. She's probably taken drugs that haven't been invented yet." An emotional response to a factual question, but I think we understand what you're trying to say, Luke.'

My head had been bowed and my eyes clenched shut, but I looked up to see Josephine give Luke a warm smile.

It was like a nightmare. I couldn't understand how I'd suddenly gone from a position of extreme power with Luke to having none whatsoever.

'The next question is "Do you think Rachel abuses drugs?" and Luke has replied "Give me a break." What does that mean, Luke?'

'It means "yes",' he mumbled.

'Thank you,' Josephine said crisply.

'The next question is "When do you think Rachel's problem with drugs first began?" Luke has replied, "The dawn of time." Would you care to elaborate, Luke.'

'Yeah,' he shifted uneasily. 'I mean she had a habit long before I ever met her.'

How dare he use the word 'habit' about me, I thought, suddenly angry. As if I was a junkie.

'So what were you doing with me then?' I found myself screeching. 'If I was that bad?' Everyone in the room jumped, including me.

Luke rolled his eyes in a 'For fuck's sake' way, as if I was a hysterical lunatic. I hated him.

'Don't worry, Rachel,' Josephine smiled smoothly, 'we'll get to that. Next question: "When did you first realize that Rachel had a problem with drugs?" And Luke has replied – this is rather a long answer – "I always knew Rachel drank heavily and used cocaine . . ."'

I raged at the barefaced dishonesty of it. This got worse. I did *not* drink heavily. The lying bastard, making me sound like Oliver Reed.

'. . . "But I didn't think it was that strange because everyone I know drinks socially and smokes spliffs. For a good while we only met at night so, although she was always pretty out of it, I thought it was just a social thing. Even so, I told her I'd love to see her straight. And she said it was just because she was shy with me. I believed her, I even thought it was cute."'

'I *was* shy,' I hissed furiously.

Josephine glared at me, then continued '"But one time after she'd stayed over at my apartment there was a strong smell of booze from her in the morning. That was weird because she hadn't had much to drink the night before. Although she'd done a lot of coke. After she'd gone home, my flatmate Joey accused me of drinking his bottle of JD . . ."'

Josephine paused. 'JD?' she asked.

'Jack Daniels,' Luke supplied.

'Thank you,' said Josephine. '". . . which I hadn't. But

I couldn't believe Rachel had drunk it, especially not first thing in the morning."'

Suddenly, my rage abated. I was mortified. I didn't think anyone had noticed the dent I'd made in the whiskey I'd found in Luke's kitchen that morning. I wouldn't have touched it only I'd woken with an awful coke comedown. I'd been out of Valium and I'd needed something to take the edge off the horror and paranoia.

'". . . And one morning after I'd left my apartment to go to work I had to come back. I'd forgotten I had to wake Joey because his clock radio was broken. I found Rachel doing a line of coke in bed. She'd taken it from Joey's stash."'

'So she'd stolen it?' Josephine interrupted herself, looking up from the page to question Luke.

'Yeah, she'd stolen it.'

I wanted the ground to open up and swallow me whole. I burned and cringed with shame. I hated being in the wrong. Worse again, I hated people knowing about it. Luke hadn't said much to me that morning. Well, he'd shouted a fair bit, said he was worried about me and told me never to do it again. But I thought I'd got away with it, that he was so into me he'd decided he didn't mind. I felt deeply betrayed that that wasn't the case. And why did he have to tell everyone about it?

'I started watching her after that and, once I knew what I was looking for, I saw things were bad. She was always on something. She was never straight.'

He stared right at me as he said that. My head swam. Luke and I belonged in New York. Happy, in love. Him being in the Cloisters, trashing me, was just too surreal, like seeing cows flying.

'Right then,' Josephine said. 'Next question: "How did

drugs affect Rachel's behaviour?" And Luke has answered "It's hard to say because as far as I know she was always off her head when she was with me. Sometimes she was affectionate and cute. But a lot of the time she was confused and made arrangements and then forgot about them. Often we had conversations that she didn't remember when I mentioned them afterwards. I reckon her vagueness was Valium-related. She was different when she took coke. An embarrassing pain. Loud and rude and she thought she was gorgeous. The part I found roughest was that she became an over-the-top flirt when she was in that state. If there was any man there who looked her version of cool..."' Josephine paused, swallowed, then continued '"... she threw herself at him."'

I was appalled, hurt, ashamed, furious. 'How dare you?' I screeched at him. 'You were lucky I ever had anything to do with you. How dare you insult me like this!'

'How would you like me to insult you?' he drawled icily.

My heart nearly stopped beating in fear. Luke *never* used to be nasty to me. Who was this big, grim, angry, cruel man? I didn't know him. But he seemed to know me.

'You did throw yourself at them,' Luke insisted, tight-lipped, grown-up and intimidating. I didn't know how I could ever have thought he was a joke figure.

'Come on, Rachel,' he sneered. 'What about the time I took you to François's exhibition opening. And you went off, went *home*, with that art dealer dude.'

My face burned with shame. I might have known he'd bring that up. I'd never heard the end of it then.

'I didn't sleep with him,' I mumbled.

'And, anyway,' I added belligerently, 'it was only because we'd had a row.'

'A row that you manufactured after you clapped eyes on the guy,' Luke coolly threw back at me. I was horrified. I'd thought I'd successfully pulled the wool over his eyes. It was catastrophic to realize that he'd known exactly what I'd been up to.

'Which brings us neatly to our next question,' Josephine interjected. 'Which is "In what aberrant ways did Rachel behave as a result of her drug-taking?" And Luke has written: "Her behaviour got more and more weird. She almost never ate. And she got badly paranoid. Accused me of fancying her friends and looking at them like I wanted to sleep with them. She took a lot of sickies from work. Except she wasn't sick, she just stayed home to get wrecked off her head. She hardly ever went out, except to score drugs. She borrowed cash from everyone which she never paid back. When people wouldn't loan her any more she stole it . . ."'

Did I? I wondered.

It wasn't stealing, I thought dismissively. They could afford it and anyway, it was their fault for not lending it to me in the first place.

A short while later, Josephine paused. 'OK, that's the questionnaire read. Now, as Brigit is feeling too upset to answer any further questions today, perhaps you wouldn't mind, Luke?'

'OK,' he nodded.

'As Rachel . . . er . . . put to you earlier, what *were* you doing with her?'

'What was I doing with her?' Luke almost laughed. 'I was crazy about her.'

Thank you, God, thank you, God, thank you, God. I exhaled

with massive relief. He had come to his senses. About time! Now he'd take back all those awful lies he'd told about me. Maybe . . . maybe we might even make up with each other.

'Why were you crazy about her?'

Luke paused. It was a while before he spoke.

'In lots of ways, Rachel was great.'

Past tense, I noticed. Wasn't so keen on that.

'She had a great way of looking at the world,' he said. 'She was a blast and really made me laugh.

'Except sometimes,' he added doubtfully. 'Especially when she was out of it, she tried too hard and wasn't funny anymore, and that wrecked my buzz.'

I wanted to violently remind him that we were looking at my good points.

'I never really bought that sophisticated girl-about-town act she put on,' Luke confided.

That alarmed me. If he'd seen through me, who else had?

'Because when she was just *herself*,' he sounded as if he'd just discovered the secret of the universe, 'then she was, like, *amazing*.'

Good, we were back on track.

Josephine nodded encouragingly.

'We could talk about anything,' he said. 'On a good day there wasn't enough time in the world for all the things we wanted to talk about.'

That was true, I thought, yearning for the past, for Luke.

'She wasn't like any of the other girls I knew, she was far smarter. She was the only woman I knew who could quote from *Fear and Loathing in Las Vegas*.'

'*And* she called it, *Fear and* Clothing *in Las Vegas*,' he added.

'What point are you making?' Josephine asked in confusion.

'That she's funny.' He smiled. 'Sometimes we were so close I felt like we *were* each other,' he said, wistfully. He looked up and for a moment our eyes were locked together. Briefly, I saw the Luke I used to know. It was excruciatingly sad.

'OK, that's fine,' Josephine interrupted, impatiently cutting into Luke's dreamy introspection. 'I presume you tried to help Rachel when you found out how bad her drug addiction was.'

'Of course,' Luke said. 'But first she hid it from me, then she lied about it. She wouldn't admit what she took, or how much, even though I knew and I *told* her I knew. It did my head in. I tried to get her to talk about things. Then I tried to get her to go to a trick cyclist but she told me to fuck off.'

He blushed. 'Scuse my language, Sister.'

She accepted his apology with a gracious nod of her head. 'And then what happened?'

'She took her overdose and left New York.'

'Were you sorry when the relationship ended?' Josephine asked him.

'By then it wasn't much of a relationship,' he said.

My heart sank. It didn't sound like he wanted to get back with me. 'It was as good as over,' he went on.

My heart sank further. He kept talking about me in the past tense.

'I don't know why she bothered with me because nothing I did made her happy,' he said. 'She wanted to change everything, my clothes, my mates, where I lived, what I spent my money on. Even the *music* I listened to.'

Josephine nodded sympathetically.

455

'I knew she laughed at the gear myself and my mates wore, and no real problem there. We were used to it. But then she started ignoring me in public, like, pretending she wasn't with me. And that *wasn't* funny, no way.'

-I looked at his open, honest expression and for a second, as I had with Brigit, I felt compassion for him. Poor Luke, I thought, to be treated like that. Then I remembered I was the one who'd been mean to him, and that actually, I hadn't been mean at all. The big whinger.

'The first time Rachel ignored me,' he continued, 'I thought "OK, she's a bit absent-minded, could happen to anyone." But after a while I had to face it. It was definitely deliberate. Definitely, man! When she met up with any of those dudes who worked in those designer clothes shops, she went all weird on me, left me standing on my own like a thick. Once she left a party without saying goodbye to me. A party I'd taken her to, but she met those stupid bitches – sorry! – Helenka and Jessica there and they invited her back to their apartment.'

'So how did you feel?' Josephine asked.

'Lousy,' Luke said huskily. 'I felt lousy. She was ashamed of me. I was disposable, a throw-away person, you know? It was the pits.'

For a moment I felt wretched. Then I looked at him scornfully, and thought, Grow up. I'm the one who should be feeling sorry for herself, not you.

To my surprise, Josephine said baldly to Luke 'Did you love Rachel?' My guts clenched.

He didn't reply. Just sat very still, looking at the floor.

There was a long, tense unbearable pause. I held my breath. *Did* he love me?

I desperately wanted him to. He sat up and ran his

hands through his long hair. I tensed for his answer and he took a breath before he spoke.

'No,' he said. And a part deep within me withered and died.

I shut my eyes from the pain.

It's not true, I forcefully reminded myself. He was mad about you, still is.

'No,' he said again.

All right, I thought, we heard you the first time, you don't have to rub it in.

'If she was the nice Rachel, the one who wasn't always off her face and smarming over those fashion assholes,' he said thoughtfully, 'then I would have loved her, no problem. No better woman.

'But that wasn't the case,' he added, 'and it's too late now.'

I stared at him. I could feel grief stamped on my face. He wouldn't look at me.

Josephine paused and looked at Luke. 'Coming here and doing what you've done today, it must have been very painful for you?'

'Yeah,' he mumbled. 'I am very . . .' he paused for a long time, 'sad.'

The word resonated in the air.

My mouth and throat felt full of something. Below my chest, I had a burning feeling, but my skin was goose-pimpled and cold.

Josephine announced the end of the session. Brigit turned and left without looking at me. Before Luke left he held my eyes for a very long time. I tried to read something in his. Contrition? Shame?

But there was nothing.

As the door closed behind them, the other inmates

457

stampeded to my side, to comfort and protect me. I recognized the way they looked at me – a mixture of pity and curiosity – because I'd used it on them often enough after their ISOs had come acalling. And I couldn't bear it.

54

My half-packed bag, lying on the floor, reproached me. Mocking me for how close I thought I'd been to leaving.

I'd thought I'd be able to race out the door as soon as the clock pinged my three weeks. But Luke and Brigit's visit put paid to that. On Wednesday evening, they had barely left the premises, when I was summoned to Dr Billings's office.

Tall and peculiar, he greeted me with an appalling attempt at a smile and I sensed the news he was about to deliver wasn't good.

'After what we've heard about you today in group, I hope you weren't thinking of leaving on Friday,' he said.

'Of course not,' I forced myself to say. I wouldn't give him the satisfaction.

'Good.' He bared his teeth. 'I'm glad we didn't have to get an injunction to make you stay.

'Which we would have done,' he added.

Somehow, I believed him.

'It's for your good,' he advised.

I managed to contain my fury by fantasizing about splitting his skull with an axe.

At least, I consoled myself on my way out of Billings's office, while I was stuck there, I could set the record straight with the other inmates. It did my head in, as I wondered what they all thought of me in the wake of Luke's and Brigit's revelations.

I felt worst of all around Chris. Even though he wasn't in my group, there were very few secrets at the Cloisters. When I'd staggered back to the dining-room after group, he was over like a shot. 'I heard you were given the this-is-your-life treatment today,' he grinned.

I usually blossomed like a flower in the sun when I was with him, but this time I wanted to run away. I was deeply ashamed. But when I tried to tell him that it was all lies he'd heard about me, he just laughed and said 'It's OK, Rachel, I still love you.'

When I went to bed that night, I re-ran tapes of the two sessions over and over again in my head. I'd been devastated with sadness about Luke, about it being over. But as I remembered the terrible, vicious, hurtful things both he and Brigit had said, my grief mutated into anger. My fury burgeoned and bubbled, festered and spat. I couldn't sleep because I kept having imaginary conversations in which I floored both of them with scathing, pithy remarks. In the end, even though I was terrified of her temper, I woke Chaquie. I had to talk to *someone*. Luckily she was too dazed to give vent to her recent narkiness. As she sat, blinking like a rabbit, I screeched at her about how humiliated I'd been. I promised her that I'd get my revenge on Luke and Brigit, no matter how long it took.

'When Dermot came as your ISO, how did you cope?' I demanded, wild-eyed.

'I was raging,' she yawned. 'Then Josephine told me I was using my anger to avoid accepting any responsibility for the situation. Now please can I go back to sleep?'

I knew I'd be interrogated by Josephine in group the next day.

I'd seen her do it to Neil, John Joe, Mike, Misty, Vincent and Chaquie. She wouldn't treat me any differently. Even though I *was* different.

Sure enough, Josephine launched straight into me.

'It wasn't a pretty picture Luke and Brigit painted yesterday, of you and your life, was it?' she began.

'Luke Costello isn't the person to give an objective picture of me,' I said wearily. 'You know how it is when romances end.'

'It's just as well Brigit came in that case,' Josephine interjected smoothly. 'You didn't have a romance with her, did you?'

'Brigit was talking crap as well.' I irritably geared up for the story of Brigit's ambition and promotion.

'Shut up.' Josephine silenced me with a glitteringly angry look.

'I never said I didn't take drugs.' I changed tack.

'Drugs aside,' she said. 'It *still* wasn't a pretty picture.'

I wasn't sure what she meant.

'Your dishonesty, selfishness, disloyalty, shallowness and fickleness,' she explained.

Oh, that.

'Your drug use is just the tip of the iceberg, Rachel,' she said. 'I'm more interested in the person they described. You know – someone with no loyalty, who would ignore her boyfriend when people she wants to impress are present. A person so shallow she judges everyone on their outward appearance, with no regard to whether or not they're decent human beings. So selfish that she steals without any thought as to how it affects the person she steals from. Who lets down her co-workers and employers at a moment's notice. A person with a distorted, warped value system. With so little sense of who she is that

461

she affects a different accent with different people . . .'

On and on she went. Every time she finished a sentence, I thought she'd come to the end of her speech, but no.

I tried to stop listening.

'That's you, Rachel,' she finally wrapped it up. 'You are that amorphous, shapeless human being. No loyalty, no integrity, nothing.'

I shrugged. For some reason she hadn't got to me. I felt a throb of triumph.

Josephine looked at me scornfully. 'I know you're pouring all your energy into not cracking in front of me.'

How does she know? I wondered, gripped with anxiety.

'But I'm not your enemy, Rachel,' she continued. 'Your real enemy is yourself and that's not going to go away. You'll walk out of this room today thinking you're great for not having opened up to me. But that's not a victory, it's a failure.'

Suddenly I felt terribly tired.

'I'll tell you why you're such a horrible person, shall I?' she asked.

'Shall I?' she asked again, when I didn't answer.

'Yes.' The word was dragged out of me.

'You have cripplingly low self-esteem,' she said. 'You count for nothing in your own estimation. And you don't like feeling worthless, who does? So you seek endorsement from people you admire. Like this Helenka that Brigit told us about. Isn't that right?'

I nodded feebly. After all, Helenka *was* worthy, I agreed with that bit.

'But it's very uncomfortable,' she pressed on, 'when you've no belief in yourself. You just float, waiting for someone else to anchor you.'

462

Whatever you say.

'Which is why you couldn't trust your decision to be with Luke,' she confided. 'Torn between wanting him but feeling you shouldn't, because the only person telling you he was OK was you. And you wouldn't believe you. What an exhausting way to live!'

It *had* been exhausting, I realized with a flash of memory. There were times when I felt I was losing my mind as I tried to juggle everyone's approval versus Luke's company.

I remembered going to a party with Luke, safe in the knowledge that no one I knew would be there. But, to my horror, the first person I saw was Chloë, one of Helenka's acolytes. In a rush of mad panic, I'd turned on my heel and left the room, while Luke went after me in bewilderment. 'What's wrong, babe?' he asked worriedly. 'Nothing,' I muttered. I forced myself to go back in, but I spent the night teetering on a knife edge, trying to hide in corners, not standing too close to Luke in case anyone (Chloë) realized I was with him, furious anytime he put his arm around me or tried to snog me, then feeling totally wretched at the hurt look in his eyes when I pushed him away. Eventually, I got really out of it because I felt I'd go bonkers otherwise.

'Wouldn't it have been far nicer to stand up straight and act *proud* to be with Luke?' Josephine's voice jolted me out of that nightmare. 'Here I am, folks, like it or lump it.'

'But . . . oh you haven't got a clue!' I was so frustrated. 'You'd have to live in New York to understand, these people are important.'

'They're not important to me.' Josephine smiled broadly. 'They're not important to Misty over there.'

Misty vigorously shook her head. But of course she would, the bitch.

'There are millions of people the world over who are perfectly content without Helenka's approval.'

'Would you mind telling me,' I said scornfully, 'what any of this has to do with drugs?'

'Plenty,' she said, with an ominous glint. 'You'll see.'

After lunch Josephine started into me again. I would have given anything for it to stop. I was very, very tired.

'You wanted to know what your low self-esteem has to do with your taking drugs,' she said. 'In its most basic form,' she went on, 'if you had self-respect, you wouldn't fill your body full of harmful substances, to the point where you make yourself ill.'

I stared at the ceiling, no idea what she was talking about.

'I'm *talking* to you, Rachel,' she barked, making me jump. 'Look at how sick you were when you arrived here. Your first morning on breakfasts you almost passed out from withdrawal symptoms from your beloved Valium!

'We found the empty bottle in your bedside locker,' she said, looking me straight in the eye. I turned away, dying with shame, raging that I hadn't disposed of it properly. But before I had a chance to cobble together some feeble excuse – 'It wasn't mine' or 'My mother gave it to me, it had holy water in it' – she started expounding again.

'This goes for all of you.' She nodded round the room. 'If you placed a high price on yourselves, you wouldn't starve yourselves or cram yourselves with too much food, or poison yourselves with excessive alcohol or, in your case, Rachel, put so many drugs into yourself that you had to be hospitalized.' Her words rang out in the silent room and I had a fleeting rush of horror.

'You were in hospital, close to death,' Josephine pressed on relentlessly, 'because of the drugs you put into your body. Does that strike you as normal?'

It was strange but I hadn't given much thought to my so-called overdose until then.

'I wasn't close to death,' I managed to scoff.

'You were,' Josephine riposted.

I paused. I had the briefest sliver of time in which I saw myself from the outside. I saw how everyone else in the room perceived me. How, if I hadn't been me, I would have perceived myself. And to almost die from taking too many drugs seemed a shocking and horrific thing to happen. If it had happened to Mike, say, or Misty, I would have been appalled at how low their drinking had brought them.

But then the aperture closed up again and with relief I went back to seeing myself from the inside, with the contextual knowledge that I had.

'It was an accident,' I pointed out.

'It wasn't.'

'It *was*. I hadn't intended to take so many.'

'You were living a life where the ingestion of powerful drugs was routine. Most people don't take any at all,' she pointed out.

'That's their problem,' I shrugged. 'If they want to struggle through all the crap life throws at them, without the assistance of recreational drugs, then they're saps.'

'Where did you get such a beleaguered attitude from?'

'Don't know.'

'Rachel, to get to the bottom of all this,' Josephine smiled, 'we're going to have to look at your childhood.'

I elaborately threw my eyes heavenwards.

'It's hard being in a big family where you feel you're the least talented, least clever, least *loved* member, isn't it?' Josephine loudly demanded.

It was as if she'd punched me in the stomach. My vision clouded with shock and pain. I would have protested, except my breath was gone.

'Where your eldest sister is brainy and charming,' she said cruelly. 'The sister closest to you is a saint in human form. Your two younger sisters are more than averagely good-looking. It's hard to live in a family in which everyone has a favourite and it's never you.'

'But . . .' I attempted.

'It's hard to live with a mother who is openly disappointed with you, who has transferred her dislike of her own height on to you,' she continued inexorably. 'Other people can say you're too tall, but it's upsetting, isn't it, Rachel, when your own *mother* says it? It's hard when you're told you're not bright enough to make a career for yourself.'

'My mother loves me,' I stammered, cold with fear.

'I'm not saying she doesn't,' Josephine assented. 'But parents are human too, with fears and unfulfilled ambitions that they sometimes bring to play on their children. It's obvious the poor woman has a massive hang-up about her height which she's passed onto you. She's a good person, but not always a good parent.'

I had a burst of wild rage against Mum. What a cruel old cow, I thought bitterly. For making me feel like such a clumsy oaf all my life. No wonder all my relationships with men were disasters. No wonder – I approached this idea tentatively – I had to take so many drugs!

'So I can blame my mother for me being – *if* I am, I

mean – an addict,' I said, desperately trying to latch onto something positive.

'Oh no.'

No? Well, what are you talking about then?

'Rachel,' Josephine said gently. 'The Cloisters isn't about apportioning blame.'

'Well, what *is* it about?'

'If we can locate and examine where your lack of self-worth comes from, then we can deal with it.'

I felt a surge of fury at everything. I was sick, sick, *sick* of all of this. I was tired and bored and I wanted to go to sleep.

'How come,' I forced a swagger, 'I have your so-called low self-esteem and my sisters don't? We all have the same parents. Tell me that, then!'

'A complex question,' she replied smoothly. 'Which I have actually already answered for you on at least one occasion.'

'Have y . . . ?'

'We form our initial picture of ourselves from our parents,' she said with elaborate patience. 'And your parents are – affectionately – dismissive of you.'

Don't.

'Some people take to heart the negative messages they get about themselves. Others, more resilient, shrug off any criticisms . . .'

Actually, I realized, some of this *did* sound familiar.

'. . . You're one of the sensitive ones, your sisters aren't. Simple as that.'

'Bastards,' I muttered, hating everyone in my family.

'Sorry?'

'Bastards,' I said, louder. 'Why did they pick on me to

467

be dismissive of? I could have had a lovely life if they hadn't done that.'

'OK,' Josephine said. 'You're angry. But look at, say, how Margaret must feel, having been assigned the role of the "good" daughter. If she ever wanted to rebel, do something out of character, she'd probably feel she wasn't entitled to. She could deeply resent your parents for that.'

'She's too much of a lickarse to resent anyone,' I burst out angrily.

'You see! You're just buying into the stereotype too! But what if Margaret *wants* to resent people? Can you imagine how confused and guilty she would feel?'

'Look, who cares about her!' I exclaimed.

'I'm simply pointing out that you and your sisters were subconsciously assigned roles. It happens in families all the time. You don't like your role – that of the no-hoper, puppy dog – but your sisters probably find theirs as much of a bind as you do.

'Stop feeling sorry for yourself, is what I'm trying to say,' she finished.

'I've every right to feel sorry for myself,' I said, feeling very sorry for myself *indeed*.

'You can't go through life blaming other people for your faults,' she said sternly. 'You're an adult. Take responsibility for yourself and your happiness. You're no longer hidebound by the role your family gave you. Just because you were told you were too tall or too stupid doesn't actually mean you *are*.'

'I've been very damaged by my family,' I sniffed, self-righteously, ignoring her galvanizing speech. I caught Mike trying not to laugh. And Misty was openly sneering.

'What's so funny?' I demanded angrily of her. I'd never have confronted her, if I hadn't been raging.

'You? Damaged?' She laughed.

'Yes,' I said loudly. 'Me. Damaged.'

'If you'd had your father coming into your bed every night from when you were nine years of age and forcing his dick into you, then I'd say you were damaged,' she said quickly and shrilly. 'If you had your mother calling you a liar and belting the crap out of you when you asked her for help, then I'd say you were damaged. If your older sister left home when she was sixteen and abandoned you to your father, then I'd say you were damaged!' Her face was contorted with wild emotion and she was on the edge of her chair. Her freckles were almost hopping off her face and she was openly snarling. Suddenly, she seemed to realize what she was saying, stopped abruptly, sat back and lowered her head.

I could feel the frozen shock on my face. It was mirrored on the faces of everyone else there. Except for Josephine's. She'd been expecting this.

'Misty,' she said gently, 'I was wondering when you were going to tell us.'

No further attention was paid to me for the rest of the session. Misty had shamed me, but at the same time I couldn't banish the resentment I felt at her because she'd stolen my thunder.

After group, when I went to the dining-room, Misty was crying and, to my great alarm, Chris was almost sitting on her lap. He looked up when I came in then turned back, very deliberately, to Misty and tenderly wiped her tears away with his thumbs. The way he'd once done to me. I was as jealous as if we'd been married for four years and I'd just caught him in bed with Misty. He looked at me again, his expression unreadable.

55

With Misty's shock revelations, the huge amounts of attention that had been paid to me all week came screeching to an abrupt halt. Her childhood abuse was an all-singing, all-dancing production which took up both the Friday sessions and lots of the following week. Everyone's focus was on her, as she raged and wept, screamed and howled.

Almost with a sense of anti-climax, I found that life in the Cloisters continued in much the same way as it had before the apocalyptic visit from Brigit and Luke. O K, so I constantly fantasized about killing them both. But I still went to group, ate my meals, bickered and played with the others. I went to my Narcotics Anonymous meeting on Thursday night, to cookery on Saturday morning and I played games on Saturday night. But mostly I kept a close eye on Chris. I was frustrated by his slipperiness because while he was nearly always nice to me, it was only up to a certain point. I'd hoped that at some stage he'd have cornered me for a clinch, but it never happened. And what really bothered me was that he was as nice – sometimes even nicer, I feared – to Misty.

Despite his elusiveness, he listened patiently when I screeched hysterically about what lying bastards Luke and Brigit were. In fact, *all* the inmates gave me airspace, even if I suspected they were humouring me. I couldn't help but be reminded of the time Neil was furious with Emer.

When he'd called her every name under the sun, and everyone had gently patted him on the back and mildly agreed with him.

Chaquie was the person who stopped me from going round the bend. She stayed up with me when I couldn't sleep from fury. Luckily, her great narkiness seemed to have passed. Which was just as well because there wasn't room for two loopers in a room as small as ours.

I was much angrier with Luke than with Brigit. But I was also very *confused*. When we'd lived in New York, Luke had been affectionate and tender to me. I couldn't come to terms with the change. The contrast was just too much.

With bitter-sweet torment, I kept remembering him at the zenith of his loveliness to me, the previous November when I'd had the flu. I couldn't stop taking the memory out, unwrapping it as if it was a family heirloom and hugging it to me.

Brigit had been away for the week. In New Jersey, on a course to learn how to boss people around more effectively. An ass-kicking conference or something. Naturally, the minute she left, Luke arrived with a facecloth and a week's supply of underpants. What was the point of having an empty apartment if you didn't maximize your chances of sex in every room in the place without fear of interruption?

It was gorgeous. Nearly like being married, except I could still breathe. Each evening we rushed home to each other, cooked dinner, took long, leisurely baths together, had sex on the kitchen floor, the bathroom floor, the living-room floor, the hall floor and the bedroom floor. We left together in the morning and got the same train to work. He always had my subway token ready for me. When he got off first in midtown, he kissed me in full view of everyone on the A train and said, 'See you this evening, my turn to cook.' Domestic bliss.

On Wednesday, I felt dodgy all day. But I was used to feeling awful in work, so I didn't pay much attention. Only on the walk home from the subway station did I really start to feel peculiar. Cold and hot, achy and fuzzy.

I staggered up the stairs to the apartment, my legs almost paralysed. At the top, Luke flung wide the front door, gave me a big grin and said 'Hi honey, you're home!' He bustled me in and said 'The takeaway is on its way. I didn't know whether to get you chocolate or strawberry, so I got you both. Now, let's get you out of these wet clothes!'

He often said that, even though, of course, my clothes weren't wet.

'Come now,' he chided, unbuttoning my Diana Rigg raincoat, 'you're soaked through!'

'No, Luke,' I protested weakly, feeling like I might faint.

'Not another word, young lady,' he insisted, unzipping my jacket with a whizz, then pulling it off my shoulders.

'Luke, I feel a bit . . .' I attempted again.

'Do you want to catch your death?' he clicked. 'Rachel Walsh, you'll end up with pneumonia.' By now he was down to my bra.

'Wringing!' he declared, deftly unhooking it.

Normally, by then, I'd be feeling pretty revved up, and might even start removing some of *his* clothing. But not that day.

'Now for your skirt,' he said, feeling for the button on the waistband. 'My God, it's sopping wet, the heavens must have opened out there . . .'

He must have noticed that I wasn't responding with

my usual enthusiasm because he faltered, then stopped. 'Are you OK, babe?' he asked, suddenly anxious.

'Luke,' I managed, 'I feel a bit funny.'

'What sort of funny?' he asked, in alarm.

'I think I might be sick.'

He put his hand on my forehead and I nearly swooned from the pleasure of his cool hand against my burning skin.

'Christ!' he declared. 'You're roasting.

'Oh babe,' he said, all abject, 'I'm sorry, me taking off your clothes . . .' He frantically draped my bra around my shoulders, then made me put my coat back on.

'Come in to the fire,' he ordered.

'We haven't got a fire,' I objected weakly.

'I'll get you one,' he offered. 'Whatever you want, I'll get it.'

'I think I'd like to go to bed,' I said. My voice sounded a long, long way away.

For a second his eyes lit up. 'Great!'

Then he realized what I meant. 'Oh yeah, of course, babe.'

I stripped off the rest of my clothes and just threw them on the floor. Although I didn't have to be afflicted with flu to do that. Then I climbed in between the cool, cool sheets. For a moment I was in heaven. I must have dozed off, because next thing Luke was standing over me with a selection of milkshakes.

'Chocolate or strawberry?' he offered.

Mutely, I shook my head.

'I knew it,' he said, smiting his hand against his forehead. 'I should have got vanilla!'

'No, Luke,' I mumbled. 'Not hungry. Don't want anything.

'I must be dying.' I managed a weak smile.

'Don't, Rachel,' he ordered, with an anguished face. 'Mocking is catching.'

'No, mocking is a laugh,' I mumbled. That was what Helen always said.

'Will you be OK if I go out for a while?' he asked gently.

I must have looked distraught.

'Only to go to the drugstore,' he explained hurriedly. 'To get you things.'

He was back about half an hour later with a huge carrier bag, crammed with everything from a thermometer to magazines to chocolate to cough mixture.

'I haven't got a cough,' I said weakly.

'But you might get one,' he pointed out. 'Best to be prepared. Now let's take your temperature.

'A HUNDRED-AND-TWO!' he yelled in alarm. He began frantically tucking in the duvet all around me, even under my feet, so I was in a little cocoon.

'The woman in the drugstore said to keep you warm, but you *are* warm,' he muttered.

By midnight my temperature was a hundred-and-four so Luke got a doctor for me. It cost roughly the same to buy a three-bedroom flat as to get a doctor in Manhattan to make a house call. Luke must have really loved me.

The doctor stayed three minutes, diagnosed me with flu – 'Proper flu, *real* flu, not just a bad cold' – said there was nothing he could prescribe for me, cleared Luke out of funds, then left.

For the next three days I was in bits. Delirious, not knowing where I was or what day it was. Aching, sweating, shivering, too weak to sit up unaided to sip the Gatorade that Luke kept pressing on me.

'Try, babe,' he urged. 'You need your fluids and your glucose.'

Luke took Thursday and Friday off work to look after me. Whenever I came to, he was nearby. Either sitting on a chair in my room, watching me. Or sometimes he was in the next room, on the phone to his mates. 'Proper flu,' I heard him boast repeatedly. '*Real* flu. Not just a bad cold. No, nothing they can prescribe for her.'

On Saturday night, I felt better enough to be wrapped in the duvet and carried, *carried*, into the sitting-room. Where he lay me on the couch. I attempted to watch telly for about ten minutes, before it got too much for me. Never had I felt so cherished.

And now look at us. Best of enemies. Where had it all gone so wrong?

Assorted members of my family came to visit on Sunday. With narrowed eyes I greeted Mum and Dad, as they approached, bent double from the weight of the confectionery they'd brought. Look at them, the bastards, I thought. Trying to buy me off with chocolate. So I'm thick, am I? So I'm too tall, am I?

They didn't seem to notice the nasty vibes I sent them. After all, conversation was usually stilted and that day was no exception.

Helen had also elected to visit me again. I was extremely suspicious of her motives and I kept a close eye on both her and Chris, in case they were looking at each other too often. Even though he'd been attentive to me since the night I'd caught him comforting Misty, I was always edgy and insecure around him.

Sunday's surprise guest was Anna! I was thrilled to see

her. Not just because she was nice, of course, but because she'd give me some yearned-for drugs.

We gave each other tight hugs, then she stood on the hem of her skirt and tripped. Even though she looked very like Helen, tiny, green-eyed and with long black hair, she had none of Helen's confidence. She was a great one for tripping and falling over and banging into things. The vast quantities of recreational drugs she habitually ingested might have had something to do with her unsteadiness on her pins.

Helen was in great form, regaling all and sundry with a story about how an entire party of clerical officers hadn't been able to attend work the day after a visit to Club Mexxx. Allegedly suffering from food poisoning.

'They're threatening to sue,' she said gleefully. 'And I hope Mr stingy-arse, crappy-wage-payer Club Mexxx goes bust.'

'Of course,' she added, 'we all know that the clerical officers were just sick as dogs from *hangovers*. Food poisoning is so obvious a hangover excuse it's embarrassing. Anna there always uses it. So would've I, except I've never had a job before.'

I finally got Anna on her own. 'Have you any blem on you?' I asked quietly.

'No,' she whispered and blushed.

'Well, what have you, so?'

'Nothing.'

'*Nothing?*' I echoed, stunned. 'But why?'

'I've given up,' she said quietly, not meeting my look.

'Given up what?'

'You know . . . drugs.'

'But why?' I demanded. 'Is it Lent?'

'I don't know, it might be, but that's not why.'

'Well, what is the why?' I was appalled.

'Because, I don't want to end up like you,' she said. 'I mean, in somewhere like this!' she corrected herself frantically. 'That's what I meant, I don't want to end up in here!'

I was devastated. Totally devastated. Even *Luke* hadn't hurt me as much. I tried to compose my face so that she couldn't see my pain, but I was in bits.

'I'm sorry,' she said, a picture of misery. 'I don't want to do your head in, but when you nearly died it gave me an awful fright . . .'

'It's fine,' I said curtly.

'Oh Rachel,' she wailed quietly, trying to hold my hand, to keep me from moving away. 'Don't hate me, I'm only trying to explain . . .'

This time I shook her off, and shaking like a leaf, I went to the bathroom to calm down.

I couldn't believe it! Anna, of all people, had turned on me. *She* thought *I* had a problem. Anna, the one person I could always compare myself to and say 'Well, at least I'm not as bad as her.'

56

The days passed.

People came and went. Clarence and Frederick left. So did poor, catatonic Nancy, the tranquillizer-addicted housewife. Even up to her last day, people were holding a mirror to her face to check she was still breathing. And there was joking talk among the rest of us about buying her a survival kit for the outside world. To wit: a Walkman and a tape with the words 'Breathe in, breathe out, breathe in, breathe out,' recorded over and over again on it. I somehow suspected Nancy wouldn't be appearing in the brochure as one of the Cloisters' success stories.

Mike left, but not before Josephine managed to make him cry about the death of his father. The look on her face was something to behold – she smiled like the man used to at the end of *The A Team*. In another dimension I heard her triumph 'I love it when a plan comes together.'

Over the next ten days or so space-cadet Fergus and fatso Eamonn left too.

Nearly a week after Luke's and Brigit's visit, we got a couple of new inmates, which, as always, generated great excitement.

One was a dumpy young woman called Francie who talked loudly and incessantly, running all her words into each other. I couldn't take my eyes off her. She had shoulder-length blonde hair with two inches of dark roots on show, a gap in her front teeth that you could drive a truck through and cheap foundation several shades too dark, badly smeared onto her face. She was overweight, her hem was hanging and her skirt was red and way too tight.

My first thought was what a mess she was. But within seconds she knew everyone, was throwing cigarettes at them and had in-jokes and intimacy up and running. To my great anxiety, I saw that she was undeniably, if inexplicably, sexy. I got that familiar sick fear that Chris would shift his attention away from me.

She stood and carried herself as if she was a goddess. She didn't even seem to notice the round bulge of her stomach through her awful pencil skirt. It would've had me suicidal. Jealously I watched her, and watched Chris watching her.

When she saw Misty she let out a little screech and yelled 'O'Malley, what're you doing here, you alco?'

'Francie, you big pisshead,' Misty reparteed, all delighted, smiling for the first time in almost a week. 'Same as you.'

It turned out that they had been in the Cloisters together the previous year. The class of ninety-six.

'You've been here before?' someone asked, in shock.

'Sure, I've been in every treatment centre, mental hospital and jail in Ireland.' Francie roared with laughter.

'Why?' I asked, strangely drawn to her.

'Cos I'm a looper. Schizophrenic, manic, deluded, traumatized, take your pick. Look,' she ordered, rolling up her sleeves, 'look at them for lacerations! All my own work.'

Her arms were a mass of cuts and scars. 'There's a cigarette burn,' she pointed out conversationally. 'And another one.'

479

'So what happened to you, this time?' Misty asked.

'What didn't happen!' Francie declared, rolling her eyes. 'I'd nothing to drink, all there was at home was meths for the greyhound's feet, so I drank that. Next thing I knew it was a week later – I'dlostawholeweek, cany'believeit? I'veneverdonethatbefore – and I came to, being gang-banged by a crowd of fellas somewhereoutsideLiverpool!'

She paused for breath before launching into the tale again. 'Leftfordead, hospitalized, gotgiventhemorning-after, arrested, deported, packedoffbackhome, minuteIgettheretheysendmehere. AndhereIam!'

The entire room had fallen silent, the look on each man's face a picture as, no doubt, they yearned to be one of the boys outside Liverpool.

'Whatareyouinfor?' she gaily demanded of me.

'Drugs,' I said, dazzled by her.

'Ooooh, the best,' she nodded, her mouth bunched in approval. 'D'you go to any NA meetings?' she asked.

'Narcotics Anonymous,' she explained impatiently to my momentarily puzzled face. 'God, you cadets!'

'Just the meetings here,' I said, almost apologetically.

'Ah no! They're no good. Wait till you go to the ones outside.'

She leant closer to me and chattered on. 'Full of fellas. Fullofthem! NA is packed to the gills with men, none of them a day over thirty, and they're all mad into hugging. You'll have your pick of them. AA isn't half as good. Too many women and oul' lads.'

Up until then, the Narcotics Anonymous meetings had made very little impression on me. I usually fell asleep. But I was delighted with what Francie had told me.

'Which do you go to? AA or NA?' I asked, bandying about the abbreviations.

'All of them.' She laughed. 'I'm addicted to everything. Booze, pills, food, sex . . .'

The dining-room almost combusted from the light that sprang into the eyes of every man present at Francie's last word.

In all the excitement of Francie, the other new inmate barely got noticed. It was only after Francie and Misty swanned off to rebond that he came into focus. He was an elderly man called Padraig who shook so badly he couldn't even get the sugar into his tea. While I watched, horror-struck, it all juddered off the spoon before it got to his cup. 'Confetti,' Padraig said, with an attempt at humour.

I smiled, unable to hide my pity.

'What are you in for?' he asked me.

'Drugs.'

'You know,' he pulled himself close to me, and I tried not to recoil from the smell, 'I shouldn't be here at all. I only came in to get the wife off my back.'

I looked at him: shaking, smelly, unshaven, dissipated. In shock, I wondered, are we all mistaken when we say there's nothing wrong with us? *All* of us?

57

It took two full weeks for my world to cave in after Luke's and Brigit's visit.

In that time there were a couple of warning shudders, seismic messengers sent ahead to warn of the approaching upheaval.

But at no stage did I identify a pattern. I wouldn't see the massive earthquake that was coming.

But it came anyway.

What Francie had told me about all the young men at NA made me approach Thursday night's meeting with far more interest than I ever had before. Just in case things didn't work out for me and Chris, it would be nice to know where to find a storeroom of fellas, and what the correct protocol was there.

Off we all trooped: me, Chris, Neil, a couple of others and, of course, Francie. That night she was wearing a straw hat and a long button-through flowery frock, the buttons almost open to her stomach in both directions, revealing, respectively, a pimpled bosom and cellulitey thighs. Even though she'd only been at the Cloisters just over a day, I'd already seen her in about twenty different outfits. At breakfast she'd worn a leather waistcoat and really tight jeans tucked into terrible stiletto boots. For morning group, an orange, eighties power suit, the shoulder pads like American footballers'. For afternoon group, a PVC miniskirt and a pink sheepskin halter-neck top. Many different garments, but all shared the common characteristics of looking cheap, badly-fitting and alarmingly unflattering.

'I've millions of clothes,' she boasted to me.

'But what's the point if they're all hideous?' I yearned to ask.

As we proceeded up the stairs to the Library, spirits were high among us, far higher than they deserved to be considering where we were going.

Despite Francie's wild talk, the person sent from NA wasn't a man. It was Nola, the beautiful blonde woman with the Cork accent – the one I'd thought was an actress – who'd been at my first meeting.

'Hi Rachel.' She gave a dazzling smile. 'How've you been?'

'OK,' I mumbled, flattered that she remembered me.

'How are you?' I wanted to keep talking because I was strangely drawn to her.

'Great, thanks,' she said, with another smile that warmed the pit of my stomach.

'Don't mind her,' Francie murmured. 'The meetings in the real world are packed with lads.'

'Sorry,' Nola apologized, when we'd all taken our seats. 'I know some of you have heard my story before, but the woman who was supposed to be coming tonight relapsed on Tuesday and died.'

I went rigid with shock and frantically looked around for comfort. Neil looked at me with concern. 'Are you OK?' he mouthed and I was surprised to find he didn't seem angry any more. Not only that, but I no longer hated him. I nodded gratefully at him, my heart no longer trying to jump out of my chest.

Then Nola began to tell us about her addiction. When I'd first heard her three weeks previously, I'd been certain she was reading a script. I simply hadn't believed her. She was too beautiful and groomed to convince me she'd ever done anything cool. But this time was different. Her words rang with quiet conviction and I was riveted by her life. How she'd never thought she was any good at anything, how she loved heroin and the way it made her feel, how it was her best friend, how she'd have preferred to be with it than with any human being.

I was with her, I was there with her all the way.

'. . . until eventually my entire life centred around heroin,' she explained. 'Trying to get the money to buy it, actually purchasing it, obsessing about when I could next get stoned, hiding it from my boyfriend, lying about it when I was out of my skull. It was a terribly draining way to be, yet it filled my life so much that it seemed totally normal to live in this obsessive state . . .'

The serious look on her beautiful face, the hypnotic earnestness of her words, conveyed the horror of the treadmill she'd been on, the hell of being in thrall to a force outside oneself. Out of nowhere I was assailed by the first mini-shock, as the thought jumped into my head, *I was like that.*

My head tightened with denial and I sat well back into my chair. But the words picked me up and shook me again. *I was like that.*

Fighting to regain steadiness, I firmly told myself I'd been nothing of the sort.

But an even louder voice pointed out that I had been. And my defence mechanisms, weakened by more than a month of continual bombardment, lulled into a false sense of security by Nola's story, began to crumble.

To my alarm, I found myself on a head-on collision course with some very unpleasant realizations. In an instant it had become impossible to avoid the crystal-clear knowledge that I'd thought about cocaine and Valium and speed and sleeping tablets constantly; about getting the money for them, about tracking down Wayne or Digby to buy whatever I could afford, then finding the time to take them, finding the *secrecy* to take them. Constantly having to hide my purchases from Brigit, hide them from Luke, trying to pretend I wasn't off my face at work, trying to do my job when my head was adrift.

Horrified, I remembered what Luke had said on the questionnaire – what exactly was it? – 'If it's a drug, Rachel has taken it. She's probably taken drugs that haven't even been invented yet.' I filled with rage, as I did whenever I thought of him and what he'd done to me. I didn't want a single word of what he'd said to be true.

I felt furious, sick and frightened. Panicky, almost. So when Nola said, 'Are you OK, Rachel? You look a bit . . .' it was a relief to blurt out, 'I was like that too, always thinking about it.'

'I'm not happy,' I said, sounding slightly hysterical. 'I'm not happy at all. I don't want to be this way.'

I could feel the others looking at me and I wished they weren't there. Especially Chris. I didn't want him to be a witness to my weakness, but I was too frightened to hide it. Beseechingly, I looked at Nola, desperate to be told that everything would be OK.

In fairness to her, she tried.

'Look at me now,' she smiled gently. 'I never think about drugs. I'm free from all that.

'And look at you,' she added. 'You've been in here –

how long? – four weeks. You haven't used drugs in any of that time.'

I hadn't. In fact, an awful lot of the time I hadn't thought about drugs at all. Of course, some of the time I had. But not all the time, not the way I had five weeks previously.

With that, I had a small glimpse of freedom, a picture of a different life zipped through me before I was cast back into fear and confusion.

As Nola was leaving, she tore a page out of her diary and wrote something on it. 'My number,' she said, giving it to me. 'When you get out, give me a ring. Any time you want to chat, just give me a shout.'

Dazedly, I found myself giving her my number, it seemed the polite thing to do. Then I dragged myself to the dining-room where Eddie had spread the contents of a bag of wine gums out on the table. 'I knew it,' he shouted, making me jump. 'I just knew it.'

'What did you know?' someone asked. I listened with half an ear. *Don't let Luke be right.*

'That there's more yellow ones than any other colour,' Eddie declared. 'And fewer black ones. Look! Two black ones. Five red ones. Five green ones. Eight orange ones. And eight . . . nine . . . ten . . . *twelve*, no fewer than twelve yellow ones. It's not right. Everyone buys them for the black ones and instead we're being fobbed off with manky, horrible yellow ones.'

'I don't mind yellow ones,' another voice chipped in.

'You sick bastard,' yet another person said.

A rowdy argument broke out about the yellow wine gums, but I had no interest. I was too busy trying to assess the damage to my life. Wondering, if I had to give up drugs for a while – and it was a big if, mind – how I would cope. What would I do? I'd never have fun, that was for sure. Not that I'd been having much fun anyway, it had to be admitted. But, as far as I could see, my life would be over. I might as well be dead.

There was always the option of cutting down, I thought, grasping at straws. But I'd tried to cut down in the past and I hadn't. Hadn't been *able* to, I realized, dread piling on fear. Once I started I could never get enough.

Further dissent broke out around me because Stalin knew all the answers to the new Trivial Pursuit questions, to Vincent's perplexity.

'But how?' Vincent whined over and over again. 'But how?'

'Dunno.' Stalin shrugged. 'I read the papers.'

'But . . .' Vincent said despairingly. You could see that he was dying to say, 'But you're *working-class*, you're not supposed to know the capital of Uzbekistan.' But that wasn't the way he behaved anymore.

It was a glorious release to go to sleep that night, to escape my shocked, racing brain for a while. But I woke with a jump in the middle of the night, jolted into consciousness by another shift in my psyche's plates. This time it was a horrible memory of when Brigit caught me stealing twenty dollars from her purse. I'd been *stealing*, I thought as I lay in bed. That was a disgusting thing to do. But at the time I hadn't thought it was terrible. I'd felt nothing. She'd been promoted, I'd reasoned, she could afford it. I couldn't understand how I'd ever thought that way.

And then, to my heartfelt relief, I was OK again.

On Saturday morning, before cookery, when Chris

slung his arm around me and murmured 'How are you now?' I was able to smile and say 'Much better.'

Of course, I still couldn't sleep for thinking about how I'd get my revenge on Luke, but the future looked brighter, still intact. Not the broken-up disaster area it had been about to become.

Once again, I started to take enjoyment in the things that had made me happy since I'd come to the Cloisters. Namely, the rows. On Monday night there was a humdinger between Chaquie and Eddie about fruit pastilles. Black ones. Eddie roared at Chaquie 'When I said you could have one I didn't mean that you could have a black one.'

Chaquie was flushed and upset. 'Well, there's very little I can do about it now.'

She stuck out her tongue displaying the remains of the pastille. 'Do you want this?' she demanded, approaching Eddie with the sliver on her tongue. 'Well, do you?'

There were shouts of 'Good girl, yerself, Chaquie,' and, 'Give him black pastilles where he'll feel it!'

'Jesus,' said Barry the child, admiringly. 'I nearly like that Chaquie wan, now.'

58

Later that week it became clear that my horrors hadn't disappeared. They had simply regrouped, before launching a fresh onslaught.

It was like playing space invaders. The memories hurtled towards me like missiles. Faster and faster, each more shaming and more painful than the last.

Initially I deflected them quite easily.

Brigit crying and begging me to stop taking drugs. I destroyed it with a POW!

Borrowing money from Gaz when I knew he was skint, then not paying him back. BAM!

Coming to on the floor of my bedroom in the dim light, not knowing if it was dawn or dusk. ZAP!

Taking a sickie on Martine's day off so she had to come in to work. KAPOW!

Waking up in a strange bed with a strange man, not remembering whether I'd had sex with him.

Whoops, lost a life there.

The memories got bigger and more powerful, with less of a gap between them. Not so many lives left now. Harder to fight it all off.

Going to Luke's work party off my head and embarrassing him so much he had to take me home at nine o'clock. BIFF!

Drinking the bottle of champagne José gave Brigit for her birthday, then lying about it. CRASH!

Telling Luke that Brigit was a slut because I was afraid he fancied her. There went another life.

Going to an exhibition opening with Luke and leaving with some guy called Jerry. And another life.

Faster and faster the unwelcome thoughts came.

Calling round to Wayne's at four in the morning, and waking his entire apartment because I was so desperate for Valium. KER-ANG!

Anna saying she didn't want to end up like me. BAM!

Getting the sack. POW!

Getting the sack again. BIFF!

Forgetting to rebutton my body when I went to the loo at a party. And spending the evening not realizing it was hanging out over my jeans, with everyone thinking I was wearing an eighties' bum flap. Several lives went with that one.

Thinking I was going to die from throwing up after a night on the rip. BANG!

Getting nosebleeds every second day. POW!

Waking up covered in bruises, with no idea how I'd got them. ZAP!

Waking up in hospital wired up to drips and a monitor. Lost a life.

Realizing I'd had my stomach pumped. And another.

Seeing clearly that I could have died. And another, and another and another.

Game over.

After the following Thursday's NA meeting, when I'd been at the Cloisters nearly five weeks, my day of reckoning finally arrived.

Things started innocuously enough. We rounded up the usual suspects and off we all marched to the Library at eight o'clock.

To my disappointment, the person who'd come to talk to us was a woman. Another woman. By then I suspected that Francie was an outrageous fantasist, so I wondered if her story of 'There's boys in them thar NA meetings' was just another of her inventions. The woman's name was Jeanie and she was young, skinny and good-looking. Just as with Nola's story, every word that came out of Jeanie's mouth sent me reeling with recognition as I hurtled headlong towards the ground-opening, earth-yawning shock of seeing my addiction.

She opened by saying 'By the time I came to the end of my drug-using, there was nothing in my life. I had no job, no money, no friends, no relationship, no self-respect and no dignity.'

And I was so shaken with understanding, it felt as if the ground had physically tipped and swung beneath me.

'My drug-taking had shut down any forward impetus in me. I stayed stuck, living the life of a teenager when everyone around me was behaving like an adult.'

A bigger, more violent shock, threw me completely off balance.

'In a way, my using *fossilized* me, I was surviving in suspended animation.'

With terrible dread, I began to realize that this time the shaking and upheaval wasn't going to stop until it had reached its dreadful conclusion.

'And the funny thing was . . .' she smiled around at us as she said this '. . . I thought my life was over when I had to stop using. But I had no life!'

Take cover, this is the big one.

That night I couldn't sleep. In the same way that an earthquake can turn a house upside down so that the kitchen table stands on the ceiling, my unwelcome insights changed the position of every emotion and memory I had. Altering their relation to each other, challenging the rightness of their original position. The universe inside my head tipped and swayed, everything upended and relocated, in places that would have once seemed wrong, illogical, impossible. But, I reluctantly admitted, they were in the places they should have been all along.

My life was a wreck.

I had nothing. No material possessions, unless debts count. Fourteen pairs of shoes that were too small for me was all I had to show after a lifetime of profligate spending. I no longer had any friends. I hadn't a job, I hadn't any qualifications. I'd achieved nothing with my life. I'd never been happy. I had no husband or boyfriend (even in my despair I refused to use the word 'partner'. What am I, a cowboy?). And the thing that hurt and confused me most was that Luke, the one man who had seemed to truly care about me, had never loved me.

It was Friday, the following day, and with perfect timing Josephine started in on me in group. She knew something was up with me, everyone did.

'Rachel,' she began with, 'you're here five weeks today. Any interesting insights into yourself during that time? Perhaps you can see now that you're suffering from addiction?'

I found it hard to answer because I was in shock, had been since the night before. I was trapped in a strange, phantasmal place where I had realized I was an addict, but sometimes I found it so painful I switched back to *not* believing it.

I couldn't accept that, in spite of all the defences I'd erected since I'd arrived at the Cloisters, I'd nevertheless ended up the same as every other inmate. *How did it come to this?*

There was that air that pervades when the dictator of a country is about to fall. Even when the rebels are at the gate, no one really believes that this invulnerable tyrant is going to crumble.

The end is nigh, I told myself.

But immediately another voice questioned – What? Do you mean *right* nigh?

'Have a look at this,' Josephine said casually, passing me a sheet of paper. 'Read it out to us.'

I looked, but the writing was so crooked and unformed, I could barely make anything out. An occasional word – 'life', 'pits' – was all that was legible.

'What is *this*?' I asked in exasperation. 'It looks like it's been done by a child.'

I laboured through it, until I got to a line that said 'I can't take anymore.' My blood froze as I realized I was the one who'd written these incoherent ramblings. I vaguely remembered deciding that 'I can't take anymore' would be the title for my poem about the shoplifter who was going straight. I was horrified. Being brought face-to-face with something I'd done when I was off my head was deeply shocking. I stared and stared at the spidery scrawl. *That's nothing like my handwriting.* I must have been barely able to hold a pen.

'You can see why Brigit thought that was a suicide note,' Josephine said.

'I wasn't trying to kill myself,' I stammered.

'I believe you,' Josephine said. 'Even so, you still nearly managed to.

'Frightening, isn't it?' She smiled, then forced me to pass the note round the room.

In group that afternoon, I tried a desperate last-ditch attempt to wriggle out of being an addict.

'Nothing bad happened to me to make me into an addict,' I said. So very hopefully.

'One big mistake addicts and alcoholics often make is to search for a *why*,' she replied, quick as a flash. 'Demanding childhood traumas and broken homes.

'As far as I'm concerned,' she ploughed ahead, 'the main reason people take drugs is that they hate reality and they hate themselves. We already know you hate yourself, we've looked at your low self-esteem in depth. And it's obvious from the state you were in when you wrote that note, how much you couldn't bear reality.'

I couldn't think of anything to say. I didn't want it to be that simple.

'So, starting off from that basic position,' she said briskly, 'you take drugs and behave badly, right?'

'S'pose,' I mumbled.

'You come to, feeling wretched and guilty, your self-loathing and fear of the reality you've created magnified. And how do you deal with that? By taking more drugs. Equals more bad behaviour, more self-loathing, a bigger mess to face and, naturally, more drug-using. A downward spiral.

'But you could have stopped at any time,' she said, cutting into my thoughts of how unavoidable, how inevitable it all was. 'You could have taken control of your life, for example, by apologizing to the people you'd upset. Then you would have stopped contributing further to the pit of things you hate about yourself. And by forcing yourself to live through a little bit of reality, you'll see it's not something you need to run from. *You can stop and reverse the process at any stage.* You're doing it now.

'Call off the search for a "why", Rachel,' she finished on. 'You don't need it.'

So I was a bloody addict.

Brilliant!

There was no joy in it. No relief. It was as awful as finding out I was a serial killer.

I stumbled through the weekend and most of the next week in a state of shock. Barely able to talk to people as the words chanted in my head, *You are an addict, na na na naaa naaaah! You are an add . . .*

It was the very last thing I wanted to be, it was the worst disaster that could ever befall me.

I knew from watching the other people in my group – particularly Neil, because I'd followed him almost from his beginning – that there were distinct phases they went through until they came to terms with their addiction. First there was denial, then horrified realization, then seething anger and finally, if they were lucky, acceptance.

I'd had the denial and the horrified realization but, when undiluted, poisonous fury arrived, I wasn't in any way prepared for it. Josephine, of course, just took the attitude 'Ah, Mr Anger, we've been expecting you,' as I went ballistic in group. I was so boilingly angry at the misfortune of being an addict that I briefly forgot about the anger I harboured for Luke.

'I'm too young to be an addict!' I screamed at Josephine. 'Why has it happened to me and to no one else I know?'

'Why not?' Josephine asked mildly.

'But, but, for fuck's . . .' I spluttered, insane with anger.

'Why are some people born blind? Why are some people crippled?' she asked. 'It's all random. And you were born with the propensity to become an addict. So what? It could be miles worse.'

'No, it couldn't!' I yelled, crying tears of burning rage.

'What's the problem?' she asked, again with that infuriating mildness. 'So you can't use drugs anymore? It's not like it's a necessity, millions of people never touch them and they live fulfilled, happy lives . . .'

'You mean I can't *ever* take anything ever again?' I demanded.

'That's right,' she confirmed. 'You should know by now that once you start, you can't stop. You've exposed yourself to narcotics so often that you've permanently upset the chemical balance in your brain. Once you ingest narcotics, your brain reacts by becoming depressed, thus setting up a craving for more drugs, more depression, more drugs, etc. You're physically as well as psychologically addicted.

'And the physical addiction is irreversible,' she added casually.

'I don't believe you,' I breathed in horror.

A freshly baked batch of fury arrived, straight out of the oven. I remembered how before Clarence left, he'd been told he couldn't ever drink again, and how that had made perfect sense to me. But that was about *him*. I was different. I had only admitted to being an addict because I thought I could be fixed.

'You can be fixed,' Josephine said, and my face lit up with hope. Until the bitch added, 'You just can't take drugs anymore.'

'If I'd known that, I'd never have owned up to anything,' I screeched at her.

'You would have,' she said calmly. 'You had no choice, this was inevitable.'

I flicked through a series of 'If only' scenarios. If only I hadn't listened to Nola. If only Anna hadn't said what she'd said. If only Luke hadn't come. If only Jeanie hadn't been so like me. If only, if only, if only . . . Frantically, I searched, trying to find the place where I'd crossed the line from not thinking I was an addict to thinking that perhaps I might be. I wanted to return to that particular point and reverse history.

'You're a chronic addict,' Josephine said. 'This realization was unavoidable. God knows you ducked it long enough, but it was always going to get you in the end.

'Your anger is perfectly normal, by the way,' she added. 'A last-ditch attempt to avoid facing the truth.'

'AAAAAaaarrrrrgggghhh,' I heard myself screech.

'That's right, work through that anger,' she encouraged mildly, making me scream again. 'Get it all out, better out than in. Then you'll have much more acceptance.'

I put my face in my hands and in a muffled voice I exhorted her to go and fuck herself.

'Anyway,' she pointed out, ignoring my request, 'you were *miserable* living that hopeless, drugged-up life. Without drugs you have a future, you can do anything you set your mind to. And think of how good you'll feel when you wake up in the morning and can remember what you did the night before. And who you went home with. If you went home with anyone at all.'

And that was supposed to make me feel better?

59

I had a week or more of rampaging around like an anti-christ. In that time Neil left, humble and contrite, crammed to bursting with good intentions.

John Joe also went. Out and proud, already displaying the rudiments of a handlebar moustache.

Chris left, but not before giving me his phone number and making me swear to ring him the day I got out. For about an hour after he'd gone I glowed with delight from the attention he'd paid me, then lapsed into a sudden, surly slump.

Helen didn't come to visit me anymore. Surprise, surprise.

Vincent also came to the end of his two months, and he too was a changed man, unrecognizable from the Charles Mansonesque bully I'd met on my first day. Soft and gentle, you could imagine him standing in a forest, covered in birds. Deer, squirrels and other woodland creatures flocking to his side.

Barry the child, Peter the laughing gnome, gambling Davy, and Stalin also left. I was now one of the elder statesmen.

As each person left, we cried and hugged, swapped addresses and promised to stay in touch. I was amazed by the strength of the bonds we'd formed with each other, across age, sex and class.

I wondered if that was how POWs or hostages felt.

That we'd been to hell and back together, and were united by it.

Although people were missed when they went, their departure didn't leave a gaping hole. The rest of us swirled over the space they'd left, surrounding it, filling it up. So that soon after, say, Mike had gone, the Mike-shaped hole was filled and had flowers growing over it.

And then, as new people arrived regularly, everything was different anyway, so that you'd never know there had been a gap in the first place.

By the end of the sixth week, my group consisted of Barney, a weaselly man who looked like he stole women's underwear from washing lines. Shaky Padraig, who'd calmed down a good bit since his first sugar-scattering day. Father Johnny, a rabid alcoholic, who'd got his house-keeper pregnant. A tabloid journalist called Mary who was fat, ugly, bitter and talentless. She'd spent the last five years drinking a bottle of brandy a day, stitching up anyone she could find to write about, and now her life was in tatters. It couldn't have happened to a nicer woman.

Then there was me, Chaquie and Misty, the old-timers.

As each new person arrived, they didn't remain new for very long. As always in the Cloisters, deep intimacy was established almost before you knew a person's name. Fresh arrivals got folded into the rest of us immediately and within minutes it seemed as if they'd always been there.

I knew I really was one of the senior citizens the day I got to be head of one of the housekeeping teams. I was in charge of breakfasts, Chaquie of lunches, Angela of dinners and Misty of hoovering.

'Now,' said Chaquie briskly, 'Angela and I have already sorted out our teams.'

'When?' I asked in alarm.

'When you were watching telly,' she said, shiftily.

'You big hoor,' I complained. 'I bet you took all the able-bodied, able-brained ones and neither of you picked Francie.'

'You big hoor yourself,' Chaquie said. 'First come, first served.'

I was so touched by her saying 'you big hoor yourself' that I forgave her. She'd come a long way.

'So you sit down with Misty and share out the rest,' Chaquie said awkwardly.

I was appalled. I hated Misty. Then it struck me that the tension which normally zinged between the two of us hadn't been as electric since Chris had gone. Still, I didn't want to sit down and do anything with her and I said as much.

'Come on now, Rachel,' Chaquie cajoled. 'Act like an adult and give the girl a chance.'

'God, you've changed your tune,' I complained. Chaquie and I had soothed ourselves to sleep every night for the previous six weeks, by detailing how much we hated Misty.

'Ah, the poor girl,' Chaquie said wistfully. 'Those terrible things that happened to her, no wonder she's such an unpleasant little madam . . .'

'I'll only talk to her if you take Francie off my hands,' I bargained. None of us wanted Francie on our teams because she was stone-mad, an awful handful and a lazy bitch to boot.

Chaquie wavered, then gave in. 'All right then. God help me.'

And, very reluctantly, I went to find Misty.

'We have to sort out our housekeeping teams,' I said. She looked at me coldly.

'OK,' she surprised me by saying. 'Will we do it now?'

So we got the list of lame brains and loopers that Angela and Chaquie had left for us and shared them out. And, once I was actually talking to her, I found that in the midst of all the other upheaval that was taking place inside me, I didn't hate Misty anymore. I was no longer consumed with jealousy of her dainty beauty, I actually felt *protective* of her. A reluctant warmth passed back and forth between us.

And as we stood up from the table, having masqueraded as grown-ups, Misty touched my cheek with her hand. It was a funny thing for her to do, but I stood there and let her, feeling compassion, affection and strange friendship throb from her. A little flower in a burnt-out land.

'You see,' Chaquie smirked at me later.

'You should get a job in the UN,' I said, with fake sourness. 'As a diplomat.'

'That'll give me something to do when Dermot divorces me,' she said, thoughtfully. And for some reason we both found that hilarious and laughed until we cried.

That evening, when the housekeeping list went up on the notice board, I heard Larry, a seventeen-year-old heroin addict, who'd done time in a reform school for GBH, whine 'I don't want to be on that Rachel's team, she's so aggressive.'

Was I? I wondered, more amused than irate.

And it was then I found that a miracle had happened. Even though I still burned with rage against Luke and, to a lesser extent, Brigit, I was no longer angry about being an addict. I'd watched a lot of the other inmates move away from rage and into the calm waters of acceptance, but I hadn't for a second believed it would happen to me.

I was filled with a very unfamiliar sensation. A kind of peace.

So, I was an addict. So what? I was no longer tormented as I wished things were different. Let's face it, I told myself, I'd always known something was wrong with me. At least now I knew what it was.

For the first time I felt *relief*. It was a relief to stop fighting, to stop resisting the insistent knowledge that my life and behaviour weren't normal. And it was a relief to know that I wasn't mad or stupid or useless, all that was wrong was that I was immature and had low self-worth, which would improve by staying away from mood-altering chemicals. The future looked promising. It all seemed so very straightforward.

Over the next week a whole load of other things fell into place once I accepted all that stuff about my low self-esteem. It explained why I'd thrown myself at men who didn't want me. As Josephine said on my fourth-last day in group, 'You got them to reinforce your own sense of self-loathing.'

And it explained why most men didn't seem to want me.

'You were too needy,' Josephine said. 'You scared them away with the big, gaping hole you had in your soul.'

I was high with understanding, marvelling at the wonders of psychotherapy. I would get over Luke and have a lovely relationship with some other man.

'And now let's talk about your unhealthy attitude to food,' Josephine announced. My happiness fell from the sky like a stone.

'You abuse food almost as much as you abused

drugs,' she said. 'You were like a skeleton when you arrived . . .'

'Ah, go'way, I was not,' I joshed, hanging my head, smiling warmly with pride.

'You see!' she screeched. 'Unhealthy, very unhealthy. It stems from the same source as your drug addiction. You avoid your immaturity and defects by focusing on something you think you *can* control, that is, your weight. But you can't change your inside by changing your outside.

'All that starving and bingeing you do,' she said. I began to object, but she cut across me. 'We've been watching you, Rachel, we *know*. You're obsessed with your weight. Although it doesn't stop you going on plenty of chocolate and crisp binges.'

I lowered my head in shame.

'You've got to admit,' she said slyly, 'for all that song and dance you made about your vegetarian food, you didn't go hungry.'

But nothing could dampen my spirits for long. I was in such irrepressible good form I was prepared to acknowledge Josephine might have had a point about my attitude to food. Why not? By then I was an old hand at believing six impossible things before breakfast. I'd accepted I was a drug addict, why not throw a food disorder in for the laugh? Any other aberrations you can think of?

It wasn't a problem, because as Josephine said 'Fix the source of one, and you'll fix them all.'

'I'm really looking forward to my new life,' I sang joyously to Misty that afternoon in the dining-room.

'Go easy,' Misty urged anxiously. 'Not everything falls magically into place the minute you stop. Knowing *why* you took drugs is only the tip of the iceberg. You've got to learn how to live without them and that's not easy. Look at what happened to me. I relapsed.'

'Ah, no,' I smiled, touched by her concern. 'That won't happen to me, I'm determined to make a go of things.'

'Will you go back to New York?' she asked.

I instantly felt confused and fearful. And very fucking angry. My rosy outlook on life hadn't extended as far as Luke and Brigit, the bastards.

'I don't think I'll ever go back to New fucking York again,' I muttered.

'Are you worried about what those glamorous people will say?' she asked. 'What's your one's name? Helenka?'

'Helenka?' I hooted. 'No, she's always horrible about everyone and I couldn't be bothered anymore.'

I briefly savoured that feeling of liberation before saying gloomily, 'No, it's Luke fucking Costello and Brigit fucking Lenehan I have problems with.'

'You'll have to go back,' said Misty the sage. She was starting to annoy me. 'You'll have to make your peace with them.'

'I'll never make my peace with those bastards!'

The night before I left, Josephine took me into her office for a private session. Everyone got a one-to-one with their counsellor just before they left. Like a football team getting one last talking to from their manager before the big match.

And basically she told me I could do nothing when I got out.

'No drugs, and that includes alcohol. No starving, bingeing or excessive exercise. And, most importantly of all, stay away from relationships with the opposite sex for a year.'

I almost passed out. *I thought you were my friend.*

'But why?' I hooted.

'You've an unhealthy attitude to men. Without drugs, there's going to be a big gap in your life. A lot of people latch onto relationships to avoid being alone with themselves. You'd probably be one of them.'

Cheeky bitch, I thought, offended.

'We say the same to everyone when they leave here,' she pointed out.

Everyone? I wondered, thinking of Chris.

'It's only for a year,' she added kindly.

She might as well have said a hundred of them.

'In that case I'm going back to New York,' I said sulkily. 'Even if I don't want to be celibate there, it'd be enforced upon me.'

'No New York,' she said. 'Give yourself a year to get better.

'And are you trying to tell me you were celibate with Luke?' she asked with a sly smile.

I managed to forbear from letting rip a string of expletives about Luke, but my hatred for him was obvious from the look on my face.

'Luke is an exceptional man,' Josephine said. 'You may not think so yet, but he did the right thing by you.'

I said nothing.

'He's loyal, has integrity, intelligence and he's very . . .' she paused and kind of patted her hair 'handsome.'

I was astonished. So the old bat was human after all!

But not for long.

'Now that you're going out into the outside world,' she said sternly, 'the hard work is only beginning. You'll have to come to terms with your past and learn new responses to every situation life throws at you. It won't always be easy.'

I wasn't fazed. It wasn't that I didn't believe her, but I felt my willingness would overcome anything.

'There's still unresolved tension with your mother,' she warned. 'If you stay around her it'll probably come to a head. Careful that you don't relapse if that happens.'

'I won't take drugs, I promise.'

'No point making promises to me,' she said. 'It's not my life that'll be destroyed.'

'It won't be mine either,' I said, a mite defiantly.

'Go to your meetings, keep up the therapy and in time, everything will be very good,' she promised. 'You've so much going for you.'

'Like what?' I asked in surprise.

'We don't focus too much on people's good points here, do we?' She smiled. 'Well, you're bright, perceptive, entertaining, *very* kind, I've seen the way you've been to the others in your group, and to the new people. You've even managed to be nice to Misty.'

I reddened with pride.

'And finally can I say,' she said 'what a satisfying experience it has been for me to see how you've changed and grown over your time here.'

'Was I awful?' I asked, out of curiosity.

'You were a tough one, but you weren't the worst.'

'I hated you,' I was appalled to hear myself say. Although she didn't seem at all put out.

'There would have been something wrong if you didn't,' she agreed. 'What's that they say in the film? "I'm your worst nightmare".'

'How do you know so much about me?' I asked shyly.

'How did you know when I was lying? When any of us were lying?'

'I was at the coalface for a long time,' she said.

That told me nothing. 'How do you mean?'

'I mean, I lived with a chronic addict and alcoholic for years,' she said, with a secret smile.

I was shocked. Poor Josephine. Who could it have been? One of her parents? Or brothers? Or perhaps even a husband. Maybe she'd been married before she became a nun.

'Who was it?' I blurted out.

I expected her to say something uptight and counsellory like 'That's not an appropriate question, Rachel,' but she didn't.

Instead she paused for a long, long time, her eyes holding mine, before softly saying, 'Me.'

60

My last day finally came. Like my birthday, my first communion, my wedding day and my funeral all at once. I was the centre of attention and I loved it; the card, the speech, the good wishes, the tears, the hugs, the 'I'll-miss-you's. Even Sadie the sadist, Bubbly the receptionist and Finbar the halfwit gardener came to wish me well. Plus Dr Billings, all the nurses, counsellors and, of course, inmates.

I gave the speech that everyone made, about how when I'd first come I'd thought there was nothing wrong with me, how I felt sorry for all the others etc, etc. And they whooped and cheered, clapped and laughed, and someone shouted – as someone always did – 'Have a pint waiting for me in Flynns.'

Then they all went off to group and I waited to be collected. Watery-eyed but excited, nostalgic yet elated. Eager to begin my new life.

I'd been in the Cloisters for almost two months and had managed to survive. Pride in myself was the order of the day.

Mum and Dad came and, as we drove out through the high gateway, I symbolically took off my hat and bowed my head in remembrance, as I thought back to the day I'd arrived. Agog and expectant, on the lookout for famous people. It seemed like a million years ago, as if it had happened to a different person.

Which in a way it had.

Apart from my brief foray to the dentist, I hadn't seen the outside world for two months. So I was highly excitable on the journey back from Wicklow, keeping up a non-stop, running commentary in the back seat.

'Oh, look, there's a letter box!'

'Oh, look at your man's hair!'

'Oh, look, there's a KFC box in a doorway!'

'Oh, look at the funny bus!'

'Oh, look at that woman buying a paper!'

'Oh, look, did you see that baby's ears? They were like Spock's!'

When we finally arrived home, the thrill of it all nearly sent me into orbit. I almost had hysterics at the sight of the front door, the door that I could go in or out of *any time I wanted*. And almost had to be sedated when I saw my room. My own *room*. With no other people painting their toenails in it. My own bed. A proper duvet! That didn't smell funny! Or make me itchy!

And no more being woken in the middle of the night to fry seventy eggs. I could stay in bed all day if I wanted. And I *did* want.

I ran in and out of the bathroom, the bathroom that I had to share with only four other people! I ran my hand along the television and rejoiced that the only limit on the amount of trash I could watch was how much sleep I needed.

The hoover was standing in the hall, so I paused to have a good laugh at it. My brief acquaintance with its brother in the Cloisters had come to an end and I wouldn't be doing any more housework. Possibly ever.

I threw open the door of the fridge and looked at all the yummy things inside, and I could have anything I wanted, *anything*. Apart from Helen's chocolate mousses that she'd sellotaped a picture of two fingers onto, of course. I opened the kitchen presses, looking for, looking for, looking for . . .

And then I felt very, very depressed.

Very depressed. So, I was out.

So what?

What could I do? I'd no friends, I was forbidden to go to pubs, anyway I'd no money . . . Was the rest of my life going to be a succession of Saturday evenings sitting in, watching *Stars in their Eyes* with my mother? Listening to her whinge that Marti Pellow should have won. That he was miles better than Johnny Cash.

And was I condemned to watch my father stand up at half-past nine every night and announce 'Right, I'm off down to Phelans for a pint'? Then being forced to sing tunelessly with my mother and whoever else was there 'Phelans, nothing more than Phelans . . .'

That ritual had existed for about twenty years, but I'd forgotten about it on my first night home, when it was just me and Dad in the room. So things got a bit nasty when he announced his intention to go to the pub and I didn't burst into song. 'Don't they sing in New York?' he demanded, fixing me with hurt cow-eyes. 'Singing not *grand* enough for them?'

I rushed out to the kitchen. 'God,' I complained to Mum. 'It's worse than the Cloisters here. The looper count is higher.'

But Mum urged compassion. She said Dad hadn't been himself since *Oklahoma* had finished its run of one night. 'It kind of went to his head,' she explained. 'And now he's just back to being ordinary Joe soap.'

'But it was only a chorus part.'

'All the same, it made him feel important,' she said, wisely.

'What'll I do?' I moaned, bored and miserable. I'd only been home a day. I missed the Cloisters and wished I was still there.

'Why don't you go to one of your funny meetings?' Mum suggested brightly.

I thought of the meetings list I'd been given before I left the Cloisters and realized I didn't want to be the kind of person who goes to 'funny meetings'. I wouldn't take drugs, but I'd do it my way. So I said vaguely 'Um, in a couple of days.'

What I *did* want to do was ring Chris, but I just couldn't summon the nerve. However, on Sunday I was at such a loose end, I found myself going to Mass. That was the last straw. As soon as I got home, with shaking hands I picked up the phone and rang him.

Bitter was my disappointment when someone – Mr Hutchinson, I presumed – said Chris wasn't there. I didn't leave my name in case he didn't call me back. Then I went through the whole nerve-racking ordeal again on Monday but this time he *was* there.

'Rachel!' he exclaimed, sounding delighted to hear from me. 'I was hoping you'd ring. How's it all going?'

'Fine!' I declared, instantly upbeat, everything sunny and wonderful.

'When did you get out?'

'Friday.'

You should have known.

'Been to any meetings yet?' he asked.

'Er, no,' I said vaguely. 'Busy, you know . . .'

Busy eating biscuits and hanging around the house, feeling sorry for myself.

'Don't neglect them, Rachel,' he warned, gently.

'I won't, I won't,' I promised hastily. 'So, er, do you want to meet up?'

'We could, I suppose,' he said. He didn't sound half as enthusiastic as I would have liked him to.

'When?' I pressed.

'Before you left the Cloisters weren't you given a warning about not doing . . . well . . . anything for a year?' he asked. First I thought he was changing the subject, then I realized he wasn't.

'Yes,' I blurted, mortified in case he thought I was trying to make a move on him. 'No relationships with the opposite sex.

'Suits me down to the ground,' I lied. 'Were you told that too?'

'Yeah, no relationships, no alcohol, no scratch cards even! I'm surprised they haven't warned me off breathing, in case I get cross-addicted to oxygen!'

We both laughed long and hard at that, then he said 'How about Wednesday evening? Seven-thirty, Stephen's Green?'

'Great!'

Delighted, I hung up.

After all, there was no law against flirting with him.

61

In honour of meeting Chris, I persuaded myself to have either a leg-wax or a haircut. I couldn't afford both, well actually, I couldn't afford either, so I decided on the haircut. No point in having a leg-wax. As both Chris and I were banned from carnal knowledge, the results of it would never see the light of day. If I was going to the bother of spending money I wanted everyone to know about it.

On Tuesday morning it was in a mood of handbag-swinging, high anticipation that I got Mum to drive me to The Hair Apparent to have my hair cut by Jasmine. What was wrong with me? I had never, ever, in my whole life, left a hairdresser's not struggling to hold back tears.

But I always forgot. It was only when I found myself sitting in front of the mirror while someone disparagingly lifted and let fall strands of my hair, then heard the words 'Christ almighty, it's in *flitters*,' that it all came rushing back to me. By then it was too late.

It was so long since I'd done anything as normal as go to a hairdresser's that I viewed the tiles and mirrors and towels and bottles of The Hair Apparent with something akin to wonder. Which wasn't reciprocated – the receptionist barely glanced at me as I explained my mission. 'Take a seat at the basin,' was her advice. Then I heard her shouting 'Gráinne, Gráinne, client at basin two.'

Gráinne didn't inspire confidence. She looked very young. I would have said she was no more than thirteen, except surely there were laws against that kind of thing. She hobbled towards me on stick legs, attempted to make eye-contact and failed.

Wobbling, she put a gown on me and tucked in loads of towels round my neck. She seemed to be having trouble remaining upright in her platforms.

Then she turned on the taps and I settled back. But relaxation was not on the cards.

'Er, where are you going on holidays this year?' Gráinne asked awkwardly, like she'd been taught by the big hairdressers to do. She was clearly determined to get her diploma in cutting, tinting and poor conversation.

'Nowhere,' I said.

'That'll be lovely,' she said, kneading my skull.

We had a few short moments of blissful silence.

'Have you been there before?' she asked.

'Loads of times.'

More time elapsed, during which she scalded my scalp and sprayed the shower-head into my ears so often I nearly got water on the brain.

'Are you going with a couple of friends?' she enquired.

'No,' I said, 'I haven't got any friends.'

'That's great,' she said pleasantly.

As Gráinne scrubbed, rinsed and conditioned, I felt a certain pride that I must still look ordinary.

'Who's doing you today?' asked Gráinne. I thought it was an unfortunate turn of phrase.

'Jasmine.'

'I'll go and get . . .' She gave a strange snigger, but so long as she wasn't laughing at me that was fine. '. . . *Jasmine* for you.'

She lurched away, leaning very forward because of the shoes, and called 'Maura, Maura, your client is ready.'

As soon as I saw Jasmine/Maura I recognized her and not just because she had trimmed my hair when I was home at Christmas. She was slathered in so much dark-brown foundation that with her white-blonde hair she looked like a negative. She was kind of hard to forget.

When she passed Gráinne she stopped for an angry couple of words, probably telling her not to call her Maura.

She mustn't have recognized me because when she did the lifting and letting fall of the strands of hair thing, she said, in disgust and a strong Dublin accent 'Jays! Who done your hair de last time? It's a disaster area.'

'I got it cut here.' I cringed. I had to fight hard to stop myself speaking like her. I was ashamed of my middle-class accent, afraid that she might think I thought I was better than her. I wanted to be salt of the earth like Gráinne and Maura.

'Who done it?' she demanded.

'I think it was you,' I mumbled.

Now she was going to destroy my hair as punishment. Hairdressers belong to the most powerful profession in the universe and they didn't get that way by being nice. Sure enough, she ran her fingers through my hair and made ominous noises and tuts and tisks.

'Jays,' she said in disgust, 'it's in bits. What have you done to it?'

'I don't know.'

'Next you'll be telling me you blow-dry it.'

'Sometimes.'

'Are you mad? You can't blow-dry hair as brittle as dis. And do you *ever* condition it?'

'Of course I condition it!' I did know the rudiments of hair-care, the stupid cow.

'Well, I've only got your word for it.' She looked at me with narrowed eyes.

'When I say I condition it,' I flailed around, 'I don't actually do the hot-oil, once a week, in a heated towel type of thing. But I do use an ordinary conditioner every time I wash it.'

'I *see*,' she said, tightlipped. 'Well, you'd want to start. With hair as dry as yours, you need a serious conditioner.'

She paused.

I waited.

I knew what was coming next.

'We do a range,' she said, right on cue.

I braced myself for the sales pitch. I picked up the occasional words like 'Laboratory tested', 'Exclusive agents', 'Vital nutrients', 'Nourishing formula', 'Your only hope'.

'How much?' I asked.

It was extortionate.

'Fine,' I swallowed. 'I'll take it.'

'You'll really need the shampoo and the mousse and the non-rinse conditioner and the anti-frizz serum and the . . .'

'Wait,' I said. And then I braced myself to say the hardest words I ever had to say.

I paused, took a deep breath and said 'I can't afford them.'

Her eyes held mine in the mirror. I knew she didn't believe me. I knew she was thinking, 'Stupid, posh bitch.'

I tensed for her to grab me by the throat and scream 'WHATABOUTMYCOMMISSION?' She didn't. I tried to convince myself there wasn't any need to feel guilty. But nothing doing.

'It's up to you if you don't buy dem,' Jasmine said reluctantly. 'I tink it's woort it personally. But it's up to you.'

'I'm unemployed,' I explained, hoping that she might soften towards me.

She tossed her head dismissively, like an angry wife shrugging off her apologetic husband's overtures. 'How much of dese ends do you want off?' she demanded coldly.

'Just a trim, please.'

'No,' she said.

No?

Apparently not.

'De ends are in bits all the way up. It'll have to come off up to here.' She indicated an area around my shoulders.

I felt a twang of anticipatory loss. Every cell in my body fought against the idea of having my hair cut.

No, Jasmine, anything but short hair. Have mercy. Please.

'I don't mind if it's in bits all the way up,' I assured her warmly. 'Honestly, it's fine, I can live with it.'

'But, it's all broken and dead. And it's split all the way to the roots practically.

'Look!' she ordered me. 'Look! See how it's split all along here.'

'I see,' I said. 'But . . .'

'No, you're not looking,' she said.

I looked.

'But I don't mind,' I said, when I felt I had looked long enough. 'I'd rather have long split hair than short not-split hair.'

'You can't have that,' said Jasmine. 'You can't go round with split hair. It's not on.'

We were interrupted by Gráinne.

'Maura,' she said to Jasmine, 'Mammy's on the phone, she said she can't babysit for Elroy this evening, you'll have to come home.'

'Fuck that, I'm going out on the piss, you'll have to do it.'

'But . . .'

'Do you want your job to be here when you come in tomorrow?' asked Maura.

'Oh,' said Gráinne, her face a picture of resignation, and she limped away.

My eyes met Jasmine's in the mirror.

'Me sister,' she said, by way of explanation.

I smiled nervously.

'So we're agreed,' she said impatiently.

Maybe it would be all right, I thought. A new beginning, cutting away the dead wood and the dead hair of the past. Going forward to a healthy, honest future with healthy, honest hair.

'OK,' I said.

The hand that wields the scissors rules the world.

Helen looked up when I let myself in.

'But you've got ladies' hair,' she said in surprise. 'Why did you ask for ladies' hair?'

'I *didn't*!' I screeched.

I rushed to the mirror to see if it was as bad as I remembered. I had a white ring around my hairline where my foundation had been washed off. I had grey puddles under my eyes. But worst of all I had short curly hair. Jasmine had cut with a liberal hand, way above shoulder height. And then, to add insult to injury, had blow-dried it into short, tight, Mammyesque curls.

'I'm so ugly,' I sobbed. Huge, choking tears.

'You are,' agreed Helen.

I was glad she agreed with me. If Mum had been there saying 'It'll grow,' I would probably have become hysterical.

I thought of the yards and yards of my hair on the floor, the hair that Luke used to tangle his hands in, and I cried even harder.

'My life is over,' I heaved.

'You certainly shouldn't do any going out for a while,' said Helen.

With her words, I almost began hyperventilating. Going out! I was supposed to be going out with Chris tomorrow night! How could I, now that I was almost bald?

'I hate her,' I gasped. 'Stupid, fat, overmade-up bitch. I hate *all* hairdressers.'

'I hope you didn't give her a tip,' said Helen.

'Don't be so fucking stupid,' I sobbed. 'Of course I gave her a tip.'

I shouldn't have given Jasmine anything, except maybe a black eye, but I couldn't help myself. I even found myself murmuring 'It's lovely,' when she did the thing with one mirror behind me and another in front.

I managed to wait until I got outside before the tears started flowing freely down my face. I stood at the bus-stop and cried helplessly and felt naked without my hair. I was sure everyone was looking at me and for once my paranoia was correct.

'Who's your one with the dodgy hair?' I heard. And when I turned round there was a crowd of schoolboys studying me carefully, then sniggering. Fourteen-year-old boys at the height of their hormones and they were laughing at me!

'And it was so beautiful,' I sobbed at Helen.

'What was?' she asked.

'My hair,' I cried. 'Until that bitch got her hands on it.'

'Well, it was all right,' said Helen. 'I wouldn't have said *beautiful*, but . . .'

'And they didn't even give me any *Hello*s to read,' I wept.

'Swizzers,' Helen sympathized.

'And the fucking cost of it!' I screeched. 'My hair wasn't the only thing that got done.'

'Do you know who you look like?' Helen said thoughtfully.

'Who?' I asked tremulously, hoping for redemption.

'Brenda Fricker.'

'AAAAaaarrrrggghhhhh.'

'You know, when she was the mammy in that film,' she said.

I rushed to the mirror. 'You're right,' I bawled, almost glad things were so apocalyptic. It gave a certain unimpeachability to my position.

Mum and Dad arrived back and were invited to tender their opinion of my annihilated hair.

Mum said doubtfully 'It'll grow.'

Dad said proudly and fondly 'You look more like your mother every day.' I burst into tears again.

'Do you know who you look like?' Mum mused.

'If you say Brenda Fricker I'll kill myself,' I warned her, my eyes bright red.

'No, not at all,' Mum said kindly. 'No, what's that her name is? An actress. What's her *name*?'

'Audrey Hepburn?' I asked hopefully.

'Noooo.' Mum flapped her hands in frustration. 'Oh, what's her name?'

I wondered if she knew who Linda Fiorentino was.

'Linda Fiorentino?' I dared to ask. (A man at a party

had once told me I looked like Linda Fiorentino and I was so touched I slept with him.)

'Who? Linda who? No!' Mum danced a little jig in an attempt to jog her memory. 'It's on the tip of my tongue. Oh what was she *in*?'

'*The Last Seduction*?'

'That sounds like a terrible pile of filth. No, it wasn't that. Oh, I have it! She was in that thing with Daniel Day Lewis . . .'

My heart began to sink.

'. . . you know, poor divil of a painter . . . Christy Brown! *My Left Foot*, that was it, that was it!' She beamed in triumph.

'What was the name of the woman who played the mother?'

'Brenda Fricker,' I said dully.

62

I had a choice of knotting a rope and kicking the chair from under myself or preparing to meet Chris.

I'd have liked to put our big night out on hold until my hair had grown back, but I couldn't be sure he'd wait the necessary twelve years.

Although I didn't look so puke-making once I'd washed the matronly curls out, and smeared on three times my usual amount of make-up.

'At least it's lovely and healthy,' I consoled myself, after I'd combed my hair as flat as possible in an attempt to lengthen it.

There was a raucous shriek of laughter from Helen. 'Listen to her,' she wheezed. 'You're so sad.

'See my hair?' she invited, lifting up some of her silky, waist-length strands. 'Split to fuck. And does it bother me? Not at all!'

On Wednesday, I spent hours getting ready. Preparations began as soon as I got up (about two-thirty), and continued throughout the afternoon. Once again I washed what remained of my hair, then I shaved large parts of my body, while reflecting on the injustice of having far too much hair on my legs and not enough on my head. Of course, there was no need to shave anything, as Chris wouldn't be getting a look at me. But what harm could it do? I demanded, my stomach pleasantly aflutter.

After that I spread myself generously with Helen's Issey

Miyake body lotion. Then felt guilty, I should have asked her. And, if she'd said no, I shouldn't have called her a little bitch, I should have just accepted it as an adult. Next time I needed to steal something of hers would be my opportunity to practise, I reassured myself.

With that in mind, my hand wavered over Helen's bottle of eau de parfum . . . then picked it up decisively. Sure, hadn't the damage already been done, with the body lotion? Perfume was different, there was more of it. People might accuse you of being a selfish hoor for decimating their body lotion but they'd give a few squirts of their perfume to a total stranger, no questions asked.

Next on the agenda was, of course, the great Agonizing about What to Wear. My worry about giving Chris the right message with my clothes – sexy but casual, stylish but easy-going – was compounded by several factors. One: all my summer clothes were in New York. And two: what was considered the height of fabulous in New York might have people in Dublin crashing their cars with mirth. And, of course, the third factor, the one I couldn't really acknowledge, was that I felt very uncertain how to behave in the outside world anyway.

Mum watched my preparations with concern. What worried her was not so much that her daughter who'd recently been released from a treatment centre was going out into the drug-infested world, but something far bigger.

'Helen'll kill you,' she warned, when she saw the depleted bottle of body lotion.

'It's fine,' I said irritably.

'Who're you meeting, anyway?' I could hear the massive anxiety in her voice and that both pained and annoyed me.

'Chris from the bin,' I said. 'You know, you met him. So no need to worry, I won't be with anyone who takes drugs.'

'Chris Hutchinson?' she said in alarm.

'Yesss,' I sighed, with a great play of patience.

'Oh, be careful, Rachel,' Mum said, her forehead crinkled with concern. 'He has his poor mother's heart tormented.'

'Is that right?' Interest and fear propelled me closer to her. 'What did he do?'

'He wouldn't stop taking the drugs,' she muttered, not meeting my eyes. 'And Philomena and Ted spent a fortune on this expert and that expert, for all the good it did. The next thing they knew, his work'd be on the phone saying he hadn't turned up in a week. And he's in his thirties, Rachel, too old for his parents still to be looking after him. And there's something else . . .'

'I know,' I interrupted.

'He was in the Cloisters once before, four years ago.'

'I know,' I said again, in a deliberately soothing voice. She'd been getting a bit agitated and it was suddenly too close to the bone for me. 'He told me.'

'He nearly made poor Philomena have a nervous breakdown,' Mum said, her voice shrill and with a hint of tears in it. Time to go. 'And then there'd be a pair of them in institutions.'

I remembered the large boomy-voiced woman who'd visited Chris at the laughing house. 'She didn't *look* tormented,' I scoffed. 'She looked like a right heifer.'

'You're too quick to judge . . .' Mum's voice trailed after me. 'You think everyone's happy except you.'

Off I went on the Dart into town, my legs wobbling

like a new-born calf's. Everything was so strange and new, I felt as though I too had just been born.

Even though I wasn't going on a date and I wasn't *allowed* dates, and both Chris and I knew that, I still had that lovely, I'll-never-eat-again, stomach-tickling terror.

Everything seemed new and beautiful. As if I was seeing a spring evening in Dublin for the first time ever. The tide was in, the sea blue and calm as I passed it on the train. The sky was wide and clear, with a faded, just-washed look. The parks were bright with green grass and red, yellow and purple tulips. I sat on the train, trembling with the fear and wonder of it all.

I almost ran to Stephen's Green with the need to see Chris. And there he was, standing waiting for me. I'd known he'd be there, yet I still marvelled at the sight of him. He was gorgeous, I thought, my breath catching, and he's standing over there because he wants to meet *me*.

I could see the blue flash of his eyes from ten yards. And had ever a man's legs been so sexy? He should never be allowed to wear anything other than Levi's, I thought distractedly.

He turned his blue gaze onto me. Eyes lowered, I crossed the road to him. Then I was standing next to him, my heart beating hard, pleasurably. We were both smiling, embarrassed, tearful. Not sure how to deal with each other in the outside world.

'How're you doing?' he said gruffly and gave me a hug that was so awkward it was nearly a necklock. Spontaneous affection did not come easily to us recovering addicts in the outside world, I thought, with a pang of loss. We'd been all over each other in the treatment centre but it was different when we were among civilians.

'Fine,' I said in a trembly voice, feeling as if my heart would burst from all the emotion.

'One day at a time,' he said, with an ironic smile.

'So,' I said with another enormous, shaky smile. 'We made it, we've done the Cloisters and lived to tell the tale.'

The general vibe was that we had survived something awful and were united by it. Like the survivors from a hijacked plane who met up once a year to rake over misty-eyed memories of drinking their own urine, savaging their nearest and dearest for their bread rolls and being beaten to a pulp by a man wearing a tea-towel on his head.

'So!' he exclaimed.

'So,' I agreed.

I waited for him to say something about my hair and when he didn't the worry started to gnaw at me. It was awful, wasn't it?

'Don't you notice anything different about me?' I heard myself asking. *No, no, no!*

'You've shaved off your moustache?' He laughed.

'No,' I mumbled, embarrassed. 'I've had my hair cut.'

'So you have,' he said thoughtfully.

I cursed myself for ever mentioning it and I also cursed men in general for their visual unawareness. The only things they ever notice about any woman, I thought in disappointment, are big tits.

'It's nice,' he said. 'Gamine.'

He may have been lying, but I was more than willing to give him the benefit of the doubt.

'What'll we do?' I asked, my good humour restored.

'I don't know, what do you *want* to do?'

'I don't mind.' I simpered. 'What do you want to do?'

'What I'd really like to do is buy a quarter of Red Leb,

526

smoke it in under an hour, take you home and fuck your brains out,' he said thoughtfully.

'But,' he smiled reassuringly at my rigor-mortised face, 'we're not allowed to do that.'

'And we can't really go to a pub,' I said, clearing my throat in manly fashion, letting him know that I hadn't taken him seriously, that I wasn't going to go all girly and clingy, and pout and stamp my foot in the middle of a busy street, 'But you *said* you'd fuck my brains out. You PROMISED!' I'd learnt in the Cloisters that I'd made the mistake in the past, too many times, of being needy. And needy girls scare men away. Of that there was no doubt. So to *not* scare them away, you've got to pretend not to be needy. When you're being shown out of their flat in the morning and they say, 'See you,' you're not supposed to turn around and plead into their face 'WHEN? TONIGHT? TOMORROW? WHEN, WHEN, WHEN?' You're just supposed to say 'Mmmm, see you,' and trail an immaculate talon along their stubble-rough cheek and waft away in a cloud of tangible *un*neediness.

I wanted to act strong, even if I wasn't. Changing old behaviour patterns. Just like they told me to. Virtuous was the Rachel who turned to smile at Chris.

'We could . . . I dunno . . . go to the pictures?' he suggested.

Not what I wanted to hear.

The pictures?

The fucking pictures?

Was I reduced to this?

No, I wasn't beaten yet. They could take away my Valium, my cocaine, my credit cards, but they could never take away my soul. Or my appetite.

'We could go for something to eat,' I said eagerly. Luke and I had had some of our happiest times in restaurants. 'We're still allowed to do that, aren't we?'

'Just about,' he agreed. 'So long as neither of us pukes straight afterwards or orders five desserts or any other aberrant behaviour.'

'Where will we go?' I asked. I was pleased. I imagined a dimly lit, romantic little bistro. Our faces close in the candle-light. Talking into the small hours, the plump patron smiling fondly at us, as all the other chairs in the place were stacked on tables and Chris and I talked eagerly on, not noticing.

'Let's just take a stroll and we'll see where we end up,' he suggested.

As we rambled, I couldn't stop thinking about what he'd said. He'd like to fuck my brains out.

The silver-tongued devil.

Mmmm.

No! You're not allowed to think that way.

That's right, I'm not, I thought, sense returning to me. OK, so he was gorgeous-looking, but we were proceeding as friends. And that was all right, my down theres would close up at the suggestion of having sober sex with someone who wasn't Luke.

A bleak wind swept through me when I realized I'd never again be in bed with Luke. For a split-second I forgot I hated him.

Briskly, I forced my attention back to the here-and-now and Chris.

We went to Temple Bar, Dublin's Left Bank. Where I witnessed the completed groovification of my native city with my own two eyes. It certainly was kicking. And very attractive.

Could I live here? I wondered. It was certainly very different from the city I had left eight years before.

Different enough to live in? I felt a shiver of fear.

If I didn't stay in Dublin, where *would* I go?

Back to New York?

Back to face Brigit and Luke and the rest of them?

I didn't think so.

I turned to smile at Chris.

Save me.

We were outside a restaurant that I felt was eminently suitable. It had everything, the candles, the checked tablecloth, the plump patron. Positively obese, actually.

'How about here?' I suggested eagerly, waiting for my fantasy to become reality.

'I don't know,' Chris said, flailing his hands vaguely. 'It's too . . .'

I wanted to go there. But instead I just smiled and said 'Yeah, it is, a bit, isn't it?' And then I hated myself.

I should have said what I wanted. I'd just missed an opportunity to change old behaviour. *And*, I thought irritably, I was sick of Josephine's disembodied voice making announcements in my head.

On we strolled, passing intimate, dimly lit bistro after intimate, dimly lit bistro, Chris dismissing each one with a vague 'But isn't it a bit . . .?'

My spirits drooped and my sentences became shorter and terser with each disappointment. Finally we arrived at a raucous yellow shed. The Gypsy Kings were playing at ear-bleeding decibels.

'How about here?' Chris suggested. Tight-lipped, I shrugged, my whole demeanour saying '*Here?* Are you out of your stupid, fucking mind?'

'Come on, then,' he said eagerly, opening the door for me.

Gobshite, I thought, in silent fury.

When we got in, the noise nearly knocked me to the floor. It was then that I realized that I was getting old and that a drug-free Rachel viewed the world very differently from the Rachel who had a gram of coke doing laps in her head.

A twelve-year-old girl wearing a poncho and a sombrero greeted us with bonhomie that was so enthusiastic as to be crazed, manic. *Give that girl some Lithium.*

'For two,' Chris said, rubbernecking like there was no tomorrow. As if he was looking for someone. While we were being led across the crowded, sawdust-strewn floor, I heard someone shout, 'Rachel, Ray-chel.'

'Rachel.' The voice got nearer. I located the source, turned and there was Helen. Wearing a red frilly blouse, a very short skirt, and a sombrero hung from around her neck. She was carrying a tray.

'What are you doing here?' she demanded.

'What are *you* doing here?' I demanded back.

'I work here,' she said simply.

And then it all became clear.

'*This* is the abattoir?' I asked.

'Others call it Club Mexxx,' Helen said flicking a glance at the manic one, who was beaming from Helen to me to Chris, as though she might explode.

'Gimme them.' She grabbed the menus from the grinner. 'I'll seat them in my section.

'Now, don't think you'll be getting loads of free drinks,' she called over her shoulder as she weaved her tiny bottom through tequila-guzzling revellers.

'Sit here.' She threw the menus down on a wobbly,

wooden table that was the size of an album cover. Within seconds my hands were punctured with splinters.

'I just have to go and get that crowd of stupid fuckers some drinks,' she explained with a nod at the eighteen very drunk lads at the next table. 'Then I'll be back.'

Chris and I faced each other. He smiled. I didn't.

'Did you know that Helen worked here?' I asked in a shaky voice.

'Sorry?' he shouted above the noise.

'DID YOU KNOW THAT HELEN WORKED HERE?' I roared, releasing some anger.

'No.' He opened his eyes wide. 'I'd no idea.'

I didn't believe him.

I hated him. He didn't want to be with me at all. It was Helen he was after. No one ever wanted to be with me. I was just their stepping-stone to someone else. Someone who wasn't me.

Helen returned about half-an-hour later.

'*Adios amoebas,*' she greeted us.

'We have to say that,' she added, with a contemptuous curl of her lip. 'To make it authentic.'

'Right,' said Helen briskly. 'What do you want?'

The menu was the usual Tex-Mex stodge, with refried beans appearing everywhere.

'What do you recommend?' Chris twinkled up at her.

'I recommend that you go somewhere else, actually,' she said. 'We get staff meals here and I swear to God, they'd have to pay you to eat them. It's all right if you like living on the edge. I had a *burrito* earlier and it was a near-death experience. But if you're not feeling suicidal, try somewhere else. There's a lovely Cal-Ital place over the road, go there!'

I was almost on my feet, but Chris laughed and said 'Ah no, as we're here we might as well stay.'

So I resentfully ordered refried beans, served with refried beans.

'And a side order of refried beans?' Helen suggested, her pen poised.

'Ah, go on,' I said gloomily. 'What harm can it do?'

'OK,' she said, moving away. '*Mutches grassy arse, amoebas.*

'Oh yeah.' She was back. 'What do you want to drink? I can steal you some tequila because it's so cheap and disgusting they don't care if we nick some of it. The only thing is, you might go blind. Sorry about that, but if I'm caught nicking any more beers, I'm for it.'

'Er, no, Helen, that's all right,' I said, wanting to die with shame. 'But I'll just have a diet coke.'

She stared at me as if seeing a vision. 'Diet COKE? *Just* diet coke? No, lookit, the tequila isn't *that* bad, it might just bring on a mild bout of schizophrenia, but it passes.'

'Thanks, Helen,' I murmured. 'But diet coke is fine.'

'OK,' she said in confusion. 'Yourself?' she said to Chris.

'The same for me,' he said quietly.

'But why?' she demanded. 'You're DRUG ADDICTS, but you're not ALCOHOLICS.'

Heads turned from as far away as the Cal-Ital place over the road.

'Well?' Everybody's faces queried. '*Why* won't you have a drink? What harm can a drink do? After all, it's not as if you're an ALCOHOLIC.'

But it wasn't the time to stand on my chair and explain to them about the dangers of cross-addiction.

'Really, Helen.' Chris went all masterful. 'Thanks for the offer of the tequila, but no thanks.'

She went away and Chris and I sat in silence. I felt very, very depressed. I could only presume that he did too.

Eventually, I became ashamed of our silence. It contrasted too harshly with the raucous screeches and drunken shouts of all the people around us. I felt as though everyone else in the whole world was having fun, except me and my coke-drinking friend.

I hated him, I hated me, I hated not being drunk. Or coked-up, ideally.

I'm far too young to be marginalized in this horrible way, I thought bitterly.

I'd spent all my life feeling left-out, and now I really was.

Desperately, in a doomed attempt to be normal, I forced a conversation with Chris. It fooled no one, particularly not me.

The entire place was uninhibited, free, young, lively, colourful. Except for our table. In my mind's eye, the picture changed from day-glo colours into sepia when it came to me and Chris, from carnival music and laughter into slow-moving silence. We were out of step, we didn't belong, a frame from a gloomy, East European, arthouse film in the midst of *Bugs Bunny Goes to Acapulco*.

Much later our food arrived and we both faked delight.

We pushed the refried beans around our plates and the askew table rocked and swayed like a ship on the high seas. I leant my elbow on it and Chris's coke wobbled and spilled. Then Chris lifted the salt and the lurch that followed sent my fork tumbling to the floor. Then I lifted my elbow so that I could rummage around on the floor looking for it, seeing as Chris wasn't going to, the lazy bastard, and his plate slid almost off the table.

A very long time later, after we'd been offered and had refused some ice cream – refried-bean flavour, of course – the horrible ordeal ended and we were allowed to leave.

Chris left an outrageously large tip for Helen and was all smiles as we passed her on the way out.

She was preparing tequila slammers for what looked like an outing of prison officers. She banged glasses of tequila and Seven-up on the table and half-heartedly urged '*Underlay, underlay*' as the screws knocked them back.

I could hardly look at her. Jealousy had corroded a hole where my stomach used to be. Even though it wasn't her fault she was born both beautiful and over-confident. But I couldn't help feeling that it was all very unfair. What about me? Why didn't I get anything?

63

When we escaped into the warm evening, Chris suddenly seemed to notice me again. He slung an arm around my shoulders, in casual, friendly fashion, and we strolled through the streets.

I couldn't help feeling glad. Maybe he did like me after all.

'How did you get into town?' he asked.

'Dart.'

'I'll drive you home,' he said. And something in me warmed with gladness. I liked what he said and the way he said it, I felt *taken care of.*

'Unless you want to come back to my place first for coffee,' he suggested, with a side-long glance that I couldn't fathom.

'Er ... OK,' I stammered. 'Fine. Where are you parked?'

'Stephen's Green.'

So we strolled to Stephen's Green, in harmony for the first time that night. And when we got to Stephen's Green we discovered that the car had been stolen.

Whereupon Chris did the Dance of the Stolen Car. Which goes as follows. Walk four paces beside the empty place, then come to an abrupt halt. Walk four paces back in the other direction, again coming to an abrupt stop. Two paces in the original direction, stop, then back again. A frantic headspin to the left, a frantic headspin to the right, followed by frantic headspins in all directions, culminating in a full-body, three-hundred-and-sixty-degree pirouette. Another pirouette in the opposite direction. This is where facial directions become very important. Pop your eyes, wrinkle your forehead, let your mouth hang open. You may sing at this point. 'But where . . .? I parked it here, I did, I definitely parked it here.'

Pause. More pacing, a lot more agitated this time. Up down, up down, up down. Faster, faster, *faster*.

Another pause for more singing, this time with arms outstretched. 'Was it here I parked it . . .? Maybe it wasn't . . . But I'm sure it was, I'm fucking certain.'

Then reaching a crescendo, 'For FUCK'S SAKE! The fucking *bastards*. The fucking . . . *fucking*, fucking, dirty, fucking . . . *BASTARDS*.'

'It's only new.' (In some versions.)

'It's not insured.' (In others.)

'My father doesn't know I've taken it.' (In Chris's.)

I soothed and shushed. I calmed and crooned. I offered to go to the peelers, ring the insurance people and kill the person or persons unknown who'd stolen the car. What I actually wanted to do was get a taxi home, go to bed and forget all about Chris and his disaster. But for some reason I felt honour-bound to stick with him.

Eventually he said 'Well, there's nothing I can do, we might as well just go home. I'll ring the filth in the morning.'

I breathed a sigh of relief that nearly uprooted some nearby trees.

'Sorry about this,' he said, with a wry smile that I recognized of old. 'Do you still want to come back to my place?

'My folks are away,' he added.

My stomach juddered and I said casually 'Ah, sure, I might as well come back with you. The night is young, hahaha.'

What are you doing?

Get off my case! He's just a friend.

Even though I lived at home with my parents, I couldn't help a stab of scorn that Chris did too. After all, he was in his thirties, I was still in my twenties.

Just.

But he was a man. There was something very namby-pamby about a man living in the family home. As if he should still call his mother 'Mammy'. As if he had to hand over his wage-packet every Friday evening and ask permission to go down to the pub for a couple of pints with the lads. As if the mother was a religion-crazed lunatic who kept the curtains drawn and had little red lights burning to the Sacred Heart in every one of the tiny, musty, whispery, lace mantilla packed rooms.

Luckily, the Hutchinson ancestral family home was nothing like that. It showed signs of suburban affluence. Extensions and conversions, conservatories and patios, microwaves and camcorders and not a red light burning to the Sacred Heart in sight.

Chris took me into the kitchen and, while he boiled the kettle, I sat at the breakfast bar – of course, they had a breakfast bar – and swung my legs to show that I was relaxed and not sick with a combination of half dread, half anticipation.

I knew I'd die if something happened with him. And that I'd die if something didn't.

I could hear Josephine's voice warning me 'Your instinct is to look for someone to fix you. A man. Probably any man.' But then I looked at Chris, at the way his jeans hugged the back of his hard thighs and I thought 'Fuck Josephine'.

Chris wasn't just any man, he was far more than averagely attractive. *And* he and I had so much in common, so much shared experience. If we were allowed to have a relationship, we'd be perfect together.

He sat on another of the stools at the breakfast bar and pulled himself very close to me. We sat with our knees touching, then he made me jump by shifting his thigh so that it was positioned between both my knees, just nudging in. I was embarrassed by how loud my breathing sounded.

We'd sat that way many times at the Cloisters, and it had been perfectly safe. But we weren't in the Cloisters anymore, I realized with a frisson of alarm. As if I'd just jumped out of a plane and realized I'd forgotten my parachute.

'Now then,' Chris said with a smile that made my intestines curdle, 'there's something I've been meaning to do for the past two months.'

And then he kissed me.

64

I knew it was the wrong thing for both of us, I strongly suspected that he didn't even fancy me. But I was determined to do it anyway.

I shouldn't have.

It was one of those nightmare sex sessions when you both realize about three seconds into it that it's a terrible, *terrible* mistake.

And, in those circumstances, with twelve stone of grunting male pinning you to the mattress, how do you make your excuses and leave?

You can't pretend that you've just seen someone you know on the other side of the room.

Oh no.

You can't just look at your watch, gasp and mutter something incoherent about your flatmate having no key to get in.

Fat chance.

You're there for the duration and you've just got to grin and bear it. Grit your teeth and get on with it.

As soon as we both took our clothes off, which was an ordeal in itself, I instantly felt all the passion ebb away. I knew, I just *knew* that he'd gone right off me. I could almost smell his panic.

And I'd gone right off him too. He was all wrong. Too small. No matter what I felt about Luke, there was no denying that he had a fine body. In comparison, Chris was lacking in every department. And I mean *every.*

We were both too polite to call a halt to proceedings.

It was like having had a massive dinner, then turning up at your friend's house to find that she's prepared an elaborate eight-course meal for you. Which you have to eat even though you feel as if you're going to puke with each mouthful.

Sick with misery, I watched him do the condom thing. If you're not slightly delirious with passion, a grown man covering his lad with a piece of clingfilm just seems plain mad. Then we both reluctantly indulged in a short bout of play-acting. Nipple sucking, that kind of thing, *very* half-hearted. Then he clambered on top of me for the main event.

It felt very, very wrong to be penetrated by a penis that wasn't attached to Luke. But at least events were moving on and it would be over soon.

Wrong.

It lasted for ever.

Will he ever come, for Christ's sake, I begged the universe, as he pounded away on top of me. Naturally, there was no chance that I'd come, but I faked and faked in the hope that if he'd been waiting for me, that he might just hurry up and bring it to a conclusion.

And still he pumped and pumped and it started to hurt. I'd probably go home with *blisters.*

Then it occurred to me that he might be one of those men who feel they haven't satisfied a woman until she's come several times. So I faked a couple more to speed him on his way.

And still he kept going.

And a long, long time later he stopped . . .

Not with a deep groan, a few death-throes spasms and wearing an expression like he'd just got an almighty kick in the bollix. But with a slowing down and a marshmal-lowesque texture to his willy, that was nothing less than an admission of failure.

'Sorry, Rachel,' he muttered, not looking at me.

'It's O K,' I replied in an undertone, not looking at him either.

I would have left except I didn't want to ask him for a lift and besides, what good would it have done seeing as the car had been stolen? And I hadn't enough money for a taxi.

He pulled the condom off himself, threw it in his waste-paper basket – ugh – then switched off the light and turned his back on me. I had expected nothing else.

Luke and I used to go to sleep wrapped around each other, I remembered mournfully.

The bastard.

As I lay there in the darkness, I suddenly felt hungry. I should have eaten my refried beans.

Too late now.

I slept horribly. Fitful and light. And when I woke at about six-thirty, my feelings of failure were so acute that I couldn't bear to be there a moment longer. I grimly got dressed, picked up my bag and made for the door.

Then I hesitated as I realized that I had absolutely *nothing* else in my life that was good. I rummaged in my bag until I found a pen, wrote my phone number on a piece of paper and put it on his pillow. I didn't dare do the trick I did to Luke of scrunching it up into a ball, throwing it in a bin and saying, 'There! That's saved you the bother.' Because in this case it would be the truth.

'I'll ring you,' Chris murmured sleepily.

*

Of course he didn't.

I might have been drug-free, but nothing else had changed in my life.

I stood at the bus-stop and the people on early starts looked at my fancy-me clothes and sniggered.

Except for a teenage boy who thought I was fair game, followed me up the stairs and sat behind me on the bus, murmuring 'Knickers, knickers, I saw your knickers,' in so low an undertone that at first I thought I was imagining it. I was afraid to move seats in case people looked at me again.

When I got off the bus the driver winked and said 'You'll have some explaining to do to your mammy.' I ignored him, stepped onto the foot-path and swore to myself *I'm not going to look up, I'm not going to look up.* But I was helpless, in the grip of an instinct too strong to resist. I lifted my head. Sure enough, the revolting, knicker-obsessed boy was leering down at me. I wrenched my eyes away from his but not before I had deduced from his hand gestures that he was planning to have a good old wank for himself in my honour.

I began the short walk home, feeling dirty.

But at least someone fancies me, I found myself thinking, before I was halfway there.

I was greeted by my mother in a manner that reminded me why I had left home in the first place.

Wild-eyed and be-nightdressed, she shrieked 'Where in God's name have you been? I was on the verge of ringing the guards!'

'I stayed in Mrs Hutchinson's.' I thought if I said 'Mrs Hutchinson's' it would sound a lot more benign than, 'I stayed with Chris and we attempted to have sex but he couldn't sustain an erection.'

'I stayed in Mrs Hutchinson's and I would have come home except their car was stolen and he had to ring the insurance and the coppers and report it . . .'

I talked quickly, hoping to distract her from her me-directed rage with the story of the stolen car.

'Philomena and Ted Hutchinson are in Tenerife,' she hissed. 'You were there on your own with him.'

'Actually, Mum, I was,' I agreed cheerily. I was tired of all this. I was an adult.

And with that she went ballistic. She tried to hit me, throw a hairbrush, sit down, stand up and burst out crying, all at once.

'You slut,' she screeched. 'Have you no shame, and him a married man! And what about his three children? I suppose you gave no thought to them.'

The paralysing shock must have shown on my face, because she shrieked 'You didn't even know, did you? Well, what kind of a bloody eejit are you? A bloody useless selfish fool who always does the wrong thing.' Her face was puce and she was breathing hard. I'd gone cold with horror.

'I bet you don't even know he was forced to leave the Cloisters the first time he was there,' she screamed. 'Because he was caught having intercourse with a married woman in one of the bathrooms. And will I tell you what galls me?'

'No,' I said. But she told me anyway.

'It was bad enough, the right show you made of me with your drugs carry-on. But now you have to go and do this. You were always a selfish brat, I haven't forgotten the time you ate poor Margaret's Easter egg, do you do these things deliberately to spite me . . .'

I ran out of the room and up the stairs, while she stood

543

at the bottom, screeching up at me, 'Selfish, self-centred pup. Well you can just get out and you needn't bother coming back. Go on, pack your bags and go, it'll be a relief to me if I never see you again. Tormenting me like this . . .'

I was shaking with shock. I'd always hated fights, and I was appalled at the force of my mother's rage. Her contempt for me was horrifying. I'd long suspected I was a big disappointment to her, but it was excruciatingly painful for it to be confirmed.

Not to mention what she'd told me about Chris. I could hardly believe it. He was *married*. With three *children*. He was obviously separated, but that didn't make it any better.

I couldn't stop thinking about how he didn't fancy me enough to come. His rejection of me felt terrible, but in conjunction with my mother's rage, it was too much.

But I knew exactly what I was going to do.

First I was going to change my clothes. Then I was going to beg, steal or borrow lots of money and go out, buy a shit-load of drugs, ingest them and feel better.

I stumbled into my bedroom and slammed the door, shutting out Mum's hysterical voice. The curtains were drawn and someone was in my bed. No, two people. Helen and Anna.

Again.

Why couldn't anybody in this house sleep in their own bloody bed? I wondered wearily. And why were Helen and Anna there together? They were supposed to hate each other.

They were both deep in slumber, curled up like two kittens, cute and sweet, their long black hair tangled across the pillows, their spiky eyelashes throwing shadows on their smooth little faces.

I switched on the light, which caused immediate uproar. 'For fu . . .!' One of them sat up in shock. 'I was *asleep*!'

'Turn off the fecking light,' the other one ordered.

'No,' I said. 'This is my room and I need to find things.'

'Hoor,' muttered Helen and leant out of bed and began rummaging around in her bag.

'Are you OK?' Anna asked. She sounded surprised.

'Fine,' I said, shortly.

'Here,' said Helen, handing Anna a pair of sunglasses. 'Put them on so we can go back to sleep.'

Helen put on a pair also and they lay in bed, wearing their sunglasses, looking like the Blues Brothers.

'So,' said Helen conversationally, 'did you ride your man?'

'Yes,' I said shakily. Then paused. 'And no.'

Helen raised an eyebrow from behind her shades. 'Yes and no? Blowjobs?'

I shook my head. I was sorry I'd said anything because I didn't want to talk about it.

'Can I just remind you,' Helen persisted, 'that anal penetration *does* count as riding.'

'Thank you, Helen.'

'So was it?'

'Was it what?'

'Anal penetration?'

'No.'

'Don't you like it?'

'I don't mind it.' I'd never actually done it but I wasn't going to admit that to my much younger sister. I should have been telling *her* about such things. Not the other way round.

'I swear by it,' she murmured.

65

I cleared my mother's purse of money, netting about a hundred and thirty quid. She must have just got her housekeeping. Then I blew the dust off her credit card and took that for good measure. I hesitated about stealing money from Anna but, as luck would have it, she only had eight pence in her little Madras pouch. Helen slept with her money under her pillow so there wasn't any point trying to shake her down for anything.

I didn't think I was doing anything wrong. I was in the grip of such a strong compulsion that I couldn't stop myself. I had to get my hands on some Valium and some coke. That was all I could think of. I was being torn apart by my mother's terrible words and it was inconceivable that I *stay with the pain*.

I was hardly aware of the Dart journey into town. My blood was up, every atom in my body was screaming for chemicals and there wasn't any force in the universe that could have talked me out of it. I had no idea where I'd buy drugs, but I sensed I had a better chance in town than hanging around at the end of my road in suburban Blackrock. I'd heard that Dublin had a bad drug problem. Naturally I was hopeful.

When I got off the train, I anxiously wondered where I should head for. Nightclubs were a great place to buy coke, but precious few were open at nine o'clock in the morning. A pub would be my likeliest bet. But where? Which one?

And why weren't any of them open? I walked and walked, fear growing, need expanding.

It reminded me of one time when I'd been dying to go to the loo and nowhere was open. Running around the streets, looking for a bar or a café that might let me in. Becoming more and more desperate as the buildings shut their doors and closed their faces against me. Nowhere, literally nowhere, that could help. Once again, I experienced those same feelings of helplessness, frustration and unbearable, excruciating *need*.

To my stomach-chilling alarm, every pub I went to was shut.

Go home.

Go fuck yourself.

'What time do the pubs open?' I blurted at a man hurrying to work.

'Half-ten,' he answered, startled.

'All of them?' I croaked.

'Yes.' He nodded, giving me a funny look that in different circumstances would have made me cringe.

Wasn't Ireland supposed to be a nation of pissheads? I thought in confusion. What kind of nation of pissheads has the pubs opening at half-past ten? When the day was nearly over?

If only Dublin had a red-light district. Why wasn't I Dutch?

I pressed on into the back roads and, more by luck than judgement, found myself on a long street which appeared occasionally on the news as an example of deprivation and violence. About two people a year were shot in Dublin, usually on that very street. Apocryphal stories abounded about suburban, middle-class citizens who'd strayed there by mistake and were offered drugs one hundred and eighty-four times along a ten-yard stretch.

Bingo.

But you can never get a dealer when you need one. Maybe it was too early for them to be up. If only I had a letter of introduction from Wayne!

For ages I traipsed up and down past graffiti-covered blocks of flats. Crooked, wobbly pictures of giant syringes with a red cross through them and big 'Pushers Out' signs were painted onto every gable end. Which indicated I was in an area where lots of drugs were sold. But nobody approached me, wrestled me to the ground and forcibly injected me with heroin, the way news reports would have you believe happened constantly. (I had yet to meet a dealer who offered free samples and test-drives of their products, but they most definitely existed in tabloid-land.) Or perhaps I should find the local school where, of course, there would be busloads of dealers all loitering and hawking their wares, as if in a Moroccan souk.

I reckoned my chances of procuring drugs were highest around the few trendy, well-dressed youths I saw. But, when I tried to make meaningful eye-contact, they all turned away with a snigger and a blush.

I don't fancy you, I wanted to scream. I only want to buy cocaine. All that talk about Dublin's terrible drug problem, I thought in fury. The terrible problem is getting the fucking drugs!

Eventually, after I'd been scurrying up and down for a full hour, I forced myself to stop and *wait*. Just wait. Simply idle on a corner and look desperate with need.

People looked at me suspiciously. It was horrible.

Everyone knew why I was there and their disgust was palpable.

To be less conspicuous, I sat down on a filthy flight of concrete steps outside a block of flats that looked like a war zone. But then a woman came out with several children and grimly told me 'Get up.' I did. Fear broke through the madness of my craving. The woman was hard, bitter and frightening and there were probably more like her. I'd heard about the vigilante groups they had in areas like this. And they did lots more than paint crooked syringes with red crosses through them on every gable end. People had been hospitalized after drug-related beatings. Not to mention the annual shootings.

A voice in my head urged me to leave, to go home. I felt dirty, embarrassed, ashamed and scalp-crawlingly scared. But frightened and all as I was to stay, I was more afraid to leave.

I stood up again, leant against a wall, looked needily at passers-by and quailed as one by one they threw filthy expressions at me.

I don't know how long I loitered for, cringing and desperate, when finally a boy came up to me. In a few short sentences, in language we both understood, I conveyed to him that I wanted an awful lot of cocaine, and he seemed to be in a position to help me.

'And I need some downers,' I added.

'Temazepam?'

'Fine.'

'The coke'll take a while.'

'How long?' I asked anxiously.

'Maybe a couple of hours.'

'OK,' I said reluctantly.

'And I get a hit of it,' he added.

'OK,' I mumbled again.

'Wait in the pub at the end of the road.'

He relieved me of eighty pounds, which was daylight extortion, but I was in no position to negotiate.

As he hared off I was gripped with the conviction that I'd never see him, the coke or the money again.

I fucking hate this.

I went to the pub. There was nothing I could do but wait.

There were a few people – all men – in the pub. The atmosphere was macho and hostile and I had a strong sense of how unwelcome I was. Conversation entirely ceased as I ordered a brandy. For a horrible moment I thought the barman was going to refuse to serve me.

Nervously, I sat in the furthest corner. I hoped the brandy would calm my frantic agitation. But when I finished it, I still felt terrible, so I had another. And another.

Avoiding eye-contact, willing time to pass, I sat, sick and edgy, drumming my fingers on the brown formica table. But every now and then, like the sun breaking through the clouds, I remembered I was only a short time away from being the proud owner of a lot of cocaine. Maybe. That warmed me, before I was pitched back into the hell of my racing head.

Whenever I remembered my awful night with Chris or what my mother had said, I took another swig of brandy and concentrated on what it would be like when I'd got my hands on the coke.

After I'd been there ages a man approached me, wondering if I'd like to buy some methadone. Keen and all as I was to achieve oblivion, I knew that methadone could be fatal to the uninitiated. I wasn't that desperate. Yet.

'Thanks, but someone is already getting me some stuff,' I explained, terrified of offending.

'Ah, that'd be Tiernan,' the man said.

'I don't know his name,' I said.

'It's Tiernan.'

Over the next hour, every person in the pub tried to interest me in buying methadone. Clearly they'd had a bumper harvest that year.

My eyes were constantly trained on the door, as I waited for Tiernan to reappear. But he didn't.

Despite the brandy, my panic picked up again. What would I do? How would I get drugs now that I'd given away so much money?

Another possibility broke through into my consciousness. It suddenly seemed like a merciful rescue that Tiernan had done a bunk with the money. *You could get up and go now, go home, sort things out with your mother. This isn't irreversible.*

But then my thoughts swung back again. I couldn't imagine anything being all right, ever again. I was too far down the path I was on to be able to make my way back. I ordered yet another brandy.

So that I didn't have to be alone with my own head, I eavesdropped on the conversations around me.

They were mostly extremely dull, all about machinery and involving the sentence '. . . So I took it up to the brother-in-law for him to have a look at it . . .'

Occasionally, though, they were interesting. There was a nice one about ecstasy.

'I'll swap you two Mad Bastards for one Holy Ghost,' a tattooed man offered a raw youth.

'No.' The raw youth shook his head adamantly. 'I'm happy with my Holy Ghost.'

'So you won't swap?'

'I won't swap.'

'Not even for *two* Bastards?'

'Not even for two Bastards.'

'You see,' the tattooed man turned to the other tattooed man beside him, 'people everywhere are saying they'd rather have one Holy Ghost instead of two Mad Bastards. Holy Ghosts give a cleaner, whiter buzz.'

At least, I thought that's what he'd said.

At about two o'clock – although time had ceased to have any meaning between the trauma and the brandy – Tiernan returned. I had almost entirely given up on him, so I thought I was hallucinating. I could have kissed him I was so ecstatic.

Quite drunk, also.

'Did you get . . . ?' I asked anxiously. My breath shortened when he waved a small bag of whitish powder at me.

My heart gave a great hop and I itched to hold it in my own hands, like a mother wanting to hold her newborn baby. But Tiernan was very proprietorial.

'I get a line,' he reminded me, swinging the bag out of my grasp.

'OK,' I gasped, fizzing with rush-lust.

Hurry up.

In full view of everyone in the pub, he chopped two gorgeous, fat lines on the formica table.

Fearfully, I looked around to see if anyone minded, but they didn't seem to.

He rolled up a tenner and neatly hoovered up one of the lines. The bigger, I noticed angrily.

And then it was my turn. My heart was already pounding

and my head already lifting in joyous anticipation. I bent over the coke. It felt like a mystic moment.

But just as I was on the verge of sniffing, I suddenly heard Josephine's voice. 'You were killing yourself with drugs. The Cloisters has shown you another way of living. You can be happy without drugs.'

I wavered. Tiernan looked at me quizzically.

You don't have to do this.

You can stop right now and no harm will have been done.

I hesitated. I'd learnt so much in the Cloisters, made such progress with myself, admitted I was an addict and looked forward to a better, brighter, healthier, happier future. Did I want to throw it all away? Well, did I?

Well, did I?

I stared at the innocent-looking white powder, arrayed in a wobbly little line on the table in front of me. I had nearly died because of it. Was it worth continuing?

Was it?

Yes!

I bent over my cocaine, my best friend, my saviour, my protector. And I inhaled deeply.

66

I woke up in hospital.

Except I didn't know it was a hospital when I first came to. I struggled to swim out of sleep and up to the surface. I could have been anywhere. In any stranger's bed. Until I opened my eyes I could have been in any of the millions of beds that exist all over the globe.

When I saw the drip going into my arm and smelt the funny disinfectant smell, I understood where I was. I had no idea how I'd got there. Or what was supposed to be wrong with me.

But I had the bleakest feeling of comedown I'd ever had. Like I was standing right on the most desolate edge of the universe, staring into the abyss. Emptiness all around me, emptiness deep within me. All so horribly familiar.

I hadn't felt like that for over two months. I'd forgotten how really, truly unbearable it was. And of course the first thing I craved, to make it go away, was more drugs.

What happened? I wondered.

I had a vague memory of lurching through the bright, evening streets with my new best friend, Tiernan. And going to another pub and drinking more and snorting more. Taking a handful of my Temazepam when slight paranoia kicked in. I remembered dancing in the new pub and thinking I was the most brilliant dancer in the whole world. Kerr-ist, how mortifying.

Then I'd gone with Tiernan to another pub where we'd got more coke. Then another pub. Then maybe another, I had a vague memory, but I wasn't sure. And after that we'd gone with three – or was it four? – of his mates to someone's flat. It had been dark by then. And we'd taken a couple of Es each. Apart from a flash of a nightclub-type scene, that may have been real or imagined, I remembered absolutely nothing else.

I could hear someone crying, sobbing their eyes out. My mother. Reluctantly I opened my eyes, and it just added to the feelings of overall weirdness when I saw that it was Dad who was in floods.

'Don't,' I croaked. 'I won't do it again.'

'You said that before,' he heaved, his face in his hands.

'I promise,' I managed. 'It'll be different this time.'

Apparently I'd been knocked down. According to the driver I'd rushed right out in front of her and she'd had no way of avoiding me. The police report described me as 'crazed'. The people I'd been with had run away and left me lying on the road. I was told that I was extremely lucky – apart from a huge bruise on my thigh, there wasn't anything wrong with me.

Except that I was losing my mind, of course.

I wished, longed, *yearned* to be dead. More than all the other times I'd wished I was dead.

A rock-heavy slab of despair flattened me. A cocktail of depression made up of the terrible things my mother had screeched at me, my shame at relapsing and Chris's rejection of me.

I lay in my hospital bed, tears trickling down the side of my face and onto the pillow, loathing myself with a dull, heavy passion. I was such an utter failure, the biggest loser ever created. No one loved me. I'd been thrown out of my home because I was stupid and useless. I couldn't ever go back there again, and frankly I didn't blame my mother. Because, as well as all my other terrible faults, I'd relapsed.

That was killing me. I'd ruined everything, totally destroyed my chance of a happy, drug-free life. I despised myself for all the money Dad shelled out on me going to the Cloisters, for all the good it had done me. I'd let everyone down. Josephine, the other inmates, my parents, my family, even me. I was racked with fierce guilt, shame and mortification. I wanted to disappear off the face of the earth, to die and dissolve.

I went to sleep, grateful to check out of the living hell my life had become. When I woke up Helen and Anna were sitting by my bed, eating the grapes someone had brought me.

'Fucking pips,' Helen complained, spitting something into her hand. 'Haven't they heard of seedless grapes, welcome to the twentieth century. Oh, you're awake.'

I nodded, too depressed to speak.

'Jesus, you're really bad,' she commented cheerfully. 'Ending up in hospital *again* from taking drugs. Next time you might die.'

'Stop.' Anna elbowed her.

'Well, you needn't worry,' I managed to drag the words out. 'It won't be your concern anymore. As soon as I'm well enough to get out of here, I'm going far, far away where you'll never have to see me again.'

I planned to disappear. To punish myself with an empty, lonely half-life away from family and friends. I would wander the earth, welcome nowhere, because I didn't deserve any other form of existence.

'Listen to the drama queen,' Helen mocked.

'Stop,' Anna wailed, distraught.

'You don't understand,' I informed Helen, my heart breaking from my almost-orphan status. 'Mum told me to get out and never come back. She hates me, she's always hated me.'

'Who, Mum?' Helen asked in surprise.

'Yes, she always makes me feel like I'm useless,' I managed to say, even though the pain nearly killed me.

There was much mirth and scoffing from the pair of them.

'You?' derided Helen. 'But she's always telling me I'm hopeless. For failing my exams twice and having a poxy job. Every second day she tells me to get out and never come back. At this stage, I worry when she doesn't.

'It's true, I swear.' She nodded at my disbelieving face.

'No, it's me she really hates,' Anna said. If I hadn't known better I'd have thought she was boasting.

'And she can't stand Shane. She's always asking why he doesn't have a company car.'

'*Why* doesn't he have a company car?' Helen asked. 'Just out of curiosity.'

'Because he doesn't have a job, stupid!' Anna said, rolling her eyes.

My spirits lifted an atom or two. I tentatively began to think that maybe I wouldn't commit suicide or run away to sea just yet. That perhaps all wasn't entirely lost.

'Is she really mean to you?' I croaked. 'Or are you only trying to be nice.'

'I don't do nice,' Helen said scornfully. 'And, yes, she's horrible to both of us.'

It was glorious for that terrible apocalyptic depression to lift, even momentarily.

Helen awkwardly pawed at my hand and I was so touched by her attempt at affection that tears came to my eyes, for the eighty-ninth time that day.

'She's a mother,' Helen told me wisely. 'It's her job to shout at us. She'd be stripped of her badge if she didn't.'

'It's nothing personal,' Anna agreed. 'She thinks if she gives out shite to us that we'll make something of ourselves. Not just you. She does it to *all* of us!'

'Except Margaret,' the three of us said in unison.

I was feeling better enough to call Margaret a lickarse twenty or thirty times. 'Lickarse,' we all agreed. 'Yeah, lickarse. The big lickarse.'

'So you mean you got wrecked just because Mum told you to get out and never come back?' Helen endeavoured to understand.

'I suppose,' I shrugged, embarrassed at how puerile that sounded.

'You thick-looking wuss,' she said kindly. 'Just tell her to feck off like I always do. Or ask her who's going to mind her in her old age.'

'I'm not like you,' I pointed out.

'You'd better learn to be,' Helen suggested. 'Toughen up, you're too much of a baba. You can't go round nearly getting killed every time Mum – or anyone – shouts at you, you won't last five minutes.'

That was the warning Josephine had given me. My head clanged as I suddenly understood what she'd been on about when she said I had unresolved tension with Mum. I'd nodded and agreed with her, but I'd forgotten all the advice she'd given me the minute some of said unresolved tensions raised their heads.

I'd failed my first test in the real world.

I'd know better the next time.

'When she goes mad at you again, ignore her.' Helen beamed encouragingly, reading my thoughts. 'So what if she tells you you're crap? You've got to believe in *yourself*.'

'Anyway, she doesn't even mean it,' Anna chipped in.

'Only with you,' Helen said to her.

I felt the black, smoggy cloud of misery lift from me. It was a wonderful revelation to find out that my sisters felt as picked on by Mum as I always had. That the only difference between us was in our attitudes. They regarded it as amusing sparring, but I'd taken it far too much to heart. And I'd better stop.

'Do you feel better now about Mum?' Anna asked gently. 'She only lost the head because she was afraid when you didn't come home. That night she was hysterical thinking you might take drugs with that Chris. People say things they don't mean when they're worried.'

She added sheepishly 'I was worried myself.'

'Clean and serene, that's you, isn't it Anna?' Helen stretched and yawned. 'How long is it since you've had a drug?'

'Never you mind,' Anna said haughtily. And a squabble broke out, but I hardly heard them, because I was suddenly assailed by guilt and shame. *Different* guilt and shame from the ones that had been torturing me since I'd come to. Guilt and shame about what I'd done to Mum. Of course she'd been worried, I realized, with horrible clarity. I'd only been out of the Cloisters less than a week. I was an addict, it had been my first trip to the outside world, with a person who was a well-known bad influence, and I hadn't come home. If she'd thought the worst, she had been well within her rights. I deserved to be roared at.

She'd accused me of being selfish. And she was right.

I'd been really selfish. I was so wrapped up in myself and Chris that I couldn't see how frightened for me she'd been. I resolved to humbly apologize as soon as I saw her.

I was starting to feel quite good until I remembered that my fight with Mum wasn't the only thing that was weighing heavy on my brain.

'I'm a failure,' I reminded Helen and Anna. 'I took drugs.'

'So what?' they clamoured.

So what? I thought in disgust. They clearly had no idea how serious the situation was.

'Don't take them again.' Helen shrugged. 'It's like being on a diet. Just because you go mental and eat seven Mars bars one day doesn't mean that you can't start your diet again the next day. All the more reason to, in fact.'

'If only it was that simple,' I said sadly.

'It *is* that fucking simple,' Helen said, sounding irritated. 'Stop feeling sorry for yourself.'

'Fuck off,' I muttered.

'Fuck off yourself,' she replied equably.

She made it sound so reasonable. As if I'd just over-reacted. Maybe I *had* overreacted, I thought hopefully. That would be wonderful, to find out that everything was salvageable.

Mum arrived in the room after Helen and Anna had left. I sat up in the bed, nervous and anxious to apologize, but she beat me to it.

'I'm sorry,' she said, abject misery on her face.

'No, I'm sorry,' I insisted, a lump in my throat. 'You're right. I was selfish and thoughtless and I'm mortified about worrying you so much. But I won't do it ever again, I swear.'

She came and sat on my bed.

'I'm sorry for the terrible things I said.' She hung her head. 'I overreacted. But it's just my way, I didn't mean any harm. It's only because I want the best for you . . .'

'I'm sorry for being such a bad daughter,' I said, feeling deeply ashamed.

'You're not!' she exclaimed. 'You're not at all. Weren't you always a pet, the most affectionate, the best of the lot of them.

'My baby,' she wailed, flinging herself around me. 'My little girl.'

A torrent of tears gushed from me at her words. I fell into her arms and sobbed as she stroked my hair and shushed me.

'I'm sorry about Margaret's Easter egg,' I eventually managed to say.

'Don't!' Mum exclaimed wetly. 'I could've cut my tongue out. The minute the words were said . . .'

'And I'm sorry for embarrassing you by being a drug addict,' I said humbly.

'You're not to be,' she said, wiping my tears away with the sleeve of her cardigan. 'Sure, it could be miles worse. Hilda Shaw is having a baby. Another one. And she's *still* not married. And, wait till you hear,' she suddenly dropped her voice to hushed tones, even though there was only me and her in the room, 'Angela Kilfeather is after deciding she's a lesbian . . .'

Imagine! Angela Kilfeather, of the blonde ringlets that as a child I was so jealous of, was a lezzer!

'. . . and parades up and down the road french-kissing her . . .' Mum paused, almost unable to say it, '. . . girl-friend. Sure, a drug addict is nothing compared to that. Marguerite Kilfeather probably thinks I'm dead lucky.'

We laughed tearfully. And I made a solemn vow never to french-kiss a woman in full view of our neighbours. It was the least I could do for my mother.

67

As soon as I was liberated from hospital, Dad said that someone called Nola had rung me. Blonde, glamorous, beautiful Nola, who'd come into the Cloisters for the NA meetings. Thank you, God, I thought with shaky, heartfelt relief. I had to start going to my support groups but I didn't want to go on my own.

I rang her back and, mortified, told her about my relapse. She didn't give out to me. Just like the two times I'd seen her in the Cloisters, she was really nice, if a bit scatty. I soon found out that Nola was always really nice, if a bit scatty.

She said that maybe I'd *needed* to relapse to find out I didn't want to anymore. It was a bit complicated but, as it didn't involve me being pilloried, I was happy to go along with it.

'Forgive yourself, but don't forget,' she urged.

She took me to an NA meeting in a church hall. I was wobbly and paranoid. It was my first trip to the outside world since that terrible day with Tiernan. And I was petrified that I'd run into Chris, still smarting, as I was, from the memory of the humiliating night I'd had with him. Luckily he was nowhere to be seen.

The meeting was quite different from the ones I'd gone to in the Cloisters. There were a lot more people, all of them friendly and welcoming. And instead of just one person describing their drug-taking past, several people spoke about what was happening in their current day-to-day lives. How they were managing to cope with jobs and boyfriends and mothers without taking drugs. And they *were* coping. I got great hope from it. And sometimes when people were talking, they could have been describing me. I knew exactly what they were getting at when they said things like 'I compared my insides with everyone else's outsides.' I felt like I belonged and I was surprised that that made me happy.

Not to mention that mad Francie had been right about the ridey lads. There were loads there.

Marvellous, I thought. One of these fine young men will assist me to get over Chris.

'Don't even think about it,' Nola said with a warm smile when she caught me looking sidelong at one of them.

After the meeting, she interrogated me in the next-door café. 'What were you up to, giving all the boys the hairy eyeball?'

So, with longed-for relief, I spilled my guts about my awful experience with Chris. The dreadful inconclusive sex, the suspicion that he hadn't even fancied me, the fear that he fancied Helen, the humiliation, the feelings of inadequacy. 'And I think the best thing for me to do is get back in the saddle,' I finished hopefully.

'Ah no,' Nola said with a mildness that briefly fooled me. 'Sure, what would you want to do that for? Relationships in early recovery are a big mistake. You'll only make yourself miserable.'

I couldn't have disagreed more.

'You're too young and immature to make the correct choices!' She made it sound like a compliment.

'I'm twenty-seven,' I objected sulkily.

'Aren't you lucky to be so lovely and young?' she beamed, missing the point. Deliberately, I later found out.

'All the same,' she said jovially, 'leave the boys for a while. You're only just out of a treatment centre.'

That really frustrated me, but she was so nice I couldn't complain.

'D'you know something?' she chattered. 'This'll give you a good laugh, now, but lots of people make the mistake of thinking that NA is like a dating agency.'

Francie, you lying wagon!

'Isn't that a scream? Sure, look at the disaster it was when you went out with an addict who'd only just stopped.' Nola looked at me fondly. 'It made you relapse! Ah, you wouldn't want that to happen again, would you? You've too much respect for yourself.'

I hadn't, but I liked her so much I couldn't bring myself to disagree.

'The whole Chris thing *was* awful,' I was forced to admit.

'It was, of course!' Nola exclaimed, as if someone had been trying to suggest otherwise. 'But forget him.'

It struck me that every conversation that ever took place between two women, whatever the context, had those exact words in it, at some stage.

'I think it hurts more to be rejected by someone I kind of hero-worshipped,' I struggled to explain. 'He was always giving me advice in the Cloisters. He was so wise.'

'But he *wasn't* wise,' Nola said, with innocent surprise. 'He was full of shit.'

I was shocked. I'd thought she was too sweet to say such a thing.

'But he was, though,' she said, with a little giggle. '*Full* of it. I'm not saying it's the poor craythur's fault, but he

565

didn't behave wisely, despite giving you a rake of advice. Talk is cheap, but look at how people behave, not at what they say.'

'But he was really nice to me in the laughing house,' I felt obliged to protest.

'I'd say he was indeed,' Nola agreed sympathetically. 'Especially when you were upset?'

'Yes,' I said, wondering how she knew.

'Sure, a lot of addicts are very manipulative,' Nola said with great compassion. 'They can't help picking on people when they're at their most vulnerable. I'd say you weren't the only woman the poor divil was nice to.' She said everything in such a mild, vague voice that it took me a minute to understand just how scathing she was. And she was right to be, I realized as I was blasted with an unwelcome memory. Of the time Chris had wiped away Misty's tears with his thumbs, the way he'd done to me a short time previously. The way he'd looked at me to make sure I saw. That had undeniably been some sort of gameplaying. Haltingly, I told Nola about it.

'You see?' she said, triumphantly. 'So get over him. He doesn't sound a bit well, the poor boy. Making you think he knows it all, when he's no better than you. And so insecure, God love him, that he had to seduce you just to prove to himself you fancy him.'

Then I remembered the walk he'd taken me for in the garden at the Cloisters. The provocative things he'd said. That had been *deliberate*, I realized in shock. He'd said those things on purpose. The manipulative *bastard*.

In an instant I was raging. To think I'd blamed myself for the crappy sex with him! What a joke. He was far too focused on himself for me to have mattered in any way.

'The prick!' I exclaimed. 'Playing games with me,

getting everyone to fancy him just because he feels inadequate, leading me on . . .'

'Arra, girl, go easy on him,' Nola interrupted, as if it was the simplest thing in the world. 'It's not his fault.'

'That's OK for you to say,' I said, breathless with what I felt was justified rage.

'Would you not try to remember that he's no different from you?' she suggested kindly. 'Just an addict very early on in a new life.'

That took the wind out of my sails.

'Even though he was giving you a load of guff about how to behave, he obviously hasn't a clue how to conduct himself.' She smiled fondly at me. 'If he had half a brain he'd never have slept with you.

'No offence meant,' she added, nicely.

I muttered that none was taken.

'So, come on now, calm down,' she urged. 'Deep breaths, good woman.'

I was almost annoyed when I found I *was* calming down.

'Forgive yourself,' Nola said, just as I realized I had. 'It wasn't your fault he rejected you. And forgive him while you're at it.'

And to my great surprise, the anger I felt for Chris and the hurt he'd inflicted on me, just shimmied away. Everything had changed and I saw him as a poor sap, no more able to cope than I was. He shouldn't have slept with me, but *I* shouldn't have slept with him *either*. I wasn't a victim. I'd made the decision to go out with him, even though I'd been warned not to. And if it all went pear-shaped – as, of course, it had – I was partly to blame.

I liked that feeling. Responsible, in control.

'Anyway,' Nola pointed out, 'you went off him as much as he seemed to go off you.'

But instead of feeling victorious, I found I was thinking of *Luke*.

'What's up with you now, girl?' Nola asked.

'How d'you mean?' I asked.

'You're looking a bit, I don't know . . . *annoyed*.' My eyes were almost popping out of my head in rage, but Nola couldn't seem to deal in any emotion more negative than annoyance.

'I had a boyfriend,' I found myself saying, my eyes filling with unwelcome tears. 'A real boyfriend, I mean, not just a half-shag like Chris.'

Burning with anger, choking with bile, I told her about Luke, what a complete bastard he'd been to me, how he'd humiliated me and hurt me with the terrible things he'd said the day he came to the Cloisters.

Nola listened sympathetically. 'And you still love him,' she said, when I finished.

'Love him?' I demanded, looking at her as if she'd lost her reason. 'I fucking hate him!'

'That much?' She looked at me compassionately.

'No, I mean it,' I insisted. 'I hate his guts.'

'Even though he was fierce good to come all that way and help you see how addicted you were to the quare stuff?' She sounded amazed. 'I think he sounds like a dote.'

'Oh, don't *you* start,' I said moodily. 'I hate him, I'll never forgive him, I hope I won't clap eyes on him until my dying day. That's one part of my life that's well and truly finished.'

'Sometimes, if it's meant to be, people from your old life come back,' she said, as if it was meant to be some sort of comfort.

'If it's meant to be,' I mimicked. 'Well, I don't *want* him back!'

'You're in desperate bad humour.' She smiled indulgently.

'I mean it, I don't want him back,' I insisted to her fond face. 'But I'll never meet anyone ever again,' I wailed, flattened by sudden despair. 'My life is over.'

Nola stood up suddenly.

'Hurry up, finish that,' she ordered, pointing at my coffee, and throwing a couple of quid on the table. 'And come on!'

'Where . . .?'

'Just come on,' she said, breathless and excited.

She marched out up the street and, rattling keys, approached a silver, sporty-looking car.

'Get in, good woman,' she ordered me. Fearfully, I got in.

'Where are we going?' I asked, as she sped like a mentaller through the streets.

'Something to show you,' she muttered, vaguely. 'You'll like it.'

And she said nothing more until we came screeching to a stop outside a red-brick house.

'Out you get,' she said. Nicely, but very firmly. I no longer thought Nola was the mild-mannered sweetie she seemed on the surface.

I got out, and she marched at high speed over the gravel, opened the front door of the house and gestured me in.

'Harry,' she called. 'Harry.'

I thought Harry must be her dog because no Irish *person* was called such a thing.

But when a dog didn't come scampering, it dimly

occurred to me that Harry was the nine foot three, tanned, blond-haired ride who came into the hall in response to her summons.

'This is Harry,' she said. 'My husband. I met him when I was three years off the quare stuff, when I was eight years older than you are now. He's pure mad about me, aren't you?' She turned to him.

He nodded. 'Pure mad about her,' he told me, confidentially.

'We have a fabulous relationship.' She twinkled at me. 'Because I'd learnt to live with myself before I met him. I was an awful miserable poor eejit until I learnt that.

'Am I making myself clear?' she asked, her face a sudden picture of perplexity.

'Crystal,' I mumbled.

'Good.' She beamed. 'Great! Sometimes I seem to confuse people. Come on, so. I'll drive you home.'

And every time over the next twelve months, whenever I woke in the middle of the night thinking I would die without ever feeling the touch of a man again – and such occasions were many – I would think 'Operation Harry', and the panic would abate. After I'd been clean and celibate for a year, I could claim my free Harry.

Nola rang me and took me to a meeting the following day. It was in a different church hall, with different people, but the format was the same. 'Keep coming back,' everyone said to me. 'And things will get better.' The next day Nola took me to yet another different meeting. And the day after that.

'Why are you so nice to me?' I asked, a bit alarmed.

'Sure, why wouldn't I be?' she exclaimed. 'Aren't you a dote?'

'Why?' I persisted.

'Ah,' she sighed wistfully. 'When I saw you in the Cloisters, with your cross little face, you reminded me of me. It took me back seven years to that desperate misery. The confusion and the shocking heebie jeebies! The minute I clapped eyes on you, I thought "There but for the grace of God, go I."'

I bristled angrily. The cheeky bitch!

'You're *just* like I was,' she exclaimed fondly. 'We're no different.'

That mollified me. I wanted to be like her.

'I wouldn't be off the quare stuff today if people hadn't been nice to me back then,' she said. 'Now it's my turn. And when you're a bit better, *you'll* help the new people.'

I was both touched and irritated.

'Haven't you a job to go to?' I asked the following day when she arrived to take me to yet another meeting.

'I'm my own boss,' she said reassuringly. 'Don't worry about me.'

'What do you do?' I asked, curiously.

It turned out she ran a modelling agency, one of Ireland's most successful. And she used to be a model herself. That cheered me up. I loved it that she could be an addict, yet have a glamorous, successful career. It ameliorated the slight residual feeling that I belonged to an underclass of losers.

'There's a pile of us recovering addicts, with fierce successful careers,' she said. 'When you're a bit better you'll probably have one too.'

I found that hard to believe.

68

Everytime Nola caught me talking to a man, she sabotaged it by saying to him 'Don't go near this one, she's stone-mad, got herself knocked down and nearly killed, she's only a couple of weeks off the snow,' then whisked me away. Instead she introduced me to lots of women addicts, of whom I was initially a bit wary.

But, as the weeks passed, I found that, in the same way that I'd ended up being really fond of everyone in the Cloisters, I'd started to consider some of the NA people to be friends. I met Jeanie, the skinny, good-looking girl who'd run the NA meeting at the Cloisters the night I'd faced my addiction for the first time. And I got pally with a chain-smoking butcher (that was what she did for a living, not what she did for a hobby) who went by the unfortunate name of Gobnet.

'No wonder I'm an addict,' she said, when she introduced herself to me. 'With a name like that.' Then she dissolved into a fit of coughing.

'Holy jayzis,' she said, her eyes watering. 'Give me my fags.'

After a while I found I'd fallen into a routine of going to a meeting almost every day.

'Isn't this a bit excessive?' I anxiously asked Nola.

'Arra, no,' she said, as I should have bloody well known she would. 'You took drugs every day, why not a meeting every day? And, sure it's not forever, only till you get better.'

'But,' I shifted uncomfortably, 'shouldn't I get a job? I feel so guilty not working.'

'Not at all,' she scoffed, as if the mere suggestion was hilarious. 'What do you want to work for? Lie out in the garden, get a tan, sure this is the life, girl.'

'But . . .'

'And what would you do? You don't *know* what you want to do with your life,' she said, as if that was something to be proud of. 'You will eventually. Anyway, aren't you getting the dole?'

I nodded cagily.

'Well, then!' she sang. 'You've enough money to survive on. So think of this as a convalescence, like getting over a bad dose of the flu, a flu of your emotions. And in the meantime, get a colour on your legs!'

'How long,' I asked anxiously, 'will I have to live like this?'

'For as long as it takes,' she said airily.

'OK, OK!' she said quickly to my woebegone face. 'They said a year in the Cloisters, didn't they? Concentrate on getting better for a year and then you'll see how well you've become. Try and be *patient*.'

She was very convincing but, just to be on the safe side, I mentioned to Mum and Dad that I was thinking of getting a job. And the torrent of objections I got from them convinced me that it was OK, at least for a while, to be a long-haired layabout.

To my surprise, I didn't think about drugs as often as I'd thought I would. And I was amazed to find I had as much fun with Nola, Jeanie and Gobnet as I'd ever had with Brigit. We went to meetings, to each other's houses, to the cinema, shopping, sunbathed in each other's gardens. Everything normal friends did together, except drink and take drugs.

I was very relaxed with them because they knew how bad I'd been, at my very, very worst, and they didn't judge me. For every story of shame and humiliation I had, they could top it.

As well as the meetings, I had psychotherapy sessions with an addiction counsellor on Tuesdays and Fridays.

Slowly my internal landscape altered. I extricated myself from the mesh of preconceptions I had about myself, as though from barbed wire. It was a great day when I understood I didn't have to think I was thick just because I had a very bright sister.

My view of my past also changed as my counsellor demystified childhood situations, in the same way that Josephine had pointed out that I wasn't to blame for my mother's misery after Anna was born. Repeatedly, it was pointed out to me that I hadn't been a bad child, that I wasn't a bad person.

It was like watching a photo developing, very slowly, over the course of a year, as I gradually came into focus.

And as I changed, other things fell into place. I reckoned I was always going to have a great fondness for savoury snacks and chocolate, but the wild swinging between starving myself and stuffing myself had calmed down a lot, without me even having to try.

That's not to say that I didn't still have bad days. I did.

Things didn't improve in a smooth straight line. For every two steps I took forward, I took one step back. There were times when I just wanted to switch off, just check out of reality for a while, when relentless consciousness got me down. Nothing bad had to have happened, I just got tired of being sentient.

Not to mention times when the sadness of my wasted years just floored me for a while. And I got bouts of terrible guilt at the hurt and worry I'd caused to so many people, but Nola assured me that when I was a bit better, I'd make it up to them. Although I didn't like the sound of that either.

It was like living on a rollercoaster because at yet *other* times I was assailed by rage at drawing the short straw and becoming an addict.

As every emotion under the sun bubbled out of me in no particular order, I couldn't have survived without the meetings. Nola and the others comforted, bolstered, reassured, encouraged and calmed me. No matter what I felt, they'd felt it too. And, as they kept saying, 'We survived it, we're happy now.'

They were particularly invaluable during the great G-string wars, which blew up out of nowhere. I'd thought that, after the great bedside reconciliation, my mother and I would never fight again.

Wrong. Very, very wrong indeed.

Oh, you couldn't even begin to imagine how wrong.

What happened was, everyone knows that Visible Panty Line is a bad thing, right? No one wants to have their knickers on display through their boot-leg pants, do they? And everyone knows that the solution to this is to either wear no knickers at all, or to wear a G-string. *Everyone* knows this.

Wearing a G-string doesn't mean you're a stripper or a brazen hussy, on the contrary, it implies great modesty. But you should have tried telling that to my mother.

She appeared in my room, all abject and mortified. She had something to tell me, she said. Work away, I cheerfully invited. With a trembling hand she advanced a small scrap of black lace.

'I'm sorry,' she said, hanging her head. 'I don't know how it happened, but the washing-machine must have shrunk or shredded these knickers.'

I examined said knickers, found that they were actually a G-string, and that there was nothing wrong.

'They're fine,' I reassured her.

'They're *ruined*,' she insisted.

'They're fine,' I said again.

'But they're completely unwearable,' she said, looking at me as if I was mad.

'They're in perfect condition,' I said.

'Look!' she commanded, holding it up to the light. 'This wouldn't cover an ant's backside.' She was pointing to the front bit.

'And as for *this*,' she demonstrated the string which gave the garment its name. 'What use is this to anyone?

'What amazes me,' she confided, 'is how it shredded away so evenly, just leaving this nice straight line.'

'You don't understand,' I said, kindly. And, taking the G-string from her, explained. 'This isn't for the bum, this is for the front. And this nice straight line here is actually for the back.'

She stared at me, understanding dawning. Then her mouth began to work convulsively and her face became dark red. She backed away from me, as if I was highly infectious. Eventually, she started to screech 'You brazen HUSSY! That might be the kind of thing they wear in New York, but you're not in New York now and while you're under my roof you'll cover yourself like a Christian.'

I felt the old fear take hold. I was shaking and nauseous from the shouting and confrontation. It was horrible, it felt like the end of the world. I legged it out of the room, wanting to kill myself, kill Mum, run away to sea and ingest handfuls of chemicals.

But this time, instead of belting into town and seeking out Tiernan, I rang Nola. And she came and took me to a meeting. Where she and the others calmed me. Told me it was understandable to be upset, reassured me that I'd live through it, that it would pass in no time. Naturally, I didn't believe them. All I wanted to do was take drugs.

'Course you do.' Gobnet coughed, lighting a cigarette. 'You've never done anything upsetting without getting off your tits.'

'It's dead easy,' Nola said soothingly. 'All you have to do is learn new responses to everything.'

I couldn't help but laugh. She was so positive it was frightening.

'But it's so hard,' I said.

''Tisn't,' Nola sang. 'It's only new. Practise.'

'I'm going to move out of home,' I declared.

'Oh no.' They adamantly shook their heads at that. 'Fights are part of life, far better to learn to live with them.'

'It'll never be OK with Mum again,' I said sulkily.

And I was almost disappointed when, in less than a day, the scrap was over and forgotten about.

'The next barney you have with her will be even easier,' Jeanie advised me.

It gave me grudging pleasure when it turned out she was right.

Time continued to pass, the way it does. And still I didn't relapse. I felt different. Better, calmer.

The only bad thing that showed no sign of shifting was

the rage I had for Brigit and Luke. I couldn't explain why. God knows, all that they'd said was true. But, every time I thought about them coming to the Cloisters and saying what they did, I felt uncontrollable fury.

Everything else in my life improved, though. I no longer had to do things I hated, like steal money or borrow money with no intention of paying it back, or skip work because I was too sick, or end up in bed with some horrible man that I wouldn't have gone near if I hadn't been out of my skull. I never woke up racked with shame and guilt about the way I'd behaved the night before. I had my dignity back.

I wasn't constantly tormented with worry about when I'd next be taking something, or about where to get it or who to get it from. Mine was no longer an existence where I had to lie constantly. Drugs had put a wall between me and everyone else. A wall that wasn't just chemical, but made of secrecy, mistrust and dishonesty.

At least now when I was with people I could look them in the eye, because, unlike the last year or so with Brigit, I had nothing to hide.

I was no longer tortured by stomach-turning, vague, nameless anxiety. And that was because I wasn't letting people down or being dishonest or cruel or unkind to anyone.

And I never felt the savage depressions that followed a good night out.

'That makes sense,' Nola agreed. 'You've stopped putting powerful depressant chemicals into your body, no wonder you feel better.'

Things that I once would have died before being caught doing, brought me great joy. Like visiting my butcher friend, making dinner for my family or going for a walk on the seafront. There was huge pleasure in the simple things. Patrick Kavanagh's *Advent* came to me often, the way it had when I first entered the Cloisters. *We have tested and tasted too much, lover, through a chink too wide there comes in no wonder.*

And I learnt about integrity and loyalty to my friends. I had to, with Helen around. Whenever she answered the phone to any of the NA people, she'd shout 'Rachel, it's one of your loser, junkie friends, one of the ones who wasn't able to hack it.'

In my previous life, I would have submitted to Helen's – or anyone's – scorn and terminated contact with the NA person forthwith. But not now.

Occasionally, just for the laugh, I'd say 'What are you so afraid of, Helen?' to put the frighteners on her.

Until one day Helen bumped into Nola and me in town.

'*You're* Nola?' she screeched in palpable disbelief. 'But you look . . .'

Nola raised one eyebrow in a questioning gesture that was highly glamorous.

'You look normal,' Helen blurted. 'Better than normal. Lovely. Your hair, your clothes . . .'

'That's nothing, girl,' Nola said in her sing-song voice. 'You'd want to see my car.'

'And her husband,' I added proudly.

I never once saw Chris at any of the meetings I went to. After a while I stopped looking for him.

Eventually I forgot about him altogether.

Until the night Helen approached me, looking awkward and nervous. Immediately I was worried,

Helen never looked awkward and nervous.

'What?!' I barked at her, racked with anxiety.

'I've something to tell you,' she said.

'I *know*,' I shouted. 'That's obvious.'

'Promise you won't be cross,' she beseeched.

I realized something really terrible must have happened.

'I promise,' I lied.

'I've got a new boyfriend,' she said sheepishly.

I almost puked. I no longer wanted him, but I didn't want him riding my sister when he couldn't sustain an erection with me.

'And you know him,' she said.

I know.

'He was in your laughing house.'

I know.

'And I know he's not supposed to go out with anyone until he's a year off the jar, but I'm mad about him,' she wailed. 'I can't help it.'

'Not jar, drugs,' I said, in a daze.

'What?'

'Chris was in for drugs, not drink,' I said, not knowing why I needed to explain this to her.

'Chris who?'

'Chris Hutchinson, your . . .' I forced myself to say it. '. . . fella.'

'No,' she looked really puzzled. 'Barry Courtney, my fella.'

'Barry?' I mumbled. 'Barry who?'

'You all called him Barry the child in the bin,' she said.

'But he's no child,' she added defensively. 'He's man enough for me!'

'Oh God,' I said weakly.

'And what's all this shite about Chris?' she demanded.

'Oh CHRIS!' she exclaimed. 'The one who wouldn't do the anal sex.'

'Yes.' I watched her. Somehow I knew something had happened.

'Did he ever ask you out?' I asked. 'And don't lie to me or I'll tell Barry's counsellor that he's in a relationship and he'll be forced to break it off with you.'

I watched the struggle on her face.

'Once,' she admitted. 'Ages and ages ago. He came into Club Mexxx off his knob on something.

'I said no,' she added quickly.

'Why?' I braced myself for pain, but to my surprise felt almost nothing.

''Cos he was a creep.' She shrugged. 'Giving everyone that "oh you're so special" shit. He didn't fool me. Anyway I wouldn't go out with someone that you'd fiddled and interfered with.'

'Why didn't you tell me?' I asked, mortified.

'Because you were having relapses and getting knocked down and nearly killed and I just thought you'd be better off not knowing,' she explained.

I had to admit she'd done the right thing, at the time. I could handle it now, though.

69

Autumn whizzed by and the weather got colder and edged into winter.

Something changed. I found I wasn't angry with Luke or Brigit anymore. I couldn't pinpoint when it happened, because brotherly love and forgiveness don't wake you up in the middle of the night and do grand-prix laps in your head, the way vengeance and hatred do.

You don't lie there, fully awake at five in the morning, grind your teeth and visualize going up to the people you feel really fond of and shaking them by the hand. And saying . . . and saying . . . and saying . . . '*I'm sorry.*' No wait, and saying 'I'm *really* sorry.' (Yeah, that'd show them.) You don't lie there and plan that once you've done that you're going to smile warmly. And for a parting shot ask 'Any chance we might be friends?'

Feelings of softness and fidelity don't lap at the back of your teeth and make horrible tastes in your mouth.

For the first time I realized how selfish and self-centred I was. How horrendous it must have been for Brigit and Luke, living with me and the chaos I'd created.

I felt unbearably sad for them, for all the misery and worry they'd been put through. *Poor Brigit, poor Luke.* I cried and cried and cried and cried. And for the first time in my life it wasn't for me.

With terrible clarity I saw what an ordeal it must have been for them to get on a plane and come to the Cloisters and say what they'd said. Of course, Josephine and Nola and everyone else had been blue in the face telling me that, but I hadn't been ready to face it until now.

I'd never have admitted I was an addict if Luke and Brigit hadn't confronted me so violently with the truth. And I was grateful to them.

I remembered the awful final scene with Luke and I now understood his fury.

It had been building up over the weekend. On the Saturday night we'd gone to a party and, while Luke was talking to Anya's boyfriend about music, I wandered towards the kitchen. Looking for something, *anything*. Very bored. In the hall I met David, a kind of friend of Jessica's. He was en route to the bathroom with a small but perfectly formed bag of coke, and he invited me to join him.

I'd been trying to stay away from the snow because Luke got so narky about it. But a free line was too much to resist. And I was flattered that David was so friendly.

'Yeah, thanks,' I said, quickly belting into the bathroom after him.

I got back to Luke

'Babe.' He slid his arm around my waist. 'Where were you?'

'You know,' I sniffed. 'Talking to people.'

I thought I did a pretty good job of hiding my buzz by lurking behind my hair. But Luke pulled me up to look at him and, as soon as he saw my face, he knew. His pupils contracted with anger and something else. Disappointment?

'You've been doing drugs,' he bit.

'I haven't,' I said, opening my eyes wide with sincerity.

'Don't fucking lie to me,' he said, and stalked off.

I was shocked to see him actually pick up his jacket and leave the party. For a moment, I toyed with the idea of letting him go. Then I could get off my face without anyone breathing down my neck. But things had been so tense with us lately that I was afraid to take the risk. I ran down into the street after him.

'I'm sorry,' I gasped when I caught up with him. 'It was only one line, I won't do it again.'

He turned to me, his face contorted with anger and pain.

'You keep saying sorry,' he shouted, his breath making clouds in the freezing February night. 'But you don't mean it.'

'I *am* sorry,' I protested. At that moment I *was* sorry. I was always sorry when he was angry with me. I desired him most when I thought I was just on the verge of losing him.

'Oh Rachel,' he groaned, wearily.

'Come on,' I said. 'Let's go home and go to bed.'

I knew he couldn't resist me, that a good ride would shut him up. But when we went to bed he didn't lay a finger on me.

The next day he was his usual affectionate self, and I knew he'd forgiven me. He always did, yet I felt extremely depressed. As if I'd done a full two grams the night before, instead of just one line. After I'd taken a few Valium the bleakness dissolved and I was wrapped in a warm, fuzzy cradle.

We stayed in on Sunday night, snuggled up on the couch watching a video. Out of nowhere my head filled with a mental picture of me inhaling a lovely, long line of coke. Instantly I felt horribly hemmed in by Luke.

I shifted on the couch and tried to calm myself. It was

Sunday night, I was having a perfectly lovely time, there was no need to go out and party. But I couldn't shake the desire. I *had* to leave. I could taste gorgeous, acrid, numbing coke, I already felt the rush.

I fought it and fought it, but it was irresistible.

'Luke,' I said, my voice wobbling.

'Babe?' He smiled lazily at me.

'I think I'd better go home,' I managed.

He looked hard at me, the smile gone. 'Why?'

'Because . . .' I faltered. I was going to say I felt sick, but the last time I'd tried that, he'd insisted on taking care of me. Making hot-water bottles for my imaginary stomach ache, and forcing me to eat stem ginger for my imaginary nausea.

'Because I've a very early start in the morning and I don't want to disturb you when I get up,' I stammered.

'How early?'

'Six o'clock.'

'That's OK,' he said. 'It'll do me good to go into the office early.'

Oh no. Why did he have to be so fucking nice? How was I going to escape?

'Also I came out without a clean pair of knickers,' I said in desperation. The feeling of being trapped intensified.

'But you can collect them before you go to work in the morning,' he suggested tightly.

'Not with the early start.' Panic took hold. I felt the walls of the room were moving in on me. I stood up and began to sidestep towards the door.

'No, wait a second.' He eyed me in a peculiar fashion. 'You're in luck, you left a pair here and I put them in with my washing.

'Luke the laundress saves the day,' he added grimly.

I almost screamed. I could feel sweat pop out on my forehead. 'Look, Luke.' I was unable to stop myself. 'I'm not staying tonight and that's the end of it.'

His eyes were hurt. But hard.

'I'm sorry,' I said frantically. 'I need a bit of space.'

'Just tell me why,' he asked. 'I mean, five minutes ago you seemed happy. Was it the video?'

'No.'

'Did I do something?' he asked, with what might have been sarcasm. 'Did I *not* do something?'

'No Luke,' I said quickly. 'You're great, it's just me.'

From his angry, pain-lined face, I saw my words were falling on stony ground. But I didn't care. Already I was in The Parlour, dancing and doing business with Wayne.

'I'll ring you tomorrow,' I gasped. 'Sorry.'

Then I bolted for the door, too relieved to hate myself.

In ten minutes I found Wayne and asked for a gram.

'Put it on the slate.' I forced an anxious laugh. 'I'll be good for cash in a week.'

'Don't matter,' he shrugged. 'You know what they say – please don't ask for credit as a bullet in the head often offends.'

'Haha,' I said, thinking what a fucker he was.

I eventually managed to persuade him to give me a quarter-gram, which was just about enough to lift that stifling sensation and give me a euphoric rush.

When I got back from the ladies' he was gone.

To my alarm, the bar emptied out as everyone I even vaguely knew left. But it was only one o'clock. 'Where are you all going?' I asked anxiously, hoping to be invited along.

'Sunday night,' they said. 'Work in the morning.'

Work in the morning? You mean they weren't going on to a party, they were going home to sleep?

In a short time I was on my own, all revved up and no one to party with. I tried smiling at the few people left, but not a single person was friendly. Paranoia started to seep in. I'd no money, no drugs, no friends. I was alone and unwanted, but so reluctant to go home.

In the end I had to. No one would buy me a drink or loan me money. Even though I asked. Humiliated, I slunk away.

But when I got in and tried to go to bed, my head buzzed like a chainsaw and raced like a grand-prix car. It was worse now than it had been in The Parlour. So I took three sleeping tablets and thought I'd write a bit of poetry as I felt particularly creative and uniquely talented.

Still my head wouldn't switch off, so I took a couple more tablets.

All the pleasure of the rush had left and I was trapped with a head that kept vibrating. I felt panicky fear. When would it stop? What if it never stopped?

My terror flitted hither and thither and came to rest on the thought of work the following day. My heart squeezed with dread. I really *had* to go, I'd been in trouble so much lately that I couldn't skip it again. I couldn't be late, and I had to stop making mistakes. For this, I really, desperately needed to go to sleep immediately. But I couldn't!

Frantically, I tipped the rest of the sleeping tablets out of the jar and crammed them into my mouth.

Voices, brightness in my eyes, the bed moving and bumping, blue light, sirens, more voices, bed moving again, whiteness, strange sterile smell. 'Dumb bitch,' a voice says. Who is? I half wonder. Beeping sounds, feet running on corridors, metal banging against metal, rough hand on my chin, forcing my mouth open, something plastic on my tongue, scraping my throat. Suddenly gagging and choking, trying to sit up, being forced back down, struggling up again, retching and heaving, strong hands flattening me back against the table. *Make it stop.*

In less than twenty-four hours I was back home at my apartment. To find Margaret and Paul had arrived from Chicago, to take me to a rehab place in Ireland. I couldn't understand what all the fuss was about. Apart from feeling I'd been beaten up, was swallowing razor blades and about to die from dehydration, I was OK. Fine, almost. It had been nothing more than an embarrassing accident and I was very keen to forget about it.

Then, to my surprise, Luke arrived.

Yikes. I braced myself to be berated for doing a runner and taking coke on Sunday night. I presumed that, in the whole stomach-pumping débâcle, he must have found out.

'Hello.' I smiled anxiously. 'Shouldn't you be at work? Come in and meet my lickarsey sister Margaret and her awful husband.'

He shook hands politely with Margaret and Paul, but his face was pissed-off and grim. In an attempt to put him in better form, I amusingly related the hilarious story of waking up in Mount Solomon puking my intestines up. He grabbed me tightly by the arm and said 'I'd like a word with you in private.' My arm hurt and I was frightened by the madness in his eyes.

'How the hell can you make jokes about it?' He demanded furiously, when he slammed the door of my bedroom behind me.

'Lighten up.' I forced myself to laugh. I was just relieved he wasn't giving out to me for doing coke on Sunday night.

'You nearly died, you stupid bitch,' he spat. 'Think of how worried we've all been – for ages, not just about this – think of poor Brigit, and all you can do is laugh about it!'

'Would you ever *relax*?' I said scornfully. 'It was an accident!'

'You're mad, Rachel, you really are,' he said passionately. 'You need help, big-time.'

'When did you lose your sense of humour?' I asked. 'You're as bad as Brigit.'

'I'm not even going to answer that.

'Brigit says you're going to a rehab place,' he said, more gently. 'I think that's a great idea.'

'Are you out of your mind?' I laughed splutteringly. 'Me, go to a rehab place? What a joke!

'Anyway, I can't go away and leave you.' I smiled intimately, to rekindle our closeness. 'You're my boyfriend.'

He stared at me long and hard.

'Not any more, I'm not,' he said eventually.

'Wh . . . what?' I asked, cold with shock. He'd been angry with me before, but he'd never broken it off with me.

'It's over,' he said. 'You're a mess and I wish to Christ you'd sort yourself out.'

'Have you met someone else?' I stammered, horrified.

'Don't be so stupid,' he spat.

'Why then?' I asked, hardly able to believe we were having this conversation.

'Because you're not the person I thought you were,' he said.

'Is it because I did drugs on Sunday night?' I forced myself to bite the bullet and ask the unaskable.

'Sunday night?' he barked, with mirthless laughter. 'Why pick on Sunday night?

'But this *is* about drugs,' he continued. 'You've a serious habit and you need help. I've done everything I can to help – persuading you to stop, *forcing* you to stop – and I'm exhausted.'

For a moment he did *look* exhausted. Bleak, miserable.

'You're a great girl in a lot of ways, but you're more trouble than you're worth. You're out of control and I can't handle you anymore.'

'Oh no.' I wasn't going to be manipulated. 'Break it off if you're determined to, but don't try and blame me.'

'God,' he said angrily. 'There's just no getting through to you.'

He turned to leave.

'You're overreacting, Luke,' I said urgently, trying to grab his hand. I knew how much he fancied me, I'd always been able to win him over that way.

'Get off me, Rachel.' Angrily he pushed my hand away. 'You disgust me. You're a mess, a complete fucking mess.' Then he strode out into the hall.

'How can you be so cruel?' I whimpered, running after him.

'Bye, Rachel,' he said and slammed the front door.

70

In the days leading up to Christmas I was very jumpy whenever I went into Dublin's city centre. Luke and Brigit were probably home and I half-hoped I'd meet them. I constantly searched for their faces under the fairy lights, among the hordes of shoppers. Once I actually thought I saw Luke on Grafton Street. A tall man with longish dark hair striding away from me. 'One minute,' I muttered to Mum, then belted after him. But when I caught up, after nearly flooring a crowd of carol singers, I found it wasn't him at all. This man's face and bum were all wrong, not half as nice as Luke's. It was probably just as well it wasn't Luke. I had no idea what I'd have said if it had been him.

On New Year's Day about twenty members of my family, plus assorted boyfriends and children, were crammed into the sitting-room, watching *Raiders of the Lost Ark* and shouting 'Show us your lad' anytime Harrison Ford came on screen. Even Mum shouted it, but only because she didn't know what a lad was. Helen was drinking a gin and tonic and telling me what it felt like.

'First you kind of get this lovely warmth in your throat,' she said thoughtfully.

'Stop it!' Mum tried to hit Helen. 'Don't be annoying Rachel.'

'No, I asked her to tell me,' I protested.

'Then the burniness hits your stomach,' Helen elaborated. 'And you can feel it radiating out in your blood . . .'

'Looo-vely,' I breathed.

Mum, Anna and Claire were systematically ploughing their way through a big box of Chocolate Kimberleys and with each new one they picked up they said 'I can stop anytime. Anytime I want.'

In the middle of all the high jinks there was a ring at the door.

'I'm not going,' I shouted.

'Neither am I,' Mum shouted.

'Neither am I,' Claire shouted.

'Neither am I,' Adam shouted.

'Neither am I,' Anna said as loudly as she could, which wasn't very loud, but at least she'd tried.

'You'll have to go,' Helen told Shane, Anna's boyfriend. Shane was now unofficially living with us, because he'd been thrown out of his flat. So it meant we saw a lot more of Anna also, as she no longer had a bolt-hole to hide in.

'Aaaaawwwwww,' he moaned. 'It's just getting to the bit where he shoots the knife guy in the bazaar.'

'Where's Margaret when you need her?' Adam asked.

'LICKARSE,' the whole room chorused.

The bell rang again.

'Answer it,' Mum advised Shane, 'if you don't want to be sleeping under a bridge tonight.'

He stomped out and came back in and mumbled 'Rachel, there's someone at the door for you.'

I jumped up, expecting it to be someone like Nola, hoping she liked Harrison Ford too. Certain that she would, though. Nola liked everyone and everything.

But when I got to the hall, there, hovering by the door, looking nervous and pale, was Brigit. I got such a shock, black patches scudded before my eyes. I just about managed to say hello.

'Hello,' she replied, then tried to smile. Frankly, it was frightening. We stood in silence, just looking at each other. I thought about the last time I'd seen her, all those months before, as she was leaving the Cloisters.

'I thought it might be a good thing if we saw each other,' she attempted awkwardly.

I remembered the millions of conversations I'd had in my head, where I'd humbled her with pithy putdowns. 'So you *thought*, did you?' 'And tell me, Brigit, *why* would I want to see the likes of you?' 'You needn't crawl in here, expecting me to forgive you, so-called *FRIEND*!'

But not one of them seemed remotely appropriate now.

'Do you want to, um . . .' I meekly gestured towards the stairs and my room.

'OK,' she said, and up she went, me following, checking out her boots, her coat, her weight.

We sat on the bed and did the how-are-you? bit for a while, followed by the you're-looking-well thing. It made me very uncomfortable that she *was* looking so well. She had streaks in her hair and a groovy New York cut.

'Are you still off the . . .?' she asked.

'Over eight months now,' I said, with shy pride.

'Jesus.' She looked both impressed and appalled.

'How's New York?' I asked, feeling a cramp of pain. What I really meant was 'How's Luke?' followed closely by 'How did everything go so wrong?'

'Fine.' She gave a small smile. 'Cold, you know?'

I opened my mouth determined to ask how he was, but I hovered on the brink, desperate to know, but unable to ask.

'How's your job?' I said instead.

'Going well,' she said.

'Good,' I said heartily. 'Great.'

'Have you an . . . er . . . job?' she asked.

'Me?' I barked. 'God, no, being an addict is a full-time occupation at the moment!'

Our eyes met, uncomfortable, alarmed, then speedily flickered away again.

'What's it like living in Dublin?' She eventually broke the silence.

'Lovely,' I replied, hoping I didn't sound as defensive as I felt. 'I've made lots of good friends.'

'Good.' She smiled encouragingly, but there were tears in her eyes. And then I felt my throat thicken with tears of my own.

'Since that day at . . . that place,' Brigit began tentatively.

'You mean the Cloisters?'

'Yes. That old biddy Jennifer . . .'

'Josephine,' I corrected.

'Josephine, then. God, she was awful, I don't know how you put up with her.'

'She wasn't that bad,' I felt obliged to say.

'I thought she was terrible,' Brigit insisted. 'Anyway, she said something to me, about how nice it was to have someone to compare myself to, so that I was always the best one.'

I nodded. I kind of knew what was coming.

'And . . . and . . .' She paused, a tear splashing onto the back of her hand. She swallowed and blinked. 'And I just thought she was talking dross, I was so angry with you I couldn't see that anything was my fault.'

'It wasn't,' I insisted.

'But she was right,' Brigit ploughed on, as if she hadn't heard me. 'Even though I gave out to you, it made me feel good that you were so out-of-control. The worse you were, the better I felt about myself. And I'm sorry.' With that she burst into noisy, energetic tears.

'Don't be stupid, Brigit,' I said, trying to be firm and not cry. 'I'm an *addict*, you were living with an addict. It must have been hell for you, I'm only just realizing how awful.'

'I shouldn't have been so hard on you,' she sobbed. 'It was dishonest.'

'Stop it, Brigit,' I barked, and she looked up in surprise, her tears shocked into ceasing. 'I'm sorry you feel guilty, but if it's any help the things you said to me the day you came to the Cloisters . . .'

She winced.

'. . . It was the best thing you could have done for me,' I continued. 'I'm grateful.'

She demurred. I insisted again. Once more she demurred. And once again I insisted.

'Do you mean it?' she asked.

'Yes, I really mean it,' I said nicely. And I *did* really mean it, I found.

Then she gave me a woebegone smile and the tension lifted.

'So you're really OK?' she asked awkwardly.

'I'm great,' I said, honestly.

We were quiet.

Then she tentatively asked a question.

'And do you go round saying you're an addict?'

'Well, I don't stop strangers in the street,' I said. 'But when it's relevant I say it.'

'Like at those meetings you go to?'

'Exactly.'

She leaned closer to me, her eyes gleaming. 'Is it like that bit in *When a Man Loves a Woman* when Meg Ryan stands up in front of all the people and says she's a jarhead?'

'Just like it, Brigit.

'Except,' I added, 'Andy Garcia doesn't come running up to me at the end and try and drop the hand.'

'Just as well.' Brigit smiled suddenly. 'He's gruesome.'

'Like a lizard,' I agreed.

'A good-looking lizard, mind,' she said. 'But a lizard is a lizard.'

For a few moments it was as if nothing bad had ever happened. We were pitched back in time and space to when we were best friends, when we each knew exactly what the other was thinking.

Then she stood up. 'I'd better be off,' she said, awkwardly. 'I've got to pack.'

'When are you going back?'

'Tomorrow.'

'Thank you for coming,' I said.

'Thank you for being so nice to me,' she replied.

'No, thank *you*,' I said.

'Any chance of you coming back to New York?' she asked.

'Not in the foreseeable future,' I said.

I went downstairs to the door with her.

'Bye,' she said, her voice trembling.

'Bye,' I replied, my voice matching hers, wobble for wobble.

She opened the front door and put one leg outside, turning away. Just as I thought she was gone, she swung back and flung her arms around me and we hugged each other fiercely. I could feel her crying into my hair and I would have given everything I ever had to put the clock back. For things to be the way they used to be.

We stood for a long, long time, then she kissed me on the forehead. We hugged again. And she went off into the cold night.

We didn't promise to stay in touch. Maybe we would and maybe we wouldn't. But things were OK now.

That didn't mean I wasn't devastated by grief.

I cried for two solid days. I didn't want Nola or Jeanie or Gobnet or anyone, because they weren't Brigit. I didn't want to go on living, if I couldn't have the life I'd had with Brigit.

I thought I'd never get over it.

But I did. In a matter of days.

And I was suffused with pride that I'd gone through something so painful and hadn't taken drugs. Then I felt a strange relief that I wasn't tied to Brigit anymore. It was nice to know I could survive without her, that I didn't need her approval or endorsement.

I felt strong, standing alone without splints or crutches.

71

On into the spring.

I got a job. It was only as a part-time chambermaid in a small local hotel. The money was so bad I'd probably have been better off if *I* had paid *them*. But I was delighted with myself. I took pride in arriving on time, working hard and not stealing any money I found lying on the carpet, the way I used to. Most of the other people who worked there were schoolgirls, supplementing their pocket money. I would have found this very humiliating in my former life, but not now.

'What about going back to school?' Jeanie suggested. She was in the second year of a science degree. 'Maybe do a degree, when you know what to do.'

'A degree?' I was appalled. 'But it would take too long. Maybe four years. By then I'd be thirty-two. Ancient!'

'But you're going to be thirty-two anyway,' she pointed out calmly.

'What would I do?' I asked, as the impossible, the out-of-the-question, suddenly became not so ludicrous. Possible, even.

'I don't know,' said Jeanie. 'What do you like?'

I thought about it.

'Well, I like all *this*,' I said shyly, indicating us. 'Addiction, recovery, people's heads, their motives.'

Ever since Josephine had told me she was an addict

and an alcoholic, the idea of achieving what she'd achieved had rattled around in the back of my mind.

'Psychology,' suggested Nola. 'Or a counselling course. Find out, ring up.'

Then it was the fourteenth of April, my first anniversary. Nola and the girls made me a cake with a candle. When I went home, Mum, Dad and my sisters had made another cake.

'You're great,' they kept saying. 'A whole year without a single drug, you're fantastic.'

The following day I announced to Nola 'My year is up, now I can ride rings around myself.'

'Good girl, off you go,' Nola said, with a wryness that unsettled me.

I soon understood what she'd been getting at when I found there was no one I wanted to sleep with. No one I fancied. And it wasn't as if I didn't meet any men. Apart from the thousands of lads in NA, I'd started going on occasional nights out with Anna or Helen. Forays into the real world, with real fellas who weren't addicts and who didn't know that I was. It always came as a surprise when they tried to get off with me. Of course, I had to go through the tedium of explaining to them why I didn't drink. But even when they realized there was no hope of getting me into bed by drunken means, they still hung around.

One or two of these interested parties were even attractive, wore good clothes and had jobs in bands or in advertising.

I certainly wasn't making the most of my liberation from purdah. The trouble was, whenever I thought of going to bed with someone, the person I instantly thought of was Luke.

Gorgeous, sexy Luke. But I only spent a fraction of a second reflecting on how gorgeous and sexy he was, before rushing to remember how appallingly I'd treated him. Immediately I felt very ashamed and sad. Not to mention scared to death because Nola kept telling me to write to him and apologize. Which I was far too mortified and afraid to do in case he told me to fuck off.

'Face him,' Nola kept urging. 'Go on, he sounds like a dote. Anyway, you'll feel so much better.'

'Can't,' I mumbled.

'So what's wrong with these boys who keep asking you out?' Nola questioned me, when I'd spent a full hour whingeing to her.

'Oh, I don't know.' I shrugged irritably. 'They're either boring or a bit thick or they've got some other girly hanging around, gazing at them with cow eyes, or they think they're God's gift or . . .

'Even though some of them are good-looking,' I acknowledged. 'That Conlith is *very* good-looking, but all the same . . .' I trailed off miserably.

'They're not good enough, is that what you're trying to tell me?' Nola demanded, as if I'd just invented a cure for AIDS.

'Exactly!' I exclaimed. 'And I couldn't be arsed wasting my time, I've better things to do.'

'Janey macaroni, but you've changed,' Nola said.

'Have I?'

'Sure, think of what you were like a year ago,' she sang. 'You'd have slept with the tinker's dog, to avoid being by yourself.'

I thought about it. And with a shock I saw that, of

course, she was right. *Had that really been me?* That desperate creature? Dying for a boyfriend?

How things had changed.

'Didn't I tell you you'd get better?' Nola demanded.

'Stop being so smug,' I chastised. 'It's unbecoming.' But I smiled as I said it.

'Do you know what you have?' she asked. 'What's that it's called again . . . Oh yes – self-respect!'

72

With shaking hands I opened the letter. It was addressed to me, c/o Annandale's Hostel for Women, West 15th St, New York.

It was from Luke.

I hadn't intended to go back to New York. Ever.

But when I came to my fifteenth month of being drug-free, Nola suddenly suggested that I should go.

'Ah, go on,' she said, as if it was no bother to me. 'Sure, why not?'

'No,' I said.

'Do,' she eagerly urged. Then she turned as nasty as she could. Which wasn't very.

'If you don't go,' she pointed out, 'you'll always feel desperate whenever you think of it. Ah, go on! Go back to the places you used to go to, make it up to the people you upset.' Nola always said nice things like 'People you upset,' when she should have been saying, 'People whose lives you almost destroyed.'

'Like Luke,' I said, shocked by how excited I'd become at the thought of seeing him.

'Especially Luke.' Nola smiled.

'The dote,' she added.

I couldn't stop thinking about New York. I was obsessed with the place, and it seemed I'd no choice but to go.

And, once I saw that going could be a reality, the Luke-floodgates opened. To my horror, I realized what I'd suspected for some time. That I was still mad about him. But I was terrified that he might hate me, or have forgotten me or be married to someone else.

'It doesn't matter,' Nola urged. 'Either way it'll be healing for you to contact him.'

'The pet,' she added, with a fond smile.

My parents were appalled.

'It's not for ever,' I explained. 'I've got to be back in October to start college.'

(The people who make such decisions had decided to let me have a stab at studying psychology. I'd danced many a happy jig the day I got notification of that news.)

'Will you stay with Brigit?' Mum asked anxiously.

'No,' I said.

'But you've made it up with her,' she insisted.

'I know,' I said. 'But it wouldn't be appropriate.'

I was pretty sure that Brigit would've let me sleep on her couch, but I'd have found it hard to be in that apartment as a short-term guest. Besides, even though I now had very warm feelings for her, I thought it was somehow *healthier* for me to be independent of her when I returned to New York.

'But you'll contact her while you're there?' Mum still sounded worried.

'Of course I will,' I said reassuringly. 'I'm looking forward to seeing her.'

And then everything happened very quickly. I borrowed a pile of money, changed most of it into dollars, booked my flight, got a room in a women's hostel, because I couldn't afford an apartment, and packed my bags.

At the airport, Nola handed me a piece of paper with an address on it.

'She's a friend of mine in New York, give her a ring and she'll mind you.'

'She's not a drug addict, is she?' I demanded, rolling my eyes exaggeratedly. 'You only ever introduce me to addicts. Haven't you any *nice* friends?'

'Give Luke a big kiss from me,' she said. 'And see you in October.'

New York in July, like being smothered with a wet, warm blanket.

It was too much. The smells, the sounds, the buzz from the streets, the multitudes of people, the upbeat brashness of everyone, the huge buildings towering over Fifth Avenue, trapping the humid July heat, the yellow cabs bumper to bumper in the gridlocked traffic, the dieselly air hopping with carhorns and inventive expletives.

I couldn't handle the sheer energy of the place. Or the number of loopers, who sat beside me on the subway, or accosted me on the street.

It was all too in-your-face. I spent the first three days hiding in my room at the hostel, sleeping and reading magazines, the blinds drawn.

I shouldn't have come, I thought miserably. All it had done was open up old wounds. I missed Nola and the others, I missed my family.

Jeanie rang from Dublin, and I was thrilled, until she gave out shite to me.

'Have you been to any meetings?'

'Er, no.'

'Have you rung Nola's friend?'

'No.'

'Have you looked for a job?'

'Not yet.'

'Well, bloody well do. Do it now.'

So I forced myself to leave the safety of my bedroom, and set off walking aimlessly through the hazy heat.

Except it wasn't that aimless. In fact it wasn't aimless at all.

It was more what you might call a *retrospective* of my life in New York. A homage.

Here was the place I'd bought the lime-green mules I'd been wearing the first night I got off with Luke, there was the building where Brigit worked, up that way was the Old Shillayleagh, down there was the nasty garage where Brigit, Luke and I had gone to see Jose's sister in the crappy 'installation'.

I lurched around, staggering under the weight of memories. Crippling nostalgia washed over me with every step I took.

I passed what used to be The Llama Lounge, but was now a cybercafé. I walked by The Good and Dear that Luke had taken me to, and nearly fell to my knees with the agony of what might have been.

I walked and walked in ever-decreasing, ever more excruciating, circles until I was eventually able to enter the street where Luke used to live. Slightly pukey from nerves – although it might just have been the heat – I stood outside the building where he once lived, perhaps still did even. And I thought about the first time I'd ever been there, the night of the knees-up in the Rickshaw Rooms. Then I thought about the *last* time I'd ever been there, the Sunday night before my overdose. I hadn't known then it was my last time; if I had, maybe I would have treated the occasion with a bit more gravitas. If I

605

had, maybe I would have taken steps to ensure it *wasn't* my last time.

I stood in the baking street and pointlessly, powerlessly ached to be able to change things. I wanted to go back and make the past different. I wanted to be still living in New York, to never have left, to not have been an addict, to still be Luke's girlfriend.

I lingered for a while, half-hoping Luke would appear, half-hoping he wouldn't. Then I realized if anyone saw me they'd think I was a stalker, so I moved off.

At the end of the street, I stopped. I had to. Tears blurred my vision so much I was a danger to myself and to others. I leant up against a wall and I cried and cried and cried and cried. Mourning the past, mourning the other life I might have lived if things had been different.

I might still be there now, roaring my head off, had not a Spanish-speaking woman come out and with energetic waves of a sweeping brush invited me to piss off and stop lowering the tone of the neighbourhood.

I hoped my little walkabout had laid to rest any lingering feelings for Luke. It would have to, because I couldn't pluck up the courage to actually *contact* him.

Instead, I focused my attention on constructing the rudiments of a life. The first thing I did was get a job. It was very easy to get a job in New York.

If you'd no objection to being paid slave wages, that is. It was in a hotel, a small, Italian, family-run one. Quite nice, apart from the poxy money. Looking back, I couldn't imagine how I'd ever let myself work in somewhere as awful as the Barbados Motel.

Then I rang Brigit, nervous yet excited about seeing

her. But, irony of ironies, she'd gone home to Ireland for her summer holidays.

Over the next couple of weeks things kind of got into a routine. Albeit a very dull one. I went to work and I went to meetings and that was about it.

The girls in the hostel were mostly wholesome farm-hands from one of those down-South states that was the incest capital of the world. They answered to great names like Jimmy-Jean and Bobby-Jane and Billy-Jill. I was mad-keen to make friends with them, but they seemed a bit frightened and suspicious of everyone except each other.

The only ones who were friendly to me were Wanda, a nine-foot, peroxided, gumchewing Texan, who was having a lot of trouble coming to terms with not living in a trailer. And a beefy, short-haired, moustachioed woman, who answered to the name of Brad. She was *very* friendly, but, frankly, I suspected her motives.

It was a strange time. I felt alone, apart, separate. It wasn't entirely unpleasant.

Except that the feelings brought about by my being back in New York were still overpowering. At times the nostalgia nearly killed me.

And also the horror. I remembered going home with total strangers, and I felt panicky fear for myself. I could have been raped and murdered so many times. I remembered how I used to feel that the entire city was evil. Going back had unleashed an entire new dimension of memories. The Luke-nostalgia, in particular, showed no sign of abating. It got worse. I started to dream about him. Terrible dreams that it was two years previously and my life hadn't gone apocalyptically off the rails, and he still loved me. Of course, it wasn't the dreams that were terrible. The waking up was.

I knew I had to see him. At least I had to try. But I didn't want to because he was probably going out with someone else and I didn't think I could bear that. I tried to console myself that he mightn't have a girlfriend. But why wouldn't he? I asked myself. Even *I'd* kind of had sex with someone, and I was supposed to have been celibate at the time.

The days passed in a kind of dreamscape. I had an unpleasant task hanging over me and, being me, I preferred to turn a blind eye to it.

Old habits die hard.

I tried to use the excuse that I didn't have his number. But, unfortunately I did. What I mean is, I still knew it off by heart. Home *and* work. Always assuming he was still working and living where he had been a year and a half previously. That wasn't guaranteed, New York had a lot of through trade.

One night, when I'd been back about five weeks, and was lying on my bed reading, I suddenly felt filled with the courage to ring him. With no warning, it seemed like an outrageously feasible thing to do and I couldn't see what all the fuss had been about. Quickly, before the urge passed or I talked myself out of it, I rushed, purse in hand, to the phones in the hostel hall, almost knocking people to the ground in my haste.

Ringing from there was slightly inhibiting, what with Bobby-Ann and Pauley-Sue queueing up behind me to talk to their pet lambs back home. But I didn't care. Fearlessly I pressed out Luke's number, then when it began to ring I went into a panicky spin about what I'd say to him. Should I say 'Luke, prepare yourself for a shock'? Or, 'Luke, guess who?' Or, 'Luke, you may not remember me . . .'? Or was it more likely to be 'Luke, please don't hang u . . .'?

I was so hyper I could hardly believe it when I got his machine. ('Living on a Prayer', Bon Jovi.) After all the trouble I'd gone to, he wasn't even there.

Bitterly disappointed, yet undeniably relieved, I hung up.

At least I knew he was still living at the same address. However, the whole ordeal of ringing had depleted me something ferocious, so I decided it might be better for my nerves to write to him instead. Also, it meant less chance of him hanging up on me.

It took a hundred and seventy-eight attempts before I settled on a letter that was humble, friendly and non-proprietorial in the correct proportions. In most of the ones I binned I'd veered towards acute prostration ('I'm not worthy to live on the sole of your shoe'). But when I'd toned the apologies down I wondered if I sounded too cold, like I wasn't sorry *enough*. So they got crumpled up and thrown at the wall also.

And as for the sign-off line – 'Yours sincerely'? or 'Yours *most* sincerely'? or 'Thank you for your time'? or 'With best wishes'? or 'With warmest wishes'? or 'Love'? or 'Lots of love'? or '*All* my love'? or 'I suppose a ride is out of the question?'? Which one gave the right message? By then I was so confused I wasn't sure what the bloody message was, anyway.

Dear Luke, I wrote in the letter I eventually posted. *You may be surprised to hear from me. I'm back in New York for a short while and I would be grateful if you could spare some time to see me. I'm very aware of how badly I treated you when we were going out with each other and I would appreciate a chance to apologize in person. I'm contactable at the above address. If you don't want to have anything to do with me, I fully understand. Yours sincerely, Rachel (Walsh)*

I thought it sounded apologetic without being ridiculous; friendly without being predatory. I was quite proud of it, until the moment I'd slipped it into the box, when I suddenly saw that it was the most terrible letter ever written. It was a very hard job to force myself to walk away and not hang around to intercept it when the postman emptied the box.

I desperately hoped he'd reply. But I tried to prepare myself for the possibility that he mightn't. There was a big chance that I wasn't the important figure in his life that he was in mine. He probably barely remembered me.

Unless he remembered me all too well, and hated my guts, of course. In which case, I wouldn't be hearing from him either.

Four days in a row I lingered by the front desk around the time the post was delivered and four days in a row I was sent away empty-handed.

But on the fifth day I came home from work to find a letter had been shoved under my door. No stamp. Hand-delivered.

Luke had replied.

I held the envelope in my sweaty paw and stared at it. I was terrified of looking inside. At least he'd gone to the trouble of writing, I comforted myself.

Unless it was a page filled with just two words – 'fuck' and 'off'.

Suddenly, frantically, I found I was tearing it open, the way a tiger tears dead antelopes. I *savaged* it. And with a pounding heart scanned the letter inside.

It was short and to-the-point. Brusque even. Yes, he

said, he'd like to meet me. What about that evening at eight at Cafe Nero? Any problems, leave a message on his machine.

I didn't like the tone. It struck me as unfriendly, not exactly in the spirit of forgiveness and extending the olive branch. I suspected the camera wouldn't fadeout on this one, with us holding hands at head-level, swaying and singing 'War is Over' or 'Ebony and Ivory' or any other lickarsey songs about the end of conflict.

The letdown was terrible. I even felt he had a bit of a cheek until I remembered I'd behaved appallingly to him. If he still carried a grudge, he was quite entitled to it.

But he *had* said he'd meet me. Maybe that was just because he'd remembered a few more horrible things that he hadn't got round to saying at the Cloisters, I thought, slumping again.

73

It wasn't a date. It was more unlike a date than any other encounter I'd ever had. And to treat it like a date would be to trivialize his feelings and my maturity.

All the same, I spent hours getting ready. *Hours!*

Should I try to look attractive or mature and rehabilitated? I wondered. Try to win him over by making him fancy me again, or behave in an adult, I'm-very-different-now way? I decided on the serious, sober approach, tied my hair back, tucked a book on addiction under my oxter and wondered if Mikey-Lou would loan me her glasses.

She wouldn't, so I realized I'd have to play the you-used-to-fancy-me-once-upon-a-time card. I tried, very quickly, to glamour myself up.

But I had almost no clothes. A year and a half of subsistence wages had taken care of that. So there was no great frantic trying on and tearing off of things. No wild flinging of things onto the floor even while pulling the next volunteer from the wardrobe.

Condemned to wear my long denim skirt and a short T-shirt, I was annoyed and ashamed. I wanted something fabulous to wear. Until I realized that that was the way I was now. Simple, straightforward, hiding behind nothing. (Badly-dressed, also.) I didn't have to put on a show for Luke.

But I piled on *tons* of make-up. I put my hair up, I took

it down, I put it up again. I took it down again. I finally decided to put it up and leave it.

Just before I left, I took it down again.

'You look great!' Brad bellowed, as I left.

'Thanks,' I said nervously, not at all sure I was pleased.

I tried not to be late. It was an effort not to play games, but I forced myself not to. It wasn't appropriate. When I arrived at Cafe Nero there was no sign of him. Naturally, I suspected the worst, that he'd changed his mind about seeing me. I decided to leave.

Then I stopped, forced myself to sit down and ordered a drink. Ten minutes, I swore. That's all I'm staying.

It was utter torment. I was ejector-seat jumpy with nerves, and kept glancing towards the door, willing him to appear.

After the arrival of the twentieth person who wasn't Luke, I miserably decided to leave. I fumbled round in my bag for my purse to pay for my mineral water . . .

And then, there he was. Coming through the door. Talking to the greeter. Being told where I was. Glancing over at me.

It was a tremendous shock to see him. He was taller, bigger than I remembered. More grown-up. He still had the long hair and leather jeans, but his face was different. An adult's face.

As he strode across the café, I tried to read what he felt towards me, but his expression was closed. When he reached me there was no effusive greeting, no hugs and kisses. He just said curtly, 'Rachel, how's it going?' Then swung into the seat opposite, giving me a delicious second or two, eye-level with his leather-clad crotch before it disappeared below the table-top.

I didn't know how I could ever have thought his

appearance was something to ridicule. He was a beautiful-looking man.

I mumbled 'Hello, Luke,' or something equally inane. I was barely able to believe it was him, Luke, sitting there, on the other side of the table. Close enough to be touched.

In a way it seemed such a long, long time since I'd seen him. But in another, it wouldn't have seemed all that weird if I'd leant over and held his hand, or if he'd kissed me.

At least that was what I felt, I wasn't so sure he did.

He sat in silence, staring at me with a hostile look. And I had to steel myself to be strong. This was going to be harder than I thought.

When the waitress came, he ordered a beer and I indicated I was happy with my water, although that was far from the case. Then, clearing my throat, I launched into my well-rehearsed apology.

'Thank you for coming, Luke, I won't take up too much of your time.' I spoke rapidly. 'This is long overdue, but better late than never, well, at least I hope that's what you'll think. What I'm trying to say here is, I'm extremely sorry for any pain or unhappiness I caused you when we, er, knew each other when I lived here. I was an awful bitch of a girlfriend and I don't know how you put up with me, and you were perfectly right to be pissed-off with me.'

How I would have loved a drink! I took another deep breath. 'I would never have behaved in the terrible ways I did if I hadn't been addicted to drugs. But I know it's no excuse, it certainly doesn't lessen the bad stuff I did to you, just for you to know *why* I'd behaved so badly . . .'

I sneaked a glance at him. Impassive in the extreme. *React, for God's sake!*

'I was disloyal,' I ploughed on. 'Had no integrity and I

betrayed you and let you down. It's probably of no interest to you to know *why* I was so unreliable, but just to let you know that I've changed a lot and I stand by my friends now. Of course,' I added, 'that's precious little use to you now; it would have come in fairly handy two years ago, when I was the terrible bitch I was . . .'

On and on I went, my words falling on the stony ground of Luke's silence. At one stage he shifted himself sideways on his chair and slung his arm along the back of it. In the midst of my abjection I couldn't help a throb of realization that he was still a complete ride.

Back to the apology. I kept my eyes downcast as I slid my glass around the wet table, as if it was a ouija board.

I eventually came to an end. There wasn't anything else I could apologize for and still he hadn't said anything. Before our meeting, I'd been dreading his anger. But it would have been preferable to this impenetrable passivity. At least we'd have been communicating.

Reluctant to sit in silence, I apologized for some things I'd already apologized for. 'Sorry again about drinking Joey's JD that time, sorry for embarrassing you, sorry for upsetting your home life with my addiction . . .' Then I trailed off, there was no point going round for a second lap.

I had no option but to leave.

'I'll be off then,' I said humbly. 'Thank you for coming.'

Again, I pawed for my purse, with a view to paying and departing.

And then Luke completely threw me off my stride by saying 'Oh come on, Rachel, get off the cross! We need the wood.'

'Sorry?'

'I mean, sit down, and talk to me,' he exclaimed in a

peculiar tone that I recognized as forced joviality. 'I haven't seen you in nearly a year and a half. Tell me how you're getting on! How's Ireland?'

It wasn't so much an olive branch, as a mere olive. But it was enough. I pushed my bag away and settled back down.

Relaxed, uninhibited chat was difficult. The situation was too contrived and I hadn't had – and wouldn't be having – anything to drink. But I tried.

We warily discussed the Irish economy. Awkward talk of Celtic Tigers, foreign investment and per capita income. We were like two political analysts on the telly. When I got a chance to be funny, I grasped it in the hope of redeeming myself, of changing his memory of me. But there are few laughs to be got out of a healthy economy. Conversation lurched along awkwardly, stopping and starting, making no real progress. I didn't want to leave because being with him was a million times better than not being with him, but it was knackering.

The waitress came. He ordered another beer and I ordered another water. Her arrival derailed whatever we'd been talking about and, into our silence, Luke asked, almost shyly, 'Is that all you drink now? Water?'

'Yes.'

'God, you have changed.' He smiled.

'I have,' I said seriously. And then we looked at each other, *really* looked at each other. The blinds had snapped up off his face and I could see him, the old Luke, *my* old Luke, for the first time. We held the look for a long time. And I was confused because I kept forgetting it was now and not then.

'Well!' He cleared his throat and broke the mood. 'Thanks for your apology.'

I managed a shaky little smile.

'You know,' he said, pushing back the boundaries, 'I thought you wanted to meet me so you could give out shite for what I said that day in your rehab place.'

'Oh no,' I breathed. I was shocked he'd thought that was my motive, but I was glad we were finally talking about why we were there. Balance of payment deficits weren't really my forte. 'You were right to say all you said. If you hadn't, maybe I'd still be going around in lala denial land.'

'I was sure you hated my guts,' he said ruefully.

'Of course I don't,' I insisted. I mean, I didn't *now*, did I?

'Really?' he asked anxiously.

'Really,' I assured him. It was ironic, Luke worrying about whether I hated him.

'If it's any consolation it did my head in saying all those things.' He sighed with a great rush. 'And doing that bloody questionnaire yoke.'

'But you had to,' I comforted him. 'It was for my good.'

'Man, I hated myself,' he replied.

'You shouldn't have,' I consoled.

'But I did anyway,' he complained.

'But you shouldn't have. I was awful.'

'Ah, you weren't,' he said.

'I was.'

'You weren't.'

'I was.'

'Well, you were sometimes, I suppose,' he eventually agreed.

'Of course I was.' I smiled to hide my kick of discomfort. 'And it was especially decent of you to come and put yourself through that ordeal when we weren't even married or in a serious relationship, when you weren't even in love with me . . .'

'Hey, I *was* in love with you,' he interrupted, in a wounded tone.

'You weren't,' I reminded him.

'I was.'

'Luke,' I pointed out, 'I'm not giving out to you here, but you told everyone in my therapy group that you never loved me.

'I have witnesses,' I added, with a stab at humour.

'Oh God, I did, didn't I?' he said, rubbing his stubble in a gesture that I recognized from another life. 'I did, of course.'

He turned an urgent look on me. 'I shouldn't have said it, but I was angry, Rachel, I was very angry with you. For the way you'd treated me, and for the way you'd treated yourself.'

I swallowed. It still hurt to hear him say such a thing. Nice to know he *had* loved me once, I thought.

'Weird, isn't it?' Luke said thoughtfully. 'How time changes things. One day I'm raging with you, next thing it's more than a year later and I'm not pissed-off anymore.'

Thank God, I thought with shuddering relief.

'Even though I was angry, of course I loved you!' he declared earnestly. 'Do you think I'd fly three thousand miles to sit in a spooky room with a crowd of weirdos and trash you if I didn't love you?'

We both burst out laughing.

'You trashed me a lot,' I said. 'So you must have really loved me.'

'Oh, I did.' He nodded ironically. 'I did.'

Suddenly the mood had shifted upwards.

I asked after Gaz and the lads. Which led us seamlessly

into a series of 'Do you remember?'s. 'Remember the day of Gaz's tattoo?' 'Wasn't it hilarious the way it got infected afterwards?' 'Remember the time we made popcorn and set the kitchen on fire?' 'And Joey had stolen the fire extinguisher from work?' 'Wasn't it so handy?' 'I'd forgotten about that.' 'I'd forgotten about it too, until now.'

There was a bit of tentative arm-touching as we jogged each other's memories. Delicious, bittersweet, a faint echo of other contact.

When we'd done enough reminiscing, I wheeled out my recent achievements like a child showing off her birthday presents.

'I haven't had a drink or a drug for a year and four months,' I boasted.

'Fair play to you, Rachel.' Luke smiled with admiration.

I pulsated with pleasure.

'*And* I'm going to un-i-ver-sit-y,' I spelt out slowly, for maximum effect, 'in October.'

That nearly floored him.

'Are you really?' He goggled.

'Oh yes.' I grinned. 'To do psychology.'

'Fuck me!' he exclaimed.

We both ignored the flirt-opportunity afforded by that remark. Things were different from the way they'd been two years before. Very different indeed.

'Next you'll be telling me you're getting married,' he said, 'for the transformation to be complete.'

I smiled. The very thought!

'Are you?' he asked, when we'd sat in silence for a while.

'Am I what?'

'Getting married.'

'For God's sake, don't be mad,' I tisked.

'Haven't you met any nice lads in Ireland?' he asked.

'No,' I said.

'Plenty of eejits,' I added. 'But no nice lads.'

He laughed, his teeth white, his aura dangerous. My insides flipped.

'You always made me laugh,' he said.

'And not just when I took my clothes off?' I quipped.

I shouldn't have. His eyes kind of lit up and clouded over simultaneously. Memories and sensations came racing back. I could almost smell the way his skin used to smell when we were in bed together. The good mood was instantly dispelled. The tension back in force, accompanied by sadness and colossal, awful regret. In that moment I hated myself for being an addict, for ruining what might have been a great relationship. The grief I felt was mirrored in Luke's eyes.

We looked at each other, then had to look away. I'd thought that the day in the Cloisters was the deathknell of the relationship, but it wasn't. It was only happening now.

'Rachel,' Luke said awkwardly, 'I just want to say that you're not to feel guilty anymore about me.'

I shrugged miserably.

'Would it sound really corny if I said that I forgive you?' he asked sheepishly.

'Of course not,' I said earnestly. 'I *want* you to forgive me.'

'You know,' he said kindly, 'you weren't that bad.'

'Wasn't I?' I asked.

'Not always,' he said. 'And on a good day, there was no one better than you.

'No one,' he repeated gently, kindly, 'ever.'

'Honestly?' I whispered. His unexpected tenderness made me weepy.

'I mean it,' he whispered back. 'Don't you remember?'

'Yes,' I said. 'But I wasn't sure if I'd imagined it, what with me being off my face all the time and everything. So it was good with us sometimes?'

'Lots of times,' he said. Both of us were barely moving, even the air had stopped circulating around us.

A tear rolled smoothly down my cheek. 'Sorry,' I said, wiping it away. 'But I didn't think you'd be nice to me.'

'Why wouldn't I be?' he asked in genuine surprise. 'I *am* nice.'

Of course, he was. He was a nice man, once upon a time he'd been *my* nice man. A rush of loss momentarily withered me.

'I wasn't expecting to feel so sad,' I said.

'I was.'

'Were you?' I was very surprised. 'Just out of interest, why did you agree to meet me?'

'I was curious, I wanted to see if you'd changed. And I missed you,' he added jokily.

'And have I? Changed?' I asked, skipping over the jokey tone.

'Seems that way.' He nodded. 'I'd have to take you for a test-drive to know for sure, but it looks like you've kept all the good bits and shaken the bad bits.'

That made me proud.

'You don't look that much different,' he said thoughtfully. 'Your hair is shorter but you're still a babe.'

'And you're still a ride.' I managed to grin, yet I felt like my stomach was being torn apart.

There was no passionate clinch, no frantic lunge across the table. The purpose of our meeting was to douse the last few embers of the fire, not to rekindle the flames.

'I'd better get back,' I said. I hated leaving him, but I couldn't bear any more staring at the destruction I'd caused.

'OK,' he said, standing up, 'I'll walk you home.'

I was desperate to know if he had a girlfriend. As we strolled, I tried to ask.

'Have you . . . ?' I attempted, then stopped.

'Have you . . . ?' I said again, not getting any further.

Perhaps it would be better not to know. It would be agony if he was going out with someone else.

'You know,' he said casually, 'I haven't had a girlfriend since you left.'

In that moment, I believed in God.

'Take care of yourself,' he said, as we stood awkwardly outside the hostel.

'You too,' I said, wishing I was dead, waiting for him to go.

'Mind yourself.' He still lingered.

'I will, you mind yourself too.'

He moved his arm just a millimetre in my direction, an infinitesimal twitch, and the next thing, as if propelled from a cannon, we were in each other's arms. His legs were pressed against mine, his arms were hard around my back, my face was buried deep against his neck as I inhaled his scent for the last time. I wanted it never to stop. Then I pulled myself off him and ran inside, not looking at him again. I almost broke my neck tripping over Brad who'd been watching the whole proceedings with narrowed eyes. I didn't think she was going to be my friend anymore.

I knew the grief would pass, that I'd get over it.

The thing I found hardest was that I'd waited until it was finally finished before acknowledging how much I had loved him. But I knew that would pass too.

I'll never meet someone like him again, I kept thinking, twanging with grief.

But I would, I reminded myself. Operation Harry.

It was impossible not to wonder what would have happened with Luke if I hadn't been off my head throughout a lot of the relationship. Or, if we had just met for the first time, if we had no shared past that stopped us from having a future. But I knew there was no point thinking that way, you can't change what's happened. The best thing I could do was accept things.

And even if I hadn't won the main prize, I did have some consolation prizes to take away with me. Hadn't I found out he'd loved me once? Hadn't he forgiven me? Hadn't I behaved like a responsible adult? Hadn't we parted as pals?

The sadness I felt was as much healing as it was pain. I'd gone back and faced the messiest part of my past. I'd looked my misdemeanours in the eye and I'd found the courage to apologize to Luke. I no longer needed to feel ashamed every time I thought about him.

The ghost was finally laid.

I just wished it had been me.

But I was so proud of myself.

I was Rachel Walsh. A woman, an adult. A heifer, a babe, a lost sheep, an addict.

A found sheep.

A survivor.

EPILOGUE

I was just getting ready for bed when I heard the racket down in the hall.

It was two weeks since I'd seen Luke and I was still waiting in vain for the heartbreak to dissolve. A mature adult was a very hard thing to be. But I took a crumb of comfort from my agony. Maybe it would make me a stronger person.

I sometimes believed it.

About two seconds a day.

The rest of the time I spent roaring crying, convinced I'd never get over him. I cleaned the loos and laid the tables and hoovered the stairs at Il Pensione, tears coursing down my face. Nobody minded, they were Italian, comfortable with raw emotion.

When I heard the raised voices in the hall of the hostel, I was just wrapping up a good cry, and absolving myself from the need to officially remove my make-up.

So little happened in the way of drama there that I rushed out for a look. The noise seemed to be coming from the ground floor. I leant over the railings, and down into the hall, where a terrible scuffle was in process. Brad was wrestling energetically with a creature.

A creature that on closer inspection turned out to be Luke. My heart almost stopped.

'No men in here,' Brad was shouting. 'No men.'

'I only want to talk to Rachel Walsh,' Luke was protesting. 'I don't mean to cause any harm.'

I knew, I was utterly certain, that this was no casual visit. There had been far too much finality about our last encounter.

Then he looked up and saw me.

'Rachel,' he called, holding my eyes, despite the funny angle he was in because of Brad's headlock. 'I LOVE YOU.' Brad let go of him abruptly, clearly revolted by what he'd said. Luke was sent staggering to the floor.

I couldn't believe what I'd heard, yet I could. After all, *I* loved *him*.

'Say it again,' I called down to him in a shaky voice, as he clambered to his feet.

'I love you,' he bellowed joyously, spreading his arms beseechingly. 'You're amazing and beautiful and I can't get you out of my head.'

'I love you too,' I heard myself say.

'We can work it out,' he urged, looking up at me. 'I'll come home to Ireland and get a job. It was good with us before and it can be even better now.'

All the other girls were out of their rooms now, some in their nightdresses.

'Way to go, Rachel,' one of them called.

'Uf she doan wanchew,' Wanda the Texan shouted, 'Ah dee-ooo.'

'I love you,' he called again, advancing up the stairs. There was a burst of cheering and clapping and one or two whoops.

'And I love you,' I murmured, as I stood outside my doorway, paralysed, watching him get closer.

Down the landing he strode. Girls pulled themselves

back into their rooms as he passed, then came out again to admire his departing bum.

'Rachel,' he said, when he finally reached me. To my disbelief, I watched him get down on one knee. And the crowd went wild! He took my hand. 'I suppose,' he said, looking deep into my eyes, 'a ride is out of the question?'

AUTHOR'S NOTE

The Cloisters doesn't exist. Around the world there are many different treatment centres that deal with addiction. The living conditions, treatment methods and psychotherapy employed vary from establishment to establishment. Some are harsher than the Cloisters, some are gentler. In fact, some really *do* have jacuzzis!

During my research the one common thread I found was the recommendation that recovering addicts attend the appropriate 'Anonymous' meeting. Therefore I found it necessary to mention Rachel attending Narcotics Anonymous meetings, while at the same time taking care to preserve the confidentiality of the meetings' procedures.

Name: Stella Sweeney.
Height: average.
Recent life events: dramatic.

Marian Keyes's hilarious new novel
is available now

Love Marian Keyes?

Join the conversation online at the new, official Marian Keyes Facebook page.

www.facebook.com/mariankeyes

Expect *all* sorts of brilliant things like news, competitions, exclusive content, extracts, chat about all of Marian's books and some words from the lady herself . . .

He just wanted a decent book to read ...

Not too much to ask, is it? It was in 1935 when Allen Lane, Managing Director of Bodley Head Publishers, stood on a platform at Exeter railway station looking for something good to read on his journey back to London. His choice was limited to popular magazines and poor-quality paperbacks – the same choice faced every day by the vast majority of readers, few of whom could afford hardbacks. Lane's disappointment and subsequent anger at the range of books generally available led him to found a company – and change the world.

'We believed in the existence in this country of a vast reading public for intelligent books at a low price, and staked everything on it'
Sir Allen Lane, 1902–1970, founder of Penguin Books

The quality paperback had arrived – and not just in bookshops. Lane was adamant that his Penguins should appear in chain stores and tobacconists, and should cost no more than a packet of cigarettes.

Reading habits (and cigarette prices) have changed since 1935, but Penguin still believes in publishing the best books for everybody to enjoy. We still believe that good design costs no more than bad design, and we still believe that quality books published passionately and responsibly make the world a better place.

So wherever you see the little bird – whether it's on a piece of prize-winning literary fiction or a celebrity autobiography, political tour de force or historical masterpiece, a serial-killer thriller, reference book, world classic or a piece of pure escapism – you can bet that it represents the very best that the genre has to offer.

Whatever you like to read – trust Penguin.